the
Hidden Abbey

In Praise of the Hidden Abbey

The Hidden Abbey by Jodine Turner is both fantasy and visionary fiction, with a historical setting in the worlds of Avalon and Glastonbury Abbey, split between two separate timelines and skillfully developed to explore two lovers from a distant past reborn into modern day for a second chance. The reader is immersed into a world of magic and esoteric practices, with the Christian perception of life merging with the pagan.

In sixteenth-century Avalon, Marissa is the legendary priestess of the Isle of Avalon, an impulsive and spirited, beautiful young woman who must learn the science of becoming the High Priestess. But she has a secret love affair with a monk called Michael, the same who saved her from drowning as a child. Marissa and Michael are tasked to safeguard the Creation Bowl—the sacred vessel containing the wisdom of the ancient Goddess tradition that has the power to heal the world. But when King Henry VIII destroys all the abbeys, the treasure is at great risk and the struggle to protect it leads to the separation of the lovers. In the twenty-first century, Marissa and Michael are given a second chance. Can they rekindle the flame of the love they once experienced and lost and also bring back the power of the Creation Bowl to a world badly in need of it?

A work of great imagination and creative genius, *The Hidden Abbey* is a tantalizing narrative with great potential to entertain a wide audience. It contains hints of the historical, mystical, and the supernatural. The author paints a vivid setting and pulls readers in with the power of imagery. The characters are elaborately developed and filled with depth; they are relatable, and it is interesting how they evolve through the narrative. The author creates a powerful dialogue between the Christian religion and the ancient mysticism of the pagan world and weaves a narrative that is both uplifting and heartwarming. It is a beautifully crafted story with powerful plotlines, merging the past and the present in an adventure that is exhilarating.

—ROMUALD DZEMO, FOR READERS' FAVORITE.COM.

the
Hidden Abbey

JODINE TURNER

AVALON PUBLISHING | AUBURN, CALIFORNIA

The Hidden Abbey
First Edition released 2020

Cover Art: Renée Starr/The Beautiful Business Co
Book Design: Maggie McLaughlin/Dragon Book Design

Library of Congress Control Number:2019918654
ISBN: 978-0-9970952-4-1
eISBN: 978-0-9970952-5-8

Names: Turner, Jodine, author.
Title: The hidden abbey / Jodine Turner.
Description: Auburn, CA : Avalon Publishing, 2019.
Identifiers: ISBN 978-0-9970952-4-1 (paperback) | ISBN 978-0-9970952-5-8 (ebook)
Subjects: LCSH: Avalon (Legendary place)--Fiction. | Goddesses--Fiction. |
    Reincarnation--Fiction. | Glastonbury Abbey--Fiction. | Fantasy fiction. |
    Paranormal fiction. | BISAC: FICTION / Fantasy / Paranormal. | FICTION /
    Fantasy / Historical. | FICTION / Occult & Supernatural. | FICTION / Visionary
    & Metaphysical. | GSAFD: Fantasy fiction. | Occult fiction. | Historical fiction.
Classification: LCC PS3620.U76 H53 2019 (print) | LCC PS3620.U76 (ebook) |
    DDC 813/.6--dc23.

This novel is dedicated to the Goddess of the Stars and the Sea, She who is the evolutionary force of embodied Love.

Chapter 1

The Isle of Avalon, England
1529 C.E.

"Michael has been dead for nearly a minute."

That is, by human reckoning of time.

The words echoed within a whirlpool of magic—the message submerged, nearly soundless. It traveled along the rivers of prophecy, desperate to be discovered, reverberating with the underwater cries of a drowning boy. It seeped into twelve-year-old Marissa's dreams, flooding them with forewarning. She bolted upright in bed. Her twin sister slept on, unaware.

Marissa whimpered. "Mama!"

Her long hair, damp with sweat and tears, clung to her cheeks and neck. The portent had morphed into a waking vision. Marissa sat immobile, unable to block the grim Death Vision from unfolding before her eyes. A boy bobbed in Avalon's lake, sputtering water, his legs flailing. She watched him catch a breath and sink again, eyes wide, his mouth opening and closing. Air escaped his lips in bubbles that rose to the lake surface. Then the water claimed him again. Marissa reached for him but caught only empty air. She threw her blankets to the floor. Perching on the edge of the bed, she pressed her palms over her eyes.

Make it stop.

It didn't.

The Death Vision now linked her physically to the boy. She clawed at the neckline of her nightgown and gulped for breath. His struggle became her struggle. His terror surged through her heart. It wasn't supposed to work this way. She didn't know how to separate herself from his suffering. Only when

1

the Vision finally revealed his form floating face down in the lake did the breathlessness leave her chest.

She was too young to be having a Death Vision. She hadn't been taught how to control its power. It was meant to summon those who were trained, the Elder priestesses of Avalon, to alert them to escort the newly dead to the golden Otherworld. Why had it come to her?

Her shoulders shook with silent, racking sobs for the drowned boy.

The placid lake surrounding the magical Isle of Avalon didn't usually claim victims for its own. No one, not the priestesses of Avalon, nor the villagers of Glastonbury on the opposite shore, had ever known someone to drown in its waters. But young Michael had tempted fate. He disobeyed his father's strict orders not to wander from the hunting party. He disregarded Fr. Timothy's whispered warnings before he left home: *"Be careful in that summer country, lad. 'Tis the land of the heathen Faery."*

Michael had spent many an evening of his mere twelve years listening, enraptured, to his father's bards singing tales of the mighty sword Excalibur. Late last evening, the hunting party had camped near the legendary lake claimed to be the resting place of that hallowed sword. Around the evening campfire, the men regaled Michael with even more tales boasting of the sword's legendary prowess. Stirred and inspired, he lay awake until nearly dawn, then he took his chance. With quiet footsteps he crept away from the men sleeping in their tents. He was determined to prove himself a heroic knight by stepping into the lake's watery dominion and commanding it to relinquish the fabled treasure. If he claimed the great sword, he might finally become the esteemed young warrior his father had always wanted him to be.

Through dappled mist, Michael raced toward the lake with his fist raised high. He bounded over the marshy fen, through tall bulrushes, and crossed over a sandy shoreline.

"You will be mine, Excalibur!" he declared to the unseen forces that fueled noble deeds in young boys and men.

Flinging his cloak on a boulder, he raised his arms to his sides and jumped into the lake. The mossy rocks beneath his eager feet were slick, and his feet shot out from under him. He grabbed the branch of a nearby bush, but it broke off in his hand. When his head struck the boulder, his hopes of glory shattered.

Michael thrashed against the lake, his feet tangled in something beneath him. He kicked hard but the tethers on his legs held firm. He tilted his head back and gulped a breath, just as his older brother Roger had taught him. Then he dunked under, blind in the dark water, groping. He yanked on the long coils of underwater reeds twisted around his legs. Panic frenzied his kicks, tightening the reeds as water sloshed into his mouth.

The world around him narrowed. Water, reeds, breath. He sputtered. Coughed. His breath became a choking gasp as more water filled his mouth and rushed into his lungs. His chest squeezed and burned. He flailed his arms. His tunic caught on a spiky branch, further trussing him.

"Help!" he tried to scream, but water swallowed the plea.

His muscles quivered with the need to stop. To just rest. He flailed his arms and legs one final time.

Michael floated face down in the lake. His body gently bobbed with the lake current. No more gut-gripping fear clenching him. Instead, his mind wandered along wisps of memory. Images of his mother flashed. He pictured her silky golden hair and tender smile—just as she'd looked before the wasting illness took her from him.

His muscles twitched and cramped. As lake water filled more precious space in his lungs, other images, fragments of his life, flitted through in a final dreamscape: scenes of his older brother Roger barking out orders to drill him in swordplay; his younger brother Philip goading him into jovial roughhousing in the fields surrounding their home; his tutor, Master Ralph, pointing to a page in a book to show him the wonders of the written word. He missed them all with fervor. Even his demanding and arrogant father, towering over him, telling him to go out in the field and train with his brothers.

Michael sank into darkness, the harsh sound of his father's commanding voice echoing in his memories. He took one last gasp, a breath full of lake water, and surrendered.

Immersed in an in-between realm of lake waters and golden light, his soul flickered, then swelled, its flame yearning for freedom. A beautiful, ethereal Lady shimmered before him. Silver stars crowned her night-black hair, and midnight blue robes rustled as She leaned toward him. She smiled, capturing his gaze. He stared into her eyes, unable to look away. Not wanting to. They shone like moonlight and stars, pearly-silver swirls of mystery in motion. Their blue depths reflected kindness and compassion. Her mercy warmed his cold, dying body, and spread to fill the chilled crevices inside him. He felt such comfort from Her presence that all thoughts of family, all thoughts of Excalibur, drifted away.

She held out her hand. He took it.

Chapter 2

The Isle of Avalon
1529 C.E.

Marissa opened her tear-swollen eyes. Nighttime shadows slithered across her bedroom walls and huddled in the corners.

Stop trembling, she chided herself. *You might be young, but you're still a priestess of Avalon. You can't be afraid of shadows. Or bleak premonitions.*

She twisted around to face her sister beside her in bed, amazed her twin was still asleep. "Ciara," she cried, shaking her sister's shoulder. "Wake up!"

Ciara moaned and pulled the sheets over her head. "Go back to sleep." Her hand patted the bed, searching for the woolen coverlet.

Marissa persisted. "I've had the Vision."

"You what?" Ciara asked, her voice thick with slumber.

"The Death Vision. Me! At only twelve summers old." Marissa scrambled out of bed and unlaced her nightgown. Amidst her racing heartbeat, and despite her despair for the boy in the vision, she felt pride rise in her chest. She'd received this special divination meant for those older than her. It would show all the priestesses of Avalon that she was capable. Trustworthy.

"I have to tell Mother."

Ciara peeked over the sheets. "Are you sure it was the Death Vision?"

Marissa stamped her foot. "Yes, I'm sure!" She jutted her chin forward. "In fact, I want to have *more.*"

"Oh, Marissa, be careful what you ask for," Ciara whispered, her blue eyes filled with worry.

Marissa shook her head. "Don't you see? This might impress the priestesses. Show them all that at last I can be trusted again . . . after . . ."

Ciara completed her sister's sentence with a compassionate sigh. "After what happened to us in the Faery Realm." She rose up on one elbow and brushed her sleep-rumpled flaxen hair away from her face. "That was well over two summers ago."

Marissa nodded, glad her sister said it aloud for her. "I know. But I still haven't made up for it."

"I forgave you long ago."

Ciara cupped a hand over her heart. Marissa's chin quivered. She turned away so her twin wouldn't see, and fumbled with her laces. "You shouldn't have," she murmured.

"I still have faith in you."

Marissa spoke over her sister. "I have to prove myself to Mother."

It would be a few hours yet before the rising sun would color the sky golden and erase night's darkness. Mother always came to their room at dawn. She'd kiss their foreheads to awaken her and Ciara for the daily rituals. Marissa couldn't wait that long.

She slipped out of her nightgown, letting it fall to the floor in a crumpled heap. When she reached for her day robes hanging on the wall hook, the room suddenly spun and pitched. Her body tilted to the side. She inched backwards, her hands groping for the bed. A swirling shimmer of silver and blue, the muted colors of the stars and the sea, billowed around her, enveloping her.

Marissa heard a voice, as clearly as if her sister had spoken. But it wasn't Ciara. The voice was crystalline, like the song of a thousand stars. The Goddess of the Stars and the Sea.

"*You must save him, Marissa. Both your destinies depend upon it.*"

Marissa's body thrummed with excitement. The Goddess had called her by name.

"Our destinies?" she asked in a hushed tone. "Isn't he already dead?"

She knew that minutes in Avalon could equate to mere seconds in the world of man. Or sometimes the minutes matched, the variation brought on by the magical veils concealing the island. Maybe there indeed was still time to save him.

"*There's barely time. You must hurry! Find Michael!*" resounded before the streams of silver and blue slowly faded. The room stopped spinning. Marissa slumped forward. Ciara's voice interrupted the silence.

"Marissa? Are you all right?" Ciara leaned across the bed and wrapped her arms around her twin.

Marissa clung to her. "Did you hear that?"

"Hear what?"

"The Goddess speaking."

"What did she say?" Ciara asked, eyes wide.

"It's about the boy from the Death Vision. And me. Us."

"Us? You and me?"

"No. The boy and me."

Ciara pouted. "Not me?"

"I have to go straight away." Marissa let go of her grip on her sister's arms and bent to gather her day robes.

"Aren't you going to go tell Mother about having the Death Vision?" Ciara clambered out of bed after her sister.

Marissa swiftly slid a blue tunic over her head. "That will have to wait. The Goddess told me to save the boy. I have to do that first."

"But where are you going?"

She held off answering. Instead, she put her arms through her robe's silken sleeves, tied the cord about her waist, and grabbed her cloak. She looked up, defiance sparking in her eyes. "To Glastonbury."

Ciara took in a swift breath. "Into the world of man? Elder Vanora says it's dangerous to go there alone. A young girl, and a priestess at that. You know you need to ask an Elder's permission, and even then, they'd have to go with you."

"I can't wait to ask anyone's permission. They'd only try to stop me. There's no time for rules or I won't be able to save him." Marissa opened their bedroom door and turned briefly in the doorway. "I'll show everyone I can do this. I'll help him." She slung her cloak around her shoulders and clasped it with a silver brooch.

"I'll come with you," Ciara said, her voice tremulous.

"No," Marissa ordered. She softened her tone. "Please, no. I don't want to lead you into trouble again. I cannot. This is my task. I need to do this myself." She hurried down the hall before her sister could respond.

Marissa tiptoed through the lodge they shared with their mother, Alianore, the High Priestess of Avalon. She hoped her sister wouldn't betray her plans. Easing out the back door, she softly closed it behind her and sprinted toward the forest beyond their house. The Goddess's directive left no room for doubt—only the over-riding compulsion to make haste. She would face her mother, as well as Vanora and the other Elders' reprimands later. After she returned.

The full moon hung low, illuminating her way. Marissa darted across its silver path through the ripening apple orchards of Avalon. "No one listens to me anymore," she murmured to herself, "but they will now." Her footsteps pounded the earth, stamping it with her determination.

Barinthus, the ferryman of death, crouched, patiently waiting within the dark recesses of the Underworld, He lifted his head, his somnolent eyes now alert, and sniffed at the damp air in his cavern. A boy. Drowned. Avalon's lake, but Glastonbury side. Odd, he thought. He rose, ready to assume his eternal duty.

He presumed the Avalon priestesses had already received their prophetic Death Vision for the boy. He did not ponder the matter further. It was simply his task to collect body and soul, not to render judgment. Neither did he mourn the loss of a young lad full of promise. He'd seen many such deaths over the eons. It was merely the underbelly of the cycle of life.

Barinthus adjusted his long black cape, his grim face now hidden in the deep folds of the hood. The funerary barge was moored in an alcove, ever prepared. In two efficient steps the ferryman reached the prow.

Marissa crossed through the apple orchard onto a grassy field and continued running. She knew Barinthus would have already left the Underworld and be on his way to claim Michael's soul. Once he disembarked, she could no longer intercede on the boy's behalf. The rules of the Underworld were firm. When the ferryman docked, he would raise his lantern to find his charge in the pearly mist, collect the body, and lay it on the raised floor of his barge in preparation to travel West. It was an act of finality that could not be reversed.

Three of Marissa's Elders, funerary priestesses of Avalon, would then arrive for their customary role to help guide the soul to the comfort of the promised golden land beyond the ninth wave.

Marissa raced to reach Michael first.

The Goddess's edict had been adamant. *You must save him, Marissa!* She swallowed thickly. How exactly was she supposed to do that? She hadn't a clue. Through force of will, she balled her fists and pushed aside the upwelling of doubt threatening to lodge in her stomach.

She paused only a moment amidst the grassy plain near the lake to listen for the steady click of the ferryman's oars. Nothing yet. Only the nearby lapping of the lake and mild gusts of wind rippling through the marsh grass. But her inner senses, her deep gut intuition, felt the trace of his preordained approach.

She ran again, urgency fueling swift footsteps.

Barinthus directed his ferryboat with a flick of his wrist. The barge responded, silently gliding through the circuitous Underworld waterways. The ferryman gripped a hanging lantern on a pole with his right hand; his dark eyes staring straight ahead with single-minded purpose while the barge navigated the familiar course. First, along the River of Forgetfulness. Halfway along the River, just beyond the bend ahead, he would reach the Point of No Return, where destiny could not be revoked. Once there, he would be compelled to complete his journey to transport the dead boy, body and soul, to the everlasting golden shores of the Otherworld.

He calculated it wouldn't be long before he reached Avalon's lake.

"Oh, these cursed robes," Marissa muttered under her breath, yanking the length of her cape from a thorny hawthorn bush and shoving the hem into her belt.

When she spotted the row of ancient gnarled oaks that marked Avalon's westernmost boundary, she slowed her pace. The oak trees loomed before her, ageless sentinels with burled eyes that watched warily. She didn't have time for tree-speak. No reprieve to stop and match their unhurried life rhythm, to communicate with them in mind pictures and thoughts, or to press her hands against their rough bark and listen for a response.

"I'm on a mission from the Goddess. I must hurry," she said aloud as she sprinted between them. She owed them that much respect at least. Naturally, with her rushed words, they didn't answer back.

At the snap of a twig, she whipped around. Ciara, following her. As usual. "Wait for me!"

Marissa groaned. There was no time to argue, no time to waste. She turned and ran toward the Avalon lakeshore. A row of small wooden coracles sat tied to a landing dock in the marsh, lake waves gently lapping against their sides. She darted to the closest one and pulled on its riggings. The tightly tied ropes were slippery in her anxious hands and she grappled with them. Her stomach felt as knotted as the riggings. Despite her trembling fingers, the mooring finally released. She scrambled onboard and grabbed the oar.

Ciara finally caught up, panting. She put her hands on her knees and bent over to catch her breath. "Take me with you. I'll help. Please."

"No. I'll break the rules. Not you. I'll not get you in trouble again."

Marissa pushed off the jetty with the paddle, leaving her twin behind. The swish of her oar cut through the glassy water as she skillfully maneuvered the prow around. After a moment of forward momentum, she established a steady rowing rhythm. Row, pause, row, pause. The lake's mists shrouded everything in caped seclusion. Her raspy breath, the splash of her paddle, and the rattling cry of a crane overhead were the only sounds that broke the foggy stillness. At the halfway point between Avalon and Glastonbury, the mists thickened into a milky opaque barrier. The magical curtain, created centuries ago by the High Priestess Rhianna, concealed and protected the Isle of Avalon. Marissa had to part the veils if she wanted to pass from Avalon into the mundane world.

Marissa set her paddle aside and scooted along the wooden seats to the prow, where she kneeled. Her heartbeat sounded loud within the surrounding calm. She wiped damp palms on her robes. She had never spoken the charmed invocation aloud—the one that would raise the opaque mists. Only fully initiated priestesses were allowed to do it, though she had heard the words so many times, she knew them by heart. She closed her eyes and lifted trembling hands.

"By the name and magic of Avalon . . ." she began.

The breeze stilled and birds stopped singing while she recited the crossing invocation in a language as ancient and secretive as the Isle of Avalon itself.

As the last words melted into silence, she opened her eyes. A spiraling vortex had formed before her. The clouds above raced across the sky. It was working! She lowered her arms, and the white mists of Avalon obeyed. A glittering pathway opened into England's summer country village of Glastonbury. The world of man.

Taking her paddle in hand, she rowed the coracle toward Glastonbury's shore, only a short distance away. She had sluiced her oar through the water only once when the splash of another paddle sounded from behind. Her breath caught in her throat. Was it Barinthus? *Already?*

Glancing over a shoulder, she spotted Ciara rowing a coracle a few yards away. Marissa let out a shaky breath. Her sister had crossed the barrier with her, riding on the tail of the invocation. Seconds later, the misty portal to Avalon snapped shut behind them.

Marissa faced forward, trying to concentrate on the task, relieved it wasn't Barinthus following so closely. Still, though she loved her twin fiercely, she felt responsible for Ciara's safety. *Maybe I should first take my sister back to Avalon.* But there wasn't time. Her stomach clenched, torn between sisterly duty and the Goddess's command.

I have to save the boy. Both our destinies depend upon it, she repeated to herself—not understanding exactly what destiny but having faith in the Goddess's words. *I have to save Michael.*

There was no choice, really. She had to follow the Goddess's directive. Now it meant she'd watch over her sister while she did so.

"Keep up, Ciara!"

Peering at the reeds on the marshy Glastonbury shore, it didn't take long to find a spot where she could moor the boat. She secured the vessel by wedging it in the silt and tying it to a staked rope. When she leapt out, she landed on springy marsh turf. Seconds later, Ciara lodged her own coracle and scrambled out.

Ciara edged close to Marissa's side. "We've never been to Glastonbury on our own without Mother or Vanora."

"I know," Marissa answered, stepping behind a stand of tall reeds.

Ciara squeezed in after. "You know what Vanora says. It's not good to be alone here. There could be men who don't like priestesses, or Christian monks who think Avalon is evil. Or . . ."

"I know!" Marissa hissed.

Her twin's eyes filled with tears.

Marissa put her arm around her shoulders. "I'm sorry. Truly. But we must be brave if I'm to find this boy."

Ciara sniffled and nodded.

Marissa lifted her sister's chin. "I must go. You stand right here and help me by praying for this poor soul, and me. Chant the invocations to safeguard us."

She scanned the marshland, then gave Ciara what was hopefully a reassuring smile. Murmuring a silent prayer for courage and protection, she stepped out from behind the cover of the reeds.

She didn't know how she would find Michael. And she and Ciara were now both fully visible in the world of man.

Chapter 3

Glastonbury, England
Anno Domini 1529

Despite Marissa's orders, Ciara pursued her.

"Marissa! Come back home with me. This instant," she pleaded.

Marissa was sure Ciara's panic instilled the unaccustomed courage to challenge her.

Ciara huffed her unease. "Mother made us promise to always protect each other. How can I protect you here?" She eyed the bulrushes warily. "How can you protect *me*?"

Marissa considered the marshy landscape. "We can always go back under the reeds to hide if need be."

Two white cranes swooped low, landing a few feet away on the glassy lake. Ciara jumped back, startled by the sudden whirring rush of wings. Marissa heaved a sigh.

Their tutor, Vanora, had often remarked that the twins' birth order had forecast their dispositions. At birth, Marissa came out first, and Ciara arrived a full five minutes later. Those few short minutes determined that Marissa would be the leader and inherit the title of High Priestess one day. Ciara always insisted she really didn't mind, admitting she didn't much like the idea of telling others what to do or how to do it. Now, Ciara shivered and tightened her cloak around her shoulders, more from fright than the chill air. Watching the cranes with anxious eyes, she said, "What if that's the King of the Underworld, taken on the shape of a bird to come after us?"

"Don't be silly. What would the King of the Underworld want with us?" Her eyes scanned the lake, but there was no one.

"Maybe we shouldn't be interfering with death, and that's why he's come for us."

"Nonsense. The Goddess herself bid me to search for the boy." Marissa pointed at the pair of birds, gliding along the lake's surface. "They're cranes, Ciara. A sign of the Goddess, not a shape-shifting King of the Underworld. Look at them. They're beautiful and fluffy white. Stop fretting."

The close quarters of the reedy marsh caused her voice to echo. It mingled with the cacophony of croaking frogs, birdsong, and the breeze fanning through the willows. Early morning fog billowed across the plains and over the lake. Marissa hoped she could find the boy's body in such haze. She held a hand out for her sister. She was the faster runner and would have to drag Ciara along, if she even came. Her twin ignored the outstretched hand.

"Are you coming or not?" Marissa had no patience for this.

"Yes, but . . ."

Marissa squirmed. They could read each other's thoughts and talk within each other's minds. Being twins bonded them that way, and their priestess heritage heightened the ability. It was an innate trait from their ancient magical bloodlines. Ciara's unspoken words broadcast in Marissa's mind as if her sister shouted them aloud.

What if we are caught outside Avalon again? Even worse, what trouble might you be bringing to us once more?

Marissa winced at the subtle accusations.

"Stop reading my thoughts. You know I don't blame you," Ciara burst out, her tone contrite.

However, Marissa had seen Ciara's involuntary shudder at the memory of their ill-fated journey two years ago, when she'd convinced Ciara and their friend Shayla to leave the safety of Avalon and enter the unknown Faery Realm. Many of the Faery race could be friendly with the priestesses, as well as the occasional human, but they kept their distance, and their realm and their laws were still foreign. She had willfully pushed down the guilt festering in the pit of her stomach ever since the incident. There was no time to dwell on remorse right now.

She refocused, trying to get her bearings amidst the jungle of shrubbery, reeds, and fog. "I feel him. Michael is close-by."

By Ciara's confused expression, Marissa knew instantly her sister didn't sense a thing. A sudden and insistent tug of intuition deep in her belly forced her to keep moving forward. "If you won't take my hand, then you'll have to hurry as fast as your legs can carry you."

They headed farther down the shore, Marissa racing ahead, running alongside a thicket of reeds that bordered the lake. Cold water soaked her slippers, squishing between her toes with each step. She ignored the chill and doggedly tramped through the wet mire of the fenland, following the intuition rising from her belly. Sometimes words arose in her mind, guiding, *Run to your left. Go forward. Faster!* Sometimes her feet had a will of their own. Every so often, images of pathways formed to show her the way.

She entered the looming jungle of reeds ahead, their tips jutted high in the air. When she stepped amidst their fronds, towering stalks swallowed her from view.

"Wait up! Marissa! Where are you?" Ciara's cry pierced the marshes, prompting the throaty warble of the white-necked cranes in reply. "Oh Goddess, don't let her get hurt."

Marissa made her way through the stand of reeds, ignoring the tiny scratches the branches made across her arms.

"Don't leave me on my own outside Avalon," Ciara's whimper flitted through the rustling fronds.

Pushing aside the long stalks, Marissa stepped onto the lake's shoreline. She squinted at the water, searching, and saw a boy, surely the one she was meant to save. He was floating, half submerged in the lake. His body lay face down in the water, his tunic caught on a spiky branch.

Her heart began to thump hard against her chest as she hurried across the sandy shore. She threw her cloak to the ground and stepped into the lake, shivering with the cold. Her robes immediately grew heavy with water; she lifted them and pushed onwards. The water rose to her waist before she finally reached the boy. She yanked his arm out of his tunic to release him from the branch tethering him.

He wasn't moving. "Please, don't be dead," she murmured. Dread and hope sparred in her gut.

The boy's buoyant body floated atop the water. Marissa grabbed his arm to turn him face up. Tawny hair fanned out in the water. He didn't look much older than she was.

"Goddess, help," she prayed.

Positioning herself behind his head and hooking her elbows under his armpits, she started to walk backwards, towing him back to land, but his leg was tangled in something. She tugged hard, but he remained trapped.

A swarm of cranes flapped their downy wings and took sudden flight from the thick bulrushes as Ciara emerged on the shoreline.

"Help me, Ciara!" Marissa shouted.

Her sister gasped as she treaded into the biting cold water and scrambled back to shore. Marissa gestured to the boy's leg.

"Please! Come and help me set his leg free. Hurry!"

Ciara chewed the inside of her cheek, but dutifully trudged forward into the water.

"Here, hold him just like I am," Marissa said when her twin reached her.

She quickly transferred her grip on him to Ciara, then clamped her mouth shut and plunged down into the cold water.

Keeping her eyes open, she searched for whatever entangled the boy. Water slowed her grasping hands. Finally, she found what she was searching for. Tendrils of a water reed ensnared his foot. She yanked on his leg but the foot didn't budge. Little bubbles of air escaped her mouth. She fought the rising panic and tugged again. Nothing. She removed his boot and the leg floated free.

Marissa propelled herself to the surface and gulped in a deep breath of air. Ciara continued gripping the boy's arm to help float him along to shore.

"No," Marissa insisted, pushing long, wet hair away from her face. "Let me finish this. *I* have to be the one to save him."

Ciara moved aside while Marissa put her arms underneath Michael's heavy body and pulled him along on her own. She fought against the soggy weight of her tunic and plodded to shore as fast as she could, doing her best to avoid the slippery underwater rocks. Ciara trailed close behind. Once they reached the shoreline, Marissa laid him on his side.

"You're the better healer," Marissa said. "Now *you* help him."

Ciara knelt next to the lifeless form—his color ashen and his lips blue. "Vanora would say to pound on his back," she murmured. When she did, brackish water poured from his mouth. But he didn't breathe.

"That should have worked," Ciara's eyes widened with alarm. "I know I did it right."

"Hurry, please!" Marissa pleaded. "Before Barinthus arrives and takes him."

She cast a wild glance toward the lake and shivered with a sudden chill. She sensed his barge nearing its objective.

With trembling hands, Ciara thumped on the unmoving back again. This time she added a healing song. In a clear tone, she sang, a plea to the elemental forces of nature.

> *Spirits of water,*
> *leave this boy's lungs.*
> *Spirits of air,*
> *fill them with breath.*
> *Life force of earth,*
> *give this boy strength.*
> *Spark of life,*
> *fuel his body.*

Marissa paced in a circle around them, muscles taut. The chant rang in her ears, a desperate reminder this boy must live, that their destinies were intertwined. She bent over him. "You cannot die. Breathe! Now!" she commanded.

Despite the summoning chant, he remained motionless. Ciara turned him onto his side and again pounded between his shoulder blades with the palms of her hands, this time shouting the invocations.

> *Spirits of water,*
> *leave this boy's lungs . . .*

Marissa paid close attention to the words. She inhaled into her womb-space, the cradle of her magical power, just as her mother had taught her. Fear threatened to swallow her voice, but she fought it. She repeated the magical mantra, along with Ciara, forcing the healing song past the tightening in her throat. Their singing blended. Marissa's womb blazed with raised power, a sure sign their dual efforts enhanced the chant's magic.

But still he hadn't moved, so she changed the words. From entreaty to command.

> *Hear me now.*
> *Heed my plea.*
> *Make him live.*
> *Death's grip be freed.*

Ciara gasped and shot her an alarmed glance. Marissa waved aside the caution behind the look. Ciara pushed her thoughts into her sister's mind. *"You know we don't command the elementals."*

Marissa watched the boy, this *Michael*, closely and answered Ciara aloud. "Yours wasn't working."

Ciara replied telepathically again. *"Vanora taught us to work in harmony with the water, earth, air, and fire. To collaborate."*

"The elementals know the Goddess bade me save him."

"You know the laws of magic. What you send out comes back to you many times magnified."

Marissa answered out loud. "I've done nothing wrong. I have the Goddess's blessing to do whatever I have to do."

The boy coughed and gulped in air.

"See! He breathes!" Marissa cried with a huge smile.

His chest rose and fell.

"Sometimes a command is necessary," Marissa glanced at her sister.

Ciara gave a doubtful shake of her head, staring as he sucked in more air and began thrashing his arms.

Marissa clasped her hands together. *Thank you*, she intoned to the elemental forces. Still, fear latched alongside the triumph swelling in her chest. A chill ran down her spine. Did Barinthus approach? She craned her neck to search the lake waters for his barge.

The ferryman's barge glided along the timeless River of Forgetfulness. Up ahead was the Point of No Return. Barinthus blinked once, peering out from under his deep hood. The route forward dimmed. The siren call for his services abruptly dulled and faded. He reached into his pockets, fingering the coined tolls he had collected from recent passengers. It seemed there would be no fare exacted today. The boy lived. Face impassive, he turned his barge around and headed back down the river toward the Underworld, to wait until the next death traveler called for his aid.

Marissa cupped her hands around her ears to listen. There was no sound of Barinthus's barge propelling itself across the lake. She searched further with her 'second sight'—her intuitive inner eyes and psychic senses that could see and feel into the Inner Realms. The rivers Barinthus traveled to make his way up from the Underworld were quiet. No barge and no ferryman. She exhaled the breath she'd been holding.

The boy coughed and sputtered. When he started to vomit, Ciara held his head to the side so he wouldn't choke. She dabbed his lips with the hem of her robe and wiped his mouth clean once he'd finished retching. He moaned, but his eyes remained closed.

"My turn to tend to him." Marissa shoved her way under Ciara's arms.

She cradled his head in her hands. When she touched him, a surge of heat traveled from her hands up through her arms and radiated in her chest. She drew in a sharp breath as the heat banked in the power spot of her belly. What kind of connection was this?

"I saw you in a Death Vision," she told him softly, though she knew he didn't know what that meant.

Marissa studied his face. Yes, this was the same boy from her vision. The dimpled cleft in his chin, the straight nose, and especially the long tawny hair, the color of a lion's mane. He wore the same simple carved wooden cross on a thin strip of leather round his neck. The front of his tunic bore what looked like a family crest with a white horse pawing the air beside an oak tree, all embroidered in gold thread. There was even that tiny white scar by his left ear. This must be Michael.

A purple bruise swelled across his temple. His breathing gurgled loudly. He groaned again, his head rolling back and forth. Everything in her wanted to protect him.

He flailed his arms. Ciara sat back on her heels, satisfied he was at least breathing.

"I'm here. You're safe now," Marissa murmured close to his ear, feeling an unaccustomed surge of gentleness. She lifted his head onto her lap. He stopped flailing and grew calm within her lap's embrace. She leaned over him, her dark locks falling forward like a curtain that sealed out the world around them.

Michael's eyelids fluttered open. Marissa's face was the first thing he saw. "Your hair . . . black and shiny as raven wings," he murmured.

Marissa wasn't sure what to say.

"Are you an Angel?" he asked, his voice hoarse from swallowing lake water. His gaze was penetrating, solemn.

She laughed. "No. Definitely not."

She wondered if he could see the two Angels surrounding him, the radiant custodians who wove the threads of life into the fabric of physical existence. Golden winged, with benevolent eyes and luminous hands, they deftly reattached his pulsating life threads back to his body. Their weaving grew stronger with each breath he took.

"*See, Ciara,*" she spoke into her sister's mind. "*The life-force Angels are here. The Goddess blesses this boy. I was right to use a commanding chant.*"

Ciara watched with a soft, indirect gaze, to see the Angels more clearly.

Michael reached up gingerly to touch a lock of Marissa's black hair. Wet from lake water, it glinted all the more in the early morning sunlight. "Are you the Black Raven of Death come to claim me?" he murmured.

"No. I'm not the Death Raven. I came to save you, not claim your life," Marissa answered with pride.

Michael lay still, looking into Marissa's eyes. A coughing fit hit him forcefully, his chest rising and falling with rapid breaths.

"There was so much water. I couldn't breathe. Then I was floating." He closed his eyes briefly and opened them again with a faraway gaze. "I heard singing. It sounded just like my mother used to, and I saw a beautiful Lady with a blue cape and a crown of stars. She told me she loved me, but that I couldn't stay with her. Not yet anyhow." His eyes closed again. Marked drowsiness overcame his features.

"Yes. The Goddess of the Stars and Sea." Marissa nodded. Undoubtedly, the Goddess would be there for the boy in his death throes. Odd that an untrained boy from the world of man could see and hear Her as distinctly as the priestesses of Avalon did.

His eyes opened. "A Goddess? Really? Our priest would say it was Mary, the mother of our Lord."

Marissa shrugged. "It seems the same to me."

He looked away. "I didn't find Ex Calibur."

The boy sounded wistful, his tone disappointed. Vanora had told her and Ciara about the many boys, and even grown men, who'd searched Avalon's lake for the famous sword over the centuries. Of course it wasn't there. Silly quest. Marissa stopped the giggle rising to her lips. It had been returned long ago to the Faery Realm, its true home. The sword awaited retrieval by its rightful owner, along with its three companion magical implements—the chalice, the rod, and the stone. All four remained hidden until the affairs of the human world deemed the time right for magic to surface once more.

She didn't know why, but she told him, "You'll find something even better than Ex Calibur one day."

Looking up at her, his eyes shone. "Do you really think so?"

Marissa nodded and smiled, knowing her statement was true. Ciara, kneeling at the lad's other side, clucked her tongue as she leaned over his legs and checked for injuries, just as her Healing Teacher had taught. She sucked on her lower lip with narrowed eyes, thinking hard.

She whispered to Marissa, "He seems all right. But I fear he may get worse. I think the Healing Mistress would say to watch for signs of the brain swelling or even bleeding from the head injury."

Her words chilled Marissa. Michael was here, saved. Alive. She'd done as the Goddess asked. Surely the Goddess would watch over him now? She flung her long hair behind her back. It seemed an invisible barrier stood around her and the boy. Ciara's presence faded into the background.

Michael's stomach roiled and his chest felt thick. At least he was breathing. The fact that he hadn't been only moments before suddenly made him want to sob with relief. He was alive! He blinked hard to force back the tears. It wouldn't do to cry in front of the raven-haired girl.

Everything was turning blurry and hazy in his mind. He bit the inside of his cheek to stay alert, to stop from drifting into the pitch-black chasm that rose in waves, threatening to swallow his awareness. He didn't want to drift into that black hole again.

He looked up at the girl, his head comfortable on her lap. As if it belonged there. As if he belonged anywhere close to her. The heat emanating from her gaze warmed him, like the fire of a blazing home hearth, a fire that spread throughout his chest and kindled his heart to beat faster. The feeling puzzled him.

He frowned. What was happening? Who was this girl? Her eyes intrigued him. They were brown, flecked with amber. Like candlelight in twilight. They sparkled as she smiled. He felt a sudden urge to tell her what had happened to him in the lake. Tell her before he fell back into that black sleepy abyss that pulled him down into a place where he had no thoughts and couldn't feel his body. But disclosure of any kind to a stranger was not wise, or so his father always told him.

Yet there was something special about this raven-haired girl that compelled him to tell her anyway.

A thought flashed briefly—it would explain why she had this mysterious effect over him. Da's priest had warned him before he left on the hunting trip, hadn't he?

Doubt crossed his face. "Are you . . . Faery?" Michael asked, stammering the heathen word and making the sign of the cross over his chest.

"Of course not. Do I look Faery?" She laughed. *Such a sweet sound.*

"No, not Faery," she continued. "Although our dear friend Shayla is half Faery. She's beautiful . . . green eyes and silver-white hair . . ." She stopped at the look of confusion and fear on his face.

"What are you if you're not an Angel and you're not Faery?" His voice rasped, his throat sore from coughing.

Another girl interrupted. He hadn't even noticed her presence before. "She's my sister. A priestess. As am I." She paused and added, "If it weren't for her—for us—you'd still be in the lake."

"Wait. You're a *priestess*?" Michael turned towards the new voice. He grimaced when the movement caused his head to throb and his vision to double. This other girl's fair coloring and gentle features were very pretty. She nearly distracted him from his current situation.

"Da' says priestesses are of the devil." Michael peered fearfully at the two, as if they might sprout horns and steal his soul. He flinched and pulled back, but ended up coughing with the effort.

The dark-haired sister looked struck. "Priestesses evil? 'Tis a lie," she said crossly. "I'm certainly not evil. The villagers in Glastonbury welcome us during their Summer Solstice celebrations. Besides, you could thank me for finding you and saving your life." A flush rose in her cheeks.

"Dear Goddess, why did you ask me to save this wretch?" she muttered, pulling her legs out from under him. His head fell from her lap and hit the loamy dirt. He groaned. Guilt flashed briefly in her brown eyes.

Michael cringed. Losing the physical connection to the girl almost hurt more than the painful throbbing in his head. "Our priest says to shun the likes of you." He paused to catch a breath. "He says you steal babies. Change men into hairy one-eyed beasts, with long, sharp teeth." His eyes widened. "You won't change me, will you?"

She sat back on her legs, arms folded across her chest. "Don't be foolish." Then she grinned, eyes dancing with mischief. "Then again, maybe I can indeed change you."

"Marissa," The fair sister chided gently. "The lad merely speaks the warnings of his elders. He doesn't know any better."

Michael scowled but kept a cautious eye on the cheeky one, Marissa. "Nay! I know many things. Do you not know who I am? I'm the son of Gerard de Boulle." Another black-chasm lapped at his awareness. He clenched his fists tight, struggling to keep it at bay.

Marissa dismissed his boasting with a wave of her hand. "I don't know of this Gerard you speak of. Nor do I care."

Seemingly satisfied that Michael was alive, the other girl stood, "Come, Sister. You found him. Now we must leave. We've been outside Avalon far too long. Someone from Glastonbury will find him and help him."

Marissa remained crouched at his right shoulder.

"Wait. Don't go yet." He reached out a hand toward the girls.

He considered the one with long flaxen hair and innocent blue eyes. Her smile was lovely and kind. Surely she could not be a priestess. But the other one? Well, despite being entrancing, that black hair of hers and those haunting amber-flecked eyes might be marks of the devil. That's what his father's priest would say. But somehow, he liked them—both. Could his father be wrong about priestesses? Could his family's priest be mistaken as well? After all, it had been a kindhearted thing the fiery Marissa had done for him.

"You did save my life, so I thank you for that," he conceded.

He felt for his eyes with his fingers, then rubbed a thumb along his top teeth. "I don't think you've done anything bad to my eyes or my teeth like Da's priest warned me about. So there, that settles it. You can't really be priestesses then, can you?"

The girls exchanged glances and giggled.

He offered them his best smile. "My name is Michael. Tell me then, am I dreaming? Are you real?" He paused and said in a quiet voice, "Or am I dead and you're the heavenly spirits?" His hand reached out and pinched Marissa's arm to make sure.

"Ouch. Stop that." Marissa rolled her eyes and stood in front of her sister. "I'm Marissa."

"Ciara," the girl with the flaxen hair said, peering around Marissa's shoulder. "I helped rescue you, too. And yes, we're real. Real priestesses."

Michael glanced up at Ciara, and saw an upset expression cross her clear features. He sat up slowly, groaning with the effort. A burst of pain shot through his head and everything was spinning, but he had to say something nice. His father would tell him it was bad manners to insult someone who had helped you.

"I didn't mean anything by it," he said through increasing pain and dizziness. He paused, squinting at both girls. "I can tell you're not bad. Neither one of you. So, I apologize, but I still don't believe you're really priestesses." He wondered what his Da's priest would have him do, maybe make the sign of the cross over his chest again, and so he did.

Ciara just stared, but Marissa laughed out loud.

Just then, his stomach, full of lake water, lurched and gurgled. "I don't feel good," he moaned and quickly turned his head aside, retching. He hoped Marissa wasn't watching.

He felt a soft hand on his back. Glad for the comforting gesture, the churning in his stomach, even his fear, was instantly soothed. Was this priestess magic? Did it matter if it was? They were helping him. Helping another person was a good thing. He wiped his mouth with the back of his hand and looked up to find it was Ciara who held his head.

She gently guided him to lie back on the loamy ground. "Marissa, his head injury is worsening, just as I feared," she whispered.

A woman's voice cut through Michael's confused thoughts. "I've found them."

Chapter 4

Glastonbury, England
Anno Domini 1529

Undulating stalks were thrust aside, and the reeds parted. A regal-looking woman emerged, clutching her long silken robes above her ankles. She scanned the Glastonbury shoreline and sighted the trio a short distance away. The two sisters were still leaning over Michael in the tufted grass beside the shore. The woman's bright blue eyes darkened with concern. An elderly lady arrived next, puffing, and shaking the dew from her hem.

Marissa winced as they approached.

"You girls know you should not be outside the veil of Avalon on your own." The older one glared at the girls, then shook her head, tutting. She tucked her wispy grey hair inside her hood and patted her robes smooth. When she lifted her gaze again, it settled on Marissa.

"And you, young lass, did you learn nothing from the disaster you wreaked by visiting the Faery Realm without permission?"

The striking one who appeared first strode forward to kneel beside Michael. "What happened here?" she directed the question to Marissa.

"I saw him in a Death Vision . . ."

The other interrupted before Marissa could respond. "You had a Death Vision?" Her voice rose in pitch. "But I haven't trained you yet."

"I know. But I did have one, Vanora," Marissa replied, bobbing her head emphatically at the elderly figure.

"You had a vision of me?" Michael's lips parted in awe.

Marissa nodded to him and beamed, as if they shared an important secret.

"We will talk about your Death Vision later," The first woman said, turning her attention to the boy's injuries. Her brows furrowed in concern as she lightly probed his head wound. "The Elders shared the vision of his death. Yet here he is. Alive." He shuddered at her touch and she finally looked into his eyes. "I am Alianore, the High Priestess of Avalon. You have nothing to fear from me."

"Michael!" A man's shout carried from across the reedy marsh, faint yet distinct.

The one called Vanora turned ashen. "We have to go. We are outside the boundaries of Avalon."

Ciara scrambled to her feet. "I told you." She glared at her sister.

Marissa remained hunched over Michael. "But the Glastonbury villagers can be friendly, can they not?" she looked up at Vanora. "They celebrate Summer Solstice with us. They ask for our help in healing their ill and injured."

"'Tis not the villagers I worry about," Vanora answered. "This boy and his people are strangers. Look at the way he dresses. The fine weave of his trews. And a nobleman's family crest embroidered on his tunic." She pointed to the finely stitched white horse and oak tree on Michael's tunic. "He is not from Glastonbury."

Wide-eyed, Michael clutched the cross hanging from his necklet. Alianore, clearly in charge, stood, surveying the stretch of marsh in the direction of the man's voice.

Marissa leaned over Michael. "Shh," she cautioned, though she knew the dense, tall bulrushes safely hid them all from view.

"Why? That's my Da's man, looking for me," Michael said. He squeezed his eyes tight against the spasm of pain in his head, the dizziness, the queasy stomach, and the drowsiness prodding him toward the black chasm that threatened to swallow him whole again.

Vanora plucked Marissa's sleeve. "Come. Now. We cannot be found. It will be the death of us. Or worse."

Ciara edged to Alianore's side. She glanced nervously from Marissa to Vanora, and then up at the High Priestess.

"You exaggerate, Vanora," Marissa insisted. "I cannot leave Michael. I won't."

"You know we do not interfere in the fate of those outside the veil of Avalon." Alianore stood tall.

"I already have. I saved him." Marissa lifted her head high. She felt heat rise up her neck. Her intent was good, yet here she was, disobedient yet again.

"Do not argue with your mother, child," Vanora admonished. Michael blinked. *Mother?*

"I will deal with you, Marissa, once we return home. For return we must." Alianore was unyielding.

"You don't . . . have to leave," Michael said with halted breath. "My father's men . . . will not harm you."

Vanora snorted in disdain and turned to Marissa. "Do you not remember the Avalon marauds during the time of the High Priestess Rhianna?"

Michael let out a small moan and gingerly touched the swelling on his forehead. Marissa took his hand in hers.

"I won't leave you," she promised.

Michael startled at her touch. The words of a tune the old bard sang in his father's Great Hall, not even two weeks prior, rushed into his memory. "*A touch can tell you a thousand things. The letting go, a thousand more.*"

"These reeds will only hide us for so long." Vanora drew their hands apart and lifted Marissa up by her arm, away from him.

Michael suddenly felt utterly alone.

Marissa twisted free from the older woman's grasp and pleaded with her mother. "The Goddess sent me to save him. She spoke to me this morning. Really, she did, Mama. There is something important about him. About him and me. Something the two of us must do together . . ."

Ciara gasped. "You and Michael together?" She looked down at the ground with a doleful frown.

Alianore raised an eyebrow. "The Goddess spoke to you about this boy?" She studied her daughter's face, her penetrating gaze coming to rest on Marissa's eyes.

"Yes, Mama, She did. The Goddess bade me find Michael and save him. You must believe me . . . this time . . ." Marissa's words faltered under her mother's searing scrutiny.

Alianore gave a soft sigh and turned to Vanora. "Tame your fear. My daughter follows a directive higher than my authority."

"Michael!" This time a lad's voice called out, sounding closer. "I didn't mean to lose sight of my little brother, Sir George. Truly, I didn't."

"Hush. We don't have time for that, Roger," came the gruff reply of an older man. "Spend your worry on our search."

"We have to find him, or Father will never forgive me!"

Vanora jerked her head in the direction of the voices and pleaded in hushed tones. "Leave the boy. Those two will soon find him."

"No!" Marissa insisted. "Mama, please!" She locked eyes with her mother.

"I think I hear something," said the voice of Sir George.

Alianore raised her hand, palm forward, a gesture meant to quiet Vanora. "The Goddess spoke to Marissa. I believe her. That changes everything."

"My Da's man . . . is only looking for me," Michael said feebly as his eyes drifted shut.

"They are coming closer." The words hissed through Vanora's thinned lips.

Marissa held out her hands in a pleading gesture. "You still don't trust me?"

Vanora frowned. "As long as you continue to traipse outside Avalon's borders without approval or chaperone."

Michael opened his eyes and took a gasping breath. "Here I am, Sir George!" he yelled.

"Is that you, Michael?" was shouted in return. In the distance, the tall bulrushes rustled with the knight's movement.

Marissa clutched Michael's arm. "Stop, Michael. You have to come back with me. I had a vision of you. I saved you." She swiped at her eyes. "We're supposed to do something grand together. I don't know what it is, but I know you must feel it too."

Michael wheezed and coughed and was about to muster his energy to call for Sir George again when he saw her tears start to fall. He didn't want her to cry. But he wanted to go home. He wanted his brothers. Even his father. He wanted his mother, dead all these years. These priestesses were strange, not Christian. Still, there was something about Marissa, something he couldn't begin to understand. It was a feeling even better than his cherished book learning with Master Ralph. Despite the priest's warnings, despite his father's certain disapproval, and despite his own uncertainty, he knew one thing: he trusted her. His gut swayed in favor of this mysterious girl. The shout to Sir George died on his lips.

"Lord keep me under your protection," he murmured. He wished everything would stop spinning around him, so he could see without his vision doubling, and hear them talk without it sounding so garbled. He fought his weighted eyelids. His eyes closed despite the unwelcome black chasm looming below his awareness, awaiting him with an open maw.

"One moment," Alianore said, and bent next to Michael once more.

The cool hand upon his forehead roused him from the black chasm's edge and into wakefulness once more. Her gaze grew unfocused, distant. Michael didn't know how he knew, but he was sure she was peering deep inside him, as if she looked into his soul. It was a curious sensation, a feather-light probe.

Alianore lifted her head. "The boy's struggle is not over. It is between life and death again. I see it in him. If we leave him, he will die. Of that I am certain."

"Then he has to come with us," Marissa cried.

Alianore flicked a cautionary look at her daughter before continuing, directing her words to Vanora. "His people's methods are incapable of giving him the care he will need. Especially the care his soul requires." She laid a gentle hand over Michael's. "We can help you, but will do nothing against your will."

Michael took a shuddering breath. "You say I'll die? But they already saved me." He continued in a breathless rush. "Da's physician . . . can heal me . . . with leeching . . . and bloodletting."

"You will be back with your father in good time, my dear," Alianore said. "For now, I advise the care of our Healing Mistress back in Avalon. For good or naught, my daughters have intervened and set fate in motion. The Goddess cast this new path for you, and for my daughters as well. What the Goddess bids, I must follow. If you are to complete your healing, you must come with us." Her voice was reassuring; she clearly bore the mantle of authority. "Still, it is your choice in the end."

"Michael, call out again so we can find you," Roger shouted from amidst the dense bulrushes.

"No. Come with us, Michael." Marissa pleaded. She put her hand in his again and held tight.

Vanora spoke curtly. "If the boy does not wish to come then we cannot take him." She reached for Marissa's arm once more. Marissa tensed and grumbled a warning.

"I believe your Vision, Marissa, and wish to follow its dictate. But calm yourself, my daughter, and respect your elder," Alianore commanded. The High Priestess turned to Michael. "What do you choose? There is no time."

Marissa murmured, "Please come with me, Michael. *Please* come with me."

The tall bulrushes rustled a short distance behind Vanora. She jumped aside, covering her mouth to stifle a scream.

"Michael," Roger called out again, separated by one last towering stand of reeds.

Ciara stepped back. "They're nearly here," she whispered, her face furrowed with panic.

Michael swallowed thickly and trained his eyes on Marissa, but his vision reeled and darkened, and he plummeted into the silent black abyss.

Vanora looked down at the boy. "He is unconscious. He cannot give his permission. Let those men find him."

"Mother. Don't leave him behind to die," Marissa cried.

The tall fronds behind them rustled once more. Heavy boots stomped noisily in the underbrush. The two cranes that had been gliding across the lake gave a warbled squawk, spread their downy wings, and lifted in flight directly overhead. Alianore cast a quick glance up at them, shielding her eyes with her hand from the glare of the sun.

"Cranes. A sign from the Goddess. It is confirmed. We take flight as the cranes show us. We leave," she commanded. "Now."

Chapter 5

Glastonbury, England
21st Century, Present Day

"I don't care, Sid. This assignment sucks and you know it." Sophie paced the small quarters of her room in the Wearyall Hill B&B. Her suitcase stood in the corner, untouched. The only things she'd unpacked were her laptop and research files for her article. The items were now strewn across the wooden desk near the window.

Sid's voice came across the cell phone, unapologetic and firm. "We've already gone over this. You're up against it this time. This new assignment will appease the boys who back the magazine. It'll show them you can toe the line. Come on, it'll save your job."

"I thought you liked my investigative style. I've won awards for it, dammit." Sophie was close to yelling at her boss, the editor in chief of the liberal investigative magazine *Fact and Fiction*.

"I do. That's why I hired you. But you pushed too far on your last piece." Sid paused to exhale loudly. "Be a good girl. Just do this stint, and then we can go about business as normal. The whole thing will blow over, and you'll be back covering the assignments you love."

Sophie nearly chucked the phone across the room. "This piddling assignment is the magazine's way of punishing me. And for God's sake, lay off the *good girl* crap."

"Stop it, Sophie. Don't be a pain in the ass." Sid's polished voice was now blade sharp. "You went rogue. You go rogue, you pay the price. That's all there is to it."

Sophie stiffened. "I followed my informant's lead. My report helped expose that perverted priest. That's a good thing. A good thing, Sid!"

"I told you. You pushed too far. You didn't follow the rules. You went into a rough neighborhood at 2:00 a.m. Who does that? I don't care what info your informant had. But worse, you got your photographer roughed up, injured. What did you expect?"

Sophie closed her eyes, reawakening fresh remorse about Jackson, her best photographer. He'd suffered a broken arm and rib. Yeah, Sid was right, it had been her fault. She put Jackson in harm's way.

"You should never have gone there. Especially without telling me," Sid reiterated.

"The only thing I'm sorry for is Jackson getting hurt. Going there gave me the story I needed. My reporting helped save those poor altar boys from a shitty life of more abuse." She pressed her lips together, her anger rising. "It galls me that the Bishop covered for the priest. They got away with everything. Scot-free."

"It galls me, too, Sophie—"

"No. It can't possibly infuriate you as much," Sophie interjected.

"Stop it. You were just plain reckless and you know it."

"Reckless?" Sophie slammed her fist on the desk. "How can you of all people say that? They can twist the facts, but I know the truth. And my reward? Now I'm up against a brick wall."

"Sophie, there is no use arguing. You'll get another crack at the big stories if you play your cards right."

Sophie perched on the edge of the bed and pinched the bridge of her nose, took a long moment to calm herself. "You're right. To get back in the game, I'll do this. For now. I'll lay low and do as I'm told."

"Promise?"

She rolled her eyes. "Promise."

Sid chuckled. "That's better. Don't worry. This won't be for long."

"Better not be. I'm going to die of boredom here," Sophie grumbled, not wanting to talk to Sid about it anymore. She held the phone out at arm's length. "Sorry . . . you're breaking up. Bye." She clicked off the call.

Sophie walked to the window and pulled aside the flowered curtain. Her mind rehashed the argument with Sid—loath to admit she'd lost this battle. She stared at the countryside beyond her window. A line of houses with red tiled roofs and tiny gardens flanked by willow and oak trees bordered the B&B's back yard. The peaceful neighborhood contrasted with the sound of honking car horns and the chatter of the many visitors she'd seen crowding the sidewalks of High Street earlier in the day.

The room was on the top floor of a two-story B&B nestled on the crest near the top of Wearyall Hill. The height afforded a panoramic view of the town and the Somerset Plains bordering Glastonbury.

She lifted the window open and rested her elbows on the sill, hoping the fresh air would clear the frustration choking her thoughts. Pale magenta clouds reflected a sun soon to set behind her. In the distance, thick mist gathered and began to charge across the plains like storming ocean waves. The mist looked eerily alive, with thick tendrils stretching, reaching, grasping. It rushed towards a hill at the edge of town and broke into curling fragments against its base.

The hill was conical shaped with earthen ridges encircling it and a tower ruin atop. *The Tor.* She'd seen pictures previously from her research. The books claimed that centuries ago the Tor would have been a lone finger amidst an island swamp, pointing to the sky. Glastonbury might no longer be an island, but Sophie had to admit the Tor still rose majestically amidst its surroundings. Her B&B host had called it "enchanted." *Just another Glastonbury New Age speculation*, she thought. She smirked but didn't look away.

If she squinted, she could make out the tiny figures of tourists climbing the steps built into the hillside, heading for the tower ruin. Her gaze dropped to the base where the swarming mists parted to each side in a play of twilight and shade.

Sophie leaned further out the window. *What's going on there? Are those robed figures in a procession, arms raised to the sky? Men riding horseback with swords held high?* She frowned. She wouldn't let her imagination sink into that New Age hype of a mystical Tor. What she'd just seen was probably just tourists climbing the hill, or a mere trick of sun and cloud.

Turning, she eyed her bed with an unfamiliar impulse to crawl under the covers—tempted to indulge in self-pity at the injustice of her career problems. But she wouldn't. Not her. Instead, she'd stop by the George and Pilgrim Hotel and Pub she'd noticed on the drive down High Street to her B&B. Get a meal and a lager.

She closed her eyes. For all her bravado, she, Sophie Morrison, hated her life. At age thirty she had been at the top of her game, headed for greatness. Hell, she was already a great investigative reporter. Now, at age thirty-one, that career had crumbled to shambles. All because of an article about that perverted son-of-a-bitch priest. The Bishop's lawyer called it *slanderous* and *unfounded*.

She stood, one hand on her hip, and chewed on her lip. The abbey trustees had commissioned Sid's magazine for this piece. So here she was in Glastonbury, England, ancient Isle of Avalon. A holy land? The New Jerusalem? So said the Inn's owners, as well as the many pilgrims. She would play the good reporter and write the story. She'd eat humble pie and pay her dues. Yeah, it was a low-level assignment, a fluff piece she'd have to tolerate to climb back to the top. And she *would* claw, scratch, and wrestle her way back to prove she was still the best. She'd show them all she was still reliable, trustworthy, and smart.

Sophie walked over to the desk and looked over the assignment notes, by habit searching for the underbelly, any signs of a deeper and more interesting story. She shook her head in dismay, causing straight brown hair to finally escape the clip pinning it up. She whipped the clip free from the few strands it clung to and threw it on the bed. Who was she kidding? What sort of underbelly could even exist in this village? The assignment was to report on the ruins of the Glastonbury Abbey on the anniversary of its burning nearly 475 years ago. It was some small-town publicist's justification for an abbey fund-raiser. Her pen hovered over the fact sheet. Keeping things simple would get her out of Glastonbury sooner. She pushed her resolve. *Just go for it, Sophie.*

Okay. In 1530 AD, over eight hundred monasteries, nunneries, and friaries flourished in England under the rule of King Henry VIII. *Check.* By 1541, there were none. *Check.* Corollary casualties: over ten thousand monks and nuns dispersed or died in the widespread dissolution. Glastonbury Abbey was one of the wealthier abbeys, but only one of the many the King confiscated or burned down in an attempt to exorcise an influential Church from the governing state. Sophie's gut told her it was more likely that the King's purpose was to line his dwindling coffers. She'd follow up on that hunch. She sighed. *Damn bunch of hypocrites, both Church and State, even back then.*

Penciling in some notes on the side of the paper—reference books to look through, people to talk to at the abbey administrative office—her stomach suddenly growled in complaint over missing lunch after a scanty breakfast. It hollered, "Dinnertime!" And time for that lager. First she pulled out the one remaining folder, one Sid had given her, outlining the bio of the photographer with whom she'd be collaborating. *Crap*, she thought, opening the folder and rifling through its contents. One more person she'd need to coddle. She liked working on her own and hated having someone else's agenda slow her down.

Well, she'd have to suck it up and meet the photographer at least. She read the first page in the folder. Daniel Holbrook, an artist, photographer, and painter. At age thirty-four, he was the winner of several awards for his photography, most notably some National Geographic pieces. His resume came to a halt two years prior. Sophie smiled, recognizing Sid's handwritten note on the side. He had anticipated she would notice the break in Holbrook's career and had penned her a message. Seems Daniel lost his wife and six-year-old son in a train wreck two years ago while on assignment in Serbia. This Glastonbury project was to be his first assignment since. *Play nice,* Sid had scribbled in capital letters.

"Hell, I'm not heartless, Sid," Sophie mumbled. She wondered about Daniel. Why would a notable photographer take a minor assignment in Glastonbury after worldwide recognition?

Picking up her cellphone from the desktop, she scanned the bio, found Daniel's cell number, added it to her contact list, then pressed call. It rang four times.

"Hello." The voice was deep, gravelly. Not what one expected from an artist type.

"Daniel, this is Sophie Morrison."

Silence.

"We're collaborating on the Glastonbury piece."

"Oh, yes. Of course." He answered with an American accent.

Sophie recognized the groggy tone. "Oh, I woke you up. When did you get in?"

Daniel yawned audibly over the phone. "This afternoon. Still a bit jet-lagged."

"Well, I know the cure. No long naps. Get yourself on the locals' time asap. Care to join me for a meal and a pint?"

"Uh, yeah, sure. I can do that. Give me ten minutes to shower. I'm staying in one of the rooms at the Abbey House."

"Well, how about that. On the very grounds of our assignment."

"Yeah. My wife . . . I mean . . . a relative of hers works as groundskeeper here. He got me in."

Sophie heard something in his voice. She wasn't sure, but it sounded like her mother when her father died. That was it. Grief bled through his pauses.

Daniel continued, his words now hurried. "Let's meet at the Mitre Pub. I'm told it's a local favorite. It's on Benedict Street, right off Magdalene. At the bottom of High Street. I'll be wearing a black T-shirt . . ." His voice trailed off.

She picked up the slack. "Ok." She'd had a different Pub in mind, but what the hell, a lager was a lager. "I'm coming from Hill Head Road, so I'll be there in about ten minutes and get us a table."

Sophie found a table for two and nursed her lager while she waited for Daniel. She'd give him a pass this once for being so late. Finally, a man wearing a black T-shirt appeared in the shadowed entryway. *Must be Daniel*, she figured. Her hand froze, lips close to her glass. She knew him. Had they ever met? No, of course not. She must recognize him from the bio photo Sid sent. Though to be fair, while he resembled his picture, the man standing in the doorway of the pub was different. His tawny colored hair was much longer, and tousled. Had he even combed it after his shower? He was tall and slim, yet not the kind of slim that came from skipping meals as Sophie was prone to do. It was a natural litheness reinforced with solid muscles well defined under the clinging cotton of the black tee. He looked good in faded blue jeans and scuffed brown boots. Sophie chided herself for even noticing these things. *Hell, I might be career-minded, but I'm not blind. Or an angel,* she thought with a soft chuckle. Daniel ran his hands through his hair, which seemed to help it fall in place. He wore a wedding band, the same tone of gold as the St. Christopher's medallion around his neck.

She watched him scan the room and waited until he caught her gaze, then nodded her greeting and stood. His eyes were deep-set and blue, the color of dusk. A guarded look preceded a ghost of a smile. He strolled toward her and she gave him her usual firm handshake.

His grip was stronger than she expected. And somehow familiar. A jolt of electricity raced up her arm. She looked up in surprise and met his eyes. His guarded look slipped for an instant, revealing the same shock and confusion. In reflex, she pulled her hand away.

She was saved from comment when her order of french fries with a side of mayo arrived. They both busied themselves with the menus and ordered a pork pie apiece. Hiding her hands under the table, Sophie nervously folded and refolded a napkin. The waitress took Daniel's order for a pint of Boddingtons Ale and left.

Sophie grabbed a handful of fries and talked around them. "So, you've never been here before either?"

"No."

She nodded her head and swallowed, her composure recovered. "Help yourself," she offered, reaching for more.

Daniel didn't move, so she continued talking. "So why did you take this assignment?"

His face registered surprise. "So much for formalities," he said with a crooked grin that accentuated the dimple in his cheek.

Sophie chuckled. "Sorry. Listen, let me be frank." She wiped her hands on her napkin. "I don't intend to spend a lot of time here. On this piece, I mean. It should be fairly straight forward."

Daniel leaned back in his chair, hands folded on his lap. He crossed his leg, ankle over one knee, but didn't speak.

"I plan to read a few books on the history. I've already started. I'll talk to the abbey trustees and their folks on the fund-raiser committee. That should give me most of the information I need, with the abbey being a museum and all. Maybe I'll interview Dr. Adam Stout. He's respected for his knowledge about the abbey history, and he'll be doing a talk on the commemoration day. Obviously, I'll keep you updated on what I'm writing. That way, you can tailor your photos to my story."

"I see."

"I figure by the end of this week, three, four days tops, we can get the hell out of here."

"You have it all figured out then."

"Well, yeah. That's how I work. Plan things ahead. Especially for insignificant assignments like this."

Daniel's eyes flickered. He uncrossed his legs and leaned forward, elbows and hands on the table. "Well, Sophie. Here is how I plan things . . . I don't."

Sophie opened her mouth, not sure whether to be amused or shocked.

Daniel continued. "First of all, I'm not using photography for this piece. I'm painting. Oil, I believe, or whatever medium I choose. Maybe watercolor if the mood suits once I walk around the grounds and get the feel for what the abbey trustees want for *our* piece."

"Sure, whatever medium suits you." Sophie donned her most diplomatic smile. *God, I hate working with other people*, she thought to herself for the thousandth time.

"Secondly, my paintings aren't meant to be geared only to your writing."

"Well, how the hell are we supposed to collaborate, then?" Any sense of awe at the earlier charged handshake had evaporated.

Daniel spoke without affectation. "We collaborate by talking about what *we* want to showcase. Then we make mutual decisions about what angles we want to bring out. As a *team*."

Sophie's hackles raised. "No angles. I'll stick to the facts."

"The facts and the truth are two different things."

"What?" Hadn't she just told Sid basically the same thing on the phone? Still. Daniel was butting heads with the wrong person. She ran her tongue along the inside of her cheek, counting to ten. Didn't make it past three. "I'll write what I think is best. And you can paint whatever the hell you want to."

Daniel slowly nodded his head. He pulled out his wallet, extracted a ten-pound note, and threw it on the table. "I really don't need this kind of hassle. Glad we met, Sophie. And now we won't have to see each other until we turn our respective pieces into the Abbey Commemoration Committee."

He pushed back his chair and stood up.

Sophie's fingers tapped against the corduroy of her pants. She remembered Sid's note to her. *Play nice.* "Wait. Don't go." She struggled for words. But she couldn't blow him off, couldn't afford to mess up this assignment. Her career was on the line.

"Yes?" Daniel said, waiting for her to speak.

"Truce?" Sophie held her hands up, palms forward, an offer of peace. "Sit down. Please. Let's finish our food. I'm famished." She smiled graciously. *Fake it until you make it.* "Let me listen to your ideas. Then we can take a stroll around the abbey grounds and see what we get . . . a feel for. How about it?"

"If you think you can manage." His voice, though a bit sarcastic, was not unkind. More weary than anything. His smile seemed to Sophie to never reach his deep blue eyes.

"Listen, I'm sorry. I need this job to go well. Humor me. We'll work out something. Together."

Daniel sat back down, donning a guarded expression again. "Let's see."

Chapter 6

Glastonbury, England
21st Century, Present Day

By the time they'd eaten a quick meal, dusk had set in. Low-lying clouds turned into the muted blue-grey of late twilight, melding into a dark horizon. A few stars made their bright presence known across the evening sky.

"Sure you're not too tired? I could stroll around the abbey grounds on my own," Sophie offered.

"No, I'm curious," Daniel said. It was more interest than he'd shown in the last half hour of their stilted conversation. He added, "Besides, you can't get into the grounds after hours unless you're staying at the Abbey Retreat House. Or know someone."

His crooked grin suggested he was maybe beginning to warm up. Thank God. She couldn't bear much more of his taciturn silence.

Since the main entrance to the abbey grounds was closed for the day, the pair made their way down a cobblestone alley that ran alongside the estate, headed for the Retreat House.

"Ouch," Sophie exclaimed halfway down the alley. Her shoe had caught on the uneven cobblestones.

Daniel reached over and lightly took hold of her elbow to steady her. It tingled where he touched her. Her first impulse was to brush him off. She'd traveled to the deserts of Iraq as a reporter. She could sure as hell navigate a small-town bumpy alleyway at dusk.

"Wow, look at that." His shift in tone interrupted her annoyance.

Sophie followed his gaze. A high stone wall hid most of the abbey, except for the towering spires of its ruins. They arched heavenward, like two lofty portals, only to be severed at their highest point, the arched tip having long ago fallen from ruin.

"Dilapidated," she mused.

Daniel frowned at her, then chuckled before gazing up again. "Beautiful. Mysterious. I have to paint them."

She tilted her head back. The moon was rising, its silver glow highlighting the spires. "I suppose you're right. Mysterious and, yes, beautiful," she conceded.

They stared at the spires in silence, Daniel still lightly cupping her elbow. Sophie's reporter instincts kicked in. Something stirred in her gut, telling her in wordless whispers there was a story here. A hidden story. Her investigative hunches were never wrong.

The spontaneous moment was broken when loud voices rose in laughter and a dog barked, the sound drifting out one of the windows from the row of brick apartments on the opposite side of the alley. A group of rowdy teens exited the back door of a shop fronting the parallel High Street, adding to the clamor.

Sophie and Daniel both turned around.

"So much for beauty and mystery," Sophie said.

"We should get going anyway."

Daniel was quiet the rest of the way, and Sophie pondered the ruins. She shook her head. Yes, definitely something hidden there, but nothing she could put her finger on. She'd have to probe and explore a bit first.

At the end of the long alley, he broke the silence. "We turn here."

He led her onto Lambrook Street, releasing his hand on her elbow once they'd stepped onto the smooth sidewalk. Absorbed in reflections about the abbey's mystery, Sophie hadn't realized she'd let him continue the protective hold. She instantly missed his touch when he withdrew.

He stopped when they reached a two-story stone building with gabled windows, fronted by a massive stone gate. "This is it. The Abbey Retreat House."

The enormous gate reared above them. Four medieval looking panels were inset above the archway, carved with symbols, most notably a cruet and a pelican.

Daniel automatically answered Sophie's unspoken questions. "The cruet depicts the one St. Joseph of Arimathea brought to Glastonbury from the Last Supper. The pelican pecking its breast is a Masonic symbol."

"How do you know all this?" Sophie eyed Daniel with renewed interest.

"You're not the only one who does research," he quipped in a dry tone.

She arched an eyebrow. *So, he has a sense of humor.*

"Fine. The groundskeeper told me," Daniel admitted. "He's the 'sort of' relative I mentioned. And a real geek when it comes to Glastonbury history."

Sophie thought this groundskeeper might just come in handy as a source. They passed through the gates and circled around to the back of the Retreat House Lodge. A well-manicured, peaceful-looking garden bordered the northern end of the abbey grounds. An older man holding a rake stood surrounded by three middle-aged people with cross looks on their faces. The man, leaning on the rake, spotted Daniel and Sophie, and winked.

He looked to be in his late sixties, short white hair thinning on top, large hazel eyes rimmed with thick glasses pushed up on the bridge of his nose. Mud-spattered blue jeans and gardening gloves hanging from his belt confirmed he was the groundskeeper Daniel mentioned.

She turned to Daniel. "Your 'sort of relative,' I presume?"

He nodded, his smile deep and genuine for the man. "Yes. Barry was . . . is . . . was . . . Janet's uncle." Again, she noted the trickle of grief seep through his words.

"Looks like he has his hands full. Those people look upset," Sophie said.

She and Daniel held back, waiting.

The man was currently explaining to the trio, "I'm sorry, but you'll need to wait two hours until the lawn fertilization is safe to walk on."

One woman whined. "But being able to spend time on the grounds after hours was the reason we booked here in the first place."

"Calm down," the man at her side said, earning him a frown from the woman. "We'll find something to do in the meantime."

"I appreciate that," the groundskeeper said. "Fertilizing is something we can do best after hours when no one can walk across the grass right afterwards. Won't happen again."

"Better not," the lodger mumbled as she and her companions strode back into the Abbey House.

"Daniel!" The groundskeeper greeted them in a friendly tone. He walked over and clapped Daniel on the back. "This must be your associate?" He bobbed a nod at Sophie.

She extended her hand in greeting, immediately liking the affable man. "Sophie Morrison. Yes, I'm the reporter on the assignment. Lawn just fertilized? We were hoping to see the grounds."

"Oh, that wasn't meant for you," the older man replied. "That was just to give you the quiet you'll need to explore on your own without New Age pilgrims toning or planting crystals or whatever they do when they think no one is watching. Barry is my name. Glad to meet you." He returned Sophie's handshake.

Barry gave Daniel another affectionate pat on the shoulder, then hooked an arm through each of theirs and steered them toward a gate.

"Private access," Barry confided as they passed through and onto the grounds. "I'll give you a quick lay of the land, then you'll have those full two hours to look about on your own. While I'm *fertilizing*." He winked again. "Thought it would be helpful to you." He gave Sophie an almost shy smile.

Up ahead stood a cluster of old cedar, oak, and ash trees. Sophie marveled at the width and bough span of the cedar. It bifurcated into two trunks, offering a perfect place to sit.

"Go ahead. Try it out," Barry encouraged. "I'll light my lantern. Ordinary flashlights just don't do around here."

At Sophie's confused look, he added, "Scares the faeries away," and grinned with a mischievous glint in his eye.

She shook her head and smiled back, then sauntered over to the cedar tree and sat in the curve where the branches split into two. Daniel seated himself against the base of the tree, one arm resting on his drawn-up knee.

Barry walked over to a nearby wooden bench where he picked up an old-fashioned tin lantern and a thermos. He lit the lantern with matches from his pocket and carried both lantern and thermos to where Sophie sat palming the rough bark and sniffing the cedar resin.

"I made some warm tea with milk and sugar. Once the sun sets it can get a bit chilly out here, even in summer," Barry held the thermos up.

Sophie was glad she'd thought to bring a light jacket and zipped it up while Barry pried off two lid cups from the thermos, poured the steaming tea, and handed them each a cup. The aroma of Darjeeling drifted up. She gratefully accepted hers and took a sip, wondering how Barry had known they would want to wander the grounds this evening.

"I figured you'd be aiming to get started on your assignment right away. Get your initial first impressions and all," Barry said.

Sophie narrowed her eyes. Had he read her thoughts?

"You've always been one to look after folks," Daniel said.

She noticed how Daniel's tawny hair glinted in the last rays of the sun.

Barry sat on the bench and rubbed his calloused hands together. "All right then. Enjoy your tea, and I'll point you in the right direction."

"Would you care to walk around with us?" Daniel asked.

"No, son. I'm pretty tired. Had a long day. You'll do better on your own. Besides, I have to monitor the lodgers, so they don't sneak back out." He chuckled.

Sophie decided she didn't care how Barry knew to steer the other lodgers away from them. She was just grateful he'd managed to do so.

"Take your time walking around." Barry's voice took on a wistful tone. "It's a magnificent showpiece despite its brutal history. Special areas are marked. The open-ceilinged crypt called the Mary Chapel is a place you'll want to spend time in. There's a hidden wellspring down there. Doesn't get the attention like the Chalice Well or the White Springs over by the Tor, but it has its own . . . mystery."

Sophie's gaze roamed the abbey ruins about a hundred yards away.

Barry pointed. "With this nearly full moon you'll be able to see the ancient inscription on the east side of the abbey walls. Says Jesus and Maria. You'll like it."

"When was that inscribed?" Sophie wondered why he thought she'd like an inscription with Jesus and Maria.

"There's a more important question," Barry answered with enthusiasm. "History says it was in honor of Jesus and his mother, Mary. Though to tell you, meaning no disrespect, I've never seen a man inscribe his name next to his mother's."

"Told you," Daniel said, looking up at Sophie in her tree seat.

"What?"

"Barry's a Glastonbury history geek," he said fondly.

"Guilty as charged," he quipped.

Sophie leaned forward. "Well, I find it interesting. I must admit, I agree. It's usually lovers' names penned together. But then who is the Mary in the inscription?"

"Magdalene, of course," Barry answered.

Sophie tensed imperceptibly. There it was again. That tingling sensation, this time racing through her chest. But Daniel hadn't touched her, like when it happened before. Barry was eyeing her, his head tilted to the side. Was he looking for her reaction to his little history lesson?

Barry cleared his throat. "Now the other place you two will want to spend time is where the High Altar used to stand. Right over there, the part of the ruins closest to where we are." Barry indicated a roped-off area nearby.

"Why's that?" Daniel asked.

"Well, not only does it mark out a powerful spot, being by the Mary and Michael ley lines . . ."

"Ley lines?" Sophie interrupted.

Barry lifted his hands up and shrugged. "You don't have to believe any of this from me. Find out for yourself. The lines are supposedly earth energy vortexes, like the Chinese meridians, or how energy lines used in acupuncture are to the human body. Ley lines run through Glastonbury in several key areas."

Sophie pursed her lips, considering the idea of energy vortexes. "I'm not sure about this."

"Legends say," Barry said.

"Legends are just that. Legends."

"Legends can be true. Or not. But the fact is that there *are* legends. And sometimes they point the way to the truth," Barry said.

Daniel was silent, gazing at the ruined walls of the ancient monastery.

Barry went on, "But very interesting as well is that near the High Altar, and it's prominently marked, is where abbey history says the bones of King Arthur and his Queen Guinevere are interred."

"They're really buried here?" Daniel finally spoke up.

"King Arthur was real?" Sophie asked. She couldn't block the hint of cynicism creeping into her voice.

"Yes, there was an historical King Arthur," Barry said. "Since Glastonbury was one of the most revered and wealthiest abbeys, the decision was made to put their ancient bones to rest here."

Sophie let her mind wander and murmured, "Well, that angle could work in our favor. People love Arthurian lore. I could totally play that up."

Daniel rolled his eyes. "I thought you didn't want angles. Only unadulterated *truth*."

"A journalist's prerogative."

Barry watched them quibble before he spoke. "The far corner of the grounds is the fish pond. The abbey had its own source of fish and fowl in its day, self-sufficient in its wealth you know. But I digress. You can walk the pathway around the grounds, read the guidebook, and discover all the historical facts from the museum. I hoped to guide you to the more . . . interesting aspects."

Sophie poked Daniel with the toe of her shoe. "Yes. We've agreed facts and the truth aren't always one and the same."

Barry nodded, glancing from one to the other.

"Thanks for the guidance, Barry," Daniel said.

Sophie cocked her head, listening closely. She'd been hearing something . . . musical . . . for the last five minutes or so and had passed it off as a band at a local pub. But this clearly wasn't band music. Certainly not rock 'n' roll, folk music, or even the Celtic stuff she loved. This was a cappella. It grew louder. Men's voices raised in what was unmistakably devotional chanting. It reminded her of Gregorian chants she'd heard once at her grandmother's Roman Catholic Church when she was a young girl.

Sophie's breath caught when the musical notes prodded a hidden pocket in her chest, within her heart. Exposing closeted grief, it stirred the emotions like ocean waves churn sand, upending the places she avoided visiting inside herself. Before she could shut down the feelings, images arose in her mind's eye. She saw her father's gaunt face as he lay dying. She was young, only twelve. Then the image of her mother's pale, vacant stares, and slow withdrawal from the world afterwards. From her. Her heart grew heavy and quivered against her chest with unshed tears.

Barry continued talking, but his voice receded to the background while the chant grew louder, crystalline clear. It plowed through her personal memories, stretching, until it grasped someplace deeper within her, plucking out a memory further back in time. Burning images flashed through her mind in a searing instant. Faces she didn't recognize, but at the same time knew too well. A boy with tawny hair and deep blue eyes. A dimple in his chin. His forehead bruised. He was coughing. Water filled his lungs and sputtered from his mouth. She fought to stop herself from screaming, then, the images changed. She saw, no she felt, herself sitting beside a gurgling well, its water ochre-tinged with iron. The smell and taste on her lips metallic but pleasant and satiating. She saw herself light a candle beside the well. A deep sense of peace filled her heart where the grief had broken through only seconds earlier. Then the vision abruptly dissolved. The pain closeted away once more. Nothing but the chanting remained.

Remain calm. Her body shook. How could she explain this to Daniel and Barry? To herself? She took several deep breaths and released balled fists she hadn't realized were clenched.

A cool evening breeze grazed against her cheek. She heard Daniel swallow his tea, and Barry explaining something about the old building called the Abbot's Kitchen, still intact and worth a visit. No one noticed her slip from . . . from what? Reality? Sanity? She just had some sort of vision. No, she corrected herself, it was her imagination. Or not enough sleep. Maybe one pint of lager too many. At the very least, Daniel and Barry must have heard the music. Why didn't it affect them like it had her? They were carrying on as if nothing happened. She slowly opened her eyes and turned to Barry.

"Are there any of those New Age pilgrims you spoke about nearby? Or, is there a church close to here?" she asked.

Barry stopped mid-sentence in a description of the Abbot's Kitchen to answer her. "There's St. John's on High Street. Also, Magdalene Chapel off of Magdalene Street."

"No, this is closer." Sophie said.

"What's closer?" Daniel asked.

"Why, the music, obviously." Sophie stopped at the blank look on Daniel's face.

"What music?" he asked quietly.

"Barry, you hear it . . . don't you?" Sophie asked. The music continued to move her, arousing a sacred, if melancholic feeling in her heart.

"Ah, *that* music," Barry's steady gaze met hers. "It comes and goes. Legends say there used to be a perpetual choir at the abbey, starting with the original wattle and reed chapel. That chapel burnt centuries ago and was replaced by the abbey." Barry offered a kind smile, then stood with a groan, rubbing one knee. "Time for me to retire and for you two to be off on your own."

"Wait. What about the music?" Sophie said. She hesitated. When she tried to hear it again, it was no longer there. "That was strange. Maybe someone had it playing on their phone or iPod."

"Then how could you hear it?" Daniel said.

Sophie sent a panicked look. "You're right. I wouldn't." She shook her head, wisps of hair falling from her hair clip. "Doesn't matter. I don't hear it anymore."

Daniel raised a brow, then hoisted up from the ground and wiped bits of grass off his jeans. Sophie rose from the cedar trunk, casting furtive glances around for the source of the music.

"Barry," she called out. "What if I hear it again? What does it mean?"

Barry was already walking toward the Abbey Retreat House, his back to them, whistling. He'd left them his lantern, and it glowed, casting dancing shadows where he had placed it on the soft grass.

He looked over one shoulder. "Sometimes the truth can't always be seen."

Chapter 7

The Isle of Avalon
1529 C.E.

A throbbing pressure in his head roused Michael from the silent black abyss. The High Priestess Alianore stood beside the towering reeds on the Glastonbury shoreline, raising her arms toward the sky and tracing a symbol in the air with her finger.

Marissa leaned in to whisper in his ear. "Everything is all right. Mother is making a magical sigil to invoke the veils that will cloak and transport us back to the Isle of Avalon. To safety." Her breath was warm on his cheek. She smelled like the springtime lilacs that grew around his Da's estate.

Eyes closed, Alianore tilted her head back, fine golden hair dipping below her waist. He heard her utter words in a language he did not understand. Vanora echoed the chant in a frightened whisper. A flash of blue light burst forth, and an unearthly mist surged toward them on precipitous white waves. It settled over the shoreline, shrouding the looming bulrushes and the rippling lake.

"Michael! Where are you?" his father's soldier called in a now muffled voice.

Michael pushed himself up onto his elbows, but his muscles trembled with the weight of his body and the layers of unnatural mist swelling over him like a heavy blanket. He dropped back down to the spongy ground. Mouthing a shout, too stunned to speak aloud, he tried to call for Sir David. For his brother Roger. Wanting them to find him. He also wanted the reassuring touch of Marissa's hand again, but the opaque mist thoroughly enveloped her. He could barely see his own hand, let alone find hers.

His soul suddenly longed for the beautiful Lady of the lake, with blue eyes that radiated love. For a moment, he thought he saw her ethereal face peer at him through the thick mist. Or was it his mother he saw? He groaned and reached out a hand.

He startled when Marissa clasped the extended hand. Her hand offered comfort against the oppressive mist that was adding to the lightning bolts of pain in his head.

"We're going back to Avalon now. It will feel a little strange, but you're safe with me," Marissa reassured him.

A sudden tug in his gut lurched him forward with suction force. Swirls of midnight blue and star-spun silver surrounded him. A hard, wooden floor beneath him rocked to and fro. A boat. Waves upon the lake raced by. In a disorienting instant, all movement came to an abrupt halt. The blue and silver spirals vanished. The thick mist parted and lifted.

The black abyss swallowed his awareness, and he drifted once more.

By the time Michael woke, the rocking boat and the lake's lapping waves were far behind. A small hill rose ahead. Voices buzzed close by. Something swayed under him. He looked down his legs. Alianore held the foot of a makeshift litter. They had fashioned Marissa's blue cloak to carry him, the ends knotted together for handholds.

"Help me lift his weight, Ciara," Vanora called from the head of the litter.

His breath caught. *Where was Marissa?*

Someone squeezed his hand. He looked to his side; there she was. He breathed again.

"I haven't let go," she said, tightening her grasp. The contact soothed him, but he wanted to walk on his own. He wanted to be with Da's men and his brother. His muscles wouldn't obey the command to move. And, somehow, he knew he was far beyond where anyone could find him.

A robust middle-aged woman strode purposefully down the slope ahead. When she drew close, Alianore turned to her and spoke.

"Elyn, we have a lad who needs your care. He is the one from the Death Vision this morning, the boy who drowned in the lake. My daughters found and rescued him."

"Rescued him from drowning you say? Hmm." Elyn eyed the twins. "And you both were outside the borders without permission? Never mind, he is here, and in my care now." She patted Michael's arm with a sure touch.

Despite the reassuring gesture, Michael felt uneasy. Elyn's words confirmed he was no longer in Glastonbury. The priestesses had taken him into their bewitched land of Avalon after all. Had he given them the permission the High Priestess sought? Fear lodged its leaden weight in his stomach as Elyn bent over the litter to examine him, her soft green robes wafting across his body with the breeze. Marissa released his hand to allow Elyn room to assess him. His fear spun into panic, quaking in his chest and rising in his throat.

"I am the Healing Mistress," she said to Michael, smiling warmly and skillfully placing her hands over his chest.

Though his hand felt empty without Marissa's, Elyn's ministration instantly relaxed his tense and aching body and eased his breath. She inspected the throbbing lump on his forehead with gentle fingers. Her brow furrowed, and she frowned.

"Dizzy?" she asked.

"Yes." His voice sounded faraway, as if someone had clamped their palms over his ears and isolated him in a muted world.

"Is it getting harder to stay awake? Feeling more and more drowsy?"

He fought to keep his chin from trembling. "Yes."

The healer gestured for Vanora to step aside, and picked up the head of the litter in her own muscled arms.

"The boy is dying," Elyn said. "He must desire to live or nothing I do will help him. He must *choose* to want to receive our healing. We will take him at once to the Healing Halls."

Michael's heart lurched. His life still in danger? He didn't understand.

"I was correct then? He needs healing only Avalon can provide," Alianore asked, hoisting the other end of the litter.

"Yes, if he is to survive," Elyn answered.

"Am I really going to die?" Had he said that out loud? No one seemed to have heard him.

Elyn and Alianore each gripped a knotted end of the litter and began climbing the knoll. Ciara walked beside the Healing Mistress, while Vanora strode with Alianore. Marissa stayed close by Michael.

Elyn continued speaking, her comments directed to the High Priestess. "There will be residual effects from drowning. In his lungs. Also in his brain where he hit his head. The head injury is starting to make the brain swell, and it appears it is getting worse."

"Healing Mistress, is that why he goes in and out of consciousness now?" Ciara asked. "He wasn't this bad when we revived him."

Elyn nodded. "Yes, that is why. But it is his soul I must concern myself with first. It is in a perilous state because of what he has gone through. He drowned. Died. Because of that, I must mend his soul before I bring him to the healing lodge in the village."

Michael grimaced. He didn't like that word, *perilous*. Hadn't Marissa already saved him from his dark fate?

Marissa pulled on Elyn's sleeve. "He can't die! Don't let him die!"

"Marissa, calm yourself," Vanora said.

Marissa persisted. "He has to live. I must go into the Healing Halls with Michael."

Elyn responded, "Marissa, you belong to the School of Divination. You are not a student of the healing arts as Ciara."

Michael felt desperate for Marissa's presence wherever they were going. He needed this young girl with the raven hair to remain at his side. The other priestesses had done him no harm, but the voice of his father's priest echoed in his mind. "*Be careful in the Summer Country. It is enchanted. Heathen.*"

From the corner of his eye, Michael noticed Marissa had stopped walking. She was glowering, eyes afire, her hands on her hips.

"Let me finish, my dear," Elyn said. The litter bounced up and down under him as Elyn kept her stride. "Since it appears you found the boy, you may stay and watch what I do to help him. But you mustn't interfere—this is the first crucial step in his recovery."

Marissa ran to catch up. "Thank you, Healing Mistress," she said, with just enough contriteness to cover the outburst.

With Marissa's reassuring presence guaranteed, Michael allowed himself to look around before his eyelids grew heavy and drifted shut again. What was atop the rounded knoll before him was like nothing he'd ever seen. They were heading toward a heavy wooden door set in a circular stone wall, with an enormous apple tree towering beyond the gate. Odd, the tree both blossomed and bore fruit at the same time. The perfume of its white blooms honeyed the air. The scent of ripened golden apples laden upon its boughs would have made his mouth water if it weren't for his queasy stomach. But there was something else in the air, something he couldn't name. It was earthy, as if flowers and fruit, earth, and air, bore a message of welcome, nurturance and kinship. The feeling trickled sweet nectar into his soul, bathing him in golden warmth.

Before they reached the crest of the knoll and the heavy wooden door, Elyn paused beside a burbling spring. The Healing Mistress nodded to Vanora, who picked up a silver cup next to the spring and dipped it into the waters. She lifted Michael's head and put the cup to his lips, inviting him to swallow. He peered into the cup, closed his lips tight, and shook his head. The water was tinted red with the ochre of iron, sure to be bitter. He lifted his gaze to seek Marissa, who nodded for him to drink. Feeling reassured, he took a small sip. The cold liquid slid down his throat, fresh tasting despite the iron tinge. When he swallowed, his thirst was instantly quenched. He drank more of the satiating water, emptying the cup.

He was about to ask what kind of water it was, when the gate ahead of them creaked open. A verdant courtyard lay beyond. After they entered, the gate closed behind them, but he could still hear the mysterious wellspring splashing loudly outside the walls.

Throughout the courtyard were women with long, braided hair, dressed in robes of blue and turquoise. Some carried pitchers of the special ochre-tinged water. Others knelt beside a garden of pungent rosemary, camphor, and sage, along with fragrant blossomed red and white roses. A few women sat beside a cascading fountain, chanting softly. Still more bustled across the courtyard carrying candles and linens, following curt orders to bring supplies to various healing rooms.

Despite the nurturing scent of herb and flower, despite the steady chanting and lively activity, it was the enormous apple tree that held Michael's attention. His fatigued mind wavered between his current surroundings and memories of the apple trees back home. This tree was likely ten times the size of the ones his father owned. Was he dreaming? Regardless of feeling so awful, he longed to rub his palm against the burled trunk, sit with his back leaning against it, and bite into its fruit. But Elyn directed his litter past the tree, heading across the plaza toward an arched doorway. One of several such doors that ringed the vast courtyard, all set into the moss-covered stone wall that encircled the enormous apple tree.

Michael craned his neck to gaze at the apple tree as long as he could, though even such subtle movement made him dizzy. His heart thumped against his chest, as if it strained to harmonize with the green vitality pervading the courtyard. This strange land of Avalon truly must be enchanted, just as the legends said. Still, marvelous as it seemed, it was unfamiliar. Unsettling. He wanted the security of his Da's Great Hall, the oaken forests and rolling hills he played amidst and knew so well. He tried lifting his shoulders and head but fell back onto the litter. No strength to run back to the lakeside where his Da's men were surely looking for him. He wasn't sure he could even find it anyway.

Elyn encouraged him. "You are going to be fine, young man. I will see to that. You are safe here. And back to your home soon enough."

Did she read his thoughts? Michael swallowed around his uneasiness. His thoughts grew fuzzy. The many arched doorways and the blue-robed priest-esses around him all blurred and darkened. He swore he saw his tutor, Master Ralph, join the priestess's entourage and hover directly above him. Master Ralph appeared to look down upon him, pulling on his beard as he always did when teaching, and instruct him in a throaty voice, *"Remain quiet and attentive, Michael."* Michael blinked, tried to focus, tried to bring his muddled mind back from the edge of the black abyss. The figure continued, *"When uncertain, you must study and observe everything around you before coming to any conclusions. It is the way of a reasoning mind."* His mentor had given him this familiar guidance many times.

Master Ralph's face faded. Michael shook his head to clear his thoughts and cried out in pain at the hasty movement. He reached out, his hands grasping nothing where his tutor had been.

Marissa brushed his forehead and tucked a strand of hair behind his ear.

Michael would do just as his tutor instructed, no matter how fuzzy his thoughts were. He would fight to keep his eyes wide open—and observe.

They carried his litter through one of the arched doorways and into a cavern. On first glance, it appeared similar to ones he explored with his brothers at home in Wales. Except this cavern was not damp and cold like the ones he knew. It was warm and dry, with walls of rough rock veined with orange calcite geodes. A fire burned in a metal tripod set in the middle of the cavern, and the flames rose high into the air, lending a golden glow to the room. Michael basked in the warmth. Shafts of sunlight spilled onto the earthen floor through openings in the tall ceiling. Lit candles were set along niches in the walls, causing the geodes to sparkle like amber fireflies.

Vanora left Alianore's side and tended to the tripod's golden flame. Elyn and Alianore gently laid him onto a raised rock pallet covered with bedding to cushion beneath him. They draped cool linen sheets strewn with lavender sprigs and tiny white yarrow flowers over his body. Once settled on the padding, Michael sought Marissa. He found her standing out of Elyn's way, but close enough that he could still see her, cheeks wet with tears she swiftly wiped away when she saw him looking. She gave him an encouraging smile as Elyn laid her hands over his head and lungs again. He could feel the healer's care flood his chest with heat. Breathing became easier. Ciara stood beside the Healing Mistress, her manner attentive. Michael turned his head to watch Elyn's every move. He struggled with weighted eyelids that threatened to once more drift shut.

Elyn assessed him as Ciara bent down to gather red jasper gemstones from a container near the bed.

"Tell me why you chose red jasper," Elyn asked without looking up.

"The stone of earth. Grounding."

Elyn nodded her approval. The gems were fist sized, bigger than any Michael had seen in his father's jewel collection. She tucked them beside his feet and along his legs. Immediately, a strong pulse penetrated his feet and legs. Slow and steady, the pulse throbbed in a primal rhythm that reminded him of walking barefoot in the ancient oak forests back home.

He was sinking down into the earth, or was he imagining that? His feet seemed to sprout roots like the huge apple tree in the courtyard. The sensation made him flinch. Yet he also found it inexplicably nurturing and strengthening. But his thoughts turned woolly again, and while his feet grew into roots, his mind meandered. He dreamily wondered if Master Ralph would ever let him read his most ancient texts on Socrates. Would his brother Roger miss teaching him swordplay? Would Da' ever forgive him for not becoming a brilliant soldier?

His breath grew shallow. His red jasper tree-root legs twitched. He wondered which parts of his feet were root, which were jasper, and if any bits remained flesh and bone? He could no longer tell them apart. His legs jerked as they unexpectedly snapped free of the black earth where they'd just become embedded. Pain seared the soles of his feet where the root stems had been attached before they broke off. Michael felt weightless. He floated in the black abyss of his drowsy mind.

Elyn placed her hands on his legs and held on. "Ciara, why did I choose to bring Michael to this particular healing hall?"

Her words reverberated into the black void that ensconced Michael. He shifted his feather-light body to hear her better.

Ciara answered with a puzzled tone in her voice. "You chose to bring Michael to the Hall of Earth, Healing Mistress. I'm sorry, but I don't understand why. Since Michael drowned, why not choose the Hall of Water to heal the liquid in his lungs? Or the Hall of Air, to give him fresh breath?"

"You pose good questions. In this case, I chose the Hall of Earth because Michael died before you found him. Only for a moment, but in that moment his soul saw the Goddess. He tasted the sweetness of Her love, felt the lure of the golden Otherworld. He needs to be brought fully back into his body, to be made eager again for physical life."

The red jasper roots rose up and spiraled toward Michael's black abyss. Twining and stretching their tendrils like eager fingers, reaching into the darkness where he floated. In voiceless words, he heard the roots speak.

We are verdant green.
Remember living!
We are life-force tree sap.
Come back to us.

Elyn continued to explain. "The memory of the Goddess is strong in him, making him yearn for her. Michael must choose to live. Or, as I said, we cannot help him."

Inside the abyss, Michael heard Elyn's every word. He shivered, cold. How did Elyn know what happened to him with the beautiful Lady in the lake? How did she know he longed to go back? Even if it meant he'd be dead. *She called her the Goddess.* Father's priest had never mentioned a Goddess. It no longer mattered. He'd seen Her himself. Whoever She was. He vividly recalled Her face. Her kind eyes. The crown of stars. The serenity She brought him. He wanted that peace. His soul quivered with a fierce yearning for Her.

A translucent silver thread floated above him, one end attached to his navel. But with his soul's desire to be with the Lady, the connecting thread was swiftly releasing. Unraveling. Undoing his life. Liberating his soul. He felt so light. He began to rise out of his body. He could vaguely see the Lady's crown of stars again.

At the same time, another part of his mind watched the red jasper roots glow, beckoning him to let them spindle from the bottom of his feet and embed into the rich soil once more. The moist, fecund soil. His jasper root feet wanted to sink into the lush black earth, suckle the moisture, spread their jasper shoots.

Eyes unfocused, Elyn murmured, "Michael wars between his soul and body." His breath slowed, rattled.

Marissa sobbed quietly. "Fight, Michael. Please. Live!" she cried.

Elyn poured a vial of something spicy-scented into her palms and sprinkled it over his feet, legs, heart, and stomach. She then cradled the soles of his feet where the red jasper roots strained to regain their foothold. At the same time, the silver thread from Michael's navel further loosened its anchor to his soul, his spirit stretched, ready to soar free.

The healer's gaze remained distant. "The life-force Angels stand close by, but they do not sing yet. They are watching. Waiting for Michael to choose," she said softly.

She began to chant. Her voice grew in pitch and intensity with each word.

Earth is dear
Hold Michael near
Strength of rock, trunk of tree
Power of the Mother in the vast ocean sea.
Hold Michael near.
Roots of life
Reach down deep
Ground Michael here
Where he belongs
In your keep
Mother of wisdom,
Fill his longing
Soothe his soul
Heal his strife
Love him here
In this life.

Michael moaned. His legs stretched, his feet straining to form roots once more. His soul rose and blazed in desire to be back in the beautiful Lady's embrace again. But Elyn's song danced in his every cell. The words catalyzed memories of his life. Of the leather-bound books he cherished, of the burled oak trees, the brilliant bluebells in the fields, and the love he harbored for his brothers, Roger and Philip.

On impulse, he grabbed the silver strand rising from his abdomen and held tight to stop it from unraveling beyond repair. He hesitated in an in-between place, caught betwixt pulsing life and death's surrender. He made his choice. His soul softly sighed its wish to float free but obeyed him and consented to stay enclosed in his body. The angels, with their golden hands and radiant wings, gently took the silver strand from his hands and wove it back into his navel. Their pure voices sang a harmonic song of life. The song reverberated in his bones, warmed his muscles, pumped his heart. Breathed life into his lungs.

Michael slammed back down. As he anchored fully in his body, the pulsating in his legs intensified, growing painful. He thrashed on his pallet, flailing much as he'd done when he was drowning. His hands groped for the red jasper roots, his fingers fumbling. Fiery heat surged through his body. It coursed inside him, pitching and roiling. Elyn joined the life-force Angels and sang the strands of his life back together in lucent tones.

The unbearable heat finally settled into ember warmth, soothing to the soul. His soul nestled deep into the depths of his core. It wasn't quite like the touch of the beautiful Lady, but it echoed her gentle comfort.

His arms and legs grew heavy now. His chest tightened, his head throbbed. A golden healing force flowed through Elyn's hands.

Eyes closed, still holding his feet, she nodded. "The battle for his soul is won. Michael has chosen life," she affirmed. "But now comes the difficult task of healing his physical body."

Chapter 8

The Isle of Avalon
1529 C.E.

Michael roused from the abyss that pulled him in and out of awareness. *In. Out.* Like the rhythm of shifting tides.

In. Awake. He lay on the healing pallet and watched Elyn with a mixture of caution and curiosity. He coughed, dry and hacking. His chest felt packed tight with wool.

"What happened?" he asked, weakly nudging one of the red stones arranged along his legs.

The gemstones had cooled and no longer glowed. Elyn removed them.

She smiled and patted his shoulder. "Welcome back to your life, lad."

He wanted to ask her what she meant, but the room began to spin around him. He groaned and rubbed his forehead, closing his eyes to shut out the dizziness. The light-headed dance inside his mind left him nauseated. His skull seemed to crush against his brain. Darkness fell. *Out.*

Elyn motioned for Ciara to watch over Michael, and asked Alianore to follow her to the other side of the healing cave. Conferring in a low voice, she said, "We need to be watchful of his head injury. It will be a day or so before he's out of danger from any swelling of his brain."

Alianore cast a concerned look Michael's way. "I had to bend the rules. I interfered outside of Avalon's borders, followed my heart's wisdom to bring him back here."

Elyn laid her hand on the High Priestess's arm. "I know."

"He would have died if I had left him."

"Yes. He would have. He still may."

Alianore heaved a sigh. "There is more. Marissa had his Death Vision. And afterwards, she was visited by the Goddess as well, who told her to save him. That their destiny was tied for a larger purpose."

"Oh." Elyn nodded slowly. "You hold confidence in Marissa's vision?"

"Yes," Alianore said without hesitation.

"Your daughter has much to learn. Much to prove. But you are my High Priestess, and my friend. I trust your judgment."

Alianore gave a wry smile. "I count on that."

Elyn touched her forehead to Alianore's in the sign of respect. "Marissa is fortunate to have your guidance. There is hope for her through you."

"Thank you, my friend. But I have faith in Marissa herself," Alianore said.

Elyn didn't respond. A shadow of doubt crossed her features before she could conceal it. Michael moaned, and Marissa rushed to his side. She took his hand and sought Elyn's reaction, worry written in her face.

The healer turned back to Alianore, "I will treat his head wound and his lungs as soon as I get him to my healing lodge. If all goes well and he heals, we can send him back to his home."

"That is my hope," Alianore replied.

"But if not . . ." Elyn's mouth set in a grim line.

"I have confidence in your healing talents."

Elyn nodded slowly, eyeing Michael. "If all goes well, there should be minimal disruption in his life from his time spent here in Avalon." She turned to Ciara and Marissa. "It is time to bring Michael to my healing cottage. You girls can carry him on the stretcher."

Michael woke to a jostling motion. In. The tightly woven stretcher swayed back and forth as Marissa and Ciara transported him from Avalon's Healing Halls. The girls carried him through the courtyard with the enchanting apple tree, past the mysteriously satiating red water spring, and back down the knoll that glimmered with the muted luster of twilight. His eyelids drooped and he clung to fading consciousness. Out. In. He wriggled his fingers and his toes just to feel them move. Then lost the delicate thread that tied his mind to the world around him. *Out.* He sank back into black nothingness before they could reach the healer's lodge in the priestess's village.

In. The darkness lifted. He heard a familiar voice. "Add more feverfew to the basin, Ciara."

Michael looked around wildly, heart pounding, not recognizing the cottage room with the large sunny windows, not recalling how he came to lay on the soft cot beneath him. *Where was Marissa?*

She had been sitting on a chair by the cottage door but jumped up and stepped forward when she saw Michael open his eyes.

"There, there," Elyn wiped a cool cloth across Michael's forehead. "You are in my healing lodge," she began to say, but Michael's eyes closed. *Out.*

"Swallowing so much lake water has infected his lungs and brought on fever and delirium," Elyn explained to her two apprentices. Ciara and the twelve-year-old Faery halfling, Shayla, stood at the ready, eager to learn from their Mistress.

"But it's been three days," Marissa protested.

Elyn flicked her a stern glance, warning her not to interrupt. "Three days is not long in situations like this." She massaged her temples with her fingertips and added in a more mollified tone, "His head injury. His lungs. It all takes time to heal."

Marissa returned to the chair by the door and absently tucked her robes under her knees. She hid her trembling hands inside the folds of her tunic. It wasn't like her to tremble, but Michael looked so dreadfully pale, and his lungs gurgled in a way that made her cringe every time he breathed. She nervously ran her tongue back and forth along the inside of her cheek. She wasn't very good at waiting. But there was nothing she could do.

Elyn dipped a cloth in spring water infused with willow and feverfew and patted Michael's brow with it. Ciara added a few more of the yellow blossoms to the water. The halfling Shayla studiously watched Elyn's actions, her vibrant green eyes alight with intelligence and curiosity.

Elyn gestured to a bowl on the table near Michael's bed. "Michael's fever is still high. We need to use more meadowsweet to offset it. Shayla, if you would please." The herb's creamy white flowers gave off a sweet smell.

Shayla tucked a stray wisp of white-blond hair behind her ear and began stuffing Michael's pillow with the strong-smelling herb. She worked deftly, the morning light accentuating the subtle silvery sheen of her skin, especially her hands. Born of Faery father and priestess mother, Shayla had been raised in the priestess traditions, as were all daughters of Avalon. She had shown a talent for healing since she was a small child, an innate inclination of the Faery Races of her lineage. Injured animals and birds were drawn to her, and she tended to them instinctively, as only one aligned so closely with the natural world could.

She scattered a handful of the meadowsweet around Michael's blankets, strewing the white clusters to mask the odor of illness that permeated the healing cottage. Elyn gave her a quick nod of approval.

Still huddled beside the door, Marissa sighed and leaned her head against the doorframe. She was frustrated that Michael's lungs still gurgled despite the healing treatments. *Why didn't he wake up? Would he be all right? Would he be afraid of Avalon? Would he be afraid of her?*

Her mother said Michael needed the priestess's particular care for his soul and body to recover. He had to be here in Avalon if he was to truly heal. Plus, there was her special vision about him. She could never abandon him after that. She would protect him, just as the Goddess wanted. Also, she liked him. A lot.

No matter that her vision had shaken her down to her bones. It also thrilled her. She squared her shoulders. She'd felt proud when her mother said she was young to be having such a powerful Death Vision portent. The Goddess had chosen *her*, a twelve-year-old, untrained priestess, to receive the vision along with the older, initiated priestesses of Avalon. This might finally prove to her mother, and everyone else in the community, that she could be reliable, was not reckless, and had something important to offer. Then maybe they would trust her again after the regrettable incident of traveling, uninvited, to the land of the Faery race two years ago.

"Ciara, stir the draught please," Elyn interrupted Marissa's thoughts.

Ciara scurried over to the fireplace to tend the steaming cauldron hanging from a metal tripod. Marissa was grateful her twin was in the healing cottage with her. They relied on the security they'd always provided each other just by being near. She especially appreciated that sisterly bond now, as her stomach fluttered and her muscles tightened at Michael's labored breathing.

Ciara added medicinal plants, one by one, into the boiling water, speaking their names in an incantation.

Elderberry, apple, and mint
Ease the boy's fever within
Cleanse his blood and heal his lungs
Elderberry, apple, and mint.

Marissa noted how carefully her sister stirred the brew, how reverently she blessed the infusion with her index and middle finger in the three-fold sign of the Goddess.

Ciara turned slightly to face Marissa. "These are meant to ease Michael's fever and infection," she told her. "They need to boil, then steep."

Elyn had made it Ciara's job to tend the cauldron because Shayla, as all those with Faery blood, could not risk touching any metal with iron in it. Her half-human blood muted the harmful effects, but iron could still burn her skin. Marissa had never seen any such burns. While some of the community's metal tools contained iron from the surrounding mountains, forged by the blacksmiths of Glastonbury, the priestesses more often used wood, bone, or shell whenever they could. This was to safeguard those of their ranks with Faery parentage.

Michael let out a loud, rattling breath. The unnatural sound brought an unguarded frown to Elyn's brow. That look troubled Marissa even more. She leapt up again and held out her hand. She had to do something, anything.

"Here. Let me use the cloth."

When Elyn didn't answer, Marissa added, "Please." She tried her best to keep her tone appeasing like Ciara's, but by the look on the healer's face, she knew she hadn't succeeded.

"My dear, if you wish to minister to the sick, you need to be an apprentice under my tutelage," Elyn said.

Marissa glowered. Indeed, Elyn's rules were the accepted practice. Only those trained to tend to the sick were allowed to do so in any manner. *Couldn't they bend the rules just this once?*

"I saved the boy." Her voice rose. "Can't I just help see to it that his needs are met?" She stopped. If only she could learn to control her demanding nature, as Vanora was always reminding her. She just couldn't seem to soften her words like Ciara.

"You may have found him and pulled him from the lake. But it was Ciara who revived him," Elyn corrected, her gaze unwavering.

Marissa flinched but met Elyn's gaze. "Healing Mistress, please. I had my Vision about Michael. The Goddess told me to find him. It's my duty . . ." It was more than her duty as a priestess, she thought, fists clenching. Couldn't Elyn see this was special, that she rescued him for an important, even if mysterious, reason? And that she, Marissa, was a part of it all?

Ciara interjected. "I can stay by her side and make sure she does things just as you taught me."

Marissa shot her sister a grateful look and held out her hand for the cloth, hoping Elyn would agree, if only for the sake of her twin's kind nature.

Elyn shook her head in resignation with the slightest hint of a smile. Setting the cloth in the basin of herbal water beside Michael's cot, she gestured for Marissa to sit beside him. "All right, you two. Just this once though. But Marissa, you must follow my directions precisely. Do nothing more, nothing less. He is to take some of this water. You can squeeze the cloth so small drops fall on his lips and into his mouth."

Marissa drew back her long dark hair and tied it with a leather cord, as she'd seen the healers do. She sat on the stool beside Michael's cot and followed Elyn's instructions, carefully dripping the water into his mouth.

Elyn patted her on the shoulder. "Well done, child. Ciara, you stay here with your sister and tend the brew over the fire. Shayla, you come help me."

Ciara turned to face the fire once more, stirring the thick herbal mixture. Marissa shivered with a sudden compulsion to throw the wet cloth aside and place her hand over Michael's chest. With Elyn still in the room, she fought the impulse, trying hard to obey the healer's orders to do only as instructed. If she didn't comply, she would certainly be banned from the healing cottage and wouldn't be able to be with Michael at all. The compulsion grew stronger. Marissa sat on her hands.

The Healing Mistress gathered Michael's used poultices and motioned Shayla to follow her into the herbal preparation room. "You can finish making the unguent for Michael's chest, Shayla," Elyn said as they made their way to the other side of the cottage.

Marissa's hands throbbed. She kept them restrained under her thighs. Her gaze followed the teacher and apprentice. She watched them to distract herself, but more so to make sure they left the room. Elyn pulled aside the woolen curtain separating the main room from the smaller chamber that housed the assorted medicinals. A mix of herbal scents swelled into the cottage. Sweet, pungent, spicy, and woodsy aromas exuded from the shelves of ointments and teas. Bundles of herbs hung from the rafters to dry. The large storage room was dark, with no windows, designed to protect the potency of the herbs. Shayla lit the readied candles, set on a well-worn but clean wooden table to give them the light they needed to work.

As soon as Elyn drew the curtain closed behind them, Marissa let out the breath she'd been holding and checked on Ciara. Her twin was busy stirring the cauldron. Marissa pulled her hands out from beneath her thighs and swallowed heavily when she saw they pulsated and glowed golden. Trembling, she surrendered to the overpowering need to place them on Michael's chest.

The moment she touched him something torrential surged through her body—powerful, like the raging waterfall she and her sister often visited. The sensation coursed down her arms and through her palms, flowing into his chest. She didn't know exactly what she was doing, just that she had to do this. Should she try to direct the surge somehow or simply let it stream from her unhindered?

She decided to command the flow of power, bend it to her will. This caused her arms to shudder painfully, and the flow abruptly halted. She licked her dry lips. What should she do now? Could she hurt him? She opened her mouth to call for Ciara, but the deluge of power stifled her.

A commanding voice spoke to her, coming from everywhere and nowhere at the same time. *"Yield to the healing power. It knows what to do."*

Marissa looked around for the source of the voice. Ciara faced the fire, busy tending her brew. Elyn and Shayla were still in the medicinal room. Who'd spoken? Was it the ancestors of her priestess lineage? The Goddess of the Stars and Sea again? Her arms felt on fire. She had to do something quick. She followed the voice's instructions and yielded to the stream of power, allowing it to run its course in its own way, unconditionally. Her arms still vibrated, but the burning ceased. The pulsations became rhythmic and fluid. Her hands, as well as Michael's chest, shone like golden sunlight. Her belly grew warm, a sure confirmation she was doing something right.

Within a few seconds, Michael's breathing quieted and calmed. Marissa smiled and gradually pulled her hands away. A sudden wave of exhaustion overtook her, and she rubbed her weary eyes.

Ciara left her draught to simmer and sat on a stool close to her twin. Her eyes widened when she noticed Marissa's hands. They emanated a faint golden, undeniable healing glow.

Ciara leaned toward her and whispered, "What did you do? Elyn will be furious. Why do you always try to break the rules? You never showed an interest in healing before."

Marissa balked. "I couldn't help myself. I had to put my hands on his chest." She stopped and jutted her chin out in defiance. "I believe I'm meant to help him. It's that simple."

Ciara sighed. "I believe you, sister. I know you mean well, but the healing energy is such a powerful force. It's best to only use it with training."

Marissa stared at her hands, torn between the exultation of the healing force that had obviously helped Michael, and Ciara's sensible warning.

Ciara offered a smile of encouragement. "You know, if you defer to Elyn more, she'll give you more leeway. Try it sometime."

Marissa sighed. "I'll try. I wish I could be as patient as you."

Her hands had not stopped trembling. Jolts of energy, although weaker, still coursed through them. She tightened her fists, trying to hold it in. Her heart raced erratically, her body felt as if it would implode if she didn't do something with the residual energy flowing inside of her.

Ciara pointed at her hands. "Put them on the ground. Do it now." She jumped down from her stool and yanked Marissa's hands to the floor.

Marissa palms made contact with the earthen floor. The excess power drained out of her hands in one relieving swoosh. Her heartbeat calmed and her panic dissolved as the ground absorbed the surplus energy.

"Please don't use the healing force again until you've been properly taught how to control it. Promise?" Ciara said, straightening.

Marissa wasn't sure she could promise anything but was saved from answering when Michael moaned. The sound alarmed her, and she moved in closer. He was still asleep, skin still pale and clammy, but his movement wasn't as restless, and the coughing had ceased. Exhaling slowly, she took his hand in hers.

Elyn had told them Michael's soul had chosen to live, but his body still needed to accept the arduous task of healing. It didn't take a healer to know his life was on the line. Either this fever broke soon, or the Death Vision the priestesses had three days ago would now become reality. Marissa was not going to let that happen.

She watched and waited all afternoon, grateful Elyn hadn't discovered she'd disobeyed her. Ciara didn't tell on her, and Elyn allowed her to continue giving Michael a few drops of the special herbal water and to daub his forehead with it. Whenever Ciara walked by, she would kiss her cheek and whisper what a good job she was doing.

It was well into the night when Michael's eyelids finally fluttered open. Elyn and her two apprentices had returned to the medicinal room to prepare more poultices. He issued a soft groan and turned his head toward Marissa, sitting at his side. She carefully dripped water into his mouth, and he licked his lips. His gaze wavered before settling on her face.

"You again," he said in a low voice.

"Yes. Me. How do you feel?" She kept her voice was soft.

"I have . . . felt better." He offered a weak smile and closed his eyes again.

Marissa considered the now familiar dimple in his cheek, the purple bruise on his forehead, his long tawny hair and strong chin.

He opened his eyes again. "You're staring."

She felt heat climb up her neck. "I am not."

"I saw you."

"You're mistaken."

Michael coughed and took a long breath before he spoke again. "What are you going to do with me?"

"Do with you? I . . . I mean, we . . . are going to take care of you."

"What does it mean, you being a priestess?" he asked quietly.

Before she could reply, his eyes drifted closed, and he fell back into that feverish place she feared was sapping his life force. She chewed her lip. What more could she do to help him? She felt impatient with prayers and poultices. Goddess, she wished she had healing training like Ciara.

Maybe a powerful surge of energy would come through her again. That had helped. Her eyes scanned the room, making sure no one was watching. Concentrating, she rested her hands on Michael's chest again. Nothing happened.

Grumbling, frustrated, she pulled them away. She stared at his closed eyelids, as if by sheer force of her will alone she could bring him back to full health.

Elyn strode out of the medicinal chamber and collected wood from a storage cubby to add to the fireplace. She turned and laid her hands on Marissa shoulders. "You need rest. Your mother will be returning shortly to check on you." And gently led Marissa to a sleeping mat set up in front of the hearth.

Marissa wanted to argue, but truthfully, she was beyond tired. She hadn't slept much at all in the three days since they'd brought Michael to Avalon. She stumbled toward the sleeping mat and dropped on top of the blankets. Elyn tucked a soft cover around her.

Slumber came quickly. It wasn't long before she entered the realm of night dreams.

Orange and red flames plume high in the night sky. Men on horseback raze the abbey grounds. Monks scatter, their cowls pulled back, their robes untied. Some are cowering, some praying. Others carry buckets of water. Those with buckets form a defiant line alongside the Glastonbury Abbey, passing the buckets from hand to hand.

Orange and red flames turn the night to ash. Their heated fury threatens to lick at Marissa's hair and robes. She steps back, crouches down behind a hawthorn hedge, hiding from the men on horseback. Michael is by her side. His face twists in anguish. She cups her hands over his mouth to silence his cry.

He pushes her hand aside. "I have to help. I have to take the holy cup to safety," he whispers hoarsely.

"Then you had better be quick and you had better be stealthy."

Orange and red flames continue to billow. Stained glass shatters. Walls crumble. Men scream. The high arches of the magnificent and ancient abbey plunge to the ground.

Marissa tears her gaze from the flames to reach for Michael's hand.

He is gone.

Marissa awoke to the sound of her own scream. Her mother cradled her. "What is it, my dear?"

She couldn't erase the image of the burning abbey, or the sensation of reaching for Michael's hand and finding him gone. Sobs punctuated her answer. "A vision. Another one. An awful one, Mother! This one frightens me. It had Glastonbury's Abbey. And Michael."

Alianore brushed Marissa's sweat-dampened hair off her forehead. "Let me help you calm yourself. Then you can tell me everything."

Elyn brought over a cup of chamomile infusion. The healer and Alianore exchanged concerned glances.

Marissa pushed the cup away when her mother brought it to her lips. "No. I want to stay alert. I have to see Michael." She pulled away from her mother's embrace to return to Michael's side. Ciara was tending him, cooling cloth clutched in one hand.

"You can leave now," Marissa said.

"But, Marissa, I just got here. It's my turn to tend to him."

"I can't go back to sleep and face another dream. I need to be with him. Move." She inched her way forward, nudging Ciara aside. "Please," she added.

Ciara looked at her mother, her eyes pleading.

"Ciara, can you help Elyn make more poultices for the boy?" Alianore motioned for her daughter to join the healer.

Ciara cast a gaze at Michael with unguarded pining. Her chin quivered. "But . . . yes, very well, Mother."

Elyn slid an arm around Ciara's shoulder. "Come with me and I'll show you how to infuse the next batch of compresses."

Elyn pulled aside the woolen curtain. Ciara lit the candle tapers, their subdued light escaping from under the dividing curtain even after Elyn pulled it closed, casting a muted glow to the main room. Alianore handed the mug of chamomile to Marissa again and stood waiting until she had obligingly taken a sip or two.

"Tell me what this is all about, Marissa. You have never shown such interest in the healing ways before. You are brusque with Elyn and with your own sister as well. Powerful visions aside, I will not tolerate rudeness." Alianore's voice was tender but also filled with the command of a High Priestess. And a mother's reprimand.

Marissa felt the hot sting of tears. She didn't want to hurt her twin. She clutched the mug and didn't look up for a few seconds. How could she explain what she didn't understand? She only knew that something deep in her belly told her to protect Michael.

There was more, the most confusing part. But she wanted to hold the mystery of her growing feelings for Michael close without having to explain.

At least not until it was more clear what it all meant. She wanted her mother to believe in her. After all, she was on the verge of starting her apprenticeship as an Oracle and Seer. For two years since the Faery Realm disaster, she had tried her best to prove herself, to make up for her error of that visit. She desperately wanted to be taken seriously.

Marissa set her mug down on the floor with a little more force than she intended. "The Goddess told me to find him. And save him. She told *me*."

Alianore waited for more.

"I can't make out the rest yet. Please trust me, Mother."

"My dear, you know I never doubt when the Goddess speaks to any of us. Even the youngest in our community." Alianore stroked Marissa's dark hair.

"Thank you, Mother." Her mother's words worked to soften her stiff muscles and snappish tone.

"When you begin your apprenticeship, you will learn how to work with your gift of prophecy. You are strong in your talent."

Marissa smiled.

Alianore continued. "But you lack experience. And discernment. That is why we defer Seer apprenticeships until your first bleeding time, when you can align with the moon's power. Once you begin your bleeding cycles, you enter into womanhood, and only then can you begin this difficult training. It helps stabilize these powerful energies."

Marissa nodded, twisting her belt ties around her fingers in nervous energy.

"For now, what I can tell you is that it is not an easy gift, this second-sight," Alianore said. "It can wrack your body and jumble your mind and manners if it is not properly controlled. I care for you, my daughter. I must see to it that you are safe and not harmed by these unusual surges of untrained prophecy."

Marissa's chin quivered. Her mother was right. She did feel flustered by it all.

"When I was your age, I had to learn to develop patience and use temperance. It took practice. I eventually learned discernment. And responsibility." She smiled at Marissa's look of surprise.

Marissa swiped unbidden tears. "You?"

Alianore nodded with a compassionate smile.

Marissa sniffled. "I know I've made mistakes, but I've learned since the Faery visit. I truly have."

"My dear, it may not seem so now, but your strong will, combined with your visions, can one day become your strength."

"How?"

"Listen for your heart's wisdom before you act. Heed my counsel. And Vanora's instructions as your teacher. We know what we are doing. We have centuries of our tradition to back us up."

Marissa looked down.

"As time goes on, you will eventually learn to handle your portents with wisdom and compassion."

"But I know this vision is true. I have to do something about it. I must warn Michael. I can't let him go near Glastonbury Abbey!"

Alianore shook her head. "There is one thing you have to remember. Helping is a good thing, but you must not force a person to do anything against their free will. No matter how ominous your visions may be, you may only warn. You never know what you might put in motion when you interfere with someone's destiny."

Marissa couldn't help but ask. "You think I am being difficult? Bad-tempered?"

Alianore shrugged and raised her eyebrows.

"You don't trust me." Marissa's shoulders drooped. "Because of what happened to Shayla and Ciara in the Faery Realm. No matter what I do to make up for it, nobody has trusted me since."

Alianore sighed softly before she spoke. "You will be High Priestess one day. You are being groomed for a delicate and important purpose. Your training will be harder. You are the one who needs my counsel most of all."

"Because I'm not like Ciara? Gentle Ciara, who is always sensible and cautious." Marissa's voice was sharp beyond control.

"I did not say that."

Marissa avoided her mother's gaze. "You didn't have to."

Chapter 9

The Isle of Avalon
1529 C.E.

It was in the early hours approaching dawn when Michael next woke. True to her resolve, Marissa hadn't left his side since the terrifying dream the night before. She had dozed off and on beside the bed, her head resting on her arm. When she felt Michael stir, she eagerly leaned forward.

"Where am I?" he said. His voice sounded weak, but the glare of delirium no longer shone from his blue eyes.

"What do you remember?" Marissa asked.

He furrowed his brow. "I remember seeing you at the lake. Did you pull me out?"

"Yes. Then you got really sick, and now you are in the healer's cottage in my village."

Michael paused, nodding his head slowly. "Yes. I remember now." He studied her face. "Am I going to die?" he asked, holding her gaze.

A chill crawled across her back. "Certainly not, silly."

Michael narrowed his eyelids and looked off in the distance, as if catching the ephemeral wisps of a forgotten memory. "I think you're right." He lowered his voice. "I saw the Lady again—the beautiful one with the blue robes and the stars around her head. She told me to hold onto her robes and She would lead me back. You know, back home where I belong."

Marissa was surprised he'd had another vision of the Goddess, being untrained and not even from Avalon. "Seeing Her is a good omen."

Michael reached for her hand, at first shyly, then clasping it tightly. "I'm glad you're here."

Warmth traveled up her neck and across her cheeks, but she didn't pull away. They were silent a moment before he spoke again, "My Da's men will worry about me. They'll come looking for me."

She nodded kindly, but knew without the aid of an Avalon priestess, his father's men would never pass through the mists hiding Avalon from Glastonbury and the rest of the world.

Elyn pulled the curtain aside from the back room and peeked out, then hurried to Michael's side. "Finally awake, are you?" She spoke with a healer's soothing, confident lilt.

"I was wondering where my Da's men were," Michael said.

"Don't worry about your Da's men for now. We'll get you back to them just as soon as you are strong enough."

Marissa dropped his hand and leapt up. "But he mustn't leave!"

"Am I your prisoner?" Michael addressed his question to Elyn.

"Of course not," Elyn assured him.

Marissa put her hands on her hips. "It's just . . . you have to stay, Michael. I mean, I saved you and all."

"Now, Marissa, the boy will need to get back to his own people eventually. But don't fret, that won't be for a few days yet."

Marissa glowered, the too familiar surge of frustration and disappointment filling her chest to overflowing. "No doubt you're all going to ignore my premonition!"

She turned and ran out of the cottage before anyone could see the hot tears streaming down her cheeks.

It was nearing the Summer Solstice, and the sun held high sway. The land of Avalon responded to the warmth and light with a profusion of meadow wildflowers, purple vetch, and white mayweed. Plentiful apple trees creaked under the weight of ever-ripening fruit. Even the cool shadows of the forest burst with vitality.

The earthy scents of summer greenery filled the healing lodge. Ciara handed

Elyn the latest batch of lung mixture she'd brewed, awaiting the Healing Mistress' inspection.

"It is such a beautiful day," Marissa said, tying the window curtains back to let in air and sunshine. "May we please take Michael on an outing? Just to the meadow by the woods," she asked for the second time that morning.

Shayla stopped folding the clean linen bandages and nodded her head with vigor at the suggestion. "Oh yes, please, Mistress Elyn."

Elyn dipped her finger in the tonic jar and tasted it. "This has been properly brewed. Well done, Ciara."

Ciara beamed.

"An outing?" Elyn pursed her lips and took a moment before answering. "All right. A bit of fresh air might do you good, Michael. But you must be mindful of your health, my lad. Open your mouth," she said, placing a few drops of the newly made tonic on his tongue.

"I feel well," Michael replied, squeezing his eyes tight and scrunching his nose as he swallowed the bitter tincture.

Elyn capped the tonic bottle and scrutinized Michael as if she could see inside his body. "You are indeed much better. Still, you are not fully healed yet."

As if to emphasize her point, Michael broke into a short coughing fit. He dutifully covered his mouth with the cloth Ciara handed him.

"We will take very good care of him," Shayla said.

"You girls are not to tax Michael. Do you understand?" Elyn was stern.

They all eagerly nodded their heads in agreement.

Michael rolled his eyes. "I'm fine, really," he protested. He caught Marissa watching him. Her smile was hidden behind her hand, but her eyes twinkled—she'd conspire to make sure he'd have a fun time on their outing.

In the fortnight he'd spent in Elyn's healing cottage, he had indeed felt himself growing stronger. Though he tired easily, coughed frequently, and often had a mild headache, he had, oddly enough, never felt better. Whether it was the women's ministrations, some enchantment, or even the magical land of Avalon itself, he wasn't sure. He had watched Elyn closely. Her hands were gentle and skilled, her smile as kind as her directives were firm. He'd improved under her care and had grown to trust her, no matter how mysterious her methods were. But he suspected his recuperation and good mood also had something to do with his feelings for Marissa.

Later that summer morning, after the girls finished their chores, the four of them headed out on their outing, a lunch basket packed by Vanora in hand. They walked the short distance to the nearby meadow at the edge of the oak woods. Once the basket was stowed safely beside a hawthorn hedgerow, they began a game of hide-and-hunt.

"I'll be the hunter," Michael said.

"We name you Herne the Hunter, Lord of the Forest, the Great Antlered One," Shayla decreed.

Michael wasn't sure his Da's priest would approve of the heathen name, but he figured except for the hunter's name being Herne, it was the same game he and his brothers played. The priest wasn't here to chastise him anyway. Besides, he wanted to show Marissa just how strong and cunning he was, so he pulled on the leather cap fastened with stag antlers that Ciara handed him, tying the rope that anchored them under his chin.

"I am Herne the Hunter, Lord of the Forest. Hide from me if you can!" he boasted.

He turned facing an oak tree and covered his eyes. Counting slowly to fifty, he gave the girls ample time to hide.

"Forty-eight, forty-nine, fifty! I'm coming to find you!"

A muffled giggle gave Ciara away from her spot behind a fallen log. Michael tapped her shoulder to tag her. Then he raced across the meadow and headed into the forest to search for Marissa. The bright summer sun was muted under the leafy branches of ash and thorn trees. Thick-trunked ancient oak trees towered above him, gnarly limbs reaching wide. Marissa told him earlier that the oaks were the custodians of the woodland. He believed her, eyeing the feathery ferns and multi-colored wildflowers, hearing the scuffle of small animals and birds, all held within the oak's embrace. It was much the same in his father's woodsy country estate in Wales.

Exploring the trees and bushes, he found Shayla hunkered down inside a split-trunked oak. "I tag you, Shayla," he crowed.

Shayla smiled and stepped out from her hiding place. Michael blinked, surprised he'd spotted her at all with the strange green glimmer radiating around her body. The green glow had grown brighter when they entered the forest, and her silver skin now gleamed in sharp contrast.

Michael dashed farther into the woods, not caring that running left him short of breath. He coughed and took in the moist air. He wanted to win this game, and Marissa was the only one left hidden. He tugged aside the branches of the bordering shrubbery, searching for Ciara's feisty twin. *By God she was clever*, he thought, scanning for signs of her presence in the thicket.

After a few moments more of peeking behind trees and peering into the bushy undergrowth, he finally gave in. "I cannot find Marissa," he called out, thereby ending the first round of the game. He took off the antlered crown.

Ciara ran up beside him, shaking her head. "I have no idea where she could be hiding."

Michael knelt and peered at the forest floor, poking at the leaves and twigs, searching for signs of any recent disturbance Marissa's footfall might have caused.

Shayla paced behind Ciara, eyes narrowed in concentration. "I cannot hear her."

"You know it's not fair using your Faery hearing," Ciara said.

"I cannot help it. Not anymore at least. It just comes on me since . . ." Shayla hesitated, then continued in a voice so low Michael could barely make it out. ". . . since we went into the Faery Realm."

Ciara wound her fingers into the fabric of her blue linen tunic. "I wish it had never happened," she whispered.

Michael kept his eyes trained on the ground but listened closely.

Shayla's expression tightened into a concerned frown. Ciara pulled her aside. "I'm fine. My heart still beats unevenly, but at least it doesn't hurt anymore. I worry more about you. You know you're like a sister to me."

Shayla smiled tenderly and reached out to tuck a wisp of hair behind her friend's ear.

Ciara sighed. "I feel you slowly slipping away from me."

Michael kept his head down when she glanced over her shoulder at him.

"I know your hearing is heightened, all of your senses seem to be, and you are always daydreaming. Even the silvery cast to your skin is deeper. And your healing abilities . . . they are stronger. I can tell."

Shayla's lip trembled. "All priestesses in Avalon have innate powers . . ."

Ciara shook her head. "Yours have always been different, but more so now. It's like they're more instinctive, blood-borne, tied to the forces of primal nature. Every moment your gifts increase, I feel it take you one step away from Avalon. One step away from me."

Shayla hugged her. "I'll always be your sister-friend, no matter what." She paused and stared vacantly, in her Faery way of seeing. "She is close."

Ciara chewed her thumbnail.

It took several seconds before Michael finally noticed Marissa leaning against the birch tree several yards in front of them, arms crossed over her chest. She was chewing a wild nasturtium leaf, her lips curled in a satisfied smile.

"Still looking for me?" she asked, grinning.

Ciara jumped at the sound of her sister's voice.

Michael stood up, the movement made him dizzy. "By the saints, where did you come from?"

Shayla frowned. "I did not hear you, Marissa. Why could I not hear you?"

Marissa laughed good-naturedly. "Because I'm better at this than all of you combined." She strolled toward them, still grinning.

Michael couldn't help staring at the amber flecks in her brown eyes. He didn't know whether to be irritated or fascinated by her. When she smiled directly at him, he settled on fascinated.

She grabbed his hand, causing heat to flame his cheeks.

"Let's spin," she cried.

Ciara took Michael's other hand and motioned for Shayla to join the circle. They began to dance round and round with quickening steps.

"Not too fast," Ciara said. "Remember what Elyn said about Michael."

"I can do this," Michael boasted. Just to show them, he pulled them even faster.

Chapter 10
The Isle of Avalon
1529 C.E.

As they spun in a frenzied circle, Marissa laughed out loud, the sound of it contagious. Soon they were all giggling. A kaleidoscope of woodsy trees, blue tunics, smiles of delight, and purple wildflowers raced before her eyes. The image abruptly changed, and she blinked hard. The heat in her belly rose up and blazed. Her eyes grew unfocused, and she stared into a dreamscape she knew the others didn't see. The vision consumed her.

Ciara appeared different. Older. There was so much sadness written in the empty depths of her eyes, the melancholic set of her mouth. Shayla looked older as well, sitting straight and proud astride a horse. And Michael. He was a young man, handsome, smiling, his tawny hair and blue eyes vibrant in a way that enthralled her. He reached for her with arms opened wide. But his expression changed. His eyes filled with despair, his mouth parted in anguish, his eyes pleaded with her.

Marissa tilted her head up to the sky, unable to bear the pain in Michael's eyes. She moaned, but in their revelry, no one heard. When she lowered her head and glanced across the circle again, her companions were once more their twelve-year-old selves. She pulled her hands away, breaking the circle. Everyone fell to the ground, wiping teary eyes from so much laughing. The vision left her with a headache, along with questions for which she had no answers. Why would dear Ciara look so sad? What would cause Michael such despair? No one seemed to notice her distress. She forced herself to laugh with them to cover her confusion.

"Come on, all of you. Let's eat," she suggested once the giddiness died down. She wanted to distract them to give her time to think.

Michael's stomach rumbled in response. He coughed, a wheezy sound earning him a concerned look from Ciara.

"Yes, lunchtime," he agreed, rubbing his stomach. He jumped up, ignoring her concern.

The four of them walked arm in arm back to the clearing, inside the ring of venerable oaks where they'd left their food basket. Marissa felt the confusion from her vision dissolve with each step she placed on solid earth.

Ciara spread a worn blanket on the ground. She opened the woven food basket and busied herself with putting out cold lamb slices, a hunk of goat cheese, and a loaf of brown bread. Shayla grabbed the empty sheepskin pouch and walked toward a hidden stream that gurgled loudly behind a copse of willows.

"I'll fetch some water," she called over her shoulder.

"Look at all the food," Michael beamed when the lunch was spread out neatly on the cloth.

Marissa punched him lightly on the arm. "We need it, what with your appetite."

He stuck his tongue out and grabbed a hunk of lamb, not noticing Ciara's outstretched hand offering him the choicest cut. She dropped her gaze and slipped the piece back with the other portions.

"I'm thirsty and hot," Marissa said. "I'm going to the stream to see why Shayla's taking so long to bring water." What she really needed was to shake off the last vestiges of the disconcerting vision.

She rose and sprinted in the direction Shayla went, disappearing behind the copse of willow trees that hid the stream from view.

Ciara watched her sister leave, smiling inwardly at the unexpected opportunity for a few moments alone with Michael.

"What did Shayla mean back there?" Michael asked, his mouth full.

"Whatever are you talking about? Here, use this," she added, handing him a small, folded cloth.

"What's that for?"

"You're getting food all over your chin." She giggled and leaned forward to wipe at the bits of meat on his face.

He leaned back. "Oh, no you don't." He pushed her away lightheartedly. "You aren't getting out of that so easy. I'll ask again. What did Shayla mean?"

"About what?" Ciara lowered the cloth, averting her eyes.

"About her Faery hearing."

She sighed and sat back on her knees. "It's a secret, Michael."

"Avalon is filled with secrets. Tell me. Come on. It's me. You know me well enough by now. You can tell me."

"'Tis not mine to tell."

His tone sobered. "Then whose story is it?"

"Marissa's." *That was a mistake,* she thought. *Now, he'll never let it go.*

He lay his slice of lamb down beside him on the blanket. "Please, Ciara."

She didn't know how a boy could have such a strong hold over her. It was Marissa's story to tell—a story her sister was ashamed of. "I promised her I would never tell anyone about it. It nearly cost her the inherited title of High Priestess."

His eyes implored her. She tried to fight his plea, tried to focus on the splashing sounds of the fast-moving stream in the distance, but she lost her resolve in his penetrating blue eyes. She imagined, even hoped, he might take her hand.

He didn't. She shook off the reverie and peered around, checking if either of the two girls had emerged from the willows yet. No sign of them.

She chewed her thumbnail before speaking. "All right. But please don't tell anyone what I'm about to share with you."

Michael nodded his head and inched closer. Ciara's heart skipped when his shoulder brushed hers.

"It happened two years ago, when we were but ten years old. I'm afraid it still lives on in everyone's mind, especially my sister's. You see, she convinced Shayla and me to pay a visit to the Faery Realm . . ." Ciara faltered, expecting him to make fun of her and claim there was no such thing as a Faery Realm. His mouth set itself in a firm line. Not sure if he did it to keep from laughing or speaking, she hurried on, fearing Marissa's return from the stream.

"'Tis a long story, and a complicated one, but in the end, we were nearly trapped there. If Vanora had not found us, I don't know what would have happened. Faery premonitions and enhanced powers have bothered Shayla ever since. She is half Faery, you know. Then I nearly died. And Marissa . . ."

"What? Wait. You nearly died?" Michael's voice rose in alarm.

She blushed, pleased by his voiced concern for her wellbeing. "Well, yes. But I'm fine now. Truly. And Marissa didn't mean any harm. We *all* agreed to go into the Faery Realm in the first place, together. It's just that Marissa, well, she was blamed for . . ."

She froze at the sound of footsteps crunching the forest undergrowth. She moaned, fearing they had been overheard.

Michael's gaze swept beyond her to their two companions, who had now reentered the grove. His mouth opened, but no sound came out. She turned slowly, her heart missing a beat. The pale, icy fury on Marissa's face told Ciara that she had heard her divulging her worst secret. And surely felt betrayed by the telling.

Ciara whimpered, her chest aching with sadness for hurting her twin. She stood and held out her hand. "Marissa, I'm so sorry. You too, Shayla."

"Wait. What *happened* in the Faery Realm?" Michael looked from one twin to the other.

Shayla stared off into the distance. Ciara looked down at her hands. Marissa was stonily silent.

He persisted. "Marissa? Shayla? Ciara? Someone talk to me."

Marissa took one slow step forward, then another. The leaves on the oak trees stopped fluttering. The wind died down as if nature held Her breath and watched.

She raised her hand and gestured with a flick of the wrist. "Leave," she ordered.

"You can't command me," Ciara cried. "I meant no harm. I won't leave until I know you forgive me."

"Please. Leave." Despite the grim scowl, Marissa's eyes shone with tears she would not shed in front of them.

Ciara's lip trembled. She gathered her shawl and turned to go, gesturing for Shayla to join her. Michael rose to accompany them.

"No, not you." Marissa pointed at him.

Shayla huffed, "She might obey you like a servant, but I won't. You cannot just make us leave, Marissa. You are not High Priestess yet." Shayla glimmered and pulsed in accord with the surrounding forest. "You know this involved all three of us."

No one moved.

Ciara spoke up, eyes wide and voice hushed. "It's all right, Shayla. Let her tell Michael in her own fashion. It's better this way. Maybe it will let you heal, Sister. I shouldn't have let your secret out."

"Then why did you?" Marissa shook with anger. "Why did you tell?" She didn't wait for an answer. Eyes cast down, she gestured again for them to leave her alone with Michael.

Ciara knew her twin well. The nearly imperceptible quiver in her chin belied her commanding tone. If they stayed, it would cost her sister her self-respect, already frayed since the incident. She slipped her arm though Shayla's, silently bidding her to walk away. Shayla hesitated, but finally complied.

As the two left the grove, Marissa dropped down onto the blanket and sat on her heels with her knees bent. She tucked her hands underneath her and hoped Michael didn't see them shaking. He sat cross-legged, facing her, watching in silence. Her eyes drifted to the forest shadows, wondering how to begin. Wondering why she felt the need to tell her side of the story anyway.

But she already knew the answer. No one trusted her. Not truly. They called her reckless and irresponsible. And now, could she even trust herself? Did she even know how to be trustworthy? Because of that one Faery visit, no one seemed to put credence in her visions about Michael, no one vowed to help keep him safe in Avalon. They all told him he could leave once he was fully healed. This, despite the clear warning of his terrible fate at Glastonbury Abbey. Their doubts about her recent visions had ruptured the guilty memory she'd worked hard to seal off. It was an unhealed wound, and if it wasn't lanced, its toxins would continue to taint her and everyone she loved. She took a steady breath, just like her mother taught her since she was a child. She couldn't look at Michael and didn't bother to hide her tears.

"During the summer season, right after Ciara and I turned ten . . ." Her voice caught. She cleared her throat and began again, her words a deluge of remorse. "I accidentally put Ciara and Shayla in harm's way in the Faery Realm."

Michael shuffled to reposition his legs; he looked uncomfortable. Marissa wondered if he found talk of the Faery Realm hard to believe, coming from a priestess no less. His expression remained impassive, so she continued.

"As you already know, Shayla is a halfling, born in Avalon, and had never visited the Faery lands. But because of her Faery blood and the collective memory it carries, she has visions and dreams where she catches glimpses into that realm."

Now he squirmed. She wondered again why she felt compelled to tell him this story. What was it about this lad in particular that made her desire to bare her soul? The thought he might hate her because of what she did made her heart sink. There was no turning back now.

She closed her eyes and recalled how Shayla tantalizingly described the things she saw in her visions. The bounty of Faery dinner banquets. Tables heaped with sugary sweetmeats, succulent boar, golden honey mead, and ripe, juicy cherries. Marissa was especially fond of fresh cherries. There were crystal prism vases, reflecting light into rainbow shards, and tables adorned with red and white roses blossomed to perfection. The vivid descriptions fueled Marissa's curiosity, stoking the fires of promising adventures.

"I wanted to see everything for myself, to taste the Faery banquets . . ."

Michael stopped squirming.

"We were young. I didn't see the harm in just a visit. Naturally, Ciara reminded me it could be dangerous to go without an Elder. I admit that's what Vanora had taught us, but everything Shayla told us made it seem so welcoming and extravagant. I figured a short visit would be harmless."

"Even I've heard the stories that say you should never eat the food in the Faery Realm." He clapped a hand over his mouth.

Her heart tightened. He'd already judged her. "If you know so much about the Faery, then I needn't tell you the rest." She pushed herself up off the cloth, but Michael quickly grabbed her arm.

"No. Please. I'm sorry. I really want to hear the rest." He gently tugged her arm until she sat again.

She searched his face until she felt his willingness to believe her was sincere. "Promise you'll hear me out to the end?"

"I promise," Michael replied, crossing himself over his shoulder and chest in the Christian sign of the cross.

"All right then. One reason it can be dangerous to visit the Faery Realm is because it's close to the Otherworld, the land of the Afterlife. But I wasn't afraid." She squared her shoulders. "I thought Ciara was being too cautious, as always. I was certain Shayla could safely lead the way there." She stopped, her defiance dissolving in a flood of tears. She hid her face with her hands.

He offered a brisk nod. "I think you're brave. Just like my father's knights."

Marissa lifted her head and wiped her eyes and nose with her sleeve. "No. I was wrong. I was reckless." The opened scar bled drops of guilt and shame. "Back then I thought I was daring and bold. But now . . . every day I have to prove myself."

Prove herself to Vanora and her mother especially. Perhaps rightly so. But this penance felt never-ending. She always seemed to fall short in showing prudence. She paused to sort out how to explain to Michael to make him understand. Shaking her head in defeat, she decided to continue her story by telling him everything, exactly how it had transpired.

Chapter 11

The Isle of Avalon
1529 C.E.

"It was two years ago," Marissa began. "Ciara, Shayla, and I sat at the foot of the Tor."

She remembered how the terraced green conical hill loomed above them, its apex seeming to almost touch the noonday sun.

That midsummer day, Ciara had picked fragrant honeysuckle vines from the bushes growing at the foot of the Tor. Kneeling beside Marissa, she hummed contentedly while nimbly braiding and weaving the fragrant blossoms through her sister's raven black hair. The sacred Red Well burbled in the distance, its wellhead located just outside Avalon's Healing Sanctuary, atop the smaller knoll that neighbored the Tor. The cooling White Spring flowed directly behind them, and Marissa could still feel how it sprayed their arms and robes with chalky water droplets. The two springs merged into one unified stream a short distance away, and then coursed into the vale below.

Shayla sat on the lush ground close by, chewing on a piece of grass. She had a faraway look in her eyes, her face pensive. Ciara paused and leaned over to pluck another bloom for Marissa's hair.

She cast a glance at Shayla. "You look sad today."

Shayla startled, a guilty look on her face. "I am not sad," she answered quickly.

"Well, it's fine if you are. I mean, I hope you aren't. I wouldn't want you to be sad. But Vanora says we should feel whatever it is that we feel," Ciara stammered. "I'm sorry. I didn't mean anything by it."

Shayla pursed her lips and wrinkled her forehead. "Well, then I suppose I *am* sad."

"Humph!" Marissa huffed. "Either you're sad or you're not."

Shayla retaliated with a defiant look. "Then I have decided I am sad."

"You can't just *decide* to be sad."

"Marissa!" Ciara glared at her twin.

Marissa put her hand on her hip. "Well, sad is a feeling, isn't it? Not something you decide."

Ciara sighed and dropped the blossoms on the ground.

"Sorry." Marissa eyed her friend. "What are you sad about?"

Shayla contemplated the Tor. Ciara picked up another honeysuckle blossom and resumed twining it amongst Marissa's braid.

Shayla pointed to the low cave beside the White Spring. "Gwyn ap Nudd lives beneath this hill. Beyond the cave." Her expression turned wistful.

"Do you believe the legend? The one that says you must know Gwyn ap Nudd's Realm to truly know Avalon?" Marissa asked.

"I believe it. I wish to meet him someday. He is Faery, after all. Like me."

Ciara shuddered. "Gwyn ap Nudd's red-eared, red-eyed hounds frighten me."

Shayla turned to face her, eyes flashing. "There is nothing frightening about Gwyn. Or his hounds. He is a Faery King."

Marissa agreed. "You needn't be afraid of him and his hounds." She reached up to pat her sister's hand, causing the woven honeysuckle blossoms to shower their robes.

"Fie!" Shayla said. "You, Ciara, sound more like the local villagers than a priestess. Afraid of Faery hounds!"

"I meant no harm. It's just . . . their eyes . . . are *red*." She finished braiding Marissa's hair with trembling hands.

Shayla crossed her arms over her chest. Ciara jumped up, blossoms once more tumbling to the grass. "Don't be mad. Faery are our cousins. You are my sister-friend." She spread her arms and gave Shayla a quick hug.

"There. You see? Like I said. Nothing to be frightened about." Marissa lazily swiveled her feet back and forth in front of her. She paused, eyes narrowing as she considered the Tor beyond them. "I have a marvelous idea. An adventure." She turned to them with a broad smile. "Let's go there."

"Where?" Shayla still looked cross.

"To the Faery Realm, of course! After all, we're Avalon priestesses, daughters of the High Priestess, thus specially trained, aren't we? And we have Shayla's halfling knowledge to guide us."

"We can't do that, Marissa," Ciara said, her voice pitched high with alarm. "Faery may be our close cousins, but the Faery Realm is too close to the Otherworld."

"So?" Marissa countered. She shrugged her shoulders, unconcerned. "Avalon is close to the Otherworld, too. Our priestesses travel to the Otherworld all the time to escort the newly dead. Traveling to the Otherworld is what priestesses are supposed to do."

"An Avalon priestess must be *trained* to accompany the most tragically dead." Shayla recited one of Avalon's holy decrees. "In a few years, we three will be assigned to journey to the Otherworld as guides. I suppose it *could* be safe enough for us to visit its bordering territory now."

"Stop, the both of you. I know all that. But we priestesses are within the realm of humankind. *We* are mortal. Faery are not. They are closest to the land of the afterlife because of this. Their magic runs deeper than ours does." Ciara jerked her cloak around her shoulders. "It's too dangerous. We could die. Or get lost and never find our way back."

"Aren't you even a little bit curious?" Marissa pled. "We can explore marvelous things. Come, Ciara! It will be fine. Besides, we agreed, if you want to truly know Avalon, you must know the Faery Realm, isn't that right?"

Ciara shook her head adamantly, causing her long blond curls to bounce off her shoulders. "We've been warned since we were small, entering without an invitation or a guide could be lethal. Their land has old protective magics. Not to mention, Vanora will be so angry with us. We would basically be breaking magical law."

"We're practically related to them; they won't hurt us. And we have magic too. And we have Shayla." Marissa spun around to face their friend. "Shayla, can you take me to a Faery banquet?"

"I can try. I have never actually been to one." Shayla gracefully rose, a wary smile playing at her lips.

Marissa grasped her by both arms and pressed her forehead against Shayla's. "I know you can do this. Won't it be wonderful to see what you've only dreamt about?"

Shayla's green eyes glowed with desire. "I would like to see it. Just once."

Ciara reached for her sister's hand. "There's got to be a good reason the Elders have never allowed Shayla to visit there before."

Uncertainty cracked across Shayla's countenance. "There must be a reason, but no one has ever . . ."

Ciara interrupted. "Besides, you know what Vanora says."

"Vanora distrusts everything. Just like you," Marissa yanked her hand away from her sister's.

Ciara pouted. "Vanora says Faery might be friendlier to those of us from Avalon than to the world of men, but we still must never turn our backs to them."

"What? Wait! I am a halfling and I would never hurt you," Shayla protested.

"That's true," Marissa said excitedly. "Besides, why would anyone hurt us? We'll have a Faery with us. We'll be in and out in no time. Off to the Faery Realm!" She grabbed her sister by the waist and twirled her around.

"I don't want to get into trouble." Ciara backed away and chewed on her fingernail. ". . . But I suppose if we're with a Faery, it could be counted as being invited. And there would probably be sweetmeats at their banquets."

"Yes, you'll have so many sweetmeats. Won't she, Shayla?" Marissa smiled widely.

Shayla giggled. "And maybe, if we are lucky, we will hear the enchanted hand pipes that Faery folk love to play."

"That sounds lovely," Marissa said breathlessly. "I hear tell if you're lucky, you can catch a refrain from those pipes, just in the distance, during Glastonbury's Summer Solstice festival."

Marissa watched Ciara hesitate and her shoulders droop. "All right. I guess one visit won't hurt. One *short* visit. Just to see a real Faery banquet, and then we can leave?"

"Yes!" Marissa squealed, giving her twin a kiss on the cheek. "Then it's agreed. We're going on an adventure."

Ciara chewed on her lip.

"Lead on!" Marissa directed Shayla.

"We're going *now*?" Ciara barely squeaked out.

Shayla steered them past willow and birch trees and into a nearby clearing, a grove ringed by ancient, towering oak trees and willowy ferns. It was silent, protected from the wind. A natural magical cocoon. Shayla stopped beside a tall, stout cluster of mugwort growing wild inside the grove. The herb's purple stems sprouted green pointed leaves and reddish-yellow flowered buds. She pulled three young blossoming shoots from the top of the plant, whispering "*thank you*" as she collected each stalk. She handed one mugwort shoot apiece to her companions. "To protect our travels," she explained.

"We need protection?" The alarm on Ciara's face was evident.

Marissa rolled her eyes. "All adventures must start with some sort of protection spell." She squeezed her sister's hand and added, "Mugwort's help should ease your worry."

Ciara carefully tucked the herb in her cloak pocket.

Shayla lifted her arms to her sides. "Take my hands, both of you. I think we have to be connected for this to work, for all of us to travel across the borders into the Realm of Faery."

"You *think*? You aren't sure?" Ciara asked before she took Shayla's hand.

"Yes. Yes, I am sure. I have Faery blood, do I not? I can do this."

Ciara sighed. Once they'd all clasped hands, Shayla closed her eyes and cocked her head, signifying she was listening with her inner ears, her inner senses. She instructed them to walk sun-wise, east to west, around the inside perimeter of the oak grove.

"I think we walk this circle thrice around," Shayla said, her voice soft and her eyes unfocused.

"Are you certain this is safe, Shayla?" Ciara asked, frowning.

"Don't interrupt her. She's concentrating," Marissa scolded, squeezing her sister's hand.

Ciara sulked, but kept quiet and followed directions.

The silence within the grove broke. Marissa heard a whirring sound, light and airy. It swiftly changed and became deep and reverberating, like a drumbeat. By the time they'd finished the second circuit around, Marissa felt nauseated and dizzy. She didn't dare open her eyes, afraid she would break the spell Shayla had woven to span realms.

When they traversed the third and final circuit, Marissa's legs weakened, and she dropped to her knees. She heard Ciara groaning. She felt her sister and her halfling friend fall to the grass beside her, all three still clinging to each other's hands

Chapter 12

The Isle of Avalon
1529 C.E.

Marissa pulled her attention away from her story and back to Michael, seated quietly across from her. Bees hovered and buzzed around the forgotten food basket. The afternoon sunlight warmed her back. Michael studied her, elbows on his knees, his sliced pork and crust of bread strewn about the blanket spread out underneath them. There was no disbelief, ridicule, or even judgment in his eyes. He nodded for her to continue. She could tell he trusted her. It felt good to be believed.

Marissa resumed her tale. "When Shayla brought us to the land of Faery that day, we immediately met a Faery guardian, someone who patrols the borders of their land. Because of Shayla's Faery lineage, he allowed us to enter. It was grand to be there. At first." Her voice quivered. "But I'm getting ahead of myself." Taking a steadying breath, she went on, once more absorbed in memory.

"I remember falling to the ground after crossing the oak grove thrice." *How weak she'd felt laying on the grass, how suddenly vulnerable they'd all seemed.*

"Can we open our eyes now?" Ciara had asked in a feeble voice.

"It seems a good idea to do that," a deep, resonant voice replied.

Marissa peeked through slit eyelids. A young man with straight silver-blond hair down to his waist stood before them. He wore a light green cape, seemingly made of moss and fern, over a leather vest and trews. His eyes matched the cape. They were the same vivid green as Shayla's.

"Looks like we made it," Marissa murmured. She slowly stood. The others followed suit.

Marissa noted they were in the same oak grove as before. The same hardy mugwort bush grew inside the clearing, but its leaves were greener. The forest ferns looked softer. Marissa tilted her head up. The sky was the truest blue. Golden sunlight haloed wild pink fuchsias. All nature's colors were deeper, more vibrant than anything Marissa had ever seen before, even in Avalon.

The Faery guardian impassively observed them. His stance remained formal, standing tall with his chin upright, his right arm outstretched to the side, gripping the emerald pommel of a spear with the pointed end touching the earth. He was quite handsome. Marissa found it odd how openly he stared at Shayla.

"I know your father," he said to her halfling friend. No warmth touched his mouth or eyes when he spoke.

"You do?" Shayla whispered.

Pain and pleasure flit across Shayla's face. She had never met her father. Shayla's mother, the priestess Kendra, had mated with a man of the Faery race at a Summer Solstice ritual. As far as everyone who participated in the annual rituals were concerned, all Solstice coupling was ceremonial, not a marital bond for life. Not once had Shayla's father tried to contact her or Kendra.

The guardian vacillated, glancing behind him before he spoke. "Because of your father, I think I can allow you and your friends entrance."

Shayla remained reserved as the guardian turned and led them into the forest and farther into Faery country. Mighty oak limbs dappled the sunlight, ash trees towered above them with tall narrow crowns, and the sharp-tipped branches of the thorn trees guarded clusters of tiny white blossoms. Marissa knew them to all be hallowed, magical trees. Ciara grabbed her arm suddenly and held tight.

"You're hurting me," Marissa hissed, prying her sister's fingers from where they were gouging her skin. But she didn't push her away.

She explored the new surroundings, trying to take it all in so she could remember every detail. The air pulsed with verdant life and rang with twittering birdsong. She swore she saw leaves on the hawthorn trees unfurl and shimmer when the guard strode past.

The group walked in silence and met no one along the way. When they reached two ancient rowan trees, abounding with red berries, their guardian stopped.

"Take the path between these trees. You will reach an apple orchard, much like the one in your land. In the midst of the orchard, you will find what you traveled here for."

Then he turned and left them without glancing back. The girls linked arms and ventured between the holy rowan trees, treading the loamy path until they reached a vast orchard. The trees hung heavy with perfectly ripened apples, enticing Marissa to pluck one. She reached up but stopped, hand in midair, as she spotted the Faery banquet.

Amidst the grove, set in a small clearing, were three long tables with empty chairs lined around them. The tables were laden with a sumptuous feast of cherries, sweetmeats, roasted boar, and golden honey mead.

Marissa squealed in delight and ran to the banquet. Shayla remained quiet, but followed. Ciara trailed at the rear, chewing her thumbnail.

"Shayla, this is exactly as you described," Marissa cried.

She leaned over a vase of fully blossomed red and white roses, closed her eyes, and inhaled. Such sweet perfume. Their exquisite beauty made her want to cry. She reached into a bowl in front of her and picked out a cherry. When she popped it into her mouth, its luscious taste exploded on her tongue like no other cherry she had ever eaten.

Marissa turned to see if her sister was enjoying herself as much as she was. Ciara had chosen a sweetmeat. Crystallized sugar sprinkles left a powdered trail along her cheek. She smiled when she saw Marissa watching her.

Shayla was no different in her wonderment. She sipped from a golden goblet of honeyed mead, and a long sigh escaped her lips. "My thirst has never been so satisfied."

"I've never tasted such a perfect sweetmeat," Ciara declared. "Maybe you were right to make us come here, Marissa. There's probably so much to learn and experience here."

"Maybe?" Marissa laughed aloud. "I knew I was right. And it doesn't seem dangerous at all. I can't understand why there are such heavy warnings against traveling here. It's delightful!"

"Did you notice? The apple orchard, the forest, they all look the same, yet so different," Ciara licked the sugar from her fingertips while she spoke.

"Are you now glad you led us on this lovely adventure?" Marissa turned to Shayla.

Her halfling friend's hair shone, and her skin sparkled more intensely silver than ever before. She clung to the goblet of mead with both hands. But her eyes. It was her eyes that most startled Marissa. Shayla gazed vacantly, past the enchanted apple orchard and straight at the Tor, a short distance away. The hill's grassy covering and its terraced walkways glowed green. Suddenly, the Tor seemed to mysteriously zoom towards them, causing Ciara to jump back.

A heavy wooden door, intricately carved with spiraling symbols foreign to Marissa, slid open at the base of the Tor. Golden light streamed out, illuminating the landscape. The sound of delicate music drifted out the entranceway. She wondered if the music came from panpipes, or maybe a harp. It was more like the sound of wind moving through the trees, flowers blossoming, and grass growing—if you could hear them—all encompassed in one enchanting note. Shayla began to follow the music, walking swiftly and sure-footed, eyes still staring ahead with that same vacant regard. Marissa darted after her.

"Shayla? Shayla, are you all right?"

Shayla stopped. "Perhaps I will finally meet my father," she said, almost imperceptibly.

"I am afraid that will not be possible," a woman's voice replied. The tone was lilting but serious, and held no mirth.

A tall, lissome woman emerged from the illuminated entrance under the Tor, followed by another guardian dressed in the same formal attire. He was older than the one who had led them to the banquet. He also bore a spear with an emerald finial, this time the spear pointed up. The lady's elegant, pale green silk robes matched her eyes, and she, too, had hair the color of moonlit frost. It trailed down her back and along the ground behind her, strands of wildflowers gracefully woven between the tresses. As she glided toward the girls, apple blossoms lined the imprint of her footsteps in the mossy grass.

Marissa's mouth parted. The lady's beauty and demeanor captivated her. Shayla's face reflected the same sense of awe.

Shayla stammered a greeting. "I am Shayla, daughter of the Avalon priestess Kendra. Daughter of the Faery . . ."

The woman lifted her palm forward, stopping Shayla mid-sentence. It was an ethereal hand, both solid and transparent at once, glowing with a faint silver sheen. Each finger bore a silver ring decorated with precious emeralds.

"You are the daughter of King Laighlon, our northern Faery brethren," she purred. "I know who you are, halfling Shayla. As well as your priestess friends."

Marissa felt Ciara edge closer to her side.

The Faery lady continued, speaking only to Shayla. "Why are you here? And why did you bring them?" She pointed to Marissa and Ciara without turning her head. Her voice was cream and honey yet held a distinct note of peril.

"It was my doing," Marissa offered, in what she hoped was her most respectful yet confident manner, though her throat was dry and her palms sweating. "I convinced Shayla to bring us here." She waited for the woman to turn to her. But she did not.

She ignored Marissa, focusing solely on Shayla. "Your friends have come uninvited. And you . . . you have come far too soon."

"I have come too soon?" Shayla repeated. Her forehead creased in confusion.

Marissa felt her neck and cheeks heat. She interrupted, "Do not blame Shayla."

"Shh, Marissa. Don't anger her," Ciara whispered. She huddled against Marissa's shoulder, never taking her eyes from the lady.

"Quiet," the woman retorted. While her voice was low, it held power as if it were booming.

"We are a friendly race," she said, again directing her comments to Shayla. "But there are rules in this realm. Respect for our ways is one of them. You see, we have had many, shall we say, greedy mortal visitors who have stumbled into our realm, only to ignore simple rules made for their safety, and take advantage of our generous nature. Stealing from us, abusing our hospitality and magic, bringing their covetous and violent ways into our land." Her jaw tensed. "We wish to avoid such unpleasantries."

"We apologize for them," Marissa said, feeling shame for human misdeeds.

The lady shook her head and shrugged her delicate shoulders. Apple blossoms drifted from her diaphanous robes to the ground. "When guests are invited, they are most welcomed. When they arrive unannounced . . ."

Marissa felt the air vibrate with warning, and thunder growled in the distance. Ciara turned her face into Marissa's shoulder.

"Tell us to leave, but do not threaten us." Marissa was loud and defiant. "We're not enemies. We mean no harm. We didn't know about these rules. What are the rules you speak of?"

The guard stepped forward, but the lady motioned him back. She continued with a formal declaration, in a voice that now sounded more like song than speech. "When mortal guests arrive unannounced and partake of our banquet without invitation, they invoke an ancient and immutable curse. It cannot be helped."

Ciara squeaked, "What curse?" She dropped her sweetmeat and rubbed all the sugary remnants from her lips.

"Why is there such a curse?" Marissa asked.

"Simple protection," the Faery answered. "The magic of our land is too easily invaded and violated, without understanding or appreciation."

"We appreciate it," Marissa countered.

The lady continued directing her answers to Shayla. "I mean appreciating its inherent dangers. For your safety, it is best to come here pure of heart. Furthermore, to ingest Faery food uninvited holds dire consequences. It is not intended for humans to consume. It will satisfy, as you have seen, but it will not nourish or sustain you."

Marissa persisted. "Ask her why that curses us, Shayla."

"I can hear you, young Marissa," the lady flicked a smoldering glance her way.

Her deep green eyes bore into Marissa's. It lasted but a second. It felt like infinity. Marissa shivered as the woman's scrutiny traveled to the depths of her bones, a scraping, painful appraisal of her whole being. She willed herself not to take a step back.

The lady lifted her chin and turned her attention back to Shayla. "Our food contains the deep magic of nature, magic innate to our Realm. If humans come to us by invitation, they can be attuned and acclimated to partake of our food without harmful consequence to themselves. But dining too long on Faery banquets binds one to our world. A world whose magic your bodies and minds are not accustomed to. Our rules are for your safety. Our rules keep away artless, greedy mortals. Our curse assures they will never return."

"But what exactly is this curse?" Marissa could not bear it any longer.

Still facing Shayla, the Faery held out lovely delicate hands, emphasizing her point. "The consequences of eating our food? Anguish. Slow starvation. Entrapment here. Insanity. Even death. The curse seeks to fit the suffering to whomever it wraps itself around."

"Please address us all," Marissa demanded. She hid her shaking hands under the folds of her robe. "If we're to be cursed, then give us the courtesy of speaking to us directly."

Ciara moaned, pulling on her arm, begging her to be quiet.

The lady took her time, lifted her robes and long hair, and turned to face the twins. She smiled. It was a beautiful smile, though harsh and somehow desolate as well.

"You," she said, pointing to Marissa, "have brought this upon yourself. As well as upon these two whom you love."

Marissa's heart pounded and her eyes stung with hot, angry tears. "I told you it wasn't their fault. Don't harm them."

"It is not I who harm. Not I who metes out the judgment. The curse demands its own retribution. The ubiquitous hand of fate and fortune work in the Faery Realm as they do in the land of mortals. Your deepest fears will specify the perfect toll for your trespassing."

"But we're not of the mortal world," Marissa argued. "I mean, yes, we're mortal, but we're priestesses of Avalon. We don't belong to the world of man, nor Faery. We're in between."

As she spoke, she began to feel something invisible drape over her shoulders. A dark and heavy weight. "What are you doing to me?"

"I told you. The curse wraps itself around your greatest fears. Your deepest flaws." The woman tilted her head to the side, further appraising Marissa. "I have seen it in you. You are to one day become High Priestess of Avalon, are you not? But tell me, how are you to lead when you make heedless decisions, like convincing your sister and friend to visit this realm without invitation? Deep down, you knew the invite was essential, but you thought you were above it."

Marissa felt the accusation punch her in the stomach. The invisible cloak of gloom grew heavier around her shoulders. The weight of doubt manacled her emotions, settled inside her, and took up residence in her mind. A litany of misgivings brought merciless questions. Could she ever make wise decisions, could she ever be trusted, would she ever be a good and wise High Priestess?

Suddenly, Ciara groaned, covered her chest with her hands, and fell to her knees.

"Stop hurting her," Marissa shouted, briefly pulled out of her own despair. She knelt beside her twin, wrapping her arms around her,

"It is not I who hurt her."

"But can you stop this?"

She ignored Marissa's question, instead making a pronouncement. "Ciara, your heart is your weakness. The curse seeks it out. Be forewarned. Your unyielding and closed-off heart will bring you pain and suffering."

"No," Marissa shouted. "Ciara is the most loving person I know!"

The lady turned, shifting her attention to Shayla.

Shayla, who hadn't lost the unfocused look in her eyes, now began to softly cry. "I so wanted to see my father. Just once."

"I am sorry, dear. Your father is of noble Faery breed, King to a land that lies far north from here. He cannot be reached before you need to leave. And leave you must, before the Faery calling consumes you. It is too early for you. That is why your father never beckoned you. He did not want to condemn you to a life of torment, a life torn between two worlds, between Avalon and the Faery Realm. Longing for one, then the other, truly belonging to neither. One day your time will come. When it will be proper and safe for you to be here. You must wait for it."

She tilted her head to the side, unemotionally appraising the distraught girl, and made her second pronouncement for the halfling. "Shayla, you must strengthen your human frailties. Balance your human blood with your Faery blood. By coming here too soon you bring on the temptation to remain here. It will haunt you and make you have to work even harder to tame your unruly human emotions."

Marissa sobbed with the stark realization that she'd condemned her sister and friend through her willful insistence to travel to the Faery Realm, her carelessness in knowing there might be consequences for everyone. She felt her secure world in Avalon shatter to pieces in her heart, knowing things would somehow never be the same.

"My heart, my chest. It hurts, Marissa. My heart is racing. It hurts so bad," Ciara whimpered.

"I'm so sorry, Ciara." Marissa tightened her arms around her sister as if she could shield her from the pain. She lifted her face to the Faery lady, eyes blazing. "Please stop hurting her."

"Lady Ravenna!" Another woman's voice rang out in the orchard.

The guard they'd first met on entering the grove stepped into the clearing, followed by Vanora. She was out of breath, her face flushed, holding a lantern before her. Marissa recognized the lantern at once. It was the charmed lamp used to light the way in neighboring realms, providing map and direction.

"Vanora!" Marissa and the Lady Ravenna cried in unison.

Vanora's mouth was set in a grim line. She carefully positioned her lantern upon the orchard ground before she spoke. "I apologize for my charges, Lady Ravenna." She cast a concerned look at the three girls. "I wish we could be meeting under different circumstances, my friend."

"As do I." Lady Ravenna embraced Vanora lightly. She turned to the young guardsman. "Folimot? Explain yourself."

Folimot dipped his head in show of respect and cleared his throat. "I thought . . ."

"I do the thinking for you in these matters. You are merely my guardsman," she interrupted icily.

"Yes, my Lady." He kept his gaze lowered. "Vanora is the girls' tutor. I called upon her to invite her here. Perhaps she can explain. Perhaps they could use her help."

"You have overstepped your boundaries, Folimot," Lady Ravenna replied with measured frostiness.

The young guard did not reply but cast a furtive glance Shayla's way.

Vanora spoke up. "Spare him retribution, Lady Ravenna. I was already on my way to seek an invitation for a meeting when he found me at your borders." She turned to her charges. "I was suspicious when I saw you girls head for the oak clearing, so I followed. When I got to the grove, I found Folimot, come to warn me you were here."

Lady Ravenna was quick to reply. "I am afraid the damage is done, Vanora. You know very well permission could have been granted if their visit had been arranged and sanctioned by both of us. The curse could have been temporarily lifted. Surely they had been warned."

"Yes." Vanora said, her concerned tone mingling with recrimination. "Since they were toddlers, the stories have been told, the warnings given. And they were taught to always respect the Faery race as cousins on the path of the Great Mother."

Marissa dropped her gaze down to the mossy ground, feeling disgraced. Shayla stared into the golden goblet, still clutched in her hands. Her expression was dreamy, as it had been when she first looked into the forest. "When will I meet my father?" she murmured.

Ciara, still bent over in pain, could not subdue her whimpers.

Marissa pleaded. "Vanora, I'm so glad you've come. Please tell her it's all a mistake. I tried to tell her it was all my doing, but she won't listen to me."

Vanora's jaw clenched. "Your mother and I will deal with your transgression upon your return."

Lady Ravenna interrupted. "My dear Vanora. I cannot guarantee their return."

Ciara groaned.

Their tutor held out her hands in a pleading gesture. "They are young. Though they have broken Faery laws, they are still innocent girls meaning no harm. They are not mere greedy mortals; they are young priestesses of Avalon. Your neighbors and friends. We celebrate the holy days of Summer Solstice together. We are not hostile, nor are we enemies. We often work for a common good."

"As I have already told the girls, the curse must exact its penalties before they will be able to leave."

"But to be trapped within the Faery Realm and incur the curse without recourse? There must be something we can do," Vanora said.

Lady Ravenna's stern countenance remained, but shaded with consideration. Her eyes narrowed as she listened.

Vanora pushed further. "Shayla was born of both priestess and Faery blood. That should be enough to seal the bonds of kinship."

Folimot nodded inconspicuously.

Lady Ravenna paused, taking in the measure of Shayla before she responded. "What you say is true. Your reasoning is noted. However, know this: if there were no consequences for misbehavior in our dealings with humans—or priestesses—there could be no shared magic between us. We do not question Avalon's magic as long as you abide by our Faery magic in our land, along with our laws and punishments. This keeps both worlds in balance. I cannot prevent what the girls have set in motion. But perhaps I can mollify it. For the sake of friendship and the bonds of neighbors."

Marissa felt a trace of hope pierce her misery.

The Faery Lady lifted her penetrating gaze to include all the girls. "But be forewarned. You are never to set foot in this realm again without invite."

Shayla raised her eyes from her goblet and gasped. "Never?"

"If you do, I promise you will be trapped, unable to ever return to the human world."

Marissa's breath hitched at the harsh decree.

The guardsman Folimot spoke up. "Surely you do not make this pronouncement on Shayla. She is of noble Faery blood." Lines of worry crossed his handsome face.

Lady Ravenna pitched her voice low, but her anger trembled across the orchard, shaking apples from the trees. "My impetuous Folimot, it is not I who decides Shayla's fortune and fate. But it indeed is I who must uphold our laws this day."

He lowered his head to hide his frown. Marissa watched Ciara blanch and clutch Vanora's elbow.

Lady Ravenna held up her lovely hand, palm forward. "I am afraid this is the best I can do." She gazed at Folimot then Vanora, eyebrows lifted, willing them to accept her proclamation.

Marissa interjected, shouting, unwanted tears rising with anger and despair. "Spare Shayla. Faery blood runs in her veins as it does yours. Look at her! Her eyes are shadowed like a wraith. And what about my twin? She's in pain. Please relieve her pain. Please have mercy on them."

"That is enough, Marissa," Vanora commanded. "Lady Ravenna, in friendship I plead for leniency for the girls. Allow them to return with me. It will be better for all of us."

"It is regrettable." This time, the Lady spoke with the bare hint of compassion in her tone. "I am afraid you girls will each suffer in your own ways. Ciara, your heart is already affected. I cannot stop that. Perhaps you will carry this affliction into your future, perhaps not. I will allow you this counsel—it is your will and your choices that determine the strength of the curse upon your heart."

Ciara swallowed thickly, watching Lady Ravenna warily.

"Shayla, when it is your time, *and only then*, you will be invited back."

Shayla's eyes glistened with disappointment and tears.

Lady Ravenna cocked her head, listening to something Marissa could not hear. "Marissa, your recklessness in this venture is your weakness. Self-doubt will now torment you. Regaining the trust you require as a future leader is your task. These things I cannot change. They are now written on your soul."

Her eyes were steel though her voice softened. "But the three of you being lost in our realm without the benefit of our friendship would be far, far worse. Take my offer and leave now, before there is nothing more I can do to help you. I will have Folimot lead you back home." She turned wearily and held her hand up, warding off further discussion. The entryway beneath the Tor opened in dazzling brilliance, and she stepped through.

Marissa watched the doorway close and seal, leaving behind no indication of its presence. She felt her hope being sealed behind that door, leaving her with only guilt and sorrow for the suffering she'd caused by her brashness and foolhardy insistence to visit the Faery Realm.

The evocative music coming from behind the hidden door slowly waned. The Tor appeared to telescope back into the distance once more. The border guardian, Folimot, motioned with his emerald-tipped spear for the group to follow him. He silently led them back through the forest of magical oak, ash, and thorn. While he didn't break stride, he glanced back over his shoulder often, his eyes always seeking Shayla. The devastated halfling moved in a daze, looking behind her every few moments with such longing in her eyes it broke Marissa's heart. Marissa half carried her twin, one arm wrapped protectively around her waist. Ciara leaned into her shoulder, taking stumbling steps. Vanora brought up the rear, holding the lantern high and herding the girls with unyielding sternness.

Chapter 13

The Isle of Avalon
1529 C.E.

Marissa sniffled and wiped away tears with the corner of her sleeve. The whole story was out. Relief diluted the guilt and pain. The afternoon wind blew gently, and a squirrel scurried across the clearing. She hadn't noticed Michael put his arm around her shoulders. It felt solid and strong, like the sturdy oaks surrounding them. She shivered with the cool of the forest shade as much as the retelling of what happened in the Faery Realm.

"Do you hate me now? For what I did?" She searched Michael's face.

He didn't reply at first. She watched clouds of an unfamiliar emotion pass over his fresh-faced features. His blue eyes looked into hers. She held her breath, waiting for him to answer. What if he told her she was selfish, like others had? That she was a heedless, thoughtless person for bringing the Faery curse to Ciara and Shayla? And by convincing them to venture into the Faery Realm she proved she was impulsive and only cared about her own mindset? Michael's response could further break her heart. His hold on her heart surprised her. She had to know what he thought and scolded herself for needing it. He was only a boy. She'd known him such a short time.

She didn't understand these new feelings that pitched and rose inside her. Maybe it was because the Goddess had entrusted her with his life. At least Michael, despite his misguided notions about priestesses, seemed to trust her when no one else did. She recalled how good it felt when he had held her hand during their first encounter by the lake. Pulsing heat had remained on her palm where their hands had clasped. She rubbed the spot with her thumb and wondered if he felt it too.

He finally spoke, choosing words carefully, his eyes lowered. "I think you are . . . courageous. My mother would tell you to make your amends and unburden your heart, then move forward. At least that's what she used to say to me when my father was his most strict and stubborn. She told me to always keep my heart open."

Marissa nodded. "That's exactly what my mother tells me as well."

He continued, "Besides . . . I could never hate you." He looked up. "Never."

Clumsily, he grasped her hand, and she felt the same warmth between their palms she'd felt before. Reveling in the sensation, she smiled bashfully.

Michael rose to his knees. "I vow to protect you from any Faery harm," he declared in a solemn voice.

She gasped.

He turned crimson but plunged ahead. "I could bring you back home with me. To Wales. We could marry. I mean, once we are old enough." He stood, gently pulling her hand so she rose to face him.

"Marry? Me?"

"Yes. I promise . . . I promise to protect you. Always," he stammered.

Her heart raced in an unfamiliar way. "And I promise to one day marry you," she replied, with a certainty that astonished her.

They were silent for an awkward moment, still clutching each other's hands.

"Once I am well, come back with me, to my Da's estates," he blurted.

Marissa's eyes opened wide. "But I can't leave here. I'm to be Avalon's High Priestess."

He furrowed his brows and chewed the inside of his cheek. "This is what we'll do. I have to go back home to arrange things. It may take a while. Not too long. Perhaps I'll finish my soldier's training as I promised my Da'. Then gather my books and my sword—I'd have to have my sword to protect you, and I must always have my books."

She felt her hands tremble, caught up in the excitement surging in her heart.

"And I must say goodbye to my brothers and my father, and my tutor Master Ralph, of course. Tell them of our plans. I'll return to you as soon as I can." He grinned. "We can always visit them. I mean, I'd really miss my brothers, so we'd have to go visit. Often. You'd do that with me, wouldn't you?"

Marissa nodded her head. "I would like that." She paused, frowning. "But I fear your sword can't defend me against my burden earned from the Faery curse."

He puffed out his chest. "I said I will protect you and I will. Whatever I have to do."

She swallowed heavily. "There is more. Wait before you say that, until you hear the end of my story."

He nodded but did not let go of her hand.

"What took moments in Faery time took two days of worry in Avalon. The time boundaries between our realms are sometimes erratic. They often waver. I returned home to a reputation for being rash and foolish, for letting my whims come ahead of the safety of my sister and friend. A bad testimonial for a future High Priestess and leader of Avalon." Marissa hung her head. "But worse than that was what happened to Shayla and Ciara. Ciara has always been sensitive, and her heart proved especially vulnerable to the curse. She nearly died from a failing heart."

Michael's hand tightened around hers.

"It took Elyn's best efforts to stave off the lingering physical illness in Ciara's heart, but I fear she is still vulnerable in other ways." She couldn't stop that sinking feeling in the pit of her stomach when she thought about the curse's effect on her twin. "She's changed. I can't get through to her. She pulls away, she withdraws. Not just from me. From everyone." Marissa shook her head and sighed heavily. "Ciara and I used to talk to each other all the time without having to speak the words out loud. But now, there are times when she just won't talk to me inside our heads anymore."

The grip on her hand didn't flinch, giving her courage to finish the story. "And Shayla, she has still never met her father, King Laighlon. But more than that, by visiting the Faery banquet table, her mixed blood lured her into a much deeper enchantment. It could have held her captive within the Faery Realm if she'd stayed much longer. When Vanora showed up and appeased Lady Ravenna, it interrupted the enchantment in just enough time for Shayla to remember her priestess and human upbringing in Avalon. It literally saved her human soul."

"Saved her soul?" Michael released her hand to make the Christian sign of the cross over his chest.

She nodded. "Vanora says Shayla must always cherish her human half, no matter if she one day returns to the Faery Realm to live. It makes her who she is, a combination of both Faery and human. Her human side gives her compassion and her Faery blood gives her the deep power of nature. But she must cherish them both if she's to have any peace of mind. At least that's what our tutor warns."

"Can Shayla do that? I mean can she do what Vanora advises?" he asked, reclaiming Marissa's hand once more.

She sighed. "I hear her moaning and crying every night in her sleep. She desires the wild ways of Faery. She battles the desire to return there straightaway. Vanora says she mustn't go back until she masters her human emotions. Until she masters being both wise and compassionate."

"Couldn't she just visit the Faery Realm and learn what she needs to there?"

Marissa sucked in a breath. "Don't you see? She would jeopardize her human side if she went there again too soon. Shayla may now yearn for the Faery Realm, but she would always yearn for Avalon as well if she left too early. She'd be caught between two worlds, never belonging anywhere. You must understand. Shayla is like a sister to Ciara and me. She's family. My mother has treated her like one of her own since Shayla's mother died. She needs it to be a truly free choice—exactly when and where she decides to live out her days. That's what Vanora says anyway. She calls it an unen . . . unencumbered choice." Marissa exhaled loudly.

"What would happen if she didn't do what Vanora says she must?"

Marissa looked off into the distance. "Supposedly she would be lost. She could never be happy and never find peace. Vanora also says Shayla could become deranged. Crazy. Maybe even misuse her Faery power. It's happened before, a halfling going mad. It's a hard task for halflings. And when they fail, the friendship between Faery and Avalon, even Faery and humans, suffers because of the strain. If Faery magic is dishonored, if it is lost or even misused, then we lose connection with the earth's deepest magic. Everyone suffers without that magic."

Michael rubbed his thumb over hers.

"What about you?" he asked softly. "What has the curse done to you?"

The question was an unexpected balm to Marissa's heart, though she felt barely worthy of such concern after the damage she'd done to her sister and friend.

"I've broken everyone's faith in me. I let them down and hurt them. And I have to live with knowing that." She couldn't look Michael in the eye.

"I believe in you," he said firmly.

Festering guilt wouldn't allow her to meet his gaze. He wiped a tear from her cheek, letting his hand linger by the curve of her chin.

Her soul's angst poured out in confession. "Even my visions are questioned. I'm called foolhardy and impetuous. Vanora says I'm irresponsible. If I'm not trusted, I may never become the wise High Priestess I'm supposed to be. The times I do have a vision and just *know* I am right about something are the hardest for me. I *must* believe in my own visions. What if I fall prey to doubting my premonitions?"

Marissa thought she'd cried all the tears she could, but her sobbing began fresh with the reminder that no one had confidence in her latest and most important glimpse into the future: her vision about Michael. She released racking sobs she'd only previously let loose around her mother since her return from the Faery Realm.

"Michael, you have to believe me. If you must leave for a short while, you must return to me, to safety, within Avalon. Perhaps you shouldn't leave at all."

"I will hasten to come back to you. But I must go home first," Michael said, with apology in his eyes.

Marissa sobbed harder. "Most of all, you must stay far away from Glastonbury and its Christian abbey. Promise me! Promise me you will stay away from Glastonbury Abbey!"

Chapter 14

Glastonbury, England
Present Day

Sophie had spent much more time exploring the abbey grounds with Daniel than she'd planned. It was late, her shoulders ached, and her eyelids felt dry and heavy with fatigue. She quietly opened the front door to the B&B, turned off the porch light, and stole up the stairs to her room. She pulled off her shoes and they dropped to the floor with a thud. Still wearing her jeans and jacket, she wriggled under the covers, immediately falling asleep. The haunting chant she'd heard that evening at the abbey infiltrated her dreams.

By the time she woke the next morning, the sun already peeked above the Tor. She pushed aside the duvet covers and stretched, luxuriating in an unfamiliar sense of refreshed sleep and calm. She began to absently hum. She froze. It was the chant from the night before. The one that repeated in her dreams. The a capella notes replayed incessantly in her mind. As before, the notes mined her heart, triggering buried grief. The song descended deeper, again probing her soul with musical fingertips. She slammed the lid shut on the closeted ache in her chest, wiped the tears the chant wrested from her, and sniffed. Then scoffed. It had to be her imagination producing the achingly haunting song. Either that or she was seriously losing her grip on reality. *No one hears music sung by monks from centuries ago.*

Sweeping aside the unwanted sadness with her best-practiced finesse, she made a mental to-do list. She'd get a strong cup of coffee, line up her interviews, do some research. Start over fresh.

With renewed resolve, Sophie changed into black corduroys, topped it with a green linen blouse, and packed her satchel. Phone, digital recorder, a few pads of paper, and several pens. She threw in a bag of almonds and a bottle of water. Who knew how long she'd be collecting material for the article today, and she didn't want to continue her bad habit of missing meals. She had to stay healthy to stay focused. That was Sid's mantra whenever she overworked. And she definitely intended to stay focused, so she could wrap up this human-interest story posthaste and move forward to bigger and better assignments.

When she scrambled down the steps with all her stuff, she was met at the bottom by the B&B owner, who steered her into a cheery dining room. Sophie eyed the other guests. There wasn't an empty table left. Still bruised from her precarious career complications, and adding in the confusing emotions brought on by the chant, all she wanted was to be alone and nurse her battered feelings.

That chant was always in the background of her mind now, ready to come forward with the slightest breach of focus. She felt the beginning twinges of a headache brewing. Choosing the nearest available seat, she joined two middle-aged couples and offered up a half smile.

"We're serving eggs, fried toast, bacon, beans, and tomatoes," the owner informed her.

Sophie's stomach growled. "I'll take it all. And coffee. Strong coffee."

She tried to avoid conversation. *Too early in the morning to feign politeness. Too absorbed in my own hurt to fake it.*

"You'd think they'd serve crisp bacon, not this limp piece of pork fat," one of the men at her table said, scooting the glistening slab to the edge of his plate.

Stifling a heavy sigh, Sophie focused on eating everything the waitress set before her.

The diner to her left whispered to her companion. "I'm going to bury three crystals on top of the Tor. They have to be clear quartz and it has to be done at midnight,"

Sophie rubbed her temples, her headache in full force now. She really needed to get away from this prattling. "I have an early appointment," she mumbled as she stood to leave.

She hurried out of the B&B and strode the few blocks down Wearyall Hill's steep road, passing houses with tiny front gardens filled with summer peonies, roses, and dahlias. When she reached the bottom, she turned left along Magdalene Street, remembering Barry's mention of Mary Magdalene's name the night before. She noticed a chapel dedicated to her alongside a few shops and made a mental note to examine it more closely later. Across the street stood the imposing abbey entrance, its thick stone walls stretching their arms around the grounds like a fortress. She rummaged in her bag for the press pass the abbey trustees had sent. She would need it to gain entrance before the tourists arrived. There was still time before her appointment to interview Mrs. Henderson, the senior museum curator.

The gate attendant led her past the abbey's closed gift shop and into the museum, where she had the place to herself for a few moments. It was rather small as museums went, about the size of a hotel ballroom. She strolled quickly past the glass case against the entrance wall, containing cup shards and bits of carved stone. After the archeological display, most of the museum was filled with aisles of floor-to-ceiling pictographs outlining the abbey's historical timeline, along with artists' renditions of what the abbey probably looked like at the height of its glory days. The large pictographs helped her envision the time period she'd be writing about in her article. She temporarily lost herself in examining the artists' renderings. Something about visualizing the abbey back then formed goose flesh along her arms.

"It was once magnificent wasn't it?" a female voice interrupted.

Sophie's heart jumped and she spun around, thrown out of her reverie. But true to her nature, and after years of practice, she readily regained composure. "Mrs. Henderson, I gather?" she said, extending her hand to the petite woman in greeting.

Mrs. Henderson shook hands with a weak grip. She appeared to be about twenty years older than Sophie, probably in her early fifties. Her brown hair was styled in a blunt-cut bob, with a large grey streak down one side. The muted color offset her grey and white striped blouse and grey twill skirt. Brown eyes appraised Sophie with a piercing flash.

Sophie pasted on her best smile. "Yes, the abbey was indeed magnificent. I'm eager to hear more about it."

Mrs. Henderson's nod was curt. "I'm quite pleased to make your acquaintance. You were my first choice," she said.

"Pardon me?"

"I said you were my first choice. I wanted someone with a good journalistic reputation who would do a respectable job representing our abbey."

Sophie grimaced internally. The woman evidently did not know about her recent fall from journalistic grace. Probably a good thing.

Mrs. Henderson continued in a clipped voice. "Yes, I want a proper piece of journalism. I don't want any of this New Age mumbo jumbo in your report." She stopped to eye Sophie critically. "You aren't a New Ager are you? Not Wiccan or Druid or any of that nonsense?" She smiled as though the two of them shared a conspiratorial dislike of anything unconventional.

Sophie donned a matching plastic smile and replied, "I like to think these little stories are as interesting as the big ones."

The older woman's left eye twitched at the remark. Sophie inwardly sighed. No use letting her frustrations spill over to innocent bystanders. It wasn't the curator's fault she was in journalistic disgrace and assigned to this piece as a result.

Sophie recovered quickly, "No mumbo jumbo. That won't be a problem. Well then, shall we begin? I've prepared a list of questions."

"One moment while I gather something I've organized for you." Mrs. Henderson's rubber-soled, grey orthotic shoes made no sound as she marched past Sophie and over to a small section of tables and chairs lined up in rows. She picked up a manila folder and carried it back with her.

"I apologize, but I'm afraid I've only got fifteen minutes to spare this morning. A group of Girl Guides—I think you call them Girl Scouts in America— changed their scheduled tour day at the last minute and will be arriving soon."

Sophie must have frowned, for Mrs. Henderson hastily resumed. "Not to worry. First up they'll be with me, listening to my presentation. You'll have time to walk around the grounds in peace. No running, screaming children for one whole hour." The older woman's demeanor remained all formality and no mirth. She handed Sophie the folder. "The information sanctioned by the Abbey Charity Trust is contained here." She glanced at her watch. "I have time for one or two questions. If they're brief. And we can talk more later."

Sophie pulled out a digital recorder, and Mrs. Henderson bobbed a quick nod of approval. "I admire your professionalism."

Mrs. Henderson strode to a nearby table and pulled out two chairs, motioning for Sophie to join her. The two sat across from one another.

Sophie positioned the recorder on the table, facing it toward the curator, and clicked it on.

"Tell me about the grandeur of the abbey. Something I might not glean from the materials you already provided," Sophie suggested, nodding at the folder that lay between them.

Mrs. Henderson pursed her lips and thought for a moment. "Well, the texts will tell you the abbey was one of the wealthiest. Let me add that it was not a pompous or arrogant abbey. It regularly fed the poor with its harvest, and the monks cared for the sick and elderly from the surrounding villages in their own infirmary if needed."

"Can you give me an example of the extent of its wealth?" Sophie asked, adjusting the recorder's microphone. She picked up her pencil and notepad in case she wanted to jot down impressions.

"Well, it was wealthy enough to build a church in every village. Our abbey was even dubbed the 'Second Rome' since it outright owned one-eighth of the land in all of Somerset County. Because of that, the King couldn't rule the jurisdiction. That gave the abbey immense independent power."

"Hmmm." Sophie tapped her pencil against the wooden tabletop. "That must have upset the King."

"Not initially. The abbey paid tribute, you know, what was due to England's sovereign. However, King Henry VIII was greedy. Eventually he got rid of the ancient charters, so he could gain abbey lands."

"I thought he took control of the church to bend Catholic rule, to allow him to divorce his first queen in order to marry another woman."

Mrs. Henderson's pursed lips and steely gaze relaxed. "True enough. Henry maneuvered England's politics to raise himself as the head of both state and Church. Initially to gain the freedom to marry Anne Boleyn."

"A well-known name." Sophie squinted, concentrating, joggling her pencil between her fingers. "I've read somewhere she may have been vilified?"

Mrs. Henderson wrinkled her nose as if sniffing garbage. "Nonsense. I hope you don't intend to report that rubbish."

Sophie appeased the curator by shaking her head *no*.

Mrs. Henderson offered a thin-lipped grin. "As I was saying, Rome ruled over the affairs of its Church, which included England's churches. Henry eventually broke with Rome. His religious reform sent his Chancellor, Oliver

Cromwell, across the land, suppressing and dissolving all of England's abbeys. Remember, this was also the time of Martin Luther's Reform. Reformation was escalating across Europe."

"How did the Reform influence England, then?"

"Henry was clever. He used the rebellious sentiments to his favor. He blackened the characters of nuns and monks, spreading rumors of their disgraceful immorality. This was meant to garner the support of the people and of English Parliament against Rome."

"People believed the rumors?" She inwardly cringed, thinking about her recent article that nearly got her fired. Sure, King Henry wanted to defame the Catholic Church for his own gain, but could there have been any grain of truth to the rumors he disseminated? If her latest investigation about the depraved priest and his accomplice Bishop was any gauge, then it was possible.

Mrs. Henderson continued, "Many did believe the rumors. And others who opposed his efforts against Rome were sent to the block."

"A reign of terror."

Mrs. Henderson nodded. "He set himself up to rule supreme for his own purposes."

"Acquiring the abbeys must have filled his coffers." The information raised Sophie's hackles. King Henry VIII, and the Bishop she'd tried to nail with her investigative report—all bastards. Some things didn't change no matter what the century.

"Indeed. When King Henry became head of the Church of England, all monies formerly paid to Rome went into the King's treasuries. And it is said, his treasuries had been in real need of replenishment."

"A complicated and devious past," Sophie said, damping down her ire with words that wouldn't offend Mrs. Henderson.

The curator glanced at her watch again and stood. "This is a good start, Miss Morrison."

"Oh, you can call me Sophie." She looked up from her recorder to see Mrs. Henderson raise one brow. "Or . . . Miss Morrison is fine."

Again with the grim smile. Sophie lowered her eyes before the woman could catch her rolling them.

"I need to finish preparing for my girls' group." Mrs. Henderson turned to leave and paused. "Oh, I nearly forgot. That nice young man, Daniel Holbrook, the one we hired on as the artist and photographer to work with you—he's already out on the abbey grounds. He asked me to tell you to come find him when we finished our meeting."

"All right. Thank you." Sophie figured Daniel could be anywhere on the thirty-six-acre estate, giving her plenty of privacy and latitude. Sid's words, *be nice*, played in her mind.

She exited the museum and stood at the top of the steps leading down to the parcel of land belonging to the Abbey Trust. Before her stretched a vast expanse of grass dotted with magnificent stone ruins. The duck and fishpond she'd seen last night glistened in the distance. Past the abbey ruins stood the only intact building—the round, stone Abbot's Kitchen Barry had told them about. Beyond the kitchen were thriving apple orchards, already smelling sweet with the promise of fruit. She decided she'd stroll along the walking paths and examine the grounds again, this time more closely and on her own. Maybe she could even prove to herself there was no perpetual choir moaning in the distant background. That's when she spotted Daniel.

His back was to her, his recognizable tawny hair curling over a flannel shirt collar. He sat, one foot perched on a portable stool leg, the other foot resting on the grass. His camera bag, along with a worn backpack, lay on the ground beside his easel. He appeared focused, absorbed in his work. From her vantage point outside the museum door, Sophie could make out the tips of the iconic abbey arches already painted onto a large canvas. With a paint palette in his right hand and a paintbrush in his left, he dipped his brush into the palette and feverishly applied more paint. Large strokes of yellow. She didn't want to disturb him, acknowledging to herself how annoyed she became when anyone interrupted her creative flow.

Making her way across the grassy area between the museum and the abbey ruins, she gave Daniel a wide berth and headed for the Mary Chapel, the exposed crypt ruins situated directly ahead of her. He didn't seem to be aware of her presence. She was relieved.

Sophie had walked far to Daniel's right and was about to turn the corner on the Mary Chapel building when she stopped abruptly. Curiosity, both her curse and her blessing, got the best of her. What exactly was he painting that absorbed his attention so much he didn't even notice her presence? She quietly backtracked and stopped a short distance behind him to take a closer peek at what he was working on. She knew oil paint was a slower medium to work with, but she was amazed at how much he had already captured on canvas. She wondered if he had started painting at first light to accomplish so much. With the exception of the yellow he was currently applying, the canvas was filled with pale, monotonous colors filling in the recognizable shapes on the grounds around her. She spotted the spired curvatures of the ruined nave and the Abbot's Kitchen in the far distance, as well as the white-flowered apple orchard beyond the abbey ruins.

Something else caught her eye. She inched closer, drawn to something peculiar he was silhouetting. Despite her intentions, she ended up standing beside him. His brushstrokes created nuances and textures not apparent in the real life setting around her.

Daniel had painted the abbey in browns and grey, but the abbey was not in its current state of ruin. It was depicted in its entirety, at its zenith. The cloisters were there, as well as the long length of the vast cathedral, similar to the pictographs she'd seen in the museum. Yet different. He had managed to capture something evocative in his portrayal of the abbey's cathedral walls. Enigmatic symbols and icons hinted at secrets built right into the stone. Most interestingly, there was now a vague, nearly transparent overlay depicting a tiny wattle and reed chapel.

Sophie recalled reading about this modest chapel when she'd had those few minutes to stroll around the museum before Mrs. Henderson arrived. The original wattle and reed chapel was built by Joseph of Arimathea and his cohorts upon traveling to Glastonbury after the death of Jesus, Joseph's nephew. Joseph had returned to this summer country land, where he'd formerly conducted tin trade, a land where he knew Druids and priestesses aligned with the essence of Jesus' message of peace and love. He'd come to build the first Christian Church in England. The chapel he constructed was dedicated to Mary, the mother of Jesus.

Sophie chewed her bottom lip and frowned. How did she know all these details, these particulars not recorded in the museum display nor found in her research? She was somehow remembering facts she hadn't read yet. The museum placard did state that this chapel burnt down in 1184 and was replaced by the Mary Chapel crypt, now in ruins. She shivered, suddenly chilled. She *knew* this newer Mary chapel. She brushed aside the déjà vu. It was doubtless something she'd scanned and forgotten. She eyed what Daniel had painted. He'd portrayed the chapel with a haunting clarity that went beyond the museum's pictographs. The painted overlay had an ethereal quality, hinting at further mystery.

Daniel moved his brush swiftly, now applying orange paint. The color and shapes he created riveted her attention. Flames. Explosive, fiery flares. Sudden, unfamiliar waves of sadness rose in her chest. Her heart felt heavy, burdened. She didn't know what to make of the inexplicable surge of grief riding through her.

"Daniel? What is this?" she whispered.

He didn't answer. He stared at his canvas as if mesmerized and continued painting. Seemingly as caught up in expressing something enigmatic as she was caught up in watching what he created. When she called his name louder, he didn't hear her. The surge of sorrow flooded her chest and throat. She pressed her hands on her chest to contain the overflow of grief and turned her attention back to his painting, fighting the impulse to stretch her hand toward it, her fingers wanting to touch the flaming images. Daniel's brush glided across the canvas, spreading the flames with bold red strokes. They flickered with menace, their heat bursting through the abbey's stained-glass windows, charring the beautiful stone walls and engulfing anything made of wood.

She spotted something in the right lower corner of the painting. Her breath caught. She couldn't exhale. In the canvas landscape, close to the Mary Chapel, stood a man. Tawny hair, blue eyes, tall and muscular, wearing the brown robes of a monk. The figure grew larger, moving inexplicably to the foreground of the painting. His painted eyes seemed to stare directly into hers. His expression pulled her in. It held a look of tender love. The tenderness changed. It was replaced with terror. Then grief. Overriding grief. His gaze raked her soul.

Sophie screamed. In her mind, the now familiar chants of the perpetual choir pealed around her, drowning out her scream. She couldn't take her eyes off the man Daniel had painted, the look of anguish in his eyes. Sophie's vision blurred and everything darkened. She crumpled to the ground.

Chapter 15

The Isle of Avalon
1529 C.E.

The sun rose above the tip of the Tor, burning off the morning fog. Healing Mistress Elyn knocked lightly on Alianore's door, noting it had been left open a crack.

"Hello?"

When no one answered, she slowly opened the door to the High Priestess' lodgings. Her hand rested lightly on the rounded doorframe, fingers running along the intricately carved wood that mirrored the pattern of the moon's phases. The frame was slightly wet from summer rain showers, and she absently wiped her damp hand on her apron as she peered inside the household, searching for Alianore in the new day's light.

Although Alianore held the position of High Priestess, she'd chosen quarters no larger than any of the others within the priestess community. *A sign of her humble nature,* Elyn thought admiringly. Walls of hewn stone formed a circular enclosure that was nearly double the size of the large herb and flower garden planted in the back of each priestess's home. Alianore shared her housing with her daughters. Normally, Marissa would now be living with her fellow Prophetess students, and the two healing apprentices, Ciara and Shayla, would be sharing living space. But since the twins were the daughters of the High Priestess, they remained with their mother, offering her the opportunity to groom them. Because the girls had been inseparable since birth, the arrangement suited them.

Elyn frowned, having hoped to find them all home this morning. She wanted to give her report concerning Michael and make sure the girls were answerable for his condition. She didn't like it when one of her patients worsened for no good reason.

She called out again. "Are you home?"

Still no response. She took a few steps inside. The scent of lavender wafted up from rushes strewn on the floor. The tallowed candles on the oak table before the fireplace were snuffed, and the nighttime fire had already been damped in the inglenook, ready for the morning sun to take its place to brighten and warm the dwelling.

Elyn quickly scanned the room. The inside walls were covered from ceiling to floor with hand-sewn tapestries. She revered these tapestries and was always glad for the opportunity to appreciate them. They were ancient, woven centuries beforehand by the original priestesses of Avalon, and their pristine state was a testament to the magic and artistry of the original weavers. Alianore's largest wall-hanging portrayed the ocean, with foamy blue-green waves and a rocky beach. Each silken stitch had been magically infused with the energy of the Goddess of the Stars and the Sea, in honor of She whom the priestesses devotedly served.

Elyn touched her heart, quietly murmuring a prayer to the Goddess. "In devotion to you."

She felt a tug in her womb-space that directed her to the left. There, another hallowed tapestry hung, delineating a sacred space, Alianore's meditation corner. The embroidery bore the symbol of the Vesica Pisces, the talisman of the Avalon priestess community.

She remembered when she and Alianore had first learned about the sacred talisman. They were five years old and sitting on the knoll by the Healing Halls with their fellow priestesses in training. The Red Well gurgled beside them, cooling the warm summer air. All training took place beside the holy Red Well. Alianore's mother Sarah, High Priestess at the time, was instructing the girls.

"The talisman is our sacred symbol," she'd said. She held up a Vesica Pisces, woven across a piece of silk. "See here. Where the talisman's two interlinking circles overlap? That overlap forms a third space, shaped like a woman's vulva, but elongated. This inner circle signifies the union of opposites, the creation dance of all things in the physical world."

The words were beyond Elyn's understanding then, but she'd grown to comprehend and cherish the meaning over the years. The tapestry before her now was stitched with gold thread, and its border decorated with calcite, amethyst, and green-purple fluorite crystals, as well as obsidian and red jasper gemstones. The charmed gems were intended to provide grounded harmony and enhance the connection for those seeking mystical union with the Goddess. She felt the tapestry gently emanate a soothing yet formidable power that made her hands tingle and her belly quicken with heat. She closed her eyes and paused to breathe in the power of the talisman and the presence of the Goddess.

Opening her eyes, she noticed signs of Alianore's daily pre-dawn meditations. Upon the small altar set before the talismanic tapestry were three candles, their wax still soft and pooled inside their holders. Each morning before sunrise, eight appointed priestesses sat in a semicircle with Alianore, comprising the council of nine governing priestesses of Avalon. They gathered to commune with the Goddess and listen for the whispers of Her guidance. Then the nine would walk the rounded knoll behind the village, taking the path past the Red Well and gardens, to attend to the vigil candles of Avalon's Healing Sanctuary and Temples. The group completed these devotions long before sunrise.

Elyn straightened the meditation benches and pillows, wondering why Alianore hadn't returned home yet. She might need to visit the Elders' cottages to find the High Priestess. Alianore sometimes spent time discussing the matters of Avalon with her eight cohorts after their morning meditations. Each Elder lived in individual cottages nearby. Because of their esteemed station, the younger priestesses assisted the Elders with menial domestic chores. The younger priestesses were housed farther away, according to their initiation status and magical talents, while the youngest girls lived with their mothers until their bleeding times began. Elyn reasoned that perhaps one of the chore helpers might have seen where the High Priestess headed after her morning ritual.

The back door swung open, and Alianore's laughter floated through the cottage.

"Marissa, you're laden like a pregnant she-bear," Alianore was saying to her daughter, who followed her closely.

Marissa dumped the gathered peppermint, lavender, and yarrow from inside her apron onto the table in front of the hearth, giggling with her mother. Elyn stepped forward.

"Oh! I didn't see you," Alianore said with a welcoming smile.

Marissa turned to the healing mistress, whose face was lined with concern. "What's wrong?" Her eyes widened.

Not mincing words, Elyn replied. "I'm afraid Michael's fever is worse."

Marissa hastily untied her apron and tossed it on a chair.

"Stay put, Marissa," her mother ordered.

"But, mother . . ."

Alianore's stern gaze held Marissa in check for the moment. "What has caused this turn for the worse?" she asked.

"Well, it seems he was out past sunset yesterday." Elyn glanced at Marissa with disapproving eyes. "By the time he returned, it had begun to rain, and he was soaked through. The chill and the wet were a setback."

"Oh, no," Marissa murmured.

Elyn blew out a sigh. "You know better than to keep the boy out in the rain in his condition."

"I'm sorry, Healing Mistress. The skies were clear when we left. The downpour came as a surprise."

Alianore interrupted. "Still, I would like to think you had the sense to not keep Michael out once it started raining." She rested her hand on Marissa's arm to prevent her from running out the door to the healing lodge.

"I'm sorry. I really am. We couldn't help it. Michael and I were talking about . . . about something important. We lost track of time."

Elyn rubbed weary eyes. "I expect someone of your age and in your position to behave more responsibly."

A small sob escaped Marissa's lips. "I meant no harm." She looked from Elyn to her mother. "Can I go to him now? Please?"

Alianore nodded her head and released her daughter's arm. "But we *will* talk about this later. Elyn will think of a suitable task for you. To make up for being reckless . . ."

"I wasn't reckless this time. You don't understand." Marissa pounded her thigh with her fist.

Alianore narrowed her eyes, assessing the outburst. "I think I do understand. But keep your temper in check. Elyn, as Michael's healer, what say you?"

Elyn sighed and waved Marissa out the door.

She ran all the way to the healing cottage at the far end of the community.

When she arrived at the lodge, Michael was propped against several pillows, playing a game of Nine Men's Morris with Ciara. He was clutching one of the wooden player pieces and laughing at his misplaced move to form a mill, the three player pieces in a row meant to gain him a winning advantage. He looked up from the board when Marissa came through the doorway. His eyes lit up upon seeing her, and Marissa felt her breath catch.

"Oh, you're back." Ciara's smile dissolved.

"Come join us," Michael called out. He coughed, and Ciara handed him a cloth to wipe his mouth.

Marissa was at his side before he finished the invitation. "Elyn said you were ill again."

"I should go," Ciara muttered, watching her sister fuss over Michael. "There's healing broth to be made."

"Please stay," Michael said. "Can Shayla make the soup? I promise I'll eat it all this time."

Upon hearing her name, Shayla pushed aside the room's divider curtain and poked her head out from the medicinal chamber doorway. "I'm already mixing the herbs. It's no problem for me to fix the soup as well."

Ciara nodded her thanks and her smile returned. Marissa frowned.

Shayla considered the three of them a moment before she retreated and let the curtain fall back into place. Elyn entered the healing hut a minute later, the fresh herbs Marissa had previously gathered piled in a basket she carried on her hip. Her demeanor was somber. She scowled when Michael broke into a long coughing fit. Marissa kept her eyes lowered, not wanting to further upset the healer.

"He'll need his medicine soon," Elyn said, putting her basket on the long oak table. "But he can finish playing the board game first."

Marissa breathed out in relief at not being scolded again. She chewed her cheek and pointed to where Ciara should make her next move. "You'll win with that," she said, grinning mischievously at Michael.

"Not fair," he grinned back. "Two against one."

Ciara moved her player to the suggested spot. Marissa pointed to indicate a good next move, but Ciara ignored it.

"You'll be sorry," Marissa quipped.

Two moves down the board, Michael's player put Ciara's in jeopardy.

"Oh, all right, I give in. You win," Ciara said. Smiling good naturedly, she gathered the player pieces and stashed the game in a cupboard.

Shayla brought out bowls and spoons and dished out steaming potato and leek soup laden with parsley. After they had all eaten soup and warm bread with fresh butter, Elyn insisted Michael rest. Marissa watched him close his eyes, and his chest soon rose and fell in the gentle rhythm of sleep. Her insides vibrated with joy as she recalled the vows they'd made to each other the previous day in the glen. She decided she wouldn't let him out of her sight again for any length of time. She had to be certain he healed well so they could carry out their promises.

For the next quarter of the moon's waxing phase, Marissa skipped much of her scrying training with the Elders, to their chagrin, to stay beside Michael. Once he was fully well, there would be plenty of time to learn to magically read the images within a bowl of water, she reasoned.

She was relieved her mother had given her unusual leeway with her studies. The Goddess's decree to save Michael for a bigger, shared destiny made Marissa feel protective of him. Well, that along with the promises they made to each other in the oak grove. She smiled at how warm her heart felt when she reflected on their shared plans. Since she was spending so much time in the healing cottage, her mother charged her with learning more of the healing arts, and the value of patience. Patience and forethought would always be important for a priestess, especially one destined to become High Priestess, Mother reminded her. Marissa vowed she would learn to be patient. She really would try.

Ciara's training with Elyn meant she also spent much of her time in the healing cottage. In the rare moments Marissa wasn't present, Ciara eagerly stole time alone with Michael.

One balmy afternoon, a half moon-cycle after the excursion that caught them in the rain and worsened Michael's cough, he asked if he could possibly sit outdoors in the fresh air. The sun gently arched overhead, casting its golden hue across the wooden bench outside the healer's cottage. Marissa was required to help her mother prepare for the full moon ritual that evening, and had told Michael she'd only be gone a short while. He waited for her on the wooden bench, basking in the late summer day's warmth. He noticed his lungs still made little gurgling sounds when he inhaled, but even so, his breathing was much better than it had been.

Ciara joined him on the bench once she'd tidied up the healer's lodge. After removing her work apron and folding it neatly, she glanced sideways at him. "Tell me about life as a nobleman's son," she said bashfully.

His mood turned pensive with the question. "Da' expects me to follow in his footsteps."

"Doing what?"

"My younger brother Philip and I are being groomed to become knights. Maybe we'll even fight in foreign lands. Roger, my older brother, is already a seasoned knight. He'll take over as Lord of Mountain Manor one day. Da' says that Philip and I are to earn our keep as soldiers—guarding our lands, our ally's lands, and acting in service to the King if called upon," Michael said with practiced bravado.

"Oh, I don't think I would like that. Do you want to fight? Especially in foreign lands?"

"Of course," he answered, perhaps too quickly. Besides, he thought, finishing his sword training would help him protect Marissa. That made him smile. He could return to her a fully-fledged Knight. "It's what's expected of me."

"Yes, but do you want to?" She insisted. Her voice was gentle.

Michael looked straight ahead, his jaw tight. "What I want really has never mattered when it comes to my Da.'"

"Maybe you're made for something else."

He was silent for a long while before he spoke. "I've always known this was my role. Always accepted it. I suppose I want it. What else could I do anyway?"

"A great many things I would guess. Although I don't know much of the world outside Avalon."

His gaze lingered on Ciara's flaxen hair and pale blue eyes. The afternoon sun framed her from behind. She was so unlike her sister, with those raven black curls, eyes as dark as bottomless pools, and a temperament to match.

"You and Marissa are so different."

"Michael, don't. Please. I hate being compared to Marissa. I suppose it's only natural since we're twins, but she's so much stronger than I am. Confident and forceful."

He didn't interrupt when her eyes watered. His mother had taught him it's best to just listen when a girl cries.

She continued softly. "Marissa knows what she wants, knows which path her feet will take her in life. I think her courage will be good when she leads us as High Priestess one day. Better than me, always being afraid."

He fidgeted on the bench. "I'm sorry I upset you. You have great talent, Ciara. You're so kind. And you helped heal me."

"Healing is expected of me."

"Marissa doesn't excel at it as you do."

She giggled. "No, I suppose not. But she excels at many other important things." She hesitated. "I don't like to talk unfavorably about Marissa."

He sighed, unclear how to reassure her. He remembered once seeing his Da' pat his mother's hair when she had been upset about the loss of her favorite lap dog. Maybe he should do that. He reached out and awkwardly patted Ciara's long flaxen tresses.

She sat still. Her face took on a warm pink glow, and she smiled timidly. Michael wasn't sure what was causing her cheeks to blush. He'd offered the perfect chivalrous gesture, just as his Da' would have done. Well, there was one thing he knew for certain. "Thank you," he said.

"For what?" she stammered.

"For seeing inside me." He moved his hand from her hair to pat her shoulder. On impulse, he grabbed her hand in an appreciative gesture. He was grateful to her.

"Well, hello." Marissa had rounded the corner of the healer's cottage and stood a few feet away, arms crossed over her chest. There was no smile in her greeting.

Michael had turned at the sound of her voice. By God, Ciara was right about one thing. Marissa was full of fire and spit. Hands on her hips, her eyes sparked, and her cheeks were vivid red. She was obviously cross. He didn't understand why, but he found the girl's fury both annoying and invigorating.

Ciara jumped up, dropping Michael's hand and raising her own to her chest. "Marissa, I didn't hear you."

The look that momentarily flicked across Marissa's eyes reminded Michael of the wounded hares his father's huntsmen caught with their sharp metal traps.

She glowered. "I've been here only a moment. Long enough to see you two getting close. Holding hands? Is there more?"

"Marissa, what do you mean?" Ciara cried.

Michael glanced from one sister to the other, not sure what contention stirred between them. His mother's instructions had never taught him anything about how to deal with whatever this was. He couldn't help noticing the slight quiver of Marissa's chin. Ciara must have seen it a well. She reached for her sister's hand.

Marissa took a quick step back, words pouring out in a torrent. "Michael, what is happening here? What were you doing with her? What about our promise to each other?"

Michael stood, thoroughly confused now. "Nothing's changed. Why would you think anything's changed?"

"What promise?" Ciara's voice was low and she had turned pale.

Marissa lifted her chin. "That's between Michael and me."

Her sister winced at the words. She hadn't told anyone yet of their vow by the oak grove. She hadn't meant to sound so harsh.

"Unless, of course, Michael made the same promise to *you*." Oh, Goddess, why couldn't she keep her words from being caustic?

Ciara shook her head vigorously. "What promise? Marissa, why are you so upset?"

Michael's gaze seared into Marissa's. Their eyes locked, and she felt his surprise and growing anger across the few feet separating them.

"You doubt me?" he asked quietly.

Marissa's chest rose and fell in quick breaths. "No. Yes. What was happening here just now?"

She held up a hand to forestall him. She had trusted him, but she knew what she'd seen when they thought they were alone. She had clearly watched Michael touch Ciara's hair and pat her shoulder. And of all things, hold her hand. Now she didn't know who to trust. If she couldn't read his feelings for her correctly, couldn't stop herself from distrusting him, or even distrusting her sister, how could she ever rely on her own intuition? Her intuition about Michael, or even more, her intuition about something as big as her mystical vision from the Goddess concerning his fate, their shared fate. How could she ever gain the wise discernment her mother and Vanora always told her she'd need to develop if she were to lead as a good High Priestess? She steeled herself against the rising flood of doubt that drowned her in its wake. She wanted to stop the turmoil, but it engulfed her. She couldn't let anyone see her uncertainty. She had to be strong, as befitting a future leader. Marissa said the only thing she could think to say amid the tidal wave sinking her heart.

"I don't want to see either of you." She spun around and dashed in the direction of the sheltering oak forest.

"Wait," Michael yelled after her.

Ciara rose from the bench, stunned. She ran after Marissa, calling her name. Michael stumbled to standing, but in his weakened state, he was unable to follow. Marissa, her steps fueled by insecurity and fear, was too swift, and she easily outran her sister.

Michael blew out a frustrated sigh, then bent down, picked up an acorn, and hurled it against the side of the hut. It fell with a dull thud.

Chapter 16

The Isle of Avalon
1529 C.E.

For the next waning moon phase, Marissa stopped visiting the healer's hut. Michael tried to corner her every time he saw her in the village. He wanted to speak to her, find out why she was upset and avoiding him. Several times a day he would ask Ciara or Shayla or Elyn where she was and why she darted in the other direction whenever he came near. Shayla and Elyn both explained they couldn't force Marissa to do anything she didn't want to do. They also both agreed that her angry, remote mood was concerning.

One bright and warm morning, after grilling Ciara again on Marissa's whereabouts, Ciara merely shook her head. "I'm so sorry, Michael. I can't convince her that nothing happened between you and me on the bench that day . . ." She looked up at him, eyes questioning, even hopeful.

But Michael's attention was not on her. He was scouring the grounds, searching for her sister.

Ciara lowered her head so her hair swept across her face, shielding her. "All I know is she doesn't wish to see you. She's barely talking to me. I wish she'd believe that nothing more than friendship exists between you and me. Right?" She peeked at him from behind her hair, scrutinizing his face again, hunting for any indication she was not the only one who felt something on the bench that day.

He leapt up, having caught sight of Marissa's light blue tunic. "I'm sorry. What did you say?" His gaze followed Marissa and he fidgeted.

Ciara's heart clenched, and she sighed. "Go. Maybe this time she'll speak with you."

Michael was off in a flash but was evaded yet again.

Ciara watched him go, her breath hitching with unspent sobs. She hurried to the meditation garden beside the Red Well. When she reached the farthest corner of the garden, she slumped to the ground beside a blossoming hawthorn tree and hid behind its thick foliage.

"Ciara?" Shayla entered the garden, softly closing the gate behind her. She spotted her huddled behind the hawthorn tree, head in her hands and her body racked with sobs. She winced at the sight of her friend's distress and crossed the flower garden to kneel beside her. "There you are," she said gently.

Ciara looked up in surprise and quickly wiped her eyes. "Oh! I didn't want anyone to hear me."

"I could not help but hear you." Shayla laid her hand on Ciara's back. "But I am sure no one else did," she added quickly, shrugging her shoulders. "My enhanced hearing and all."

Ciara smiled weakly. "Of course." She bent her head again, unable to stop a fresh flow of tears. "I'm sorry. I'm being so silly, crying like this."

Shayla cocked her head to the side, studying her. "Do you cry for Michael?"

"How did you know?"

"I understand you, my dearest friend. Even if Marissa does not." There was no malice behind her words. Just stark truth, spoken plainly.

Ciara sank into her outstretched arms. "Yes, it's about Michael. Marissa, too. She's angry with me, for no good reason."

Shayla held Ciara as she spent her tears, silently stroking her soft golden hair, her heart breaking with her friend's misery. She loved both twins, had grown up beside them since they were infants and Alianore had fostered her. They had all played in the ocean and climbed the trees in the apple orchard together as children. Shayla cooked the dinner stews and ate her meals with them. As they grew older, she was nearly always by Ciara's side, learning the ways of an Avalon healer as Elyn's apprentice. It was for this twin whom she bore the deepest affection. She wasn't sure why. Maybe she felt Ciara was more fragile and needed more protection than the strong-willed Marissa.

Still, as much as Shayla's heart felt the burden of Ciara's one-sided love for Michael, she couldn't bear to see Marissa hurting either. The twins loved each other as only those who shared a womb before birth can. Despite Marissa's stubborn pride, Shayla was sure it would tear her apart to realize the boy she loved, who obviously loved her back, had broken Ciara's heart with his unrequited affection. She couldn't watch this kind of insidious rivalry tear the bonds of sisterhood. Something had to be done about it. They were her family, and she couldn't bear to watch the strain between them. It was ruining everything, ripping apart the special companionship the three girls had always enjoyed.

Ciara lifted a tear-stained face. Shayla smiled tenderly, wiping Ciara's damp cheeks with the corner of her robes.

"I'm fine. Really, Shayla."

"No, you are not. You cannot lie to me."

Ciara leaned back against the hawthorn trunk. "No, I never could. But I have to be fine with this. Michael chooses Marissa. It is plain to see, except to Marissa."

"That could change," Shayla said, brushing hawthorn blossoms from her friend's hair.

"What could change?"

"Michael's feelings."

Ciara gave her friend a wan smile. "Now who is lying?"

Shayla stared into the distance, an idea forming in her thoughts. Ciara stood and smoothed her robes, sweeping away bits of dirt that clung to them. She pulled her hair back and began to braid it, tidying herself up so no one would suspect her tears.

"Wait." Shayla turned to Ciara.

"What is it?"

Hoping to cheer her friend, she was about to divulge her idea, then thought better of it. It would be best if neither sister knew of her inspired plan.

"Let me help you. You are braiding it crooked," she said instead, keeping her scheme to herself. She stood and lifted her friend's long flaxen hair into her hands. Ciara managed another weak smile and left the weaving to Shayla's nimble fingers.

After the plait lay neatly down her back, Ciara said, "I better get back to the healing hut before Elyn misses me."

"You are going to be all right."

"I will be." Ciara sniffled then lifted her head high. She turned and walked the path leading to the garden entrance and paused. "Thank you, Shayla. For understanding. I guess there are some things I can't talk to my sister about anymore." Over her shoulder, she added, "That's the hardest part." She didn't wait for an answer.

As Ciara made her way out the healing garden's gate, Shayla's heart wrenched. Human sorrow was too hard to bear. She sometimes wished her Faery ability to detach from emotions would grow as strong as her other bourgeoning Faery capabilities. She rubbed her temples with her fingers. "You are right, Ciara," she whispered to herself. "There are things better left unsaid, kept secret. So what I am about to do, I do for you, my two dear friends."

Chapter 17

The Isle of Avalon
1529 C.E.

Shayla took Ciara's previous spot, settling beneath the garden's imposing hawthorn tree. The gnarled and thorny tree was known to be sacred to her Faery folk. Yes, *her* folk. She could no longer deny the pull of her bloodline.

Marissa's lack of foresight two years ago, convincing her to lead the twins into the Faery Realm with the promise of adventure, had ended in suffering for Shayla. Since the disastrous trip, she was troubled with inexplicable surges of Faery power. She could now do things, see things, hear things, that weren't possible for human mortals. Magical things Ciara and Marissa couldn't do, even with their priestess heritage. Because of that one bit of contact with the Faery, that one visit that sang like a luring siren call to her half-Faery blood and bones, she was no longer content. She barely slept, food tasted pale in comparison to the Faery banquet, her thoughts were consumed with everything Faery. Emotions surged and swelled, and she didn't know what to do with them. One thing was certain. She was angry with Marissa for the quickening of this Faery desire. Very angry.

She heaved a tormented sigh and leaned her head against the hawthorn tree's sturdy trunk. She would always love her friend, no matter if she was angry, would always adore her foster-mother Alianore, and cherish her Avalon upbringing. But she was no longer sure she knew how to live with her soul at peace in the world of humans, even priestess humans, as magical and close to the Faery Realm as they were. She wasn't sure where she fit any longer.

Vanora kept reminding her, as magical as her blood was, she had to make sure she held on to her human compassion, and was discerning and wise with her enhanced Faery powers.

Well, she deeply loved Marissa and Ciara, but they were making such a miserable mess between themselves. She sighed and picked up a handful of the soft white hawthorn petals and let them drift through her fingers. She could tap into her priestess healing skills to help her friends, but instinct told her Faery magic was the more powerful way to bring the three of them back to the way things were before Michael arrived. She wanted them happy again. Close, like they used to be. She could use her mushrooming Faery abilities to make things right again.

She tilted her chin up to let the delicate hawthorn blossoms fall upon her face, breathing in the scent of the hawthorn tree. The tree was known as the bearer of good fortune, but more importantly, capable of removing a thorn from one's heart. A thorn of sorts had certainly inserted itself in the heart of her dearest friend, Ciara, and had obviously poisoned Marissa's good sense as well.

This plan would help them all. Shayla was sitting in a potent earth spot, a spot of inherent Faery power—under the hawthorn tree, with a small creek forking into two rivulets just beyond the tree, sourced from their most sacred Red Well farther up the ridge. Such crossroads would magnify any enchantment conjured. She felt the natural power thrum and vibrate inside her. Still, she hadn't a clue how to invoke the Faery magic or exactly what to do with it once it was summoned. On instinct, she closed her eyes and turned her body to face the hawthorn, wrapping her arms about its trunk.

"Speak to me, Spirit of Hawthorn. I am one with your spirit, one with the earth. I need your help. Tell me how to remove the thorn entrenched in a beloved human's heart. My dearest friend, Ciara."

To her surprise, it was not the spirit of the hawthorn tree that answered her plea, but one of her own kind—a Faery, full-blooded—whose image and voice rose in her awareness.

"Shayla of the Faery *and* the Avalon Priestesses," a male voice said. Shayla opened her eyes and turned toward it. A vague shimmer slowly solidified into a Faery being who stood beside the hawthorn. A handsome young man encircled by the green-tree aura, tall and lithe, with long silver hair, and piercing green eyes.

"Who are you?" she whispered, while she worked to focus on his shimmering form, one arm still wrapped around the trunk.

"I am called Folimot."

"Oh! We met two years ago. You are the guardian who led us into and out of the Faery Realm."

"Yes." A small, mysterious smile played at his lips. "You have linked with the sacred Hawthorn. I am its steward and I heard your plea." He bowed. "Daughter of Laighlon, King of the Northern Faery Realms."

Shayla gasped and stood. "You know my father? Please, tell me how I can meet him."

"The Faery Queen Ravenna already clarified why you cannot. He will not interfere with your human upbringing until the time is right. Such is the bargain made with an Avalon priestess should a child be conceived from mating with Faery during the holy Summer Solstice celebrations. Your father wishes only peace and happiness for you. Not torment."

"But I *am* tormented," she whispered. "More so without him."

"I have sensed your torment. Your blood sings with the song of Faery. It grows stronger, does it not?"

Shayla nodded mutely.

"You were born of both bloods, but one day you will have to choose. Faery or Priestess. One realm or the other. An important decision." Folimot shook his head. "But that day is not today. Today you have called upon the sacred Hawthorn to help those whom you are concerned about. As its guardian, I hear your plea. I am aligned with Hawthorn's deep nature, its spirit of healing one's heart."

"Then you will help me?" she asked, locking onto the young man's gaze. She was afraid he might simply shimmer away.

"Yes." He reached his hands out to hers, and she met his grasp with her own. "I, Folimot, nephew to your father, the great King Laighlon, pledge my assistance. However, I ask you this. Are you sure you wish to use Faery magic? It is far more potent than human magic, even priestess magic, and sometimes comes with unexpected consequences."

She searched his face. Her *second sight*, her intuitive knowledge, warmed her belly, assuring her she could trust her kin standing before her. *Faery magic comes with unexpected consequences.* She shivered.

She had been so certain she wanted to do this. But should she? She recalled Ciara's tears, Marissa's anger and hurt. Michael's presence in Avalon had affected them all. She shook her head. Things were out of hand. They needed to be remedied. She had to do something. She *would* do something, no matter the cost to herself.

"I have felt consequences from my venture into the Faery Realm. I will accept the possibility of more because I wish to use Faery Magic. I will take special care with it. This is a very important request." A flush of hope rose within her chest. "Would it be possible to ask for my father to meet me outside the Faery border?"

His green aura dulled. "I am sorry. I cannot. I have risked enough coming to your aid in this way."

"You have risked yourself for me?"

He looked away. "Lady Ravenna told you it was too soon to involve you in Faery ways. You are not ready. Yet. She would not approve of my assistance with Hawthorn magic, much less with ensuring a meeting with your father."

"Then why did you come to me?" Shayla asked, confused.

Folimot's gaze returned to her, deepened, and his jaw muscles tightened. She saw something in his expression, something that said he swallowed back hidden words. Instead of speaking what Shayla sensed, he answered, "Humans need to develop their minds and master their emotions to handle the potency of our Realm. Even you, with your halfling blood. You know your connection has already brought you suffering and confusion." He took a step back, letting go of her hands. "Perhaps I should not have come at all."

"Oh, no. Please do not leave."

His countenance brightened at her words.

She blinked back tears. "Meeting my father, even hearing about him, is more than I could have hoped for anyway. And that is not the reason I called for Faery magic today."

Folimot's eyes flickered with racing emotions that Shayla could not name.

"I will help you, Shayla. But know this. Your desire for our realm will only grow. You must strengthen yourself. It will help if you practice your priestess ways with focused intent. And even then, I tell you, it will be true love that finally eases your way back to the Faery Realm."

"True love? How?"

"I have said too much." He grew silent and lowered his eyes.

She swallowed thickly. "I am willing to take on ... consequences. For my friends."

He studied her and nodded slowly. "All right. Name your desire."

"I would like ... I would like ..." She paused, closed her eyes, and concentrated on exactly what she would like for heart-broken Ciara, to restore the camaraderie between the three of them. "I would like to ease my friend's pain. I would like our visitor Michael to leave soon and forget his visit to Avalon. To forget Marissa and Ciara for good."

"Once this Michael leaves Avalon and the veil is drawn again, his memories will naturally diminish," Folimot pointed out.

"The veil is not enough to accomplish what is needed. I want my friends to be free of the unfortunate heartache caused by his presence."

"I do not deign to understand human turmoil. But I have one last question: why do you wish to do this?"

"Because I love them both," she said without hesitation.

He persisted. "And what else?"

She choked back a sob. "Marissa and Ciara are like sisters. If they don't get along, where does that leave me?"

"You are honest. Then it is simple. There are no trinkets or amulets, potions, or rituals involved. Merely conjure up their faces in your mind."

Shayla brought Ciara to mind first, envisioning her friend as if she stood directly before her. She built an image of her delicate features: pale blue eyes and a gentle smile, long flaxen hair that reflected light, be it sun or candle flame. Caring hands that had already helped to heal so many, and her loving heart. Shayla flinched when she sensed Ciara's heart. It appeared to be slowly closing with sorrow.

She took a breath before raising the image of Marissa. Dark, glossy hair framed fiery brown eyes that glowed with amber flecks. Her straight back and uplifted chin, her contagious laughter and bold nature. Both sisters so different. She would protect them with her life if need be, her love for them was that deep. Finally, she summoned Michael's image, with his tawny hair, deep blue eyes, and ready smile. All three stood before her in her mind's eye.

"I am ready," she said, her voice steady as she concentrated.

"Say these words."

Folimot clasped Shayla's hands once again. She was surprised at how tenderly he held them, and how it lifted her heart. He spoke softly, in an exotic language she recognized from the brief visit to the Faery Realm, and from her subsequent otherworldly dreams. It was more song than spoken word.

Her mouth went dry. She hesitated, suddenly torn. She wondered, was she doing the right thing? She liked Michael. But he brought discord. And heartache. She must help the twins. Make all three of them a happy family once again.

She refocused on the spell. While she thought she'd never be able to pronounce what Folimot directed her to say, she was surprised how easily the sounds rolled off her tongue. Three mysterious words repeated three times, once for each person whose heart was involved in the ill-fated triangle. One round for her beloved friend Ciara, the next for Marissa, and the last for Michael. This way he would forget the two sisters entirely and never attempt to return to Avalon to sow more unhappiness. Three words she hoped would remove the twins' heartache and distress.

"Wait," Shayla burst out. "Muddling Michael's memory cannot happen until after he leaves Avalon. Otherwise it will never go unnoticed. Make it so that for him, only once he leaves, his Avalon memories become like a dream that quickly fades."

Folimot lifted his hands from Shayla's. "To make sure this happens in precisely the way you intend, add this single word." He spoke the word softly, drawing invisible sigils in the air between them. She didn't know if it was her imagination, but did the hawthorn tree dim with the gesture, and drop a few leaves?

She forced herself to tear her eyes from the tree, closed them, and sang the last spiraling tone, copying his hand gesture. The sound rang softly around them, and she felt a sense of completion. Her spell was cast. The priestesses would not easily recognize it, as it was sourced from Faery. The knot she had felt in her stomach from watching her friends suffer unwound. She breathed easier and felt her smile to be genuine when she opened her eyes and looked once again at Folimot.

"Thank you. With Michael gone, never to return, and his memory of Avalon faded, my dear friends will be free of their misery. As will he. All will return to normal. We will be as we used to be before his arrival."

Folimot cocked an eyebrow, but returned her smile, then began to fade. "Please, do not go," she pleaded.

"I must." His words echoed softly. "I have crossed the borders without permission and have been gone too long. I do not wish to draw attention to our meeting."

"I do not want any trouble for you," she said, shuddering with the memory of crossing the border before without permission. "Will you come again?" she asked, feeling suddenly shy.

This time his smile grew broad, warm, but again secretive. "Yes. We will meet again. I am not at liberty to tell you where or when. But we are destined to do so."

"Destined? What do you mean?"

"It will unfold in good time," was all he replied.

"Wait. If you cannot help me see him, will you send my father a message?" Shayla pleaded. "Please?"

Folimot's shimmering form had already faded, leaving behind a shower of delicate white hawthorn petals.

Chapter 18
The Isle of Avalon
1529 C.E.

The late summer sun rose above the Tor and warmed Elyn's healing lodge. Michael kept watch out its window, always on alert for Marissa. Honeybees hummed, seeking their sustenance, the sweet nectar of the red and white roses that grew outside the lodge. Their heady perfume mixed with the fragrance of ever-ripening apples. If it were not for the fact that he had still not spoken with Marissa, he might have felt content. But the ache in his heart had become a fast friend, accompanying him throughout the last of his days in Avalon.

"Cough for me," Elyn ordered.

He forced air from his lungs and grinned at her. "See? I am truly well now."

"I will be the judge of that," she said lightly, ruffling his hair.

Michael dodged her affectionate gesture, thinking himself too old for such a thing. It was something he usually did to his younger brother. He suddenly missed Philip.

"He is indeed better, is he not, Healing Mistress?" Ciara ventured with a concerned look on her face.

Elyn chuckled. "Michael, you must be the most looked after patient Avalon has ever had."

Shayla stood to the side and watched, arms across her chest, bearing an unreadable expression.

"Well, there you have it. I can go home now," Michael said.

Shayla brightened and stood taller. Ciara leaned back against the wall and sighed quietly.

Elyn examined the faded bruise and faint scar on his forehead. "Anymore dizziness?"

"No."

"Nausea? Headaches?"

"No. And no." He turned his head and smiled at Ciara, tossing a rolled-up strip of linen her way. "And you needn't worry so much, Ciara."

She caught the linen and giggled. Shayla remained quiet.

Elyn clucked her tongue. "Fie! You can stop your folly and conduct yourself properly. Those are my clean bandages."

"Yes, Healing Mistress." Michael lowered his head but peeked up to grin at the two girls. He hazarded a glance at Elyn and saw her trying to hide a smile.

"Your head injury has healed, your lungs sound healthy, your fever is gone, and your cough is no longer wet and rattling. Yes. You can go home now, young lad."

Michael grew solemn. He was eager to see his brothers. Still, heaviness lodged in his chest. Not from the coughing illness, but from Marissa's absence. She'd spurned him. He'd done something unforgivable to her and he didn't know what it was. The pain of it had not lessened with the passing days. He'd promised his heart. That day in the oak grove, they'd vowed to marry. He didn't understand what had changed. Healing from her rejection was worse than healing from nearly dying.

He turned to Elyn. "I wish to thank you for everything you've done for me. Without your aid I would have died."

Ciara rushed over to pat his shoulder, just as he'd patted hers two weeks ago when offering reassurance and comfort.

"Your fine healing cured me," he said, pausing to take in all three healers, "and Marissa saved me from drowning. I would like to thank her too," he added, feeling the longing for her company rise up within him. An awkward silence ensued.

He glanced out the window again, hoping Marissa would walk by on her way to the Seeress Hall. No sign of her. He sighed, resigned to the fact that even if he did catch a glimpse, she'd likely turn the other way and hurry on.

He jumped down from the examining table. "My father will likely send a fine recompense for taking such good care of me. Coins, or perhaps the fruits of our upcoming harvest."

"We do what we do because we are priestesses of Avalon. Payment is not required. But I would not turn it down either," Elyn added hastily. "There are things our community might use from the outside world. Extra linen, or unguent bottles perhaps." She busied herself corking two small vials of amber liquid.

Ciara took the bottles and handed them to Michael with instructions. "Take this one in the morning. This one at night. A few drops in water."

He wrinkled his nose but held his hands up in surrender. "I'm sure they will taste vile, but I'm only better because of your mysterious tinctures. I'll do as you command, m'lady."

She blushed. Elyn shook her head and smiled.

"Can we help you gather your things?" Shayla abruptly interjected.

Ciara frowned. "Wait! There's no rush. Michael will have a grand midday meal before leaving. I'll tell Cook to prepare something special. A true farewell feast." She turned to him. "You would like that, would you not?"

"Mmm." He responded with an offhanded nod. He stared out the open door, following a fleeting figure with raven-dark hair, dressed in blue robes. Marissa slowed her steps. His heart sped up. She cast a furtive glance inside the door and they locked gazes. Her eyes softened, then grew steely almost immediately. She spun around and hurried past the healing hut.

"Ciara is offering you a feast, Michael," Shayla said curtly.

"It's all right, Shayla," Ciara said.

"What?" He pulled his attention back to Ciara, trying to calm his racing heart and his, once again, dashed hopes. "Oh, I'm sorry. Yes, a feast would be very nice. Thank you. You're always so kind." He offered Ciara a sincere, if distracted, smile.

Late that afternoon, the community of priestesses gathered around Michael in the dining hall. Remnants of a fine meal were scattered amongst the tables. Ciara had asked Cook to prepare Michael's favorites: parsnips in herbed cream sauce, bread served with honeyed butter, crusty pigeon pie, hard-boiled eggs covered with saffron and flavored with cloves, and plums stewed in rosewater. Michael had filled his trencher plate twice, savoring each bite. The food in Avalon was even better than the hearty meals his Da's cook prepared at their Mountain Manor. He sat back and belched, showing his appreciation.

Shayla strode up to his table, a small packed bag in hand. "Michael, you have been a good patient and a fine friend and playmate these last two months." She held up his bag. "Alianore awaits you at the barge."

Michael accepted it readily. "Thank you, Shayla." He searched her face, realizing something. She had changed in the last few days. She was still a compassionate caregiver, ministering to the resolution of his cough and fever, but she had become aloof. She didn't play board games with him and Ciara anymore. Nor did she take her morning meals alongside him any longer.

Then there was Ciara. She, too, now behaved strangely. He often caught her staring at him. He knew she was upset because her twin ignored her. It hurt him to see her suffer from the snub. She'd become his confidante in Marissa's absence. A good friend. He sighed, licking the buttery breadcrumbs from his fingers. Maybe he had just outstayed his welcome.

Marissa was pointedly absent from the feast, with the explanation that she was beginning a three-day visionary initiation in the Seeress Hall. Michael knew it was just an excuse. The knowledge cut into his heart.

It was hard to leave her, especially going away without making up or even saying goodbye. He was hale and robust again, time for him to go home. More importantly, how could he stay in Avalon if Marissa continued ignoring him? She left him no choice but to depart.

The women of Avalon walked him down to the edges of the lake that separated Avalon from the outside world. Each of the priestesses hugged Michael farewell and gave him a token of affection—flower garlands, bright ribbons, and beaded charms. He placed them in the special silken pouch Ciara had made him for such things.

He turned back to give Avalon one last glance. The crystal-veined stone walls of the Healing Halls he had visited upon his arrival glistened in the distance. He remembered how frightened he'd been of the magical ways of the priestesses and their unfamiliar healing methods. Those very methods had saved his life. He was no longer afraid of these women, no matter what his Da' or people might think of priestesses. Despite being secretive and enigmatic, they were kindly, and had helped him and nurtured him back to health.

His eyes wandered past the village lodgings, toward the Seeress Hall, anticipation filling his breath. If only Marissa would come down to the shore and bid him goodbye. One last embrace from her might soothe his heart. But he had lost her, lost something precious, and he despaired at their parting. He swore he saw movement at the Hall window, but the figure swiftly moved away. Was it Marissa, watching him? Did she care for him at all?

Alianore placed a gentle hand on the small of his back to guide him to the barge that would take him through the borders and back to the world of man. "My daughter is stubborn and willful. She is wrong to turn you away, but she has a loving heart. She will come around."

Michael looked up into her knowing eyes. "Do you really think so?"

Alianore nodded sagely. "I know my daughter well."

"But how can I ever see her again? How can I get back here to Avalon? And when?" He knew he couldn't simply return on his own. He didn't have the magic to find Avalon's borders, much less part their obscuring mists.

Alianore's gaze was tender. "My daughter will find the truth in her heart. She will find a way. If it is meant to be, she will find you. Trust that."

His jaw muscles tightened, and he blinked back tears. His Da' would say it was unmanly to cry, though he hurt inside like never before.

Ciara approached. She tied the strings of the small silken pouch holding his treasures and placed it around his neck. He noticed that she, too, fought back tears. She hugged him tightly.

"Farewell. Happiness and health to you, Michael."

"And to you, my good friend."

She turned and joined her mother at the bow of the barge. "I'm coming with you to see him off," she said, looking straight ahead.

Alianore raised an eyebrow but did not turn her away.

Shayla approached Michael shyly, eyes downcast. "I wish you the best in your life." She placed a small hawthorn twig with one tiny white blossom in his hand.

"Thank you," he said. Though he still wondered what made her seem distant, even distressed the past few days, he was relieved she bid him a caring goodbye. He sniffed the hawthorn flower. The blossom's scent made him feel light-headed. He hoped he wasn't feverish again. No dizzy spells had afflicted him for many days now. He shook off the hazy sensation and tucked the blossomed stem in the loop of his tunic's buttonhole.

"I'm ready," he told the High Priestess. He stepped onto the barge and waved at those on the shoreline.

Alianore instructed him. "We are taking you to the exact spot on the lakeshore where we found you. Jack, the son of Glastonbury's blacksmith and a good friend to us, rode to Wales to give your father the message that you were taken in by the village folk and nurtured back to health. Upon Jack's return, he told me your father will send two knights who will await you and bring you home."

"After all this time, my father has not come for me himself?" Perhaps he should not be surprised. This would be his Da's way of handling things. Unemotional. Detached.

"The veils distort time. Although it has been two months in Avalon, only two days have passed for your father."

"Still, it was two days . . ." Michael replied, looking down.

Alianore kissed his cheek. "Remember us. You are well loved here."

Her words settled into his heart—a balm to his father's indifference and Marissa's absence.

She turned to face the bow. With Ciara by her side, she lifted her arms to begin the parting invocation that would raise the pearly mists and allow the barge to carry Michael back to his world.

He stood facing forward, hands clutching the silken pouch about his neck. The barge began to move slowly, picking up speed as fog turned to wind that propelled them forward. Michael's hand tingled and he looked down at his pouch. To his surprise, it had flattened. He quickly untied the strings to find the gifts inside had all disappeared. He tried to recall what the gifts were, tried to remember the faces of the priestesses who'd given them to him. But his thoughts were growing muddled, the gifts and faces blurred. He glanced toward the prow of the barge. The distant shore drew close. He could see two men on horseback, and he recognized their faces, Sir George and Sir David. The two women at the bow were now dim outlines, slowly fading and blending into Avalon's mists.

"Ciara," he called, alarmed.

She turned, giving him a sad smile before she faded from his vision.

Desperate now, he shouted. "Marissa!"

No one answered. The barge banked itself on the shore of its own volition, bereft of its priestess navigators. Michael shook his head, trying to clear his muddled thoughts.

The pouch he had clutched only moments before was gone. He pulled open his cloak, searching for it. A small hawthorn twig with one tiny white blossom fell to the deck of the barge.

"Michael!" Sir David shouted. "Here we are, boy. You're returned, thank the Lord."

"Looking safe and sound," Sir George added.

The knights dismounted and ran to Michael. He stepped off the barge, fiercely missing his Da', his brothers, and all his friends from Mountain Manor.

Sir David lifted him in a gruff embrace. "We thought we'd lost you, boy."

"Your Da' was beside himself," Sir George said, patting Michael on the back once David had put him back on the shore again. "He sent out search parties."

"Your brothers were worse. Philip would not eat," Sir David put in.

"I'm fine, truly. I was hurt badly, but I was healed. There were these women. They helped me." He furrowed his brow and rubbed his forehead, the spot where he'd hit his head two months prior. Wait. Hadn't it been only two days? "I think they were healers. I . . . I'm not sure. They brought me back on that barge."

Michael turned to point to the barge. It was no longer there.

Marissa stealthily made her way to the lake. She felt a sudden chill and drew her cloak tightly around her. Kneeling low behind the cover of bulrushes, she watched the barge depart, her tears flowing with its departure.

This boy who had changed her life was gone. Despite herself, her heart silently begged Michael to remain in Avalon. He had made such lovely promises in the oak grove. She had returned his love. They vowed themselves to each other. How could he have deceived her? With her sister no less? Ciara denied it, but Marissa knew what she'd seen that day. Michael tenderly caressing Ciara's hair, lovingly patting her back and holding her hand. Just like he'd done with her in the oak grove.

A new doubt slithered along her spine and nested in her heart, snuggled against the mistrust that had been living there these last few days. Had she been wrong about Michael and Ciara? If so, had she just made the biggest mistake of her life? Maybe she should have cooled her stubborn anger and reconciled with Michael. She trembled with the realization. It was too late.

"I cannot help myself. My heart is yours, even if you no longer care for me," she whispered.

Blowing him a kiss, she added fervently, "At the very least, heed my warnings. Believe me, I beg you. Stay away from Glastonbury Abbey."

Chapter 19

Glastonbury, England
Present Day

Sophie opened her eyes. Daniel was leaning over her with a concerned look. *How blue his eyes were, like the ocean at dawn,* she thought. Squinting against the bright sun that haloed Daniel's tawny-colored hair, she reached up and touched a strand. His face registered surprise, then his gaze locked with hers. It was a long moment before Sophie turned away. She shook her head. *What's gotten into me?*

The abbey's curator, the prim Mrs. Henderson, approached Daniel and handed him a dampened cloth. He reached down and wiped Sophie's brow with it. The cool moisture relieved some of the panic rising in her chest.

She licked dry lips, and rose up on one elbow, pushing aside the moist cloth. "What the hell happened to me?"

"You tell me," he said, handing the cloth back to Mrs. Henderson. "One minute I'm painting, and the next, you fall like a sack of flour."

Sophie scowled. "Like a sack of flour?"

"Well, no one faints elegantly. Are you sick? Did you eat?"

"Shall I ring for a doctor?" Mrs. Henderson asked.

Sophie shooed away their words, annoyed at the whole situation. She'd never fainted once in her life, and she'd seen some horrific things in her journalistic career. But nothing had shaken her like the man in Daniel's painting. Or the look in his eyes. She opted for innocent humility as far as Mrs. Henderson was concerned. She had to get rid of the woman and find out what the hell Daniel had painted that had sent her into such terror. Mrs. Henderson had just told her in no uncertain terms this morning that she wanted nothing but the facts in Sophie's magazine article for Glastonbury's commemoration fund-raiser. No mumbo jumbo. She was sure Mrs. Henderson would consider being spooked into passing out from a painting to be mumbo jumbo.

Sophie put on a sheepish smile and said, "Too much coffee, not enough food. And jet lag. I have water and a sandwich in my bag. I'll be fine."

She tested her legs by kneeling before she stood. No wobbling or shakiness. "See? Good as new. I promise to check in at the end of the day and let you know how I'm coming along on my piece." She smiled, took Mrs. Henderson by the elbow, and gently steered the curator back toward the museum. "Really, I'll let you know if I need anything. Thank you for your concern."

"Well, if you think you're all right, I'll just get back to my desk. The Girl Guides will be arriving soon."

"That's right. Shouldn't miss that. We'll speak later."

Once Mrs. Henderson headed for the museum, Sophie turned to find Daniel propped against his stool, arms crossed over his chest and a look of amusement crinkling the corners of his eyes. "Couldn't get rid of her fast enough, eh?"

"Well, what do you think? I just fainted away at the sight of your painting and there's no way I can let her know that juicy bit," Sophie hissed, putting her hand on her hip.

Daniel's amusement faded. "What startled you about my painting?"

"You tell me. I remember I was looking at your canvas. At the flames . . . at that man," she said, pointing a finger that began to tremble. She stuffed her hand in her jacket pocket.

He turned to face his work. "It is unsettling, isn't it?"

"Quite," she said, afraid to look at the painting again, yet drawn to it at the same time.

His hand was on his chin, stroking the stubble growing there. He looked like he hadn't shaved since she'd seen him the night before.

"I don't know what came over me while I painted," he said. "Those yellows, oranges, and reds . . . it was like my brush had a will of its own."

"I knew it. I knew something felt odd. That's why I came closer. Then I saw the man, that monk, and I lost it."

He turned to face her. "Any idea why?"

She exhaled loudly and shook her head. "Daniel, I don't spook easily, so this has me thoroughly confused."

He shuffled his feet and looked down at the ground.

"What? You know something. What is it?" she demanded, her tone sharper than she'd intended.

He held up his hand in a gesture of peace. "Hold on a minute. I'm not withholding. Not really, anyway."

Sophie pinned him with her best steely glare.

"Okay," he said. "It's just that, well . . . no, you'll only think I'm making it up. That I'm one of those nutters who believes in séances and carries crystals. Mumbo jumbo, as our curator Mrs. Henderson says."

"Can it get any worse? I'm hearing music and chanting that no one else hears. I'm keeling over from looking at a painting, for God knows what reason. Out with it."

Daniel sat back on his stool with a sigh. "All right. For two years now, since Laura's death really, I've seen . . . ghosts." He mumbled the last word.

She narrowed her eyes. "Ghosts?"

He looked up, his expression beseeching her not to laugh, his shoulders set back in defiance in case she did.

"Sophie, just listen. It took me by surprise. I thought I heard someone talking to me right before Laura and the baby went on that train, trying to warn me against their journey. I turned around to see who was talking and nobody was there. I blew it off as being overworked and over-protective."

Sophie softened her stance. Daniel was sincere. He wasn't the deceptive type. He sounded haunted. Not by ghosts so much, but if her instincts were right, by guilt. She waited while he took a breath, staring vacantly into the distance.

"But that voice, whatever it was, was right. That prediction came true. After my wife and baby died in that horrible accident was when I really started hearing and seeing things. I couldn't walk by a hospital, a convalescent home, and yes, even a cemetery, without someone—someone not really there, someone no one else noticed—following me, talking to me. They were as surprised I could see and hear them as I was."

Sophie wasn't sure what to say. She could tell he really believed all of this.

"But you know the damnedest thing of it all?" He lost the vacant look and stared at her directly, as if he was trying to bore into her the seriousness of what he was about to disclose. "With all the ghosts I see, there hasn't been one bloody time I've seen Laura. Or my baby. Not once." He raised his hands and let them fall back down to his sides again.

His jaw clenched and unclenched, and his blue eyes grew dark and shadowed. "It's like I'm being punished for not listening to the warning. If I can see ghosts, why can't I see my wife? She's dead. My baby is dead. Why don't they appear to me?"

Sophie felt no satisfaction in her spot-on assessment of Daniel. His loss and grief had torn his life apart. But his guilt was more eroding.

"Daniel, you couldn't have known the prediction was real. Hell, you couldn't have known the voice you heard was real."

He stopped her with a wave of his hand. "I've been through all that reasoning, Sophie. I even got so furious that I cursed the disembodied voice that warned me in the first place. I blamed it, ghost, demon, angel, whatever it was, for my loss. My ranting nearly cost me my sanity. After that, the ghosts stopped appearing." He huffed a faint laugh. "It gave me time to put my life back together again."

She nodded, feeling it was wiser to listen than to placate, challenge, or even sympathize.

"As I said, I stopped seeing the ghosts." Daniel rubbed his hand across his face and over his eyes. "Until last night."

Chapter 20

Glastonbury, England
Present Day

Late-morning sun shone through Sophie's B&B window, highlighting a swirl of dust motes.

Sophie balled up her first drafts and tossed them in the garbage can. "Damn," she muttered.

The room suddenly felt confining, much like her editor's restraints around the writing of her magazine piece. Sid said the article needed to bring her back into credibility in the world of journalism if she wanted to salvage her career. He would never give her the okay to veer off into the realm of . . . well, ghosts, perpetual choirs no one else could hear, and mysterious paintings that cause fainting spells. He wouldn't believe this stuff anyway, and neither would her readers. Hell, she barely believed it herself. But it had happened. To her. The whole incident was creating one huge writer's block.

She had to clear her head and get back to reality. Focusing on images of blazing abbey infernos, mysterious monks, and choirs whose songs haunted her subconscious, was not going to bring her closer to said reality. Nor would accepting Daniel's tale of seeing a ghost at the abbey ruins.

Sure, she reasoned, *if such things existed, the abbey had a right to be haunted.* Its legendary history, for the most part holy and peaceful, was also wrought with turmoil and tragedy. But she simply could not subscribe to the theory of ghosts, much less use Daniel's report of sighting one, in her article. He claimed the alleged ghost appeared as a monk, clothed in brown robes tied at the waist with cording. He even noted details of the apparition's appearance, recounting the monk's tawny hair and blue eyes, just like the monk in his painting.

She tapped her fingers on her desk. Her thoughts narrowed and grew focused. What she needed to do was to write down the facts of the abbey's recorded history as she knew them. In outline form, using pen and paper. That was her answer. Old-fashioned handwritten script took more time, but it was that slower pace of scrawling words on paper that always diffused her confusion and clarified her thoughts. She snapped closed the cover on her laptop, fished in her briefcase for a pen and notepad, and set them on the desk. She pulled the clip from her hair and shook out her long, dark mane, letting it fall freely down to her shoulders. Then she stared at the yellow, lined legal paper, arranging in her mind the historical facts she had acquired, waiting for the flow of words to commence.

Her focus blurred, and she absently rubbed her eyes, hoping she wasn't too tired to write. The pad and pen were haloed with diffuse luminosity, much like the sun had haloed Daniel's head when she peered up at him after fainting earlier that morning. She blinked several times to clear her vision, wondering if she was going to pass out again.

"Whoa," she murmured, as all thought stopped and swiftly morphed into unfamiliar images inside her mind. She found herself in a golden meadow, running free like a child. Tall spring wildflowers brushed against her legs as she ran, their sweet scent and the warm sun overhead tempting her to drop down and roll around in the soft grass.

"I'm Herne the Hunter, Lord of the Forest! I'll find you, you can't hide forever," a boy's voice rang out, his laughter punctuated by raspy breath. She had to keep running, had to hide before he found her. She stifled her laughter lest he hear her. The woods were just ahead, the thick-trunked oak trees offering the perfect cover.

Sophie jerked awake, dropping her pen. "Oh, crap, did I black out again?" Her heart lurched. But she hadn't fallen to the floor or even slumped against her desk. She was still sitting erect on the high-backed, wooden chair. The room was now darker, twilight's shadows flitting in the corners. She wondered how much time had gone by. Turning on the desk lamp, she checked her phone clock. Five hours! Her heart was racing now.

Calm down. You'll be better if you get a bite to eat and a drink of water, she reassured herself.

The back of her neck ached, like it did when she'd been writing for a while. She reached her hand around and rubbed where it hurt.

When she glanced down at her writing pad, her eyes went wide. "What the hell is this?"

Pages of scribbled notes lay scattered across the desk. She scooped them up and counted them. Ten. Not one of them was in her handwriting. The words *Avalon, abbey,* and *King Henry*, were prominent among a sea of free-streaming sentences. Had she gathered research notes and forgotten about them? Did Sid include these in her work packet? She reached for her briefcase and dug into the file Sid had provided. No, there'd been no mention of handwritten notes for her use, and she truly didn't remember seeing any beforehand anyway. She sat back, and with trembling hands, picked up the pages one at a time to put them in a pile, then began reading the first page.

It started with notations in an old-fashioned cursive script and detailed what seemed to be a monk's daily life at what he called 'The Blessed Abbey of Glastonbury.' It was a communal timetable of sorts, labeled at the top of the page, *Benedictine Horarium.* The schedule organized daily prayer times, reading times, study times in the library, sleep time, meal time, even the rotation of monks who arrived in shifts of twelve to keep the perpetual choir from faltering. *Perpetual Choir?* Sophie gasped and jumped up from her chair.

Her heart knocked against her chest like a jackhammer. So she *had* heard singing last night in the abbey grounds. She wasn't making it all up. She immediately censured the whole idea anyway. *Hold on,* she told herself. *How can you rely on notes that inexplicably appear in front of you to validate something that sounds crazy to begin with?*

She gripped the edge of the desk, still clutching the page she'd read in her other hand, and slowly sat down. She had to know more.

The notes on the next pages described three Benedictine vows: stability, obedience, and a simple life of chastity, poverty, and surrender to their Lord Jesus. Then the entries became more personal in nature. Her lips parted in disbelief. The writer, whoever he was, boasted that the Benedictines were preeminent scholars. He wrote how what he loved most was his time spent in their voluminous library, soaking up the collection of books in between his monastic duties. More intimate still, he spoke of the early-morning call of birdsong in the apple orchard at dawn when he set out to harvest apples, and how their sweet scent reminded him of a particular Summer Solstice celebration, a cherished memory. Of the time he'd spent an unforgettable evening with a beautiful girl of raven-black hair.

Sophie's hand flew over her chest. There was something familiar in the monk's description. The moment was fleeting. Her breath hitched as she tried to grab hold of the elusive image that had flitted through her mind with the monk's words. An upsurge of sadness lay heavy in her chest. Then the feelings and images disappeared, sinking under a dark quicksand of oblivion.

"Pull yourself together, Sophie," she murmured. She fought to regain control of her emotions, her heartbeat, her breath. She closed her eyes but grew curious again. One more page. She reread the last page and frowned. This had to be wrong. A Summer Solstice celebration didn't sound like a Christian holy day. The monk went on to speak of the consolation he sought after that Solstice. He found a measure of it in tending the stock of fish in the abbey's pond, and in the comforting cocoon of silent meals shared in camaraderie with his monastic brothers.

She stared at the pages in her hands. She could only take in so much before her reasoning mind screamed that this was all nonsense, that it must be some kind of hallucination. Throwing the papers down on the desk where they scattered—some floating to the floor—she jumped up, grabbed her keys, and bounded down the stairs to the street. She had to be outside, had to touch and smell and listen to the cacophony of crowds in the High Street market. Anything more real than those foreign handwritten pages.

She headed for a touristy tearoom, the *Galatia*, and ordered an espresso and a scone. While waiting at the table for her order to come, she realized she couldn't stomach the intrusion and small talk of other tourists after all. She flung some pound notes on the table and left before her order arrived.

The typical High Street bedlam heightened her breath to shallow gasps. She wasn't finding what she needed to calm her disorientation. Turning around, she walked down another lane. Her lack of direction found her striding toward the abbey with a sudden compulsion, strong in her gut, to be amidst its ruins.

A young woman in her late teens, a museum attendant Sophie hadn't met before, was at the entrance gate. When she saw Sophie approach, she smiled brightly and said, "We're closing in a few moments, miss," her voice sounding, to Sophie's ears, a few octaves above chipper.

Sophie rolled her eyes and muttered under her breath, "Dial down the perky." She pulled her entrance pass out of her purse and flashed it at the attendant. "Please. I'm the journalist writing the piece on the abbey's history. I won't be long."

The attendant hesitated and looked over her shoulder toward the museum. "I'm sorry. Mrs. Henderson says I'm to let no one in after hours."

An older man in dirt-smudged dungarees stood up from where he was kneeling, beside rows of daffodils planted just inside the entrance gate. He laid down his trowel and pulled off his gardening gloves. Sophie recognized him instantly. His eyes had that unusual gleam she'd noticed the evening prior when they'd met.

"Barry, hello there." She gave him a sincere smile. She liked Daniel's uncle-in-law.

Barry nodded at her, his face crinkling into a kind smile. "It's okay, Beth. This is the museum's journalist, Sophie Morrison. Mrs. Henderson won't mind her being inside for a few moments. I'll take care of it."

"If you say so, I suppose that's okay then." Beth let Sophie inside the abbey entrance, closing the gate behind her. "As long as Mrs. Henderson won't mind," she added, her expression once again bright. She spun on her heels and darted back into the gift shop.

"Thank you, Barry. As I said, I won't be long," Sophie said.

"That's just fine; take your time. What Mrs. Henderson doesn't know won't hurt her," Barry replied, and winked.

Sophie chuckled at his irreverent manner. Now she knew why she liked him. She lingered to admire the blooming primroses, pansies, and violets. Barry obviously had a prolific green thumb.

"You all right, lass?" He asked, scrutinizing her. "A bit pale, I'd say."

As if to debate the pale color, she felt heat rise up her neck, and cursed how her blush could so easily give her away. "Yes. No. I mean, yes, I'm fine. Really." Hastily she put on her practiced, steady professional face. It wouldn't do to let anyone know she was falling to pieces.

"Oh, nearly forgot this." Barry picked up a small bouquet of flowers and greenery sitting next to his gardening tools. Offering it to her with an enigmatic smile, she took it, holding it up to her nose and sniffing. She recognized the sharp scent of rosemary.

"They're lovely. But what's this for, Barry?"

"I find flowers always help me when I'm confused."

What? How did he know? The bouquet had two other flowers tied together at their stems. One bore small, white clusters, and the other fluttered with creamy-white, delicate petals that bowed low, touching their thin, long leaves. They were both dainty, charming.

"Rosemary for remembrance," he said.

Yes, she'd heard that before.

"The other is baby's breath. For everlasting love."

Before she could puzzle out the purpose of giving her everlasting love, he added, "And the creamy white is oats blossom. Stands for the witching soul of music."

"The witching soul of music?"

He shrugged his shoulders. "I saw how much the music last night upset you."

"Um, thank you, Barry," she mumbled.

How odd. Still, the flowers felt comforting in her hands.

He slowly pulled on his gardening gloves and said, "He's in the Mary Chapel." Then he turned and knelt beside the daffodils once more, giving them his focused attention.

"Who's in the Mary Chapel?" Sophie asked, then stopped. "Oh." He meant Daniel. Was that why she felt compelled to come to the abbey?

She flicked a glance over her shoulder, toward the chapel. Bouquet in hand, she left Barry to meet up with Daniel.

Barry shook his head as she left, and gazed across the abbey ruins. "Best you're gentle with these two," he admonished softly to no one in particular.

Sophie knew he hadn't meant her to hear him. She added this cryptic comment to the enigma of the confusing pages of writing she'd left in her room, along with Barry's weird comments about his bouquet. *Nothing makes sense.* She slowed her steps as she made her way toward the chapel, taking time to gather her thoughts and composure before seeing Daniel.

She would have preferred the expansive apple orchard or the cedar tree-lined abbey paths. But here she was. She squared her shoulders. *Okay, enough stalling. Best to confront whatever's happening to me.*

She trooped the rest of the way to the ruins of the Mary Chapel, her mind made up to tell Daniel about the perplexing pages. *He might be the only one who'll believe me.*

Chapter 21
The Isle of Avalon
Summer, 1535 C.E.

Marissa sprawled on the grassy mound beside the holy well of Avalon, its mists reflecting tiny rainbows in the sunshine. She tapped her foot against Ciara's, a friendly gesture that belied how long it had actually been since she and her twin had shown any display of sisterly affection. Shayla, sitting cross-legged beside them, bent forward and watched, her eyebrows arched. Ciara inched her foot away. Marissa sighed, missing the closeness the three of them once shared.

She believed Ciara suffered as she did over the loss of their special sisterly bond. Oh, she knew they still loved each other fiercely, but they had lost their shared mindreading communication, and there was no longer the same comforting ease to their camaraderie. Ever since Michael left. A full six summers ago.

Ringed in a semi-circle behind the three young women sat a group of younger students. Marissa listened as they giggled and whispered amongst themselves in their excitement to observe the day's lesson. Alianore and Vanora, seated in front of the group, clapped their hands lightly, bringing them all to attention.

Vanora spoke first. "Today we will talk about the upcoming Summer Solstice Celebrations. Summer is a time of fecundity both in nature and in the bodies of the young women who have started their bleeding cycles." She pointed to the younger girls. "You are here to begin learning about your role as a priestess in the ritual. For the future, when you are eighteen summers old, like these three." She pointed at the twins and their halfling friend. "And you three, as newly initiated priestesses, can help us teach today."

The younger girls, none of whom had experienced their first blood flow yet, tittered and looked around shyly. Marissa had heard these lessons since she was a young girl, like the ones who sat behind her, and could recite the teachings by memory. She rolled onto her side and leaned over the spring, running her fingers through the iron-tinged water. The spring burbled, its flow continuous since time immemorial, and its waters cool and clean.

At the head of the well, a gnarled hawthorn tree and an apple tree shaded them all from the noonday summer sun. Marissa breathed in the scent of their perpetually blooming white and pink blossoms, feeling the vibrancy of nature's fertility stirring her belly and blood—perfect for rousing the desire needed for the upcoming Solstice Ritual, when young men and women celebrated the mating rites of summer. Too bad her mind and heart weren't aligned with the greening vitality all around her. She'd always looked forward to participating in the mating rites for the first time, but they wouldn't be the same with anyone but Michael. And he wasn't here to participate. She looked down, fighting the longing that had only grown since he'd left Avalon, taking her heart with him. Now she shielded her sorrow with a veneer of prickly brusqueness. She couldn't help it. It was the best way she knew to protect her broken heart.

"Why is the well water tinted red?" Alianore asked the group, her voice soft like the breeze that rose up and crested the mound where the small group was assembled. The lessons always began this way, with this question. A question meant to honor and remind them of their community's source of wellbeing, the holy well they had revered since the first priestesses arrived in Avalon centuries ago, survivors of the demise of Atlantis.

She repeated the question, her eyes resting on Marissa. "Marissa, will you tell us?"

Marissa had learned about the Red Well the hard way, when she was taking her first baby steps and nearly tumbled headfirst into the wellspring. It had been Ciara's screams that alerted their mother, who'd turned her back for only an instant. It was Vanora who'd promptly lifted the young Marissa up and out of danger.

She answered the question by rote. "The red color is from the minerals. But in Avalon, it is the blood of the Mother, emerging from the underworld to nourish our body and soul."

"And? What else?" Vanora piped in. Their tutor wasn't really paying close attention. Her focus was on mending her dark blue, silken stole, the beaded one she wore during ceremonies.

Marissa had an irrational urge to roll her eyes at the Elder, but she was eighteen summers old now, too old for that sort of behavior. Still, Vanora's constant patronizing tone wore on her nerves. She knew her Elder had her best interests at heart, intending to properly groom her to one day fill Alianore's shoes. But still. She sat up and rolled her head side to side to ease the ever-present tension that burrowed in her shoulders since Michael's departure from Avalon. She reminded herself to focus. She must act responsibly and prove herself proficient in priestess lore, ready and eager to one day be a leader.

She answered as was expected. "The water is used for healing, as well as for scrying so we can see into the future."

Vanora looked up from her stitching. "Scrying is not only to see the future. It is to read the actions of others in the present as well."

"Of course it is," Marissa snapped.

"Marissa, tame your temper when speaking to an Elder," her mother scolded.

"Yes, Mother. Forgive me, Vanora. I confess to feeling anxious about the upcoming ceremony." She offered her hands, palm up, to Vanora.

Her tutor nodded acceptance to the apology. "What other magical underpinnings does our holy Red Well have? Shayla?"

Shayla's head jerked up. *Preoccupied again*, Marissa thought. She'd never known another priestess to daydream as much as her friend.

"Umm . . . all blood and all tears shed on earth flow into the Underworld River of blood and tears. We see them above ground as the red and white springs of Avalon."

"Good . . ." Vanora said. Her voice droned on in further instruction about using the waters for scrying.

Marissa turned her attention back to thoughts of Michael. She certainly knew the purpose of scrying well, and not only because she had been formally initiated into the arts of seership one summer ago. How many times had she poured the holy water into her shell bowl and gazed into the shimmering fluid, setting her intent to learn of Michael's whereabouts. She'd even knelt down on all fours next to the spring, scrutinizing its watery depths, begging the Goddess for some sign of his return. But in six years she had not been privy to any such information. No images appeared to show her where Michael was or how he was doing. It baffled her. It was almost as if something was blocking her watchful eye. Some sort of obstruction she couldn't discern or move beyond.

All she saw when scrying were the orange and yellow flames from her previous dream. That same vision from six years ago when Michael had been recuperating in Elyn's healing lodge. The one in which he disappeared amidst the fiery wake. Although she never spoke of the vision again once Michael left, it still held her in fear's clutch. What did it mean? Was he all right? Whenever the image broke into her awareness, her gut churned and her breath caught in her chest. But she had no way to help him if she couldn't find him.

She blamed herself. She wished she had listened to Ciara, who begged her to bid him goodbye when it came time for him to leave Avalon. But back then she was still angry with her sister, even angrier with Michael, thinking him to be misleading both of them by pairing up with Ciara behind her back. Despite all they'd promised to each other that day in the oak grove. More than anger, she suffered the loss of him. Her young heart had fervently believed the vow they had spoken to each other. To be together one day. She still cherished that vow and held it in her heart.

Vanora interrupted the lesson and lifted the robe she was working on to show the girls. "You will decorate your robes like this," she said, pointing to the lapis blue beads, silver embroidery, and tiny shells she had fastened onto her own mantle. "Naturally, everyone's will turn out a bit differently. You will be creating your own patterns, working beads and shells into your robe, and then invoking the magical properties of each gem and stone through prayer and chant."

Marissa absently nodded her head. She had already completed her robe. Royal blue silk, with her chosen gemstones beaded onto the material as well as sown into its seams. Rose quartz to open the heart, the foundation for the holy rites. Garnet to enhance the pleasure of physical lovemaking and boost fertility. And calcite to connect it all to the Goddess, for passion was one of Her sacred gifts for the Solstice.

She swallowed back the unbidden images that rose up in her mind of sharing the rite with Michael. He wasn't here, and it only hurt more to imagine him so. She questioned his promises to her. Why hadn't he returned to her? But she never doubted the fledgling feelings he'd catalyzed in her. The feelings she'd nurtured in the silence of her heart, away from the curious questions of her mother, or the sorrowed look in her sister's eyes when she thought no one was looking. Despite her blank scrying bowl, Marissa held onto the hope that dangled before her, with iridescent wings as beautiful, and fragile, as the dragonflies that graced the mound she sat upon now. She would be with Michael again one day. No. She *must* be with him in the future.

Marissa straightened her spine and curled her legs beneath her tunic. "I'm sorry, Vanora. I suppose my mind is elsewhere."

Alianore and Vanora exchanged glances.

"You've already apologized, Marissa." Alianore's brows creased again in what seemed ever-present worry as she considered her daughter.

Ciara piped in. "We're all preoccupied, Mother. With Summer Solstice coming up and knowing we're to participate in the rituals for the first time."

Shayla pulled her knees up to her chest and rested her chin on them. Her long graceful arms wrapped around her legs.

Alianore turned to Shayla. "Are you not looking forward to the ceremony?"

"I . . . it's just . . ." Shayla balked.

"You want to mate with someone of the Faery Realm, don't you?" Ciara reached out and patted her friend's back.

Alianore smiled. "Well, there's nothing wrong with that, Shayla. Priestesses can join with whomever they wish. You know very well that's how you came about, my dear."

"Our Goddess simply wishes you to embody Her in the ceremony," Vanora added. "As long as you fulfill your ceremonial role to evoke the experience of Her within your lover, then you've accomplished your duties as a priestess. No matter whom you choose, we are all Her children. Faery or human, we all carry Her divinity inside us." She paused. "Although, I must say, I haven't heard of many Faery of late in the Solstice ceremonies. They're rather unpredictable, aren't they?"

Marissa frowned when she saw Shayla's expression fall. Vanora could really be tactless.

Ciara jumped in. "Our Faery cousins will be present, you'll see." She scooted closer to her friend.

"Well, in my youth, young priestesses awaiting their first sacred mating were much more enthused than the three of you," Vanora chided.

Ciara chewed on her lip and Marissa stared at the gurgling wellspring.

"We *are* eager for our duty. And excited. Really we are," Ciara said, as a faint blush spread across her cheeks.

Vanora continued. "I would have thought you three would be more excited. Especially you, Marissa. You are always so keen and curious to be involved in the world outside Avalon. And Ciara, I know you're concerned about the dangers in the world of man, but be assured, it's safe to cross the veils to participate on this one day of the Solstice rituals."

Marissa closed her eyes and sighed. Vanora was trying to be reassuring, but she was not helping things.

Vanora persisted for the sake of the younger girls present, their bright faces eager, all looking forward to the day when they would have their own opportunity to partake in the Summer Solstice Rites. "This is the one day priestesses are protected when they venture outside our misty borders," she told the girls. "The abbey will turn a deaf ear and blind eye to the celebrations because they know the importance of local tradition. They know which holy days to bend to their way and which ones to leave alone. There will be no interference from them. The monks won't even realize you are priestesses of Avalon, although the local folk will likely know."

One of the younger girls, timid Leesa, raised a hesitant hand. Vanora nodded for her to speak.

"Why will they need to be cautious then?" she asked, pointing to the three older initiates.

"It is wise not to flaunt our priestesshood. While our ways are tolerated during these local festivals for the sake of peace, they are not accepted in general. We've always warned you that priestesses may be feared and demonized." Vanora turned to the three older girls. "You three are to blend in with the other maidens from the local villages who will also be celebrating and looking for their evening's mate. Don't stand out, don't get into trouble." She raised her eyebrows at them.

Alianore had been watching her daughters and their halfling friend. "My daughters three, we've prepared you well. I don't think this talk of caution is what troubles you." She waited for an answer, and when none came, she continued. "Simply choose a lover to revere the fecundity of the summer, the abundant gifts of the Goddess. This is not the same as picking a life mate or even handfasting."

Marissa's insides clenched. How did her mother read her thoughts so well? Alianore's gaze caught each of the girls in turn, settling on Marissa. Marissa wondered how she could voice her yearning for Michael in the Solstice Ritual, but also as her chosen life mate. Vanora interrupted her thoughts, her eyes back on her sewing.

"Marissa, please teach our young pupils about the role of a priestess in the Solstice Rite."

Marissa swallowed her sadness to speak. "We are the ones who must keep the Goddess alive amongst men. One way we do this is to initiate the village boys of age into sacred lovemaking. For us, it is always and foremost honoring the Goddess, the Creatrix of all living things. It is about embodying Her. The Solstice celebration also has practical purpose. Because we are charged with carrying on our lineage, we need the seed of men to grow in our wombs."

Forcing her tone to be jovial, Vanora added, "May you three bear the fruits of your unions two weeks hence."

Marissa knew Vanora meant to bless the possibility of joy and ultimately, pregnancy. For her, there was only heaviness in her chest, the yearning in her belly. She would go through with her ceremonial duty, but she wasn't sure how her heart would bear her grief, for the sacred ceremony wouldn't feel complete with anyone other than Michael.

Chapter 22
The Isle of Avalon
1535 C.E.

The Solstice lesson ended while the sun still held sway in a cloudless afternoon sky. Marissa sighed, struggling with the flood of memories about Michael, memories that only worsened the heartache.

Vanora gestured for the group to follow her. "Come now. There's tea and honey cakes in the main lodge for everyone."

The younger students eagerly rose and dashed off to see who could reach the hall first. Marissa remained seated.

"I'd like to stay here by the well a while longer," she announced. She wanted to be alone, tap into the wellspring's sustenance, soothe her sorrow, and perhaps scry one more time before the rituals. Catching a glimpse of anything at all would be a balm to her heart.

Shayla shrugged her shoulders and slipped her arm through Ciara's. Ciara glanced back at her twin, her eyes questioning, but she turned and they left. Only Vanora and her mother lingered.

Alianore put a hand on Vanora's shoulder. "Go on ahead. I will only be a moment."

Marissa contemplated the wellspring's bubbling red waters, waiting for her mother to leave. Instead, Alianore eased back down onto the grass with her usual grace. At first they didn't speak. Her mother let the silence stretch comfortably, until Marissa finally looked up from her well-gazing. In the distance, a crane took flight from Avalon's lake. It rose in a stately arc, its bugling call fading as it flew higher.

Alianore spoke softly. "The crane moves comfortably between water, earth, and sky. A good lesson from the Goddess."

Marissa didn't want another lesson just now. Her mother studied her until she finally met her patient eyes.

"Is this about Michael?" Alianore asked.

Marissa nodded, not bothering to stop the tears that began to fall. She found she needed her mother's comfort after all. Alianore leaned over and gathered her daughter in her arms, just as she'd done when she was a child. She stroked her hair and waited until her tears ran dry. Marissa sniffled, and hugged her mother tightly before she pulled away.

"Will this ache ever go away?" Marissa asked.

Alianore's expression was filled with compassion. "You are my beloved daughter. I would like to tell you it will go away, even take the pain for you. But I cannot, or I would be telling a lie."

"What am I to do then?" Marissa pleaded. "Six years! No contact, no messages. Maybe he has forgotten about me."

Alianore shook her head. "You've scried for him?"

"I see nothing."

"We do not know what is happening with Michael We can only guess. But there is one thing you must do, my child."

"What's that?" Marissa asked eagerly.

"You must keep your heart open. Amidst all your hurt, frustration, and your sorrow, you must do this one thing above all."

Crestfallen, Marissa sighed. She'd hoped for something more practical and direct. "Great. I don't see how that's going to bring him back to me." She immediately felt sorry for her caustic remark.

Alianore sat quietly, letting Marissa feel her remorse.

"I'm sorry for being abrupt with you just now, Mother."

"I know."

Marissa sat up straight. "All right. I'm listening. I'm to keep my heart open."

"And do it even when you feel like you do not want to. Especially then."

"It's hard."

"Yes. But if you do not, you will end up like Ciara, with her heart beginning to coil tight. Unable to fully receive the love in her life."

Marissa felt a fresh pang of old guilt. She clasped her hands tightly together on her lap. "If I hadn't coaxed Ciara to go to the Faery Realm, her heart wouldn't have been cursed."

Alianore lifted Marissa's chin with her finger. "It is true, the Faery curse could have indeed been avoided. That was your part. But the curse did not impose anything on Ciara that was not already a seed germinating within her. It only brought forth that which had potential. A weakness of sorts."

Marissa felt a tiny crack in the hardened brick of guilt that had always weighed heavily in her stomach since their Faery misadventure. Could it be true? She'd never allowed herself to consider what her mother was saying. Her own stubborn impulsivity wasn't given to her by the Faery Lady Ravenna. It had always dwelled within her. And Shayla's longing for the Faery Realm? That, too, was something Shayla harbored long before the Faery curse.

Marissa nodded slowly. "The curse didn't create the suffering." She paused. "Even if that's true, it did make things worse. It magnified our weaknesses."

"Marissa, it threw light on your weaknesses and forced you to face them head on. How you face them, what you do with the curse, is entirely within your free will. Being consumed with guilt has prevented you from seeing the larger and deeper truths."

"Why didn't you tell me this long ago? Make me understand it. Save me from my guilt?" Accusation edged Marissa's words.

Alianore tenderly put a hand on her daughter's arm. "I have attempted to do so many times. It is only now that you seem ready to hear it and take it in."

Marissa's anger slowly dissolved. It was not her mother's fault, or responsibility, to undo what she had brought upon herself.

Alianore continued, gentle yet firm. "Yes, it is true you acted rashly by convincing Ciara and Shayla to enter the Faery Realm with you. But the facts and the truth of the matter are two different things, my daughter."

Marissa's brow furrowed with confusion.

"There are deeper and larger hidden forces at play in our lives, my dear. It is our job to listen to the voice of our intuition and align with these divine forces. Intuition will always guide you to the better course of action and the most loving way to respond to your challenges."

Marissa sighed. "Will I ever be as wise as you?"

Alianore gave her a faint smile and squeezed her arm. "You are my strong daughter. If you apply yourself as I have taught you, there will come a time when you will be stronger and more powerful than perhaps any of us."

Marissa inhaled sharply, surprised. "I don't feel that way."

"Rely on your strength. And trust in the Goddess."

Marissa kept silent for a few moments, eyes once more riveted to the wellspring's flow. There was so much to learn. So much she had to accomplish and become before she could ever be the High Priestess she needed to be. She chewed on her lip, her thoughts returning once more to her sister.

"Ciara was always so open and loving. I miss that in her."

"Your sister is still kindhearted to others, especially in the healing wards. I have faith she will find her way back to her heart in her personal relationships and open it once more. That is why I give you warning not to close off yours. It is much harder to open again once it is shut tight. And it is only through an open heart that you can truly love, that you can feel your intuition, that you can hear the voice of the Goddess." Alianore leaned over and kissed Marissa on the top of her head.

"I will leave you to your thoughts now," she said, smoothing out her robes.

"Mother?"

Alianore arched her brow, waiting.

Marissa cleared her throat. "I'll try my best."

Alianore rose. "Simply do," she said, and left.

Marissa lay back in the grass beside the well, watching the clouds overhead, listening to the robin's birdsong and the well water gurgling beside her. She let the afternoon drift by, absorbing what her mother had said, thinking about this new perspective, and allowing it to take root in her thoughts. She began to feel guilt's harsh edges soften within her. She adopted her mother's sagacity, and when her guilt tried to revive itself, she returned to her heart. Focusing on keeping her heart open, she let herself feel the love there for her mother, for Ciara and Shayla, for all those in her priestess community, again and again. And when she thought of Michael, and felt the hollow ache of missing him, she placed her sorrow upon the altar of her heart. Felt her grief through her heart's alchemical vessel. Surrendered her heart to the heart of the Goddess. She put her hand over her chest to help keep her attention there, for the sadness could so easily pull her back into its own isolated fissure. She intentionally practiced the Path of Love.

When she finally sat up and stretched, the sun was curving toward the horizon, the afternoon sky heading toward dusk. The apple and the hawthorn tree at the head of the wellspring glowed with twilight's tinges of muted green and gold. Twilight, not truly day nor night, was when the veils between the worlds of the seen and unseen were thin. *The perfect interval to scry one last time before the Summer Solstice Rites*, she thought. Maybe this time when she practiced the art of seership she might finally find Michael.

Feeling hopeful, she gripped the silver cup that always lay beside the Red Well and dipped it into the waters. Bringing it to her lips, she drank deeply. The cool water slid down her throat. Satiating. She let the vital earthly blood of the Goddess nurture her, body and soul. She remembered that Michael's lips had touched this very same cup when he'd first entered Avalon to be healed. The recollection wrenched her out of her heart and dropped her into a pit of sadness and longing.

She took a deep breath and pulled her sadness back into her heart space. Her sorrow didn't go away. But it was met, and held, within her heart. It was a hard balancing act. She did it anyway. Over and over until she could remain there even a bit longer, and eventually persevere without wavering.

When the tide of her grief ebbed, she went to work, calling on all her abilities as an initiated prophetess. Sitting on her knees, she extended her arms and invoked the seven directions. To her right and her left, before and behind her, above and below her. The flow of the directions' elemental powers—air in the East, fire in the South, water in the West, and earth in the North—rose and interwove in a surge of power that made her body tingle and her hands heat. She placed her hands on her heart, moved them down to her belly, and breathed into her womb-space. Her sacred heart-flame flared and arced into her belly, kindling the embers of power there. With her next breath, she connected her womb-space to the center of the earth to anchor and stabilize her.

Aligned with heart, belly, breath, and womb, she began to scry. With eyes half-lidded and gaze unfocused, she used her inner eye to peer into the wellspring. The red-tinged water burbled and stilled, swirled, and stilled again. In the moment of stillness, Marissa leaned further in. She set her intention. *Find Michael*. She waited. Expecting nothing and hoping for everything.

His face did not appear in the smooth waters. Disappointment edged its way into her thoughts. She breathed into her heart to keep her hope alive. The air grew charged around her. The breeze caressed her cheek. She inhaled the surrounding scent of roses and apple blossoms, and waited some more. Finally, the water stirred and rippled with flashes of silver and blue. Within the rippling water, Marissa saw the Goddess's face appear in an ocean of nighttime stars. A beautiful face, eyes bright with compassion, dark hair tipped with more stars. Her blue mantle cupped the night sky.

"You came to me," Marissa cried, her devotion undulating through her body.

"My daughter." The Goddess breathed out words that sang the melody of the heavens above and percussed the rhythm of the earth's heartbeat below.

"I am yours," Marissa said. Exquisite peace suffused her mind.

The Goddess smiled. It warmed Marissa's soul, sparking the flame of sacred love in her heart anew.

The Goddess spoke. "I have heard your cries of sorrow. I know what you seek. But I will show you something you *need* instead."

The soft breeze grew into a blustery wind, whipping Marissa's hair behind her. The spring water churned. Wrapped in the protective blanket of the Goddess's love, Marissa's stomach lurched as she was transported into a vision. This time, instead of just seeing the images in the water, she became a part of them. She saw and felt herself standing on the shore of the ever-eternal ocean, her arms raised high.

A sea of stars rode the night sky. The Goddess gathered them into a pitcher and poured them into the watery ocean on the earth below. The stars streamed steadily along the glowing path from the Goddess's night sky womb into Her watery earthly womb. When the stars mixed and merged with the ocean water, they solidified, finding form. From this alchemy emerged a huge cauldron, rising from the ocean waters to hover above the waves.

Marissa recognized the cauldron at once from the ancient creation stories she'd listened to since she was a child. "The perennial womb bowl of creation," she whispered, mesmerized.

With a flash of silver and blue, the large cauldron refashioned itself into a small wooden bowl. The Goddess reached down, plucked the bowl from the ocean waves, and set it on the shore beside Marissa.

Then the Goddess spoke again, her voice traveling along a silver star beam and booming with power. "I am Creatress. From my womb all things are born and reborn anew."

The words resonated through Marissa's blood, the life-flow waters within her body. The sound stirred the ethereal waters of her soul and seeped into her bones.

I am deep within all that I create.
I am divinity within matter.
I flow.
I enliven.
I generate.
I restore.
I am embodied love.
I am collaboration.
I am intuition.
I am harmony.
If anyone calls for Me, I will come.

The bowl next to Marissa began to shine bright silver, akin to the starlight from which it was created. The Goddess spoke again, Her words ringing the song of a thousand stars.

I am the Creation Cauldron
This bowl has forever been My symbol.
Symbol of My Sky womb,
My Earth womb,
My Ocean womb,
Women's womb.
My birthing womb.
Symbol of hope.
Of love.
Of holy creation.
One day to once again be known and revered by the world.

Marissa felt tears stream down her cheeks. The beauty and power emanating from the bowl ignited her from within.

"I do not show you your beloved Michael. But I show you your shared destiny with him. A destiny in service to Me."

Resting on the sand, the bowl blazed with silver flame. Alchemy of star and sea. When the flame died down, what remained was a simple wooden bowl, ancient symbol of the Goddess of the Stars and the Sea and reliquary of her power.

Marissa had always known she and Michael shared a mysterious destiny, but this magnificent and primordial bowl left her confused. "Please! What does this Creation Bowl have to do with our destiny?"

When the Goddess answered, the blue and silver swirls surrounding Marissa swelled, then lapped at her feet like ocean waves.

"Humankind once knew and celebrated Me. My ways, the Path of the Sacred Heart, was honored." Her voice echoed a millennia of mourning for the loss of humankind's love.

"We honor you as such here in Avalon."

"Avalon upholds my ways. The world of man does not. They no longer recognize me."

Marissa knew this to be true. It had been so since long before her ancestor, the High Priestess Rhianna, veiled Avalon, shielding it from a world that no longer revered the Goddess.

The Goddess's tears fell like rain. "Humankind does not know me. I am shunned, vilified, and My ways disparaged. But it is My ways that can heal all strife and end all suffering. There will come a time when man's destructive, divisive, domineering actions will bring ruin to My beautiful earth, unless the world of man returns to Me and lives by the Path of the Sacred Heart."

Marissa felt a second lurching sensation in her stomach. She found herself funneled out of the eternal ocean shore. Her body shunted back beside the Red Well, where she knelt on her hands and knees in the grass. She was nauseated by the sudden shift but leaned over and examined the well water anyway. Images from the world of man flashed in quick succession. She gasped and covered her mouth to stifle a cry.

Men on horses fighting. Blood, carnage, death, more fighting.

Was this Michael's battle? She shook her head. No, she didn't see him in the image. The men in this vision were dressed in unfamiliar garb. More scenes followed, appearing with dizzying speed.

A king's crown sat upon one man's head, a stout man with red hair and dangling jowls, followed by another king and yet another, in a swift series of crownings and deaths, crownings and deaths. Clouds sped across the sky. The sun rose and set. The landscape changed. Villages, towns, and cities grew in size and scope and number of people, again dressed in peculiar manners. What didn't change were the images of men fighting and shedding blood. Enmity, violence, and corruption permeated every image, highlighted by blackened hearts that ignored the suffering of the poor and ill who cried for mercy. In the next vision, the earth shook, then cracked open, and cities fell. The land was raped asunder by men operating mechanical devices Marissa had never before seen. She cried out, not wanting to see more. But further images loomed in watery spectacle. Animals tormented and dying. Razed, leveled land where trees once breathed in greening vitality. Oceans and rivers, life-blood of the world, grey and dead, toxic.

Marissa fought to retain her scrying stance, gulping in deep breaths. Her heart bled tears for the suffering shown in the visions racing before her eyes. Suddenly the vision of earthly turmoil stopped. It was replaced by the image of the simple wooden Creation Bowl.

The Goddess spoke again. "The fate of the world, the peace of man, relies upon the way of the heart. You are to safeguard this bowl in the world of man. It is a symbol of renewed hope and a reminder of My ways. It is a vessel of mystical power whose very presence will catalyze this knowing in humankind. It will quicken the Path of the Heart—when the time is right."

Marissa frantically looked around her. She had last seen the bowl beside the ever-eternal ocean in the first part of the vision. "Where's the bowl now?"

"It is destined to come into your possession."

More questions came out in a tumble. "How do I safeguard it? When is the right time?"

The Goddess answered with golden patience. "The time is not yet ripe. Safeguard my Creation Bowl for the future, for the era when humankind will be open and willing to receive My love and My help."

Marissa sat back on her heels, reeling with the weight of what was being asked of her. "Why Michael and I? Why is this *our* shared destiny?"

The Goddess's words whispered on the wind. "You were born for this. As was Michael. This is a merging of you who revere me in Avalon, in unity with him from the world of man. Michael holds the seed of potential of what can be when My ways are followed. The two of you, a perfect blend."

Marissa's heart raced. "But I haven't seen Michael in years. Does this mean he'll return?"

The blue and silver ephemeral swirls began to fade. The wind died down. Birdsong once again trilled.

"Don't go. I have so many questions!" Marissa cried.

"This is all you *can* understand for now. Follow My path. The Path of the Sacred Heart. You will discover the answers and all that you seek on this path." The Goddess's voice faded, the visions dissolved, the power ebbed. The Red Well burbled as normal in the now cool night air. Marissa rubbed her arms with the chill and wrapped her cloak around herself. She held her arms around her middle to stop from quivering after the influx of such powerful energy. Questions assailed her, but she was unable to think clearly. So tired. She curled on her side on the soft grass. The last thing she saw before she fell into a deep, dreamless sleep was the Goddess's sky womb, Her deep blue mantle holding the ocean of silver stars.

Chapter 23

Mountain Manor, Wales
Summer, Anno Domini 1535

Michael planted the tip of his sword into the dry earth and leaned into it. He was panting heavily from training, with his older brother Roger as his opponent. The heat of midsummer's noonday sun added to his efforts, layering a sheen of sweat across his brow and down his back. He was sure his father was watching, either from the solar window or the great hall of their huge country residence. He didn't mind, really, though his father had exacting standards when it came to battle skills, and he was sure his abilities were currently being gauged. He had learned the art of swordplay from his brother and the other Knights under his father's command, those loyal to the family of Gerard de Boulle.

"Your parry is well done, Michael," his brother said.

Roger was well trained and experienced, and showed little exertion. His brown hair still in place, unlike Michael's, and not a drop of sweat upon him. "Next time, try blocking more like this." He hoisted his sword and raised his right arm to his side. "This will give you momentum."

Their younger brother Philip took the opportunity of Michael's distraction to knee him in the calf, causing Michael to drop like a sack of grain. Philip's good nature took the sting out of his antics, and Michael couldn't help but laugh. He sprung up and charged his lithe, muscular brother, whereupon they fell to wrestle in the dry dirt of the training field.

Roger's tone brought them up sharp. "This is no time for your folly. You act like undisciplined stable boys, not the grown sons of our father and liege."

Still laughing, Michael freed his hold pinning Philip to the ground. "Oh, come now, Roger. You used to like to tussle with us. When did you become so serious?"

Their older brother's mouth set in a stern line. Michael wondered at the source of his brother's bad mood. Roger was always the more serious one, often quiet and reserved, but not prone to flare in temper or be ill-natured. Today he wasn't himself.

He hefted Michael's sword from where it pierced the ground. "I grew serious when you turned eighteen summers, when Father needed us to be strong enough, cunning enough, to protect our lands here and abroad," he said with disapproval.

"But Father maintains his own retinue of soldiers," Philip interjected.

"That's right. No paid mercenaries for him. Loyal knights all," Michael added. "So, why rebuke us?"

"While we may live in the West Country, that doesn't mean we don't feel the English Crown's oppression, taking its toll on us and our freedoms. We need to be fighting ready. That includes preparing you two."

Michael sensed something more underneath the warning. He shrugged, figuring Roger would tell them in his own time.

Philip deflected the scolding with geniality. "You're quite right, big brother. We shame our father if we don't train well, but Michael will be knighted within a few years. He has a squire of his own. I'm not too far behind him. Not a small feat for men of our youth." He smiled cheerily, then clasped Michael's forearm and offered to help hoist him off the ground. Michael consented to the friendly gesture and stood.

Roger's countenance did not change with his brother's affable efforts. "Philip, you're too easygoing to be a cunning soldier right now. A serious skirmish or two will cure you of that. You're both still inexperienced. But, Michael, it is you I'm concerned about. Ever since you were lost six summers ago . . ."

Michael stuck his palm forward to stop Roger. "No. We won't discuss that again. Why do you insist on bringing it up? I was returned home, and I'm fully recovered. Hale and whole. A winter cough now and then is common enough amongst the healthiest of us."

"It's not a winter cough I concern myself with." Roger frowned. "Though the two of you can hardly make it through a winter without falling ill since you can't remember to properly wrap your feet inside your boots."

"You sound like mother used to, as well meaning as she was. May she rest in peace." Michael lowered his head and made the sign of the cross in respect. "Still, why such fussing over me? Stop it."

Roger pounded his fist on his thigh, startling Michael. "You become so easily distracted from your duties as second born."

"What! I've done everything you and Father have asked. I've honed my battle skills. I practice every single day."

The rage Michael kept hidden flared. He had obediently acquiesced to his father's will and dutifully spent hours, nay, years, to become a skilled Knight to satisfy his father's wishes and gain his meager approval. Michael turned and punched the hay bale behind him, the one used earlier that morning for archery practice.

"Keep your temper," Roger warned.

"No! I've had enough." Michael's blue eyes turned dark as his mood swiftly soured. His brother might have something on his mind, but he'd gone too far. "I've learned how to use a sword. I've learned how to shoot an arrow true." His muscles tensed as his anger rose. "I've even learned to fire that damned hand culverin, though I swear shooting it is more of a danger to me than to any poor foe. I have the respect of our men-at-arms. What more do you want of me? Has Father set you up to badger me? If he's not pleased with me, he can tell me so himself."

Roger's aggravated gaze raked over Michael. "This has nothing to do with Father. It's about your role as heir presumptive. You're second in line after me to inherit all of this." He spread his arms to encompass their surrounding vista. "Our lands. Mountain Manor."

Michael slowly swiveled his head to take in the dominion so familiar to him. Rugged green mountains reigned over the vale where their estate lay. Oak, ash, and pine woodlands ringed a meadow dotted with bluebells and yellow primroses. Sparkling, clear streams meandered in the shadow of the foothills. His anger could not dampen familial pride. The fierce, independent nature of the Welsh was ingrained in his family.

Their Welsh estates were bordered by England on their southern edge, giving the border regions the nickname, the Marchlands. The property had been granted to their ancestor, the renowned knight Jacques de Boulle, thirty years after the conquest of the Norman King William in 1066. It had been held honorably by the de Boulle family ever since. Michael's elite Norman line mixed with Welsh nobility over the centuries, gradually becoming more Welsh in nature and bearing.

Roger continued. "You need to appreciate all that our ancestors built, all that our father has maintained. And learn how to manage it."

"Undoubtedly, I appreciate it," Michael snapped. Managing it all was another matter altogether.

In his mind's eye, Michael heard his aged tutor lecturing him in his rough voice, concern burning in his eyes. *"You need to learn about the political tides of change, Michael. You have the mind for it. Manor lords all over England have been substituting tenant farming for feudal serfdom for many years now. Tenant farmers have no fighting responsibility to their lord the way a knight given land for his services does. And now, knights of loyalty are replaced with paid professional soldiers. All you have to do is listen to your father's messengers. Sit at his council table."*

His tutor, Master Ralph, may have been aged, but he was learned, with a keen intellect, discerning ears, and piercing eyes that observed everything. He never missed a bard's revealing songs in the manor hall, or the political rumors that filtered through to Mountain Manor. He infused all the news with his sharp ability to put snippets together to form a picture of the out-side forces that might affect his liege and his liege's offspring. His insights were one of the reasons he had been retained in the de Boulle's service for so long.

Emboldened by his outrage at Roger's remarks and his smoldering anger toward his father, impassioned by his beliefs, and ever one to debate, Michael spoke his mind. Things he'd been ruminating over since he was old enough to reason and discuss matters with his tutor. "I appreciate my inheritance. But Father hangs on to an old way that will no longer serve us in the future. Master Ralph says there is a rise in trade, and money now holds more value than land holdings. There are peasant revolts. These things are happening all over England. Though England's upheavals affect us less here in the West Country, they will one day change how we live. They will change everything in Wales. Including here at our manor home."

Haughty with ancestral pride, Roger declared, "Nothing will change for us. Not for a long while at least. That may be true in England, but we are Welsh."

Michael sighed heavily. He would not give in. Not when he knew Master Ralph's perspective to be the more astute and sagacious. Influenced by his tutor's lectures about the rising tide of social change, he rose to the bait. "Master Ralph says to mind his words—the King's reach is still long. It will extend to everyone here in Wales eventually."

"Don't be so gloomy, Michael," Philip ribbed.

Michael groaned. "Not you, too! Master Ralph says we are to learn from history. Things are shifting."

Roger's voice grew impatient. "You misunderstand what I'm trying to tell you. This is about you, Michael. You've been dutiful enough, but you're distracted. Since your disappearance, you're often daydreaming like a girl. And neither you nor Philip has seen a serious skirmish yet. You're still untested."

Philip watched his brothers quietly, arms over his chest.

Michael's blue eyes turned steely. "Daydreaming like a girl? Trying to insult me now, Roger?"

"Nay. It's an observation. Even though you work toward it, I sense your heart's not in becoming a Knight."

Michael's irritation with his brother's foul mood didn't cloud the truth. While his father hounded him to embrace his duties as a Knight, his tutor had infused in him a love of books and study. He never wanted the life of Knighthood. He wanted . . . what did he want? Not this. Fighting wasn't in his blood. There was something else he wanted but couldn't quite reach, something that haunted his dreams. Besides, why was Roger being so antagonistic?

"I've done all that is required of me as second born. Besides, Master Ralph says the knighthood is dying. It's heaving its last breath." Challenge and dissent snuck into his tone. He took a step toward his brother, fists clenched.

"Wait," Philip broke in. "Michael is indeed a good soldier, and much better at bow and arrow than either of us. Don't you at least agree with that, Roger?"

The older two ignored Philip's conciliatory attempt and circled each other, glaring, fists at the ready. Michael's knuckles clenched tight with fury. Philip grabbed his arm to hold him back. Michael shook him off. But he reigned in his urge to punch his brother. Mainly because he wasn't sure if his anger was with Roger, or the truths Roger had laid bare about where his heart lay—in books, not the Knighthood.

In a sharp tone, Roger replied, "Lands will always need to be protected. The Knighthood is not dead. Not here on our father's estate. Da' will keep the old ways. His soldiers are faithful to him. He's their liege lord. They're loyal secondly to King Henry only because of their allegiance to our father. I intend to uphold the traditional ways as well. As should you. For Sir Jacques, our forbearer!"

Philip hovered beside Michael, waiting. Michael hesitated, clenching and unclenching his fists, watching Roger warily. He couldn't argue with Roger's ardent family loyalty, but Roger had insulted him unfairly. Daydreaming like a girl? Fie!

Fists still tightened, Michael called out, "Just what do you accuse me of, then, Roger?"

Roger took a step forward, pinning Michel with his fierce countenance. "This—you have to fully engage with your training and become an even better soldier than I am."

Michael arched his brow in surprise. "Better than you? Why?"

"You need to take your head out of your history and philosophy lessons, your Latin and Greek books. Your studies of such things should have ended when our tutor turned you over to me to train. You must keep perfecting your fighting skills. And you need to concentrate on the ledgers, accounts, and means of running our estates."

Though Roger had not hit him, Michael felt his brother's words punch him in his gut. How could he ever give up his cherished books, his learning?

"But clearly, those are the things you're endowed to perform, Roger," Philip said, stepping between his brothers. "Yes, Michael and I must train to protect Father's estate, but we leave these lordly matters you speak of to those who are meant to inherit such managerial responsibilities. Meaning you."

Roger raised his hands in the air, exasperated. "That's just it," he said, turning to Philip. "What if something were to happen? To me?"

"What? You're invincible," Philip exclaimed, his face ready to break into his usual smile despite the tension in the air.

"You still haven't answered me. Why do you insult me?" Michael asked, straining his muscles, ready to pounce.

"Because I never wanted this."

"Wanted what?" Philip asked.

Michael kept his fists at the ready, but pulled back a bit.

Roger raised his voice. His eyes shone wet, his mouth grim. "I'm the one who's taken care of you two, since Mother died and Father traveled, leaving us alone. Perhaps that's made me too protective now."

Michael slowly released his fists. He knew too well that even when their father was present, he was distant and withdrawn, or gruff and stubborn. Roger had indeed taken it upon himself to see to his and Philip's needs, the three of them forming a tight-knit bond. His anger deflated.

He placed a hand on Roger's shoulder. "Wait a minute. What are you saying?"

"I'm saying that father received a messenger this morning. From France." Roger rubbed his hands across his chin.

"When? I saw no messenger."

"Nor I," Philip said.

"You were in the study, Michael. And you, Philip, who knows where? In the barn with the milkmaid?"

Philip blushed. "Nothing happened. Yet, at least," he added, with a twinkle in his eye.

Roger sighed and continued. "The messenger brought news that a serious conflict has broken out in France. Our Uncle David's lands there are in danger. As well as father's lands that Uncle David oversees as Bailiff."

"Why is there conflict?"

"Does not Master Ralph teach you about social class conflicts and civil unrest in France as well as England?" There was a hint of sarcasm in Roger's voice.

"Stop your mockery and give us the news, brother," Michael said.

Roger nodded, his head lowered in defeat. He stepped between the two and hung his arms about his brother's shoulders, but his expression was forbidding. "The Protestants are uprising. Their civil unrest runs even more rampant in France than in England, or even here in Wales."

"What does that mean for us?" Michael asked.

"Father wants me to travel to France."

"You've always been a valiant soldier. Honorable. Why does that trouble you?"

Roger looked at them somberly. "I'm to take the two of you along."

Michael grew solemn. "So, we're to finally go to battle?"

Roger nodded. "To protect our interests there. As well as help protect Uncle David's." He gazed at his brothers with unguarded affection. "That's why I push you to train so hard now." He tightened his jaw, looked past his brothers to the distant mountain ranges. "I knew well you'd one day see battle. I'd hoped that day wouldn't be upon us so soon."

Michael felt a rush of affection and any remaining vestiges of anger dissolved. He exhaled softly. Despite Roger's accusations to the contrary, he had long ago resigned himself to his familial duties to Mountain Manor. But he had never in his eighteen years been tested as to his capabilities in executing his role as protector. Oh, he was loyal and grateful for the comfort of his life, but perhaps Roger was right. The time for daydreaming was over. There was no choice really. The realities of his responsibilities now suddenly lay like a heavy mantle across Michael's shoulders.

Chapter 24

Wales
Anno Domini 1535

The stables at Mountain Manor smelled of horse, straw, and dung. It was just after dawn, and the stalls hadn't been mucked out yet. Michael ignored the pungency and worked on tightening the rope binding his gear to his packhorse. He would be carrying his longbow and was glad for it. Its bow stave was strong, made of wild elm from the forests surrounding the estates. He collected the elm wood with his brothers two years ago, and had let it dry and season before it was fashioned into a bow. The French crossbows he'd likely encounter in their skirmish overseas would be slower and would not shoot the distance his Welsh longbow could. Or so his brother Roger informed him, having been to France once before, five years ago when he was twenty, and had been knighted on the battlefield.

Michael planned to also carry his two-handed sword by his side. His secondary weapons—spear, battle-axe, and mace—were wrapped and enclosed in the sturdy leather bags he was securing to his packs. The dagger his father gave him when he returned from his disappearance six years ago was housed in a sheath banded to his thigh. He wound rope around the sack carrying his hand culverin, much as he distrusted the damn long-barreled, lead bullet shooter. At least they didn't travel with their father's canon. It took nearly twenty horses to pull the thing. His uncle would likely have one or two at his disposal in France, but Michael was told it would not even be needed. This familial call to arms was to quell unrest, not fight a siege as they'd first thought.

Roger strode past, nodding his approval. "Well done, brother. A well-prepared soldier is a successful soldier."

Michael had heard his father say the same thing to his men in the days he still led them into battle. The words sprang as naturally to Roger's lips as they had to their father's. Roger moved on to supervise and check the progress of the other twelve men in the retinue when Philip caught Michael's eye.

In a low tone, Philip said, "I admire Roger. He deserves respect. But he's gotten so serious. Sometimes when he orders me around, all I remember is us rolling in the dirt, play-fighting as boys, and I stifle the urge to laugh like we did then."

"Aye. It's a different Roger now," Michael agreed.

Philip looked their brother's way. "I suppose responsibility does that. Well, not for me. I aim to be knighted, but I will never turn my smile into a perpetual frown like he's done."

Michael cuffed Philip in the arm and pointed to their packhorses. "We'd better get back to this—"

"—or there will be hell to pay," Philip finished for him.

Both grinned and returned to the task at hand. Michael hoisted a second leather satchel against the other side of his packhorse. It was old, its leather creased, but still in good shape. It had been his father's, given to him after he'd stopped participating in battle forays five years prior. Michael set about attaching it securely to his horse's saddle ring with a segment of twisted rope. He would stow medicines common for battlefield use inside the satchel. The local wise woman, Mistress Helen, would soon be arriving to provide said remedies, as she had done for the past forty years in service to the de Boulle family. His father did retain a proper physician and trusted the learned man to bleed and purge the ill. But according to his father, with the exception of amputation, it was the ways of the old woman that best treated battle wounds. Especially after the surgeon barber's amputation services. And more so in those "damned foreign lands," as his father referred to any domain outside Wales, where he believed one could not always count on help from unfamiliar medicinals.

The light touch of a hand upon Michael's arm startled him from his packing. True to form, Mistress Helen had hobbled over in good time for him to stow the items she brought him.

"Why do I never hear you approach?" he asked, grinning affectionately at the older woman.

Mistress Helen tucked a stray wisp of gray hair into her coif. She was never one to properly cover her linen cap with a hood, thus her piercing brown eyes and wrinkled skin, tanned from hours tending her gardens, stood out. Her knowing eyes appraised Michael now. She handed over the bag of medicines she had made ready.

"Go over their uses with me," she ordered.

"Once more? Why?" he complained.

"You may be our young lord, going off to yon' France to battle, but you are still a lad to me. A student of my skills." She clouted him lightly on the ear.

"Ouch," he yelped. "Enough. Before I need these herbals for myself!"

He couldn't hide his smile, despite Helen's stern manner. Taking the satchel from her, he leafed through the small pouches within. He squeezed each pouch to ensure it was full, then opened them one at a time.

The first pouch he inspected contained feather-like leaves and tiny white flowers.

"Yarrow," he recited.

"Correct. And what is it to be used for?"

"Prized to stop blood flow and heal wounds. This is the one Da' swears by."

Its application had staunched a deep arm laceration his Da' had obtained in his first battle raid. Mistress Helen nodded in curt approval.

The second pouch he checked held comfrey. He remembered finding its broad leaves along the riverbank that ran though the estates. "This one is to be used as a compress for fractures."

Then there was henbane, to be administered in cautious doses as an anesthetic in the case of—he shivered at the thought—the dreaded amputation. He ran his fingers over the bag containing the common garden hollyhock. Its pink and red flowers reduced fevers. He remembered well when he and his brothers, as well as many of the house staff and villagers, suffered from influenza during a wet, cold winter three years ago. While his father's doctor bled and purged the most severe sufferers, Michael was certain it was the old healer's ministrations of chicken broth with onion and garlic, and her tea containing hollyhock, honey, and a bit of mullein, that was most helpful in their recovery.

The last pouch contained a special formulation of Mistress Helen's. She had made Michael angelica tonic for his tendency toward lung chills. She had laughed when Michael told her his father's aged priest called the herb, 'The Root of the Holy Ghost.' Helen had scoffed, saying it was used long before the Holy Ghost set foot in Wales.

Clean linen cut in long strips for bandages was packed alongside the herbal pouches. There was plenty in the pouches for all fourteen men, and it was Michael's job to carry this portion of the group's supplies.

Philip watched the whole exchange, his back against the stable wall, arms crossed. "I've never understood why you're interested in all this," he said, pointing to the medicinals.

"Don't be rude," Michael scolded.

Philip glanced over at Mistress Helen. "No offense."

She ignored him.

He continued. "You've been obsessed with them since after you disappeared." Michael shrugged. "Doesn't matter. Someone has to know what to do with these. And we can't rely on your addled brain for that."

Philip head-locked Michael in the crook of his elbow. Michael jabbed him in the gut.

"We can't be seen roughhousing," Michael warned with a wide grin.

Philip released him just as Michael's destrier, Storm, neighed from his stall in the stables, calling for attention. The dusky-grey war steed stood head and shoulders over the packhorse Michael was loading. Storm was regal in bearing, as was his stud line that ran all the way back to his forefather, the magnificent charger, Wind. He offered Storm a conciliatory glance. When Storm's snorting didn't stop, he checked to see if Roger was watching and snuck a quick, affectionate pat to the steed's neck, worried his older brother would chastise him for getting distracted from his tasks.

"Sorry, boy. Patience. You'll have me with you soon," he whispered in his horse's ear.

He walked to the adjoining stall and gave another hasty, affectionate pat to his chestnut palfrey, his usual travel mount. Michael murmured that he'd be back soon, promising the horse a long ride across the meadows of Mountain Manor. Tradition and common sense dictated that he would normally ride long distances on the palfrey, saving his destrier's energy for the battlefield.

But for this journey, the palfrey was to be left behind, for ease of overseas travel.

When both horses had calmed, Michael resumed packing. Once satisfied his satchels were secure, he led Storm out of the stall and saddled him. Roger had authorized the village blacksmith to create new harness fittings and iron shoes for Storm, as well as for all the Knight's horses, as was befitting the wealth of the de Boulle's estates. Michael was glad for Roger's generous forethought—the fittings were critical for long travel and warfare from horseback, and their craftsmanship was of good quality.

The sun was just rising over the trees when all the men were finally outfitted and readied, their horses whinnying and prancing, as eager as the soldiers to be off. Michael's father arrived and stood at Roger's side, giving last minute instructions and advice. Once Gerard had personally spoken to each of his men, he strode over to his two younger sons. He was grey haired, his muscles no longer bulked as they once had, but he was still a forbidding presence to be reckoned with, as always.

He addressed the two young men brusquely. "You boys . . . ahem . . . men . . . listen to your brother. He's experienced, and if you follow his orders, as you should, you will come to no harm and will bring honor to Mountain Manor."

Gerard's eyes showed an unaccustomed measure of warmth. It surprised Michael.

"Now, off with you," He finished in a gruff voice, and slapped the rump of Philip's horse, setting it on its way.

He gave a sharp nod to Michael. "You as well." He spoke crisply. "I expect you to come back knighted, like your older brother. Be well, son."

Michael's eyes searched his father's. Gerard hadn't called him *son* since his mother had died in childbirth. She had been old for pregnancy, but had carried the babe to full term, though with some frailty. A difficult labor proved too arduous. Her death still haunted his father. Gerard's allotment of stoicism, as well as enthusiasm, had seemed to run out with the loss of his wife and stillborn son. It was soon thereafter that he stopped joining in battle raids and skirmishes, and turned the running of the estates over to Roger.

Once the soldiers were headed off in procession, the Lord de Boulle waved.

Philip pulled his horse alongside Michael's as they trotted into the valley below the manor. "Da's acting strange," he said.

"I noticed," Michael answered. "But it's our first battle. Maybe he's more nervous than we are."

Philip gave him a sidelong glance. "Thanks for the vote of confidence." He shook his head, but his smile remained undiminished. "I'm not afraid. We've had the best training. We have each other to rely on. Da' knows that. There's no need for any of us to worry."

Michael fell silent, ruminating on what his father's unusually affectionate behavior might mean. His father baffled him. He loved his Da'. Feared him even. But the man had never had a kind or encouraging word for him, and was never one to coddle. Despite the fact Michael's two-day disappearance years ago had prompted his family to fear him dead at the hands of bandits, his father's reaction to his homecoming had been very different than his brothers', or even the men-at-arms'. Gerard had merely looked him over and muttered, "Well it looks like you're fine. Good." And life went on. Except his father then insisted Michael put aside his treasured scholastics and pick up training as a knight instead. Da' had decided in his absence that it was time he learned how to better defend himself.

Michael narrowed his eyes, noting the shadows in the forest looming ahead. His thoughts continued to drift. He found it odd that in those early days after returning, no one made mention of his mysterious time away, nor the fact his strength and agility were twice what they were before he'd disappeared.

While he had been sorely disappointed at having to formally give up his beloved studies for training as a soldier, he made up for it during the first year by sneaking into Master Ralph's cottage to study in secret. As time went on and his training in arms grew more demanding, he was unable to find the time to steal away. To his relief, Master Ralph would slip a book to him every now and then, usually something by the great Greek philosophers, Aristotle or Plotinus, or even the Catholic philosophers, St. Augustine or Thomas Aquinas. He savored all his opportunities to read.

So, he had kept his mind stimulated and persisted in his studies despite his father's decree otherwise. He really didn't mind learning how to defend himself or attack his enemies. It challenged his body as learning challenged his mind. He was just not certain he had been attacked and kidnapped by bandits as his father assumed. It was a plausible explanation, but he simply didn't remember much about it. His recollections were clouded at best. He only knew he had almost died, and that his Da's men found him unconscious, laying on the banks of Avalon Lake two days after he'd gone missing.

Upon his homecoming, he had no way of accounting for his newfound strength and agility. There were other strange things as well, like his perplexing dreams. His brothers, who shared his sleeping quarters, teased him about his nightly ordeals, saying he moaned and tossed in his sleep, crying out and murmuring incomprehensible names.

Michael both dreaded, and oddly, cherished the nightmares. In these vivid dreams, he was mortally injured, and someone beautiful and strong always brought him back from the brink of death. An angel? Maybe Mother Mary, the mother of our Lord? Several women appeared consistently, both old and young, and all wearing deep blue silken robes. They took him in and nursed him back to health. What troubled him most about these dreams, the thing he struggled to remember upon waking, were the faces of two young girls. One fair skinned with flaxen hair, the other with brown eyes and hair black as raven feathers. While the fair-haired, blue-eyed lass sparked softness in his heart, the dark-haired one with the piercing gaze touched his soul. The problem was, he had no waking memory of having known either one. He longed to know who the two girls were who haunted his nights.

Michael knew he faced weeks, if not months, of sleeping in the open in tents amidst his soldier comrades. He worried if his dreams continued, he might cry out each night and embarrass himself.

Philip's horse whinnied and beside him. Michael remained quiet throughout the morning, not paying attention to a word his brother said, until finally Philip cantered off to ride alongside Roger. When early dusk settled, the band of fourteen men set up their evening camp within the western borders of the summer lands of Somerset County in England. They had left the heavy forest of elders, oak, and thorn behind, and now only a few hawthorn and elder trees ringed the clearing chosen for the night. The group unloaded packs and allowed the horses to graze on sweet grass before securing them to the trees.

Two men went off to hunt rabbit to roast for the evening meal. The older, grizzled Sir David was the best cook among them and was elected to tend to the meat once the hares were skinned and gutted. Philip gathered wood for the fire, and George, another of the hardened de Boulle knights, bid his squire to unwrap a few loaves of hearty brown bread they must eat while still fresh.

After the meat was set to roast, Michael lounged against a nearby hawthorn tree. He grabbed one of its fallen branches, carefully pared away the thorns, and began working it—trimming away dead leaves, baring the bark from the soft wood, and pushing out the core of the branch to create a hollow tube. Perfect for a makeshift flute, for music and singing to pass the evening. He noticed George eye him under hooded lids.

"What are ye' making young lad?" he asked in his wary way.

"A pipe."

"From hawthorn? Are you sure you want to be doing that?"

"Aye. Why not?" Michael said, preoccupied with not catching his fingers on any remaining thorns before he cut them away.

"Why not, you ask? Only because hawthorn trees call the Faery folk. Especially if you were to play music on a pipe carved from its branches. Is that not so, David?" George nodded to his comrade. Then he spit in his palm, rubbed his hands together to cast off evil spirits, and made the sign of the cross over his chest.

"Fie!" Michael shook his head. "We're a Christian household. Da' says we should ignore those superstitions. Priest says they're devil's tales."

"Well now, your father is my sworn liege, a fine knight indeed, with his own saintly priest of the Church in his service. Still, those Faery folk will come if called." George cast a cautious glance around him. "You mark my words."

Michael suppressed a chuckle. The gruff, brawny soldier afraid of Faery folk and pipes?

The roasting hare dripped juices, and David patted down the spattering of flame. "Your father's priest would say the Faery, if indeed there are any, would have to answer to the power of our Lord Jesus Christ."

Philip dropped down on the mossy ground between Michael and George, and leaned back on his elbows. His eyes held mischief.

"I don't know anything about that. All I know is hawthorn makes a fine pipe," Michael said.

He respected the hawthorn tree. Mistress Helen had taught him about its healing berries and edible blossoms. There would be no red berries until fall, but the tree's blooms were full and fragrant, still tender, and ready for the taking. Michael did just that, stuffing a few in his mouth as George watched with guarded disapproval.

Philip grabbed a few hawthorn leaves as well and chewed them avidly. "I'm damn hungry, George, with all the time David's taking to cook our rabbits," he said, munching loudly. "Here, have some hawthorn leaves. It'll curb your hunger." He flung some leaves at George.

George leaned back and made a quick sign of the cross. David guffawed.

Roger shook a finger at Philip. "Respect your elders." He walked over to George and clapped him on the back. "Now, my friend, put your superstitions aside. There's no harm from that hawthorn tree and you know it. Just to prove it, I, for one, will gladly sing to the accompaniment of my brother's pipe."

Philip peered closely at Michael's rough, hand-hewn pipe. "Poorly made I might add, but it will do for an evening's entertainment."

Michael gave Philip a flicker of a grin before he hunched over the makeshift flute, carving out small holes for air and sound.

"And what are *you* in such a good mood about?" George asked Philip, still surly, but falling under the spell of his lively charm.

"Good food, good company, the prospect of a round of song . . . and the news that my brother Roger has a surprise for us.".

"What surprise is that?" David asked, poking a pointed branch into a haunch of rabbit to keep it from falling into the fire.

Roger rolled his eyes at Philip. "Leave it to you to ruin my surprise." His tone was serious, but his eyes held an unusual sparkle.

"Well, out with it," George said.

Roger held up his hands. "All right, all right. Early evening tomorrow, we'll stop in Glastonbury . . ."

"What in the world for?" George interrupted. "Nothing but a village and an abbey there. Nothing for us soldiers."

"You can go to the abbey to pray for protection from the Faery," Philip teased.

David snickered and pounded George on the back.

"We're going to stop there because it's Summer Solstice, my friend," Roger announced.

"Thought we didn't go in for those heathen holidays," George said.

"This one we will mark." Roger tried to suppress a smile. "My younger brothers have never partaken of Glastonbury's festivities."

Michael paused his carving and looked up. Philip caught his eye and shrugged his shoulders.

"Aha!" David's chuckle turned into a full belly laugh. He pointed at the two youngest brothers.

"Why are you laughing at us?" Michael asked.

"I don't want to spoil Roger's . . . mmm . . . gift. Let him be the one to tell the two of you the details."

George's churlish expression dissolved when he laughed. "You mean the two of you lads are as yet untested? This is too good."

Michael put his knife and hawthorn branch down and stood. Glastonbury only held confusing, foggy memories for him. Memories of nearly dying. He hadn't been back since that fateful day six years ago. Though he had to admit, there was something he couldn't name, something deep in his gut that felt compelling about the town.

Michael turned to Roger for an explanation. His brother coughed and fidgeted.

"Do you mean to enter us in a soldier's tournament for the festival?" Michael asked, feeling impatient with the blatant hesitation.

George laughed louder, slapping his thigh. "Tournament? No, Michael. He means you lads are virgins."

"But tomorrow night, no longer!" David bellowed.

Philip's face flushed. He stood by Michael's side.

"And who says we're virgins?" Michael countered. He clearly remembered a discreet rendezvous or two with the blacksmith's daughter.

"That's right," Philip said, standing taller.

Michael turned to gape at his brother. He knew Philip flirted with the dairymaid, but his little brother had had . . . encounters? Well, he supposed, why not? He just thought Philip would have told him about it.

Philip looked at Michael with a sly smile. "Just a few times. Nothing to brag about. I'm a gentleman after all," he whispered.

George and David's laughter grew louder, with the other men around the cooking fire joining in.

Roger called out. "Wait!"

His command stopped all but a few chortles.

"I never said you lads were virgins. But virgins or not, a man has a right to experience the young maidens of Glastonbury on the Summer Solstice."

Roger turned to his men, pointed to them one at a time. "You've all had that privilege, have you not?"

The men all nodded or answered 'yes' in lowered voices. Still, their mirth was barely repressed. George made another sign of the cross on his forehead, chest, and shoulders. "Bless me, Jesus, 'twas a long time ago, in my youth."

This only served to kindle more raucous merriment.

"A man deserves a full night of pleasure before facing his enemies in France. Isn't that right?" Roger asked, looking around at the men, then settling his gaze on his brothers.

Michael and Philip both grinned. Philip strode over to Roger and shook his hand. Michael ignored the rowdy comments hurled at him and sat back down to resume his carving. Maybe it wouldn't be such a bad idea to return to Glastonbury after all.

Chapter 25

England
Anno Domini 1535

Roasted and gnawed rabbit bones, crumbled heels of coarse brown bread, and the cores of sweet apples picked from the surrounding wild orchards, were strewn about the camp site. The evening air was only mildly chilled, typical of southern England summers, so the men had relinquished their cloaks and lounged in linen tunics and ankle length woolen brais.

Michael licked juicy rabbit grease from his fingers and wiped his mouth with the back of his hand before he took a swill from the shared jug of hard cider.

Roger reached for the jug once Michael had finished and turned to the hefty David. "Cook Gwenda at the Manor couldn't have made a better meal." He lifted the jug. "Cheers."

David's lips turned up in an awkward smile.

George chuckled. "Go on, David. For tomorrow's dinner we want to see you wrap a ladies' cooking apron round your fat middle like Gwenda does."

The men howled while David turned crimson at the jibe. "We'll see who laughs loudest and whose stomach growls the most when I refuse to cook tomorrow's dinner," he grumbled, pointing at the grizzled George. His embarrassment only served to make the men laugh that much harder. They raised the jug of ale to enjoy more swigs.

Michael stood and stretched his legs, sore from riding all day, and strolled over to the hawthorn tree on the other side of the firepit. He picked up his carving knife from where he had left it before dinner, on the forest ground beside the half-whittled flute. Turning the knife's curved blade tip forward, he resumed carving the branch into a crude but adequate instrument. The concentration required helped him fend off the churning in his gut whenever he thought about the upcoming battle in France.

It wasn't so much losing his life he feared. He felt capable and strong. Roger had trained him well, both in offensive and defensive parries. He was properly armed, given the longbow and blade his sturdy destrier carried for him. He was in the company of an experienced group of men, and his father's knights were loyal and tough. They would fight together with the precision and close comradeship born out of many battles fought side by side. His older brother made a good leader for the small retinue and fostered that brotherhood. Michael stole a glance at Roger, sitting across the firepit among the other soldiers. Roger exuded a confident demeanor, always.

No, Michael didn't dread the upcoming battles. This heaviness in his gut came from Gerard de Boulle. His father was an exemplary knight. Though Michael was still a bit young at eighteen, Gerard expected, indeed pressed, for Michael's knighthood upon his return. Being knighted meant he would truly shed his cherished dreams of study and the learned life.

Philip came to join Michael on the quiet side of the pit. He sprawled on the grassy ground, belched loudly, and played at poking the fire with long, thin branches.

Not looking up from his work, Michael nevertheless appreciated his younger brother's company. He whittled out the last hole on the flute, eager to finish and test it with a simple melody his father's bard had taught him as a boy.

Loud laughter rose from across the camp. The men raised their jug of ale and cheered.

"Not bad at all for our first day of travel. Roger says two more days to reach the sea, then we board the ship to France," Michael said to Philip.

"And evidently, before our sea travel there is Glastonbury," Philip said with a broad smile. He poked Michael in the ribs with his wooden stick.

Michael shook his head at his young brother's conduct. "Grow up." His mild scoffing was overlaid with affection for his little brother's enthusiasm. "Our brother surprises me at every turn," Michael said in a low voice. "First, rough and strict, then this news of the Solstice. I would never have guessed he would let us stop over for the festival. Still, he could have been more discreet about the two of us."

"You think too much. Can't say I am all that upset. Who wouldn't look forward to Glastonbury at Summer Solstice?" Philip leaned toward Michael and added in an undertone, "Roger told me that each and every young lad is guaranteed to be chosen by a maiden for the evening's . . . celebration."

Michael granted a quick smile in return, and Philip took up poking at the fire with his stick once more. Michael was indeed looking forward to the festival, though Glastonbury still made him uneasy for some inexplicable reason.

He sensed Philip craved more jovial company than he could offer this evening. He turned to his brother before he could rise and join in the camaraderie on the far side of the firepit.

"I would ask a favor, brother," Michael whispered, turning his back to the other men for privacy.

Philip stopped poking at the fire. "Anything." He smiled his genial smile, and it warmed something worried inside Michael, the part that held secrets even he was not privy to. The secrets that tortured him in his dreams.

Michael cleared his throat. "Umm . . ."

Philip rapped his stick on Michael's thigh. "Well, what is it? You've never been one for a loss of words with me."

Michael looked Philip in the eye. "You know how I dream? How I am prone to nightmares?"

Philip nodded his head. His grin was replaced by an expression of compassion. Or possibly concern. Michael couldn't tell which. As long as it was not pity.

"Well, do me a favor. If you hear me toss and turn, if you hear me begin to mumble, or God forbid, call out, I want you to wake me immediately. Jab me in the side, roll me over, slap my face. Anything. Just don't let me carry on."

"I'd do anything to slap your face with your permission!" Philip teased. The twinkle in his eyes faded and he said, "By all means, I have your back."

Michael saw no pity in Philip's eyes. Only the complete love of a brother and the promise of protection.

"And I always have your back as well, little brother." Michael reached out to rumple Philip's hair, something he'd done since they were young lads.

Philip batted Michael's hand away but softened the gesture with a grin. "None of that. I'm no longer a child," he murmured, then stood to join the fellowship of the soldiers on the other side of the campfire, leaving Michael to his thoughts and carving.

Michael watched Philip walk around the firepit and cross to the other side. When he finished testing his flute, he would join him, set up a round of song and music, forget his melancholy. He put his lips to the roughly-hewn flute and blew, fingering the instrument's holes, and drawing a few notes. He was pleased with the high, sweet sound. Good enough for a soldier's evening around a campfire. He sheathed the knife he'd used for carving and glanced over to the lively group of men. Movement caught his eye in the forest off to the left.

He jumped up, about to shout a warning to the others, but the words died on his lips and he stopped cold. The figure in the woods blinked in and out of sight, much like a candle flame flickering in the wind. Michael squinted his eyes, trying to see more clearly. A luminescent-looking man stood next to the gnarled hawthorn tree he'd taken the branch from to carve his flute. It was like no man he had ever seen. His form was vague, lit from the inside with an opalescent green cast. Silver hair flowed down to his waist, and he wore mossy green-tinged robes. His upturned green eyes stared directly at Michael. This was no bandit. Not even human.

The stories his mother had weaned him on, the stories of the heathen spirits of the night, the superstitions George had warned him about, all flooded his mind. Chills ran along his back and sank into his bones.

He dropped the hand-carved pipe to the ground and quietly backed up, reaching for the sheathed sword he'd laid on the ground beside him while he carved. He held the gaze of the shining man while he slowly knelt on one knee to retrieve it. The figure didn't move, didn't attack. In fact, he radiated calm within the luminescent glow of his body.

Michael cast a quick glance across the fire-pit. David was telling a story that held the men's rapt attention. No one appeared to see the glowing entity, for if they had, they would have cried out as he nearly had. He knew if he were to call out now, they'd think he was mad, they'd think the peculiar things he'd babbled about when he first came home from his disappearance six years ago were upon him once more. He'd worked hard to be seen as credible, to be the son his father would be proud of, to be a respected comrade-in-arms. He wasn't about to trade that in for a hallucination most likely brought on by too much hard cider. He shook his head, trying to clear his vision. It did no good—the form solidified and approached him, practically gliding across the loamy ground.

"Those who play a pipe made from the sacred tree of hawthorn will see the world with different eyes. Although, to be proper, you should have offered a gift in exchange for the hawthorn branch you took," the man said. His voice was low, soft, silken even, and carried a mesmeric tone.

"Who are you?" Michael whispered. He was unable to control the tremble in his voice. He stood, sword forgotten.

The man ignored the question, lifted one brow, and appraised him. "Your flute sharpened your sight. Quite interesting. Only a rare few are able to see us anymore."

"Do you mean I called you by playing my flute?" Maybe George was right and the old superstitions were alive in the woods in the dark of night. Maybe he'd indeed called one of the Faery by carving a flute from the branch of their sacred hawthorn tree.

The man scoffed. "Faery do not come at Men's *beck and call*. We are always here, merely a step deeper in the forest, a step closer to the green world than you are. We can choose to respond. Or not."

"So, you're Faery then," Michael breathed in sharply, trying to keep his voice low and appear casual. Since the others gave no indication they'd seen the man, it would not do for them to see him talking to thin air.

"Faery." The luminous being gestured at the spoken name as if swatting a fly. "It is what *you* call us. We are the First Ones. The Shining Ones. I am Folimot, Guardian of the Hawthorn."

Michael gulped. "What do you want, coming here to me?"

Folimot raised his chin and sighed. "Are all humans so thick skulled and cloudy brained?"

Michael felt the heat of anger surge up his neck. "Hold your sharp tongue. I am Michael de Boulle, knight in training, and have many men I could call to my side in an instant."

"It would do you no good. And it is certainly not my intention to bring discord . . ." Folimot stopped midsentence and further scrutinized Michael.

"What is it? Why are you looking at me like that?"

"Oh! It is you!" he said, peering closer. "You of all people should know nothing of me. Shayla will be most disappointed if our meeting weakens her spell by your knowledge of me. I have no wish to sadden her." His expression turned tender.

"Shayla? Who's Shayla?" Michael swallowed thickly. "Why does that name sound familiar?" Sudden images of his nighttime dreams, the mysterious girls in blue silken robes, surfaced in his awareness.

Folimot held out his hand in a gesture of peace, a conciliatory movement that replaced his earlier arrogance. "Forget we met. Forget you have seen me. Forget for your own good." His green eyes held Michael's in earnest.

"How can I? You know something about my dreams, don't you? You can help me, can't you? Tell me! Did I meet you when I . . . disappeared?" Michael asked, his words tumbling out in his excitement. Perhaps the riddle of his dreams could finally be solved.

"I am sorry, Michael de Boulle. We should have never met. I must leave."

"Wait!" Michael pleaded.

Folimot's form flickered. "Forget me," he said in a voice that intoned and commanded.

Michael lunged for him, but the Faery had disappeared. He grabbed the flute from the forest floor and played an urgent short tune to call him back. To no avail. Folimot was truly gone. Michael threw his flute to the ground.

"Help me find him," he shouted over his shoulder to the other soldiers. He couldn't lose the one person who could tell him what his dreams meant. No matter what it cost him in credibility.

The men all bolted up, the more seasoned among them already fingering the hilts of their swords kept always at their sides. They turned in the direction Michael pointed, forming a semi-circle line of defense. Michael bent down and yanked his sword from its scabbard.

"Where? What was it, Michael?" Roger yelled, his right arm swinging his sword before him as he scanned the woods. The other men stood rigidly on guard, eyes surveying the dark woods. They advanced a few feet as a unit, on the offense now, ready to enter the forest.

"Into the woods. Didn't you see?" Michael shouted, his body electric and tingling with battle readiness.

"What was it, lad?" David asked

"I don't see a thing," George added in a gruff voice.

"What did you see?" Roger repeated brusquely.

Michael hesitated. He couldn't say it was Faery. "I don't know. Something. Something big and moving."

"Spread out, two by two. Search. Yell when you've found something," Roger ordered.

"I'll go along as well. He was right there in the tree line. He ran into the woods," Michael insisted. "I mean, it. *It* ran into the woods."

Two of the men lowered their swords.

Philip looked at Michael, as if he could sense his growing uneasiness. He followed Michael's gaze back into the shadow of the trees, then turned his head to his brother once more, brows creased, looking for confirmation as to what was alarming him.

Michael grimaced and held up his sword arm. No one else had seen a shining man. They were ready to help but didn't know what the target was. His gut clenched. Folimot was someone who belonged more to his haunted, nighttime visions than his waking life. He swore their conversation was real, knew that Folimot could help him remember. He started for the woods.

Roger interceded. "You don't go alone, and you only go on my orders."

"But I must find him," Michael said, advancing forward.

"I *said*, you move on my orders, and only on my orders. What's wrong with you, Michael?" Roger held him back by his arm.

David said in a low, firm voice, "A soldier listens to the orders of those above him, lad."

Michael wrenched his arm from Roger's grasp. He would never be able to explain what finding Folimot would mean to him. He also knew he must obey his brother. The realization sunk in that a search party for a Faery that could simply fade away would be of no use anyway.

Roger forced a smile. "I think my brother has had too much ale."

Humiliated and frustrated, Michael picked up on his brother's save. He feigned a stagger and slurred. "That must have been it. Sorry, so sorry. I swore I saw something."

"Hold back my first order. George and David, only the two of you will go and search for our mysterious intruder." Roger eyed Michael sternly.

The others grumbled, a few laughed off the apparent error.

"Better alert than missing something important, lad," David said with a nod.

David joined George and they snuck off into the shadowed trees. Michael stood by the forest line and heard George mutter. "First the lad disappears as a boy. Under my watch. Blamed myself for it that day, I did. He comes back strange if you ask me. Now this. He sees things not there."

"You don't know that," David replied. "Could have been robbers. Even a wolf. Better to be safe."

"I say the lad was stricken by the heathen Faery when we lost him those years ago. Never been the same since."

Michael felt heat rush to his face. He wished he could hide in the shelter of the forest darkness. Hide from the ridicule of the soldiers, from the stern look in Roger's eyes. But mostly from the knowing that, yes, he was different. He saw things in his dreams and the torture of that was bad enough. Now to see Faery, to see what others didn't in his waking time? Either he was going mad, or everyone else was. No matter what, he would have to work harder to prove himself capable and reliable. Yet again.

Resigned, Michael sat back down, picked up his flute and stared into the woodland. Waiting for another glance of the glistening figure. Part of him hoped to God in heaven Folimot would reappear. Another part of him wondered if he should take the Faery's demand to heart and forget he ever saw him.

Chapter 26
Glastonbury, England
Anno Domini 1535

Marissa stood on Glastonbury's shore with Ciara and Shayla beside her. The three waved with feigned courage to Alianore and Vanora, who had remained on the barge. Marissa surprised herself by how much she already missed her mother's presence and calm manner. The Elders would stay on Avalon's side of the veil to hold vigil for the girls' first Solstice ceremonies. The three young women stepped away from the lake's bank and the portal of thick, pearly-white mist closed. They watched it fully disappear before they made their way to town in silence, still feeling the potency of the ceremonial rites they'd undergone in preparation for the evening.

The scent of anointed rose oil and spikenard, mixed with the resinous incense of frankincense and myrrh, clung to their skin and robes. Marissa inhaled, allowing the heady fragrance to ground her in her otherworldly alignment and her connection to the Goddess.

Ciara held her hand. Her sister's grip was tight, betraying her unease upon entering the town of Glastonbury and the world of men. Shayla walked on Ciara's other side and clung to the twin's other hand.

"Look at us," Marissa laughed, trying to ease the tension she knew they all felt as the village square came into view with its large oak tree and communal well. "You'd think we were going to our executions, not to a night of merriment. We have a sacred duty to perform., so on we go, with rightful joy in our hearts."

Ciara looked over at her, blue eyes round with fear. The town square was filled with villagers, young men and women, as well as old. The village girls were dressed in either distinctive vermilion or bright yellow tunics, their normally plaited hair set free to cascade down their backs. Marissa had foregone her silken blue robes and slippers, as had Ciara and Shayla, to dress in the same rough-hewn linen as the village girls in order to blend in. Marissa smoothed her tunic and tucked a strand of her long hair behind her ear.

She thought the music uplifting. Some of the older villagers plucked dulcimers or played melodies on pipes and flutes. There was a hurdy-gurdy with its hand-cranked, droning strings providing accompaniment to the melodies of the flutes. Some of the village girls clasped hands and began to dance around the central well, snaking through the musicians to parade before a group of young men, most of whom eyed them nervously.

Shayla's gaze swept slowly back and forth, taking in the crowd and festivities. Marissa couldn't shake the feeling that her friend was looking for someone in particular.

She tried again to calm them all. "Mother and the Elders have prepared us well. They've told us what to expect and how to participate. There's really nothing to fear, is there?"

When Ciara only chewed her lip, and no one answered her, Marissa shook her hand loose from her twin's. "Come on, Sister. What's the matter with you?" Her tone was sharp, but her impatience had more to do with her own anxiety than her sister's. Still, she hated the look of hurt that replaced the fear in Ciara's eyes. *So much for the peace and serenity we invoked before we left Avalon*, she thought.

Shayla glared as she turned to face Marissa. "Stop being cross. You know Ciara doesn't like the idea of entering the realm of men. It makes her nervous."

"I'm sorry," Ciara said. "I guess I just don't trust any place but Avalon. There's too much going on here." She covered her ears with her hands, blocking out the raucous laughter and music coming from the village square.

Marissa sighed and pushed aside her irritability. "Yes, it is noisy here," she agreed, and offered Ciara an appeasing smile.

Marissa surveyed the village square for a less crowded spot. Stalls had been set up with vendors selling sweet treats, while the other side of the square was lined with peddlers of colored ribbons, and bouquets of violets, daisies, periwinkles, and pale pink primrose. All meant to woo a maiden and entice her to choose the young man who might proffer such lovely gifts to be her evening's lover.

The sight only served to sadden Marissa. Their first foray back into the realm of men, on an evening meant to celebrate joining in sacred union with a man, was only serving to make her longing for Michael grow stronger. She'd never been able to rid her heart of the wrenching ache of him leaving Avalon and never returning. Her yearning for him hadn't diminished in the six years since he'd left. Most of all, her dread sprang from the fateful vision she'd had about him at Glastonbury Abbey. The one nobody seemed to believe. Before her hidden despair drowned her in its gloom, she turned to her sister.

"Time to join in," she said with contrived enthusiasm.

The three approached the crowd just as the older village men began to beat tambours in a primal, sensual rhythm. Young men stood to the side, swaying to the music, eyeing the village girls. The girls returned the appraising stares. Older women quivered their tambourines and approached the young men and women, shaking the instruments seductively, indicating their approval of a promising pair for the late evening's coupling.

Marissa suddenly felt she wasn't ready to plunge right into picking a mate for the celebration. She purposefully turned toward the aroma of warm potato and onion pasties, sun-drenched apples, and fresh baked honeyed cakes, all mixed with the fermented smell of cider and mead spiced with cloves and meadowsweet.

"Maybe we should have a treat first," Marissa said, "to entice the mood." She led her sister and friend to a nearby stand.

The choices available made her stomach growl. The three of them had fasted in preparation for the evening, but now were finally allowed food. The baker held up several of his choicest honey cakes. Marissa pointed to three cakes. Yes, she admitted to herself, she was stalling. She also hoped to reconcile the slight she'd given Ciara for being vexed. For truthfully, the one and only time she had ever been truly upset with her twin had been long ago. Six years—the time she thought Ciara was trying to steal Michael away from her. She scowled. *Humph*. Turned out Michael belonged to neither of them now, despite the promises he'd made to her in the oak grove. She'd long ago forgiven her sister for their misunderstanding, desiring only to return to the special attachment only sisters, moreover twins, shared. Well, they'd nearly returned to that attachment. Still, Ciara remained fairly closed-off, even to the mind talk they had always shared so freely.

As the baker wrapped the cakes for them, Marissa turned to her sister. "Ciara, I am the one who should apologize. Stay by my side until we grow accustomed to the noisy, blunt ways of this world. Then we shall pick out fine young men, one for each of us. And we will enjoy sharing the sacred rites as only a priestess can."

"You're right," Ciara said, smiling weakly. "But, remember, Vanora says we must not let on that we are priestesses."

Shayla squinted into the distance, her gaze still searching, and replied without looking at her friends. "We won't run into any trouble. Glastonbury may be a Christian town now, but most of the folks want the Goddess involved here just as much as we do. They still believe in the old ways. They still leave offerings of ribbons and food at the holy wells, don't they? Besides, Vanora says we can turn to Brother Gregory from the abbey if anything should go wrong."

Marissa put a hand on her hip, feeling irritation flame up once more. "Stop it. What in the world can go wrong? We're here to celebrate. Why are you putting unfounded and frightening ideas in Ciara's head?" She paused, studying Shayla. "And, for goodness sake, you've been preoccupied with the crowd since we got here. Exactly who are you looking for?"

"No one. Just scanning the crowd for young men," Shayla stammered.

Ciara giggled.

A lad brushed by them and let out a lewd whistle.

Marissa sighed. "I'm sure this was easier long ago when we could be priestesses in the open, to officiate at the festival. If I get one more vulgar whistle, I'm going to punch the fellow who does it."

Ciara gasped. "You wouldn't!" She covered her mouth and giggled at Marissa's bold threat.

"I would. Seems everyone has forgotten the meaning of the ritual. Forgotten that the Goddess is the one who created pleasure and beauty and that we are to honor Her. I don't see any evidence of honoring the Goddess here." She spread her arms to encompass the town square and all its merrymakers.

"*We're* here, Marissa. You know we're here to *help* them remember," Ciara said. "Any man we pair with will know the Goddess through us. She'll never be forgotten as long as we're here."

"You've always been the wise one among us."

Marissa turned back to the stall owner and gave him his coin. The three nibbled their treats as they strolled past the serene abbey grounds and toward the vale where the red and white springs of Glastonbury merged and flowed down in unison toward the abbey. The odor of smoke and burning wood rolled hazily over the vale. Shayla pointed to a low-lying bonfire atop the Tor, the rounded hill that spewed Glastonbury's white spring at its base, a mirror-image of the Tor in Avalon. Some of the younger men who would be participating in the evening's celebrations were busy feeding the bonfire flames with sacred oak branches. The older men tended to the containment of the sparks and blaze, keeping the flame low. Marissa could hear them chastising the younger men, calling out to them to treat the fire with caution and respect.

"Are you going to jump the flames?" Shayla asked.

"Definitely!" Marissa replied at the same time Ciara said, wrinkling her nose in distaste, "Only if I have to."

"Coward," Marissa teased. "We have to keep up appearances at least. All the couples jump over the flame for blessings."

"For purification and boons," Shayla added.

Marissa winked, "Before they go off into the woods together."

Shayla moaned in mock pleasure and Ciara blushed, shaking her head. "Keep focused, ladies. Focus."

"Might you ladies be thirsty?" a man's voice said from behind them.

All three startled and turned.

"Oh! And who might you be?" Marissa said.

"I'd be Brother Gregory," he replied, beaming. His brown eyes sparkled, matching the cheerfulness of his smile.

"So, you're the famous Brother Gregory? The monk from the abbey?"

"One and the same." He held a wooden tray with three mugs of apple cider. "Here. Each of you take a beaker. 'Tis the best cider around. Made it ourselves, from our very own orchards at the abbey." He handed each girl a mug.

Marissa accepted hers and tasted a cider so sweet it slid pleasingly down her throat. With a satisfied sigh, she watched the monk from under lowered lids. His cowl hung down the back of his plain brown robes, tied at the waist by a piece of braided leather. He was older than her mother by maybe one score, but no more. His hair was deep brown, noticeably streaked with gray, and tonsured in the fashion of the religious order of the abbey.

Ciara clutched her mug tightly. "Are you here with us because something is wrong?" she asked, worry edging her voice.

Brother Gregory chuckled. It was a soft laugh, but came from deep in his belly.

"Nay, nothing is wrong. You must be Ciara the Gentle, with the eyes as blue as the sky. Is that right? Don't let me worry you. I'm innocent in my intent. Your mother and Vanora asked me to watch over you."

"They don't trust us?" Marissa sulked.

"Nothing like that at all. When I first came to the abbey many years ago, I met your mother. Before she became High Priestess. She came to town just as you three are doing now, to take part in the ancient rites that our people have revered for centuries."

"You're all right with us being priestesses, then? With us celebrating the ancient rites of sacred union? Even though you worship the Christian God?" Marissa asked.

Brother Gregory's infectious laugh rang out once more. This time he smiled so broadly that his eyelids creased until all Marissa could see were his lashes. She found herself smiling in return.

"Assuredly, I am fine with the ancient rites. Your secret is safe with me." He winked. "And just to be fair, I'll let you in on a little secret of my own. A secret about the abbey."

Marissa leaned forward. "A secret. What secret?"

Brother Gregory lowered his voice. "There are some of us at the abbey that revere the heavenly Mother as well as our Lord and all the saints."

"But you worship one they say is a virgin. You call her by the name of Mary. Certainly that's not one and the same with our Goddess who promises the pleasures that the Virgin never knew," Shayla said, her tone failing to hide her disapproval.

"Shayla! Show Brother Gregory respect," Ciara chided.

"Yes, we do revere the Virgin Mary. But what is in a name? Many of us in the abbey also know Her as the Star of the Sea. As you know Her."

Shayla stared into the wooded grove of oak, ash, and hawthorn trees to their right, at the base of the Tor. "Oh," She faintly exclaimed.

"What is it, Shayla?" Ciara asked.

"He is here! I have found him. Folimot is *here*." Her face glowed. She smoothed her robe and patted her silver-blond hair.

"Who?" Marissa demanded. She followed Shayla's gaze and saw a striking young man with long silver hair and an iridescent glow about him, standing at the edge of the woods.

"Faery," Marissa whispered. Her memories of their disastrous foray into the Faery Realm surfaced, causing the muscles in her stomach to clench.

"I have to go. He may not stay long," Shayla murmured. She sprinted off without a backward glance before anyone could stop her.

"No. Wait!" Marissa cried. "It's not safe for you to be around Faery. Remember?" She couldn't let her friend be hurt by another encounter with Faery. She would not be to blame for that again. She thrust her cider mug into Brother Gregory's hands and started to run after Shayla, but Brother Gregory called to her and his words stopped her.

"Marissa. You know that Faery have joined with priestesses in the Solstice Rites for centuries."

Marissa felt his strong and calming tone pacify her. She hesitated, looked back at Brother Gregory and then forward to the spot where Shayla had disappeared into the woods.

"But Vanora says she has to be careful. Especially since she visited their realm."

Ciara walked up to Marissa and gently reached for her arm. "Come now, Sister. Shayla knows to be careful. And our visit to the Faery Realm was long ago and best forgotten."

Marissa blinked and took a deep breath. She had to get control of her fear. She had to get past her guilt for how terribly things had gone wrong for everyone. The bad memories were muddling her judgment.

Brother Gregory watched her with a compassionate expression and placed her mug of cider back into her hands. Marissa wondered just how much her mother had told the monk.

Ciara leaned into Marissa and whispered, "Did you hear what Shayla said? She knew his name! How does Shayla know a Faery man? She never mentioned him to *me*. Did she mention him to you?"

Marissa shrugged her shoulders and stood on her tiptoes, trying one more time to see the pair, but the crowd had moved to block her view.

"I'm as surprised as you," Marissa said, "but she got her wish to enjoy the sacred rites with the man she desired." Guilt was replaced by the familiar aching pit in her chest, the one she had whenever thoughts of Michael arose.

Marissa brought her mug of cider to her lips and swallowed down her grief with a hefty gulp of the sweet apple juice. But she sputtered and choked when she spotted a tall, young man with a head of tawny hair standing at the white spring a short distance away. It wasn't the color of his hair as much as the way the he tilted his chin and laughed. The sound was familiar, cherished, and it caused her chest to tighten. Her instincts sharpened. Before she had time to ponder or think, and—Goddess forbid—before another girl chose him, she shoved her mug into Brother Gregory's hands yet again, and ran off, much as Shayla had.

"Well, helping you three find suitable young men is not going to be a problem at all," Brother Gregory said, smiling down at Ciara. "The ritual preparations appear to have a strong effect on you three."

"Excuse my sister and my friend. I can't imagine what rudeness has come over them to leave so suddenly like that," Ciara said.

"Hmmm. This is the way of Summer Solstice. Young girls and lads may think they choose their partners at random. But tonight, lovers know whom they are meant to be with. As if the attraction is set in the stars. That is why your mother has me watching out for you. To guide you to your star."

Ciara frowned as comprehension dawned. Her sister's behavior could only mean one thing. Her heart felt suddenly heavy and tight. Michael must have returned.

Chapter 27

Glastonbury, England
Anno Domini 1535

Dusk settled, catching the last rays of the sun to cast a subdued glow on the forest greenery. Folimot clasped Shayla's hand and led her deeper into the woods, behind a copse of flowering hawthorn trees. Their blossoms lay like a luxuriant white blanket on the woodland floor, their leaves covering the pair in a latticework of shade and dappled light.

Folimot scanned the surrounding area. Though only priestesses would be able to see Faery without assistance, he nevertheless wanted to make sure no one saw Shayla speaking with someone who wasn't visible to the world of man. He was bound to protect her at all costs. It was his oath-sworn duty, though she was unaware. More than that, she had become precious to him.

"You came." Shayla's voice touched him like a gentle breeze. "I prayed you would be here."

He gazed solemnly into her green eyes. "I told you when we first met that destiny was ours. I've known all along." A full head taller, he smiled down at her with tenderness. Until meeting Shayla, he had been unaccustomed to such delicate emotions. The feelings both surprised and delighted him, made his chest feel expansive. Maybe the tumultuous world of man held some worthy treasures after all.

"You knew we would one day be here together?" she asked.

His hands trembled. "I hoped." He would wait to tell her everything until she seemed more at ease.

"Sit," he said, motioning to the nearest hawthorn tree. He knelt and patted the ground beside him.

Shayla sat, and Folimot encircled her in his arms. He sighed with the pure pleasure of her nearness—the smell of lavender in her hair, the scent of rose oil on her skin, the resin of sacred frankincense that clung to her tunic. When he saw that she didn't pull away, he settled in more comfortably, his back supported by the tree trunk, and she leaned into his side.

His blood thrummed with the familiar synergy he shared with hawthorn, the tree he was both steward of and drew his magic from. The full moon rose, emanating a silver glow that reflected off each leaf above, creating points of light as if the tree were lit with tiny candles just for their pleasure.

Folimot reached out with his Faery senses, breathing as one with the woodland and its wildlife. Red-breasted robins hopped through the needles on the forest floor. Tiny goldcrests peeked out from amidst the bush next to them. Thrush and brown wrens flitted between the leaves above. All mingling their birdsong in a twilight chorus, their trills muffling the boisterous merrymaking in the town square far below. He was acutely aware of the passing footsteps and light laughter of other lovers finding their own private spots along the earthen ridges of the forested Tor that rose above them like a sentinel pointing to the stars. Soon he and Shayla would join with the surrounding nature, in the vigor of summertime's fertility.

After a few moments of silence, she lifted her face to look at him directly. "You will be my lover for tonight, won't you? I mean, that *is* why you are here?" she asked boldly, though her voice wavered.

Folimot couldn't hide the gladness that crept into his reply. "Yes, that and much more. If you will let me." Surely no other Faery had ever treasured his charge more than he.

"And much more?" Shayla's eyes were wide and trusting, her face so close to his.

He turned to her. "Well, you see, there are certain things you ought to know." He marveled at the beauty of the woman he held in his arms. He'd waited so long for this. "First, I must tell you that I am the nephew of Gwyn ap Nudd— "

"The Faery King who is said to rule under Glastonbury Tor?" Her voice held awe.

"Not said to. Does," he asserted. "Yes, the same." He smiled ruefully. Man or priestess, all were alike in their fear and fascination with Gwyn.

"Go on," she said, eyes shining with excitement.

"As I said, I am Gwyn ap Nudd's nephew. By marriage. My father and your father are court members and distant cousins. They both serve Gwyn. Your father as King of the northern realms; my father as King of the westerly islands."

"Wait. You know I have always dreamed of knowing more about my father. I cannot believe this is finally happening tonight. Thank you." She paused, letting the silent tears gathering in her eyes flow down her cheeks. Folimot caught a teardrop on his fingertip.

She reached for his hands, cradled them in hers. "Tell me more."

He continued, the warmth of her touch muddling his thoughts, melting the confidence of his planned speech. "You and I . . . we were . . . promised to each other when you were a baby." *There. Now she knew.*

Shayla sat back. "Promised to you as a baby? I do not understand. I have been brought up in Avalon. As a priestess. I am the daughter of Kendra." She claimed her human heritage with obvious pride and affection.

"Yes. Your mother, as a priestess of Avalon, had the right to keep you with her and raise you as her own. This has been the way for centuries between our people. We are allies. But there is one difference. Because Kendra mated on a night such as this with the son of a Faery King, who is now a King himself, it is our right to reclaim you after your first coupling. It will soon be time for you to return. Is that not that wonderful?" Folimot's radiance pulsed with excitement.

"Yes! Wait. No! Reclaim me? What does that mean?" she asked in a strained voice.

He watched her face cloud with emotion. He sensed her confusion and it bewildered him.

She pulled back, releasing his hands from hers. "You do not know how much I have longed for Faery . . . but . . ."

Ah, but I do know. I've been but a breath and a thought away from you for a long time, he thought.

She continued. "But I never imagined I would be *obligated* to return. Tell me, does this mean I have to give up Avalon?"

She was becoming visibly agitated, balling up her tunic in her hands.

"How could my mother have duty-bound me so? Do I have no say in the matter? Did she know she did this?"

"Your mother would have known this when she joined with your father. He would have told her. You carry his *royal* Faery blood. Because of that, you now must return to your own people."

"Is this why I dream of Faery? Why the pull is so strong that it sometimes weakens my thoughts? Turns my heart away from those I love to hunger for places I have never even been?"

Folimot nodded, glad Faery blood ran so strong in her veins. "You are to return to us straightaway. Forevermore."

She hesitated, and with an anguished cry, shook her head. "No."

His breath caught. "What do you mean, no?"

"I told you I yearn for the realm of my father. I even yearn for you. But I have roots in Avalon. My friends. My mother. To *never* see them again? I will not be ordered to return to the Faery Realm forevermore . . . it cannot be demanded of me."

His shimmering essence dimmed. "But you must. I thought this was your deepest desire."

"It is. But I will not be commanded. It is to be my choice." Shayla abruptly stood and wrapped her arms about her waist as if to contain her distress. "And to leave Avalon forever tears my heart." Her face softened. "I am grateful I am welcomed back, but I must be allowed to return on *my* terms. Which means I will come when I choose to, and may visit Avalon to see my loved ones. I will always have priestess roots. That can never be erased. I have been taught I must balance my halfling blood, priestess and Faery. Both are inside me. I cannot totally abandon one for the other."

Folimot stood as well. He didn't understand her sudden resistance. He had never heard of anyone contradicting the Faery tradition. "Shayla, we are bound to each other by our family's oath. This is beyond us."

"I still want to know more about my father, but I will not be told what to do. I am half human after all. A priestess and a sovereign woman. This is what has been ingrained in me since birth. Not Faery law."

Though it was not in his nature, Folimot could not help but plead his case with one more bit of information she couldn't have known. "Since I was of an age to do so, I have been assigned to watch over you."

Her eyebrows arched. "So, I am your duty? Nothing more?"

"Of course not. Not only duty. I mean, yes, you are more. Much more." His confusion was marring the brilliant silver of his countenance. He stood still and breathed in the perfumed blossom and leafy green of the hawthorn surrounding them. He allowed the chorus of twilight birdsong to buoy him. It served to calm his senses, so overwhelmed by Shayla's volatile human emotions. "I have grown to adore you."

Her face softened. "You say you have watched over me?"

"At your father's request. Since we were oathbound."

"Since I was a baby? But how? How old are you?"

The question perplexed him. "In human years, I am your age. In Faery, much older. When you return to us, you will not age as humans do, either."

She covered her face with her hands and began to cry softly. He did not understand what was happening, what was distressing her. He had expected her to acquiesce, willingly. To rejoice with him.

"Shayla, daughter of King Laighlon of the northern realms, I have come to bring you home for good," he declared formally.

"Will you force me?" she asked, looking up and gazing directly into his eyes. Straight into his heart.

"Force? Why, no, indeed not." He let out a long sigh. "But this is what has always been expected. After tonight, it is time for you to return."

Shayla's expression turned pensive, her eyes distant. "The Faery realm calls me, deep in my bones. I see memories that aren't mine. I see a land of exquisite beauty and the secrets only nature holds. In visions, I see my father in his realm. He is tall and strong, with long silver hair and eyes as green as the five emeralds in his crown. He holds his hand out to me. And there is a signet of a white horse upon his signature ring."

"Yes! Yes, that is him, Shayla. That is your father."

"I am drawn to come. As I have always been drawn. But not tonight. It must be in my own timing. Our two communities can cooperate in this, can they not? To never be allowed to visit Avalon again is too harsh a sacrifice. The rules must bend."

He murmured softly, "It is our tradition. Our wisdom. Although it is not high law."

"Good. If it is not high law, then we will change tradition. You and I together.

For us. For all humans and all Faery. All halflings." Her eyes brightened. "Please understand. There is a force in my human world that is as compelling as the force that calls me back to you. It is the love I have for my mother Kendra and all she wanted for me as her priestess daughter. It is all the abilities and sovereignty I inherited from her. It is also the love for my High Priestess Alianore and my dear sister-friends, Marissa and Ciara. Especially Ciara." She put a hand over her heart. "I must make sure she will always be all right."

"Ciara . . . the girl I helped you protect with Faery magic years ago." He hesitated, momentarily unsure how to tell her this latest piece of news. He had been dreading it. "I came across Michael recently. The one you wished to protect her heart from."

Shayla's eyes widened and her body visibly tensed. "Marissa nor Ciara must ever see Michael. The spell we cast has to hold. Their hearts must not suffer because of him. And our sisterhood bond cannot be jeopardized again." She grabbed his shoulders. "Where? Where did you see Michael?"

"In the forest surrounding Wales. Do not worry. He does not remember your friends, Marissa or Ciara. Just as you wanted. He does not remember Avalon."

"How can you be sure?"

"If he had remembered, he would have knowingly and in full awareness returned to Marissa, is that not so? The spell we conjured holds strong." He wouldn't worry Shayla by telling her that he, the one who created the spell at her request, just by having met Michael face-to-face one day ago in Wales, may have loosened the grip of the forgetting spell they had spun in Michael's mind. So went Faery law.

"So, he went on with his life in Wales. That is good, is it not? Did he seem happy?" she asked, sounding more relieved.

He couldn't dampen her hope. "Yes. Happy and healthy." He put his hand on her arm, tenderly tracing his fingers across her skin.

A lightning bolt of potent desire crackled between them. Shayla trembled as its embers fanned to blazing. It quickened her heartbeat. Her breath hitched. There was power in them being oathbound, but stronger yet was this burgeoning feeling in her heart for Folimot. Her desire for him, her yearning for the Faery Realm rose in a tidal wave of pressure within her. It warred with her love for her dear ones and her life as an Avalon priestess. She felt herself drowning in dual waves of desire and love. Still, she clung to her demands, her conditions for her return to her other blood land.

"I must be assured that tradition will bend to allow me to visit Avalon. This must be agreed upon before I leave to go anywhere." She sighed, her breath unsteady. "Once that is guaranteed, I will come with you." She averted her eyes and her cheeks blushed. "After tonight's celebrations, I mean."

Folimot felt like he could breathe freely again. "I will personally bring the request to your father to delay your return back."

"No. Not a request. My conditions. I will not leave so suddenly. And I will not be bound to never return. It would break my heart."

He gazed at the hawthorn trees around him, gathering his thoughts, aided by their wild strength. Would the king allow this? The short time Shayla needed would be but a drop in the ocean in the ageless time of Faery. Her condition to visit Avalon did not seem so extreme a bend in tradition to him. Her father could be brought to understand. When he finally faced her again, he smiled, wiped a tear that had escaped down her cheek to pool on the corner of her lip. "It will be as you say then."

He took the green, shimmering mantle from around his shoulders and held it out. It reflected the colors of twilight sun and rising moon flickering through all the greenery of the forest. "This mantle now belongs to you. When you are ready, wear it for safe passage into the Faery Realm."

Shayla reached out to touch it, mesmerized by its wildling green hues. Folimot bent to meet her lips and kissed her softly. His wild, nature-sourced Faery blood met her priestess power—flint summoning fire.

He laid the mantle aside and pulled her down, onto the leafy, blossom-strewn ground beneath the hawthorn. The hawthorn copse lent its enchantment and unique fecundity to them as they surrendered to each other and joined in the way of the Goddess.

Chapter 28

Glastonbury, England
Anno Domini 1535

The residual light of dusk hung over the town of Glastonbury, casting dancing shadows around the gurgling white spring and surrounding oak trees. Marissa hesitated, her heartbeat caught in her throat. Maybe it was not Michael she had glimpsed. She chided herself. Why would he be here, after all? Still, hope surfaced. Well, why not here, she reasoned? Come back to her after all these years. Why not, indeed. The thought bolstered her resolve.

She quickened her stride, heading directly toward the young man with tawny hair who stood beside the spring. He turned, his brow creased as if concentrating. His eyes scanned the crowd gathered around the spring, young men and women hoping to find a partner to celebrate the fruitful power of life on this Summer Solstice eve.

Yes, it's him, she thought. The blue eyes, the dimple. It was undeniably her Michael. She was close enough to leap into his arms. But her heart fell, and she stopped when he finally caught her eye. There was no recognition reflected in its azure depths.

Still, he stepped forward, haltingly at first. The young man next to him who resembled him in coloring and stature, only slightly younger, grabbed his elbow and looked at him questioningly, then glanced over to where Michael was staring. At her. He let go of Michael's elbow with a nod and a quick pat on the back.

Michael walked toward her. Marissa did not move. Her throat was dry, her heart quaking like a wild bird captured in the confines of her chest. His puzzled gaze pierced her, sharper than any arrow. *How can he not recognize me?*

"Hello. Who are you?" he said, his voice low.

"You don't remember?" she asked, her response a mere whisper. Had she changed that much in six years? From girl to woman. Her heart, now leaden, sank to the bottom of her stomach, her arms and legs immobilized in despair. Years spent longing for him, remembering their promise to each other. And now this? She silently dared the fates, insisting there could be no way on the Goddess's bountiful earth he had forgotten. They had shared so much so deeply back then, even at their young age.

"No." He shook his head. "I don't remember. But I have indeed seen you. I'm sorry, I know this sounds strange." He peeked fervently behind him, at the young man who bore his resemblance, as if gathering courage from his approval. The lad smiled at Michael cheekily and sauntered away. Michael turned back to Marissa.

"I choose you," she stammered. Then she said it louder, bolder, bypassing the tremble of her body, hiding the quiver in her voice. "I am Marissa, and I choose you."

Unexpectedly, he chuckled, his half smile replacing the trepidation in his expression. He tilted his head to the side, the same way she remembered him doing as a boy in Avalon.

"I *choose* you," she repeated, nodding quickly for emphasis.

"And I choose you," he replied.

His eyes never left hers. They questioned and probed. "I know you," he said.

"Of course you do," she replied, encouraged.

He continued, his voice charged with excitement. "In my dreams. You're the one in my dreams."

Marissa felt her ire flare. "Michael, stop it right now. I was no dream. I am no dream now."

He leaned closer. "I met someone yesterday. I'm not jesting, but I'm sure it was a Faery, named Folimot. He spoke of Hawthorn magic." Michael glanced at the nearby blossoming hawthorn trees. "Did he send you to me?"

"Who? Folimot? How do you know *Folimot*? If you remember him, then you remember Shayla. And then you must remember me." Her eyes narrowed. "Don't you?"

He looked around nervously, then grabbed her hand and led her away from the crowd. She beamed. Now things were going in the proper direction.

He guided them toward a stand of birch trees. As they approached the copse, they heard the unmistakable sound of lovers' sighs deep within the brush. Muffled moans, intimate laughter, the rapid breathing of bodies pleasuring one another. Michael's face flushed crimson and he lurched in the opposite direction, pulling her behind him. Marissa smiled to herself. Embarrassed, was he? Well, maybe he was naïve to the ways of lovers. She felt her face heat as she savored the thought of showing him the joys and pleasures of the Solstice celebration and the ways of the Goddess.

He strode deeper into the woods, choosing a solitary oak to stand beneath. Heavy, gnarled boughs towered over and dipped around them, with the bursting leaf of summer to enclose them in a cocoon of privacy. Her senses heightened by the ritual preparations and her promising encounter with Michael, Marissa felt the thrum of the tree's vitality reach out to encompass her. She opened her being to receive the touch of the oak's green vivacity and felt the Goddess enter her through the earth she stood upon. The vibrant energy spiraled up from the ground and into her feet, her legs, her waist, her chest, her arms, her head . . . her pelvis. Ah, it vibrated and throbbed there. Then traveled to the center of her heart and circulated. The energy surge happened in an instant. She trembled. So, this was the quickening her mother and Vanora prepared her for.

She turned to him, ready and expectant. Forgetting and forgiving the gash his initial lack of recognition had chiseled into her heart.

His jaw tightened and his eyes opened wide. The look of bewilderment and agony doused the fire in her belly.

"Michael. Please." She reached up and caressed his cheek.

He stumbled back, his alarm palpable in his faltering movement. "I have . . . so many questions."

With her will and her breath, Marissa banked the flow of exaltation already coursing through her veins. It took a moment to tell her body and heart to pause their anticipation. He was obviously not ready. Rather, he appeared distraught and confused. He seemed . . . different?

"I don't know you, but I do," he stammered, his words tumbling out without breath to support them. "I've seen you every night since I returned home six years ago. In my dreams, I mean. But I did not know who you were. You haunt me." His hands fell limply to his side. "You haunt my every waking and sleeping moment. And I don't know who you are."

"You truly don't remember me, do you? How can that be," she said. "We spent months together when you were recuperating in Avalon."

"Avalon," he repeated. With furrowed brow, he stared into the deep woods, pursuing the elusive thread of hidden images, curtained within the deep crevices of lost memory.

Marissa frowned. Avalon's mists would not totally obscure the time he spent there. The veil was not designed to shackle memory. What could induce this level of forgetfulness? Collecting her thoughts, she reached inward until she connected with her intuition, her second sight. She connected with her heart, linked heart to belly, and breathed the embers of wisdom held within her womb fires.

Michael's lips parted. He exhaled slowly, still gazing into the distance. Marissa sensed him hunt something in his mind. As she intuitively scanned him, she began to see what he saw. His memories were a puzzle, like the puzzle game pieces his tutor had shown him as a boy. But his mind's pieces were scattered. She felt him strain to refocus. Some pieces coalesced. His memories captured an image of antlered stag horns tied to his head. A game of *Hunt and Chase* played with three young girls. The image wavered. Resurfaced. The pieces joined again to produce another image. He pictured a girl with raven-colored hair. Her! They were sharing secrets and promises. Plans. Holding hands. The image wisped into nothingness. He groaned and struggled to capture the elusive memories again.

Marissa used her training as a seer to further probe Michael's inner world. Her well-practiced psychic awareness floated along his blood, into his bones, and then deeper, into his soul landscape. Just above the golden luminosity of his pristine, pure life force, she found something. Something foreign that didn't belong. She stopped, breath catching, her muscles stiffening. Tenacious green vines grew profusely on hawthorn trees outside the cave of his memories. She knew at once that his recollection of their time together had been purposefully tampered with. But how? Every pore of her body felt the foreign intrusion as an earthy, emerald charge. The same taut, visceral sense she had felt during her childhood foray into the Faery Realm. Her priestess instincts honed in on the feeling, on its silken texture. She perceived the honeyed taste of Faery magic. She exhaled slowly. Michael's memory had been bound with some sort of Faery enchantment. She was sure of it. Was this payment for her blunder in bringing Shayla and Ciara into the Realm of Faery when they were but children? Was his memory loss Faery revenge for breaking their laws and entering the Realm without invitation?

No, that couldn't be. Vanora smoothed things over with Lady Ravenna back then, righted the wrong Marissa had committed. And they all had paid with the curse. Then, how did this Faery magic happen? Who did this to him? She ached to bring him back to his full awareness of her. Of them. She pulled up and out of her inner probe, opened her eyes, and examined his face, desperate to find answers there. He watched her, his jaw tight.

He was older now, but she knew every line, every indentation—the dimples paired alongside his mouth, the beauty mark beside his left eye, the small scar by his ear. She had memorized the whole of him six years ago, and had called upon that store of knowledge in her mind's eye every day since then.

He reached for her and whispered, "I don't care who you are, if you're real or not. Because I do know you. From my dreams. And that's enough for me."

She laughed softly. "You told me once you didn't believe I was real."

He searched her face. His eyes brightened, their inner light doused, then lit again, like a flickering candle illuminating the pages of his memory. She willed him back, willed him to remember.

"Is it you . . ." His words were a question. No, a statement.

He hesitated, shook his head, his expression a tumult of confusion. Then, suddenly, he lifted her chin and kissed her. A long lingering kiss that ignited her soul and set fire to her body.

He leaned his head back. "Did you say I told you once I didn't believe you were real?"

"What?" she murmured, lost in the surging sensation of his kiss.

Michael gripped her shoulders, boring into her eyes for a long moment. His voice splintered. "You are . . . you are . . . Marissa."

"Clearly, I am."

"No, I mean, it's you. The priestess. You saved me when I drowned."

"Yes, yes! That's more like it." A profound understanding dawned on Marissa. She couldn't breathe for the sheer force of it. Their love was more powerful than whatever Faery magic had chained his memories. Vanora and her mother had never taught her about this. There was powerful magic in love. "Kiss me again."

Before he could say more, she reached up and drew his head to hers, kissing him on the mouth, nose, eyes, cheeks, and neck. She felt his fire meet hers in perfectly matched desire. She could feel the Goddess's hands reach down, alighting just atop their heads, to bless their joining. Her body throbbed once again in anticipation of the pleasures they would soon share—body, heart, and soul.

"Do you remember anything more?" she asked, softly laughing and nibbling on his ear with her teeth, relishing how he trembled in response, how his hands possessively encircled her waist and dropped down to cup her buttocks.

Michael smiled broadly, eyes twinkling, and the look of despair fled his expression, replaced by one of mischief. "Yes. I do remember! Damned nuisance of a girl you were. Always bossing me, always had to be right. Stubborn." He added softly, "And beautiful, even back then."

Marissa wrapped her arms around him and kissed him again. She held him tight and whispered, "Let's bring back more of your memories."

He nodded, pulling her down with him to lie beneath the oak tree. To create new memories.

Ciara watched in secret from behind the cover of a tall, leafy ash tree some distance away. When Marissa and Michael knelt on the forest floor, she averted her eyes and turned away. Wiping tears away, she pushed her shuddering sobs down where she could no longer feel them rack her heart. She was happy for her sister, truly she was. Her twin had finally gotten her true love back. She scolded herself for her own wistful desires for Michael, and withered at the sight of their reunion.

An idea struck her. She would go back to the white spring and find the lad who looked like Michael. And do her part for his Summer Solstice initiation.

She dabbed her wet eyes with the sleeve of her blue linen kirtle, lifted her chin, and marched straight toward the spring and the young man Michael had left behind. She found him leaning against the thick trunk of a heavily leafed oak tree, watching the thinning crowd of young men and women milling about, still searching for partners. He appeared at ease, his arms crossed, and one knee bent with a foot braced along the tree's trunk. Despite the amusement in his blue eyes, she picked up a trace of nervousness as she approached.

She smiled, hoping it looked genuine, for her heart felt flat. The lad pushed himself away from the tree with his foot and smiled in return. She swallowed down the ache in her chest and wondered if she had been indeed wise, or more likely foolish, to choose the one man who looked so much like Michael.

"I choose you," they said in unison.

Surprised, Ciara inhaled sharply, but the lad laughed. "Then I suppose we are agreed," he said, and bowed to her.

"I suppose so," she answered softly.

She felt awkward in the ensuing silence.

"Philip. My name is Philip de Boulle, and I must say, I find this whole situation a bit unnerving. Until you, that is." He coughed and looked down.

She swallowed back her surprise. Michael's brother? Well, naturally, she'd spotted the resemblance straight away. "Well then," she said, suppressing the quiver in her voice. "Let's calm our nerves with a walk before we . . ." She sighed and held her hand out, glad it wasn't quaking in the way her insides were. "I'm called Ciara. Shall we walk?"

Chapter 29

Glastonbury, England
Anno Domini 1535

Dawn broke and the sky was pale, with hints of orange clouds on the eastern horizon. A few stars straggled, and the full moon set. Morning song of red-breasted robins filled the forest, and Marissa stretched in languid satisfaction. Still wrapped in Michael's arms, she turned to face him, draping her leg atop his. He lifted his hand and gently caressed her cheek. Holding her, they clung to each other without words.

Michael broke the silence. "I love you, you know. I always have, since the moment I opened my eyes on the lakeshore and saw you looking down at me. Your long black hair covering the two of us . . ." He tenderly lifted a length of her hair, wove his hands through it, drawing her mouth to his, kissing her deeply.

After a long moment, she leaned back. "There's something I must say. I'll never mention this again, but I must say it now."

He nodded for her to continue, his eyes still half-lidded with desire.

"I'm so sorry for how we left things those many years ago. My refusing to talk to you or even say goodbye. I should never have believed Ciara could part us. I was young and headstrong then."

"Then?" he said with an easy grin.

Marissa laughed, the sound coming from low in her throat. "Yes, I believe I've always been direct in stating my wants."

She took the opportunity to show Michael once more just what she desired. Last evening's coupling had been a Solstice ritual intended to invoke sacred union through communion with the Goddess of the Stars and Sea, to acknowledge and celebrate the Goddess's presence in all pleasure, especially in that of making love. In the evening's ritual, she had formally invoked the Goddess through prayer, chanting, and anointing each other with oil of frankincense and rose she'd carried in her robe's pocket. This morning, the hallowed fragrance still lingered on their bodies and in the air, and their joining promised to be just as rich and distinctive. This time, though, their years of banked longing made them desperate for each other in a different manner.

"I never want to lose you again," she murmured into Michael's ear, running her hands along his skin, feeling the need for him as vital as the air she breathed.

"I don't understand how I could have ever forgotten you. Us," he said, his lips meeting hers, his voice husky and inviting.

She moaned in pleasure at the waves of sensation building inside her from his finger's caress and the silky fondle of his tongue. Eager to join with him, she gently nudged him onto his back and straddled him.

Her breath, *and oh Goddess*, her heartbeat, raced beyond control. She explored his body as he explored hers, their fingertips memorizing every inch, discovering the ways to pleasure each other best. When she opened to receive him inside her, all thought, all questions, were forgotten. She took him in fully and gave back to him completely. Michael was with her entirely once more.

Inside her, the ancient prayer arose, evoking the sacredness inherent in their physical joining. A holy act made more perfect because it was sourced in their destined love. With deep, easy breaths, she stirred the power in her belly, summoning the alchemy of consecrated lovemaking. The embers kindled and blazed in response, igniting the power coiled at the base of her spine. The raw power flamed and uncoiled. She felt the red arcing spiral of heat undulating up her spine and knew it entwined with the white spiral in Michael's. On this cord of pure ecstasy, their spirits traveled up into the heavens, penetrating the star womb of the Goddess. Silver star-song pulsated to the rhythm of their body's dance and chimed with the Goddess's blessings as She received the spirit of their loving.

The spiraling cord of their union descended back down into their bodies, settling into their blood, their bones, kindling the primordial stardust residing inside their deepest core, where their flesh conjoined the stars within. Their union quickened their souls, the earthly womb of the Goddess herself.

Marissa felt her womb-space throbbing, sending roots of energy deep into the earth to connect with the source of all sustenance. From that center, the Goddess's love flowed back up and into her. The enlivened love spread throughout her body. Love, human and divine, flamed in her heart. Fanning that flame with sharp, quick breaths, she used it as a bodily gateway to unite her soul and spirit. Together, she and Michael met the Goddess above them, within them, and below them. As the Goddess's presence entered him, he drew in a breath filled with awe.

Invigorated by the Goddess, and Michael's acknowledgement of Her, Marissa's second sight flared. She saw her heart open and radiate waves of golden tenderness, linking her with Michael and animating his sacred heart. She closed her eyes and invited the Goddess to embody her once again, as She had the evening before. This time she went beyond embodiment and *became* the Goddess. Suddenly, she was filled with the warmth of Her love, deep and expansive, as she became Her. The Divine Presence vibrated in her body, her belly, her heart. Her eyes met Michael's and she dwelled there, seeing him through the eyes of the Goddess, feeling him through *Her* heart. Before her was a strong, caring, devoted, courageous man, and her devotion went out in blessing.

The Goddess had made Herself known to Michael through their lovemaking. He embraced the divinity Marissa embodied. She saw it reflected in his eyes, felt it in his body.

"The Lady emanates through you," he whispered. "I adore you."

"I love you," she said. Was it herself or the Goddess speaking? It made no difference. As their lovemaking climaxed in unity, she heard the voice speak again. "And I will love you forever."

In a burst of luminosity, they touched the sanctity seeded in their deepest core and ignited the spark of sacred union. Absolute, unreserved, total love. The air stilled, the forest silenced, as they floated in an eternal moment of one body, one heart, one soul. Then peace showered them in a glittering blanket, soft as the hawthorn petals they lay upon. And they banked its embers inside themselves.

Lying entwined in each other's arms, they listened as their breaths grew even and the beating of their hearts slowed to a steady rhythm. Marissa's body became her own once more. Her own heartbeat, her own breath, alive within her chest. Separating after joining so completely with Michael left an unexpected hollow in her heart. But knowing how their loving united them, that they would be forever joined in the Goddess, and would do so again and again, consoled her spirit. *Making love in the ways of the Goddess*, Marissa smiled.

Their bodies glossed with perspiration and the scent of loving filling the air, Marissa tilted her head back from where it had comfortably laid on Michael's shoulder. "We'll be together for always, yes? Just as we promised in the oak grove those many years ago?" she asked, her voice faltering. She needed to hear his promises anew.

Michael lifted her chin. "Yes. Just as we vowed as children."

She smiled and saw her joy reflected in his eyes, but there were so many things she needed to discuss with him. Her enigmatic vision of their shared destiny to be sure, but first, other matters that needed clarifying and resolving for them to be free to be with each other for the rest of their lives. "You know I'm to be Avalon's High Priestess one day."

"I remember." He frowned. "But—can a High Priestess marry? Can you still marry me?"

She lay back, stretching his cloak over them when the morning breeze stirred. "We don't marry in Avalon."

"Then how are we to be together?"

"I take you as my consort. Priestesses call their mates consorts."

"Consort means the same as husband?" Michael was busy slowly tracing his finger down her throat to her chest. She closed her eyes as his hand cupped her breast.

"Yes, in a manner I suppose. It's a partnership favored and recognized by the Goddess, not one made official by the rules of men." she murmured, arching her back.

"Could we . . . would you come with me to Mountain Manor and have our priest marry us as well?"

She rode the sensations he kindled in her with his touch. "If that makes you happy. Yes," Marissa replied, trying to focus on his words.

He smiled. "Now that I've found you again, I don't intend to lose you." He bent over her, trailing his lips down her neck to her chest, his mouth replacing his hand over her breast.

She struggled to speak, but her nipples throbbed under the gentle flicks of his tongue. "I can't think if you keep doing that," she moaned.

He stopped caressing her, and she took a long, steadying breath before she answered him. "I don't intend to ever lose you again either. We are meant to be. Destined. Do you remember feeling that when we met?"

Michael nodded solemnly. "Yes. I remember somehow knowing it was a destiny bigger than us. But I still don't know what that means."

"Nor do I, exactly. Yet. I just know that we share a fate. The Goddess gave me a vision about it. About Her cauldron of creation, a holy bowl."

He leaned his head back. "A bowl? Tell me."

"We've been given a serious task. One that deserves our utmost attention and time to discuss. Let's wait until we're dressed, and when I'm not nearly as tempted to take you into me again. Please." She nuzzled into him once more. Their shared destiny would have to wait just a bit longer, until she could calm her body and clear her mind.

They kissed and clung to each other for a long moment.

Marissa broke the silence, wanting one thing settled for certain. "We shall also hand-fast. It's our way in Avalon to pledge our love for a year and a day."

"You wish to be with me for only a year and a day?" Michael rose up on one elbow.

She chuckled. "No, I wish to be with you all the days of my life. We can renew our vows every year. Or, after a year and a day, we could declare our vows to last for always."

"I suppose this hand-fasting is binding, like a Christian marriage?"

"It's a commitment of our hearts and souls."

He twirled a strand of her hair and let it fall again. "I would still like a priest to marry us as well," he said. "Though I suppose after all the time we've lost, I really don't mind who makes it official, or how we pledge ourselves. Just as long as we do so."

"Then we shall marry in the way of your religion. But since you're here now, we'll hand-fast. It's simple. We do it in private."

"In private? We can do so here and now?"

Marissa nodded. She pulled two single strands of her long hair, tied one around Michael's wrist, one around hers, and joined them in a simple knot. Then she scooped up oak leaf and moss, sprinkling both on their knotted wrists.

Turning to him, she said, "I declare my vow to you for a year and a day and beyond. I do so now."

He reached up to trace his finger over her lips. "As do I."

"So be it. There, it is official."

"Just like that?"

"Just like that. We can complete the rest of the ritual later, tying our hands with ribbons to symbolize our union. There are words we speak before the Goddess."

"But we are truly pledged now?"

"Yes, Michael," she said tenderly.

"I like pledging to you this way. I mean, there is my priest's ceremony to come, too." He bent to kiss her, then stopped. "Are there other traditions in Avalon I should know about?" The twinkle in his eye belied his serious tone.

Marissa felt the heat of his body and snuggled in for more. He wrapped her in his arms and she sighed in pleasure.

"Yes, there is another matter you must know. We spoke about this long ago, in the oak grove. As a priestess, more so as High Priestess, I will need to live in Avalon." She hesitated, chewing her lip. "But you do not." She looked at him, gauging his reaction, hoping he would protest and want to stay with her.

"I don't understand. If you must stay in Avalon, then how are we to be together? Must I live in Avalon, too?"

"It's your choice. Avalon is a hidden realm of women. Female priestesses. But we have always taken consorts, down through the ages. Many, but not all of them, have lived with us. Though our children, both boys and girls, do." She cast her eyes downward, waiting for his response. She could tell he was considering her revelation.

"There's truly nothing in my life that holds me back. I'm not in line to inherit lands. I don't wish to pursue soldiering as my life's work, despite my father's wishes." He squinted, nodding his head. "I think I would like to live in Avalon. I could visit my brothers as I wished?"

Marissa nodded. "Anytime you wish."

"Could I follow my studies? Are there books in Avalon?"

She laughed softly. "More books than you can imagine. Books you have never heard of before." She paused. "You would live in Avalon only because nothing holds you back to your life in Wales? And you'd come only for the books?" she teased.

"Of course. For those mysterious books you speak of." He could only half hide his playful grin.

"Michael?" Her chin trembled despite her best efforts.

"What is it?" He kissed her chin.

"Don't ever leave me again," she whispered.

He looked into her eyes. "I won't. I mean, after my obligation in France. Just this once, and only for a short while. I head for France today, for my family."

Marissa pulled away sharply and sat up, her heart hammering in her chest. "France? Today? What obligation?"

"My brothers and I have been called to defend our family's lands in France. There are uprisings. Religious uprisings. I'm part of my father's retinue, sworn to uphold and defend our holdings."

She grimaced. "The ways of battle don't interest me. I wish they didn't interest you so."

He sighed. "Soldiering isn't my passion either, but I have a duty, a promise, and my honor to uphold. For my family."

She rose to her knees. "What about your duty to you and me? To our shared destiny? We've wasted enough years apart. We've pledged to each other *again*. Stay with me and we can live without these onerous battle-driven duties. Imagine. Would it not be lovely?" She leaned forward, tracing her hand down his chest, and lower still.

He groaned softly. "There's nothing I'd like more. I promise you, I'll return to you. We'll never be parted again. Ever. And when I come back, we'll have the life together we've dreamt of."

"Fie!" Marissa leaned away and jumped to her feet. "The truth of the matter has nothing to do with the facts. You must act from the obligations of your heart, not some misguided sense of duty." Her black hair curtained her chest and torso, the tresses rising with her uneven breath. She wanted to understand this sense of obligation. But she could not. "What about us? Will men never learn? They fight, they always fight. For what? For more lands and power, riches, and dominion over everyone and everything. If that is the way of men, I want nothing of it."

She stood, eyes flashing with anger. Michael rose and stood before her, his eyes still filled with love, but matching her fury with his strength. He stood tall, feet planted solidly on the ground, facing her full on.

"Do you think I'm not aware of the wickedness of which you speak? I loathe what my father aspires for me. I abhor the shedding of blood to get it. But I have this one sworn duty to my father. It will be my last duty to him, for I'm sworn to you now."

She tossed her head, flicking her hair behind her. The early-morning sun outlined the niches and valleys of her body. Michael's jaw clenched in an effort to bite back the desire that his body could not hide.

Her indignation crumbled. "Please don't go. I'm afraid. Afraid if you leave you won't come back," she confessed.

"Nothing can keep me away."

She took a step back, looked up and locked her gaze with his. "Choose me, Michael." She said the words with all the strength and love she could muster. "Choose us. Choose our love over bloodshed and killing, and a soldier's obligation."

He stepped forward, keeping the distance between them close. "I do. I do choose you and me. But I cannot make good on that choice until I return."

"Then go. If you must go, leave now." She turned away from him, batting at the hot tears coursing down her cheeks.

"You don't mean that. Don't send me off in this way."

When she didn't respond, he backed away, jaw still clenched. She heard him slowly exhale, pick up his clothes, his mantle, then a rustle as the clothes dropped to the ground again. Leaves crunched underfoot and suddenly his arms encircled her waist. She tried to pull free, but he reached for her again.

"I love you more than life itself, Marissa. But you must understand a man's honor. I gave my word. I will go to this battle with my brothers. I cannot let them down. I would never forgive myself. And I will return. After that, I pledge a life together. Give me this willingly, with your heartfelt blessing. Wait for me. I will return to you."

He gripped her shoulders and turned her gently. She flung herself into his arms and buried her face in his chest. She wept until she felt dry and empty inside. She inhaled deeply, taking in the smell of him—leather and oak leaves, apple cider, and musky remnants of their passion—storing the scent in her memory to draw upon when she needed to recall their loving in the long days he would be away. Until he returned to her. Once again, she would have to wait.

Marissa sniffed and tilted her head to look up at him. He kissed the remaining tears from her cheeks, his mouth following down to where their salty wetness pooled on the corner of her lips and on her neck. She trembled at the heat of his touch, the urgency of their bodies yearning to come together, but took his hand to stop him. She would extract one more vow from him first. The most important one.

She straightened and stood tall. "If you must go, then promise me one more thing."

"I'll promise you anything in my power to promise." He kissed her forehead and stroked her cheek with his fingertips.

She paused, recalling her terrifying, fiery vision from years ago. She arranged her words carefully. "Believe in me and my vision. Promise me you will never set foot in Glastonbury Abbey."

"I believe in you, Marissa. You saved my life, didn't you? All based on your visions."

She persisted. "Then promise me."

"How could I be part of the abbey when I mean to wed you, and bed you to the end of my days? I could never be a chaste monk with you in my life."

Marissa swallowed thickly and whispered again, "Promise me, Michael."

He raised his hand and crossed his heart to seal the vow. "I promise. And I promise my heart to you. For always and forever."

Chapter 30
Glastonbury, England
Anno Domini 1535

The sun peeked around the side of the Tor, anointing the hill with a crown of light. The town, as well as the Solstice Eve lovers ensconced in the shadow of the woodland, was slow to rise and greet the day. All was quiet except for the occasional call of a crane beside the marsh. Ciara waited for her sister and friend along the misty shoreline of Avalon's lake, the appointed place they had agreed to meet the morning after the celebrations.

The waiting gave her time to bind her broken heart, so that its hurt would be invisible to Marissa. She owed her sister her joy, not her personal sorrow. She had never truly lost Michael, she told herself, because he had never been hers. The effort to conceal her disappointment squeezed her from the inside, making it painful to breathe. She felt hardened and brittle at the same time, like frozen glass primed to shatter. She turned her thoughts to Philip, wanting to find solace in her priestess duty well fulfilled. Though Philip was a de Boulle, brother to the man who did not return her love.

She had not been Philip's first lover, though he was hers, but she was still able to introduce him to bodily pleasures only priestesses were trained in. Vanora and her mother had been right. Awakening her young man to the revelations of the Goddess was sacramental. She had embodied the Goddess and felt the Goddess alive in her. She had reveled in the sensual stirrings of her own body.

Philip had been tender and sweet. He learned well the things she taught him. He came to know the pleasures of the Goddess, the powers of life and love that flowed from Her, through Ciara, to him. Ciara was changed from the experience, and sensed Philip was as well. She had done her duty. Perhaps in time, the remembrance of his sweet ways would ease the cavernous ache in her chest where she carried her one-sided love for Michael.

She turned at the sound of rustling reeds and spotted Shayla making her way through the marshy ground towards her. Her friend looked subtly different. A more brilliant hue to her green eyes, perhaps. Or was it a pale shimmer of silver opalescence round her. She wore a gossamer green mantle about her shoulders, trimmed with living flowers. Bluebells, pink primroses, and pale-yellow hollyhocks fluttered in the gentle lake breeze as she walked, leaving a trail of flower petals in her wake.

Ciara ran to her friend and hugged her. When they pulled apart, she looked into Shayla's green eyes and saw, to her surprise, unfathomable sorrow.

"Shayla, what is it? What sadness chases you after such a night?"

"I know I cannot hide my feelings from you of all people. Oh, Ciara," Shayla cried, moving into the circle of her friend's arms once again.

"I must . . . I have to . . . we are oathbound . . . but I cannot leave! I have always dreamed of this, but I just cannot. Not yet. But I want to. So very badly." Her words were punctuated with sobs.

Shayla wept in a way Ciara had never encountered from her before. Even more desperately than those nights when her half-Faery friend woke from dreams that kindled her desire to be close to her Faery-kind, when she'd been prohibited to do so. Ciara waited until she quieted, until the sounds of sniffling ceased, then led her friend to a boulder they could lean against.

"Folimot came for me," Shayla began.

"Folimot? Wasn't he the guardsman who let us into the Faery Realm? I haven't thought of him in years."

Shayla chewed her lip and cast her eyes downward. Ciara sensed she hid something, but did not push her friend.

"Yes. He is from the Western Realms of Faery. He is my betrothed. We have been oathbound since birth."

"Have you always known this? What does this mean?"

Shayla's eyes watered again. "I only discovered it last eve. What it means is that I am being called back to the Faery Realm—for good."

Ciara's heart clenched. Her dearest friend leaving Avalon? She could not help her response. "Lady Ravenna said you would one day be called back.

I know you've waited for this, but you've been brought up in Avalon. As a priestess and healer."

"I know. As much as I have desired to discover my birth heritage and my father, to follow the calling that sings in my blood, how could I ever bear to part from all those I love in Avalon? Especially you, my dear friend."

Ciara felt a yawning emptiness climb its way up from her depths. She wasn't sure she could hold her grief, her loss. First Michael. Now Shayla. She closed her eyes against the tide of emotion filling her body with an undertow threatening to submerge her. Grief streamed through her, despite her knowing this was about destiny and not her personal desires.

"Shayla, you must do what your heart decrees. You know that." She opened her eyes, took hold of her friend's shoulders. "I don't know if I can be brave enough to ever give that advice again, so hear me now before I take it back and beg you to stay in Avalon."

"Avalon is all I've ever known. You are my sister as surely as you are Marissa's. Oh, I do not know what to do. My desire to be with my Faery kind and my love for you, for Avalon, battle inside me."

Ciara's gaze softened. "We'll ask my mother. She has raised you as her own and knows you well. And as our High Priestess, she carries the wisdom of our lineage."

Shayla nodded her agreement. "You are right. Agreed, we will ask her." She cocked her head, appraising her friend. "How was your evening?"

Ciara blushed. "You're not going to believe who I chose."

"Who?" Shayla asked eagerly.

Ciara sighed. "Michael's brother, Philip."

"What?" Shayla exclaimed.

A loud crunching of dried grass underfoot was followed by a shout of greeting. "Sister! Shayla! I've arrived!"

Shayla threw her a questioning look, but Ciara quickly put a finger to her lips as Marissa approached them, waving her hands in greeting.

"I've found him. Michael has returned," Marissa said as she drew closer.

Shayla inhaled sharply. A mixed look of surprise, concern, and pity mirrored in her eyes.

"How can this be? Ciara, I am so sorry," Shayla sputtered.

Ciara shook her head brusquely. "No. Hush. Please!" She clung to the rhythm of her breath, flowing with its tide. She stood to greet her sister, a smile firmly planted on her face.

Marissa drew near. Ciara braced herself, waiting for her sister to pick her up and spin her around, or to laugh and twirl with her arms reaching for the sky. Instead, she saw the joy in Marissa's eyes vying for pain also present. Her smile could not fool Ciara. Their bond, her own empathic senses, screamed at her that something was wrong. Had the Summer Solstice brought them all nothing but sorrow?

"Isn't it wonderful? Finally! My Michael is mine again."

Ciara flinched, though she couldn't help but feel genuinely happy for the sister she loved so dearly. No matter the cost to her own heart, Marissa's happiness meant the world to her. Still, her twin's eyes and words did not match.

"I'm most pleased for you, my dearest," Ciara said. She looked over her shoulder. "Aren't we, Shayla?"

"This is a grand day, indeed," Shayla replied in monotone, never taking her eyes off Ciara.

Ciara noted that Marissa was so caught up in her news she had not detected Shayla's hesitation, nor her own. Ciara would forever keep her feelings to herself. She would not mar her twin's happiness. Still, she wondered why Shayla hesitated in her well wishes.

Marissa pulled both of them into an exuberant embrace. "All will be well. You'll see."

Ciara peered at her twin. "Marissa, are you well? What troubles you amidst such grand news?"

Marissa leaned back, holding Ciara and Shayla at arm's length. Her facade crumbled. "Michael leaves again . . . but he will return. He didn't even recognize me at first. Not at all. It was Faery magic. Faery bound his memory . . . some horrible Faery spell. I could sense it. Oh Goddess, I'm sorry, Shayla. I didn't mean *Faery* are horrible." Marissa's hand rose to cover her mouth.

Shayla's skin was ashen. She blinked several times then stared at Marissa with a look of shock.

"Shayla?" Ciara said, brushing her friend's arm lightly.

Shayla shook her head. "I am all right," she stammered. "I guess I am surprised, that is all."

"Well, the curse is broken," Marissa said.

"Broken," Shayla repeated. "How . . ." She swallowed back her words.

Ciara peered at her, wondering what was causing her sudden upset and curbed words.

"It appears love is the power that antidotes Faery magic. I must tell Vanora and mother."

"Yes, that is important to know," Shayla muttered.

"But Michael is leaving again? Why?" Ciara asked.

Sadness once again clouded Marissa's features. "He goes off to battle the French, for some piece of land or religious ideal. Which means he'll be gone from me again." She lifted her chin and shook her hair behind her. "But he's promised to return. And it won't be six years this time. He'll come back to me healthy and whole and in good time." She wiped an escaped tear and forced a smile.

Ciara encouraged her sister's bravado. For Marissa's sake as well as her own, but mostly for Michael. For his safety. She would pray every day for it. "Then assuredly, it won't be long before you're reunited again. Look how fate brought you together. You defied a curse by the strength of your bond." She put her arm through Marissa's and patted her hand.

"Ciara, what would I do without your bright cheer? You always know what to say to make me sweep aside my despair. I love you, sister." Marissa kissed her twin's cheek, then turned to Shayla. "As well as you, dear friend. The three of us, together always."

Ciara overheard Shayla's soft whimper at her sister's words. Marissa, oblivious, gathered Shayla close as well.

"Do tell me of your adventures. Shayla," She rested a hand on her shoulder. "More about this Folimot you so eagerly ran off to? And, Ciara, who did you pair up with?" This time, her enthusiasm matched her smile.

Ciara envied her expansive mood. "Well, my darling sister, Shayla found herself a Faery lover just as she desired. And I? I found a most congenial and likeable lad. He . . ." She stopped herself. She didn't want to reveal that last evening's lover was Michael's brother, that he looked so very much like Michael. She wanted to keep him a secret from Marissa. Something she could hold onto and examine, something of her own apart from her twin, something that wouldn't be pulled into Marissa's vivacious orbit. At least until she could reconcile her feelings for Michael. Instead she revealed, "I had a most enjoyable evening of initiation and loving with my Solstice partner."

Shayla eyed her closely.

Marissa beamed. "Is it not the most wonderful thing? Oh Ciara, how did you get on? Did you like him? Did you favor him?"

Ciara raised her palm, gesturing for her to halt her questions. "Marissa, I just met the lad. You know as well as I that our Solstice matings are not normally meant for lifetime involvement, if that's what you mean. I mean, except for you and Michael, of course." Her voice trailed off.

"You're right. I expect too much from a Solstice evening's joining. You did your priestess duty. But I can't help asking." Marissa leaned in closer to Ciara. "Could it mean more?"

Ciara grimaced.

Shayla gave a sidelong glance to Ciara and coughed. "I had a lovely evening as well."

Ciara sent her friend a private look of thanks for sparing her from Marissa's further interest.

Marissa put her arm through Shayla's, her other arm still entwined with Ciara's. "Ah, dear ones, let's part the mists and call for our barge to take us home to Avalon. Then I want to hear all the details from each of you. Don't leave out anything."

Ciara's insides cinched, tightly binding the cords of her heart. Shayla remained quiet, her eyes downcast. Marissa strode forward with her usual tenacity, looking straight ahead, jaw set firm. The three reached the lake's edge and lifted their arms high, perhaps not quite with their usual synchronization, Ciara noted, to part the mists and call for the barge that would return them home to Avalon.

Chapter 31

Glastonbury, England
Present Day

Sophie walked down the short set of steps into the abbey's Mary Chapel. The chapel had once been an underground crypt, centuries ago, and was now open to a sky bruised dark lavender by early twilight. Cold moisture coated the crypt's stone walls, giving off a faint scent of mineral ore along with a residue of incense. She halted at the head of the long nave and squared her shoulders.

Shore up, Sophie, she thought. *Best to confront what's happening. And Daniel needs to know about it. Crap, he's probably the only one who'll believe you about the freakish pages back in the room.* Knowing he'd listen with an open mind felt surprisingly good. She realized she was beginning to trust him.

She gave her eyes a moment to adjust to the dim light. Dusk cast furtive shadows down the nave, outlining an enormous alcove at the other end. She tread softly across the ancient, tiled floor towards the alcove. It sheltered a stone altar faced by two long, stone benches. As she came closer, she made out the form of a man sitting there. Tawny-colored hair curled along his neck told her it was likely Daniel. His straight back and broad, muscled shoulders confirmed it. She arched a brow and grinned, amused by how she so easily slipped into appraising and appreciating his physique.

Daniel's head was bowed, and she thought he might be meditating or praying, or whatever one did in a place such as this. Not wanting to startle him, she sat quietly and slid along the bench until she was a few feet away. He didn't look up.

"He said you'd come." Daniel's voice was low.

Sophie found herself whispering her reply. "Yes, Barry told me you were here."

When he didn't answer, she continued. "We have to talk. Something happened to me this afternoon. Something that doesn't make sense . . . again."

She closed her eyes, deciding how to explain what had transpired since she left him at the abbey that morning—the bizarre journal entries mysteriously penned as she sat unconscious at her desk in the B&B. When she opened her eyes again, he had swung his body around, so he straddled the bench with his back facing her.

"No, not Barry," he said, pulling on his denim jacket.

"What?"

"It wasn't Barry who told me you'd come," he repeated, pausing only slightly. "It was Michael."

"Who's Michael?" In her mind she ran through the names and faces of the people she'd met since arriving in Glastonbury. Generally, she was good at recalling such things, but she couldn't place a *Michael*.

"He's here now." He tilted his head, looking up at a space in front of him. An empty space.

Sophie felt her skin prickle. "Daniel, there's no one here but us." She stood and peered into the dim recesses of the alcove just to assure herself they were alone.

"He says he was a monk at the abbey in the year of the Lord, 1539 . . . and . . . he speaks of someone he calls his dear priestess . . . his beloved."

She stepped to his side. "Daniel, look at me."

No response.

"Are you playing a prank? It's not funny. Stop it."

He nodded his head at the emptiness in front of him, saying, "Yes, I'll tell her."

"Enough of this craziness. Who are you talking to?" she demanded.

"I told you already. It's Michael. The spirit I met last evening. He really is here."

"A spirit? You don't mean a ghost, do you?"

He squinted over his shoulder at her. "I suppose so. Though he doesn't like to be called that."

"Oh, he doesn't? Well then, what should we call him? What should we call *this*?" She raised her arms and made an expansive sweep of the vacant spot in front of Daniel. "A joke?" Her anger felt far better, more familiar, than this utter nonsense that left her flustered and uneasy.

He faced forward again and cocked his head. "He says . . . to just call him Michael."

Sophie rolled her eyes.

He abruptly lifted a hand. "Wait."

She raised her voice. "I will not wait."

Daniel spoke over her. "He says he missed something in the Horarium. The names of the fellow monks he sang with in the perpetual choir. Walter, Peter, Geoffrey, Roland . . ."

Her hand shot out to grab his shoulder to stop him. Or maybe to steady herself. Her baffling penned pages spoke of an Horarium and a perpetual choir. Her heart began the same hammering she'd felt earlier that day in her room.

He continued. "He says the abbey's library was magnificent. So many books. More than he'd ever seen, and all in one place. He studied many of them before the abbey fell."

As Daniel relayed Michael's words, alarm tightened Sophie's stomach. The stories were verbatim the pages written in the unfamiliar handwriting back at her B&B. When he began to speak of Michael's 'dear priestess,' her legs nearly buckled, hardly able to hold her upright.

This was outlandish. She wanted him to help her make sense of what happened in her room, not add more madness to the matter. She searched herself for the strength she normally relied on when things got beyond her control out in the field on assignment. She supported her knee against the bench, stood as tall as she could manage, and dredged up her journalistic courage. She'd push through her panic and use her expertise to get to the bottom of all this.

"How do you know about the Horarium?" she asked Daniel crisply.

He shrugged his shoulders. "Hmm? I don't know what an Horarium is. I'm just telling you what he's telling me."

She tried another route, voice trembling. "Okay, Daniel, think about it. Michael can't be a monk. He's calling someone his dear priestess, his beloved. Priestesses were considered heathen, even dangerous in the eyes of the Church during King Henry's time. How could a priestess be a monk's . . . beloved? How could a monk even have a beloved?"

He stared once more into the void, infuriating Sophie. She thrust her arms out to the side. "Dammit Daniel, ask him *that*." *Crap, I just asked him to ask a dead monk a question for me.*

He responded immediately, his speech halting, but his voice calm. "Michael says the Church still had its rules, but there were some things it couldn't control. Priestesses of the Goddess were one of them, ancient traditions were another. He says it is a story he will tell if you will listen." He raised his gaze to Sophie and whispered. "And he says, then, maybe, you'll both begin to remember."

She snorted. "Begin to remember? That's it. I'm done here." She realized she'd rested her hand on Daniel's shoulder and she snatched it back. If she walked away now, she could hold onto at least a veneer of sanity.

"It's easier to hear him when you touch me."

The comment froze her in place. "I'm not participating in this farce." She clasped her hands tightly together to stop them from shaking. *What if this monk, this Michael, is real?*

"Ah. He said the apple blossoms fell like snow clouds the Summer Solstice he was with . . . with Marissa." His tone turned tender. "His dear priestess."

Ache and desire exploded into Sophie's awareness like a detonation that filled her abdomen with fire. She wrapped her arms around her middle. The honeyed scent of apple blossoms perfumed the air around her. She clenched her fists and dug her nails into her palms to induce pain, a more reliable reality. Swallowing hard, she shoved all other feeling and sensation down, clamping an iron lid on them. Then she lowered herself onto the bench beside Daniel.

His body stilled, his voice became a soft caress. Through Daniel's sometimes faltering words, Michael spoke again about his intense and forbidden passion for the woman named Marissa. His pleading sincerity rooted Sophie to the bench, ensnared as though ropes bound her.

I have to put a stop to this nonsense, or leave, she told herself. But she somehow couldn't go. Grief and longing gripped her heart. Daniel had managed to convey Michael's deep anguish that pleaded for her forbearance now. She wiped the tears streaming down her cheeks, surprised at her body's reaction.

Sophie spoke, not sure she really wanted to converse with a dead monk, but she aimed her words at the empty space in front of Daniel, where Michael purportedly stood. "Who are you?" she asked softly.

If he replied, she heard nothing. Daniel answered momentarily. "He says, 'Recognize me. I have always been yours.'"

Her heart clenched. "I'm telling you, I don't know who you are," she insisted, less confidently now.

She didn't need to see the ghost to sense how crestfallen he was at her response. It resonated in the timbre of Daniel's voice as he echoed Michael's reply. "Remember when we played Hide-n-Hunt as children, how we ran across the fields of primrose and grass? The day you told me how guilty you felt over jeopardizing those you brought into the realm of Faery. We chose each other that day, made our promises. Young as we were." Daniel sighed before he continued. "It is a choice I have never forgotten." His voice lapsed for a moment. "I mean, Michael says it's a choice he's never forgotten."

Sophie felt a wave of pressure pass through her chest, a ball of sadness that lodged deep in the caverns of her heart, into spaces she never knew existed. She grabbed Daniel's shoulders and swung him around to face her.

A sob pierced her voice. "Who *are* you?"

He stared at her. Through her. "I'm your Michael."

Her hands dropped limply to her lap. She couldn't speak at first. Finally, she forced her reply around the heaviness in her chest, past the weeping that continued to climb from her heart to pour from her eyes. She angrily swiped the tears away with her hands. It was too much to feel this, whatever this was that Michael's words engendered within her. She wanted to know more. She also wanted to run, but remained seated. "Please. Stop this. Whatever you're doing to me, stop it."

Daniel breathed the name, "Marissa . . ."

A deep keening surfaced from Sophie's depths. She clamped her mouth shut to swallow it back. If she let it out, she feared it might slash her soul in two.

"Remember me," the voice beseeched. "Remember me. Daniel knows."

Her voice fought through layers of clenched muscles and heartache to choke out a response. "But I don't remember you." *This isn't real. This isn't real. Pull yourself together. Why does it feel so real?*

"You must remember us. You and me, my dear priestess. And more importantly . . . I beg you, tell my story."

The air sparked, charged with Michael's despair. Sophie shivered. "I am not your dear priestess."

Daniel's voice quavered, eyes still staring ahead into nothing. "Oh, but you are."

She gulped, her throat dry. Tender feelings, intimate feelings infused her heart. Feelings she couldn't rationalize.

"Michael says that first you must know the abbey has secrets. He knows them. He says the true story must be told. You know the true story. You just have to remember it."

Sudden orange and red flames appeared in Sophie's mind's eye. She gasped and jumped up, blinking hard to erase the image. It swiftly faded, leaving her heart pounding. In its place she beheld a simple wooden bowl gleaming silver under a night sky. That image faded as well, leaving her even more confused and agitated. She moaned and rubbed clammy palms along her pant legs.

Am I going crazy? No! She'd always prided herself on her logical mind and practical nature. *Maybe reality is not what I think it is.* She remembered Barry's cryptic comment: *The facts and the truth are two different things.*

She began to pace back and forth. Maybe she ought to just listen to what Daniel, or Michael, had to say. He claimed there was a buried story. The *true* story, he had called it. She wavered, her journalistic instinct piqued. She gathered the pieces the inexplicable grief had shattered within her, brushed them into a pile and hid them in a corner of her heart to be dealt with later.

"True story? True story of what?" she asked, twisting to face Daniel.

"What happened to the monks of Glastonbury Abbey. King Henry's men came not only to claim the abbey, but to desecrate it . . . and the monks therein."

"Desecrate the monks?" She shook her head, her thoughts vacillated, leaning towards hard reason again. "Wait. We can't rely on what this Michael says. He isn't real." Yet, his words etched themselves in her mind like lines of sentences in an article, so clearly she could see them, hear them, feel them.

"He says there's more. Veiled teachings. A secret treasure. A hidden abbey."

Her fear slowly deflated, replaced by curiosity. *What if this were true?* "Okay. Fine. What are these secrets? Can we verify them?"

"He says we must finish what we started. We must find the sacred bowl. Now is the time to show it to the world. The world is ready, and the world needs it."

She jerked her head back, startled. "What in the heck does that mean?" The image of the bowl she'd seen not a moment ago flashed again in her mind.

"He says to first promise to tell his story." Daniel's voice dimmed. His body slumped forward.

Sophie leapt to kneel beside him, clutching his arm. "Daniel? Daniel?"

He blew out a long, shaky breath before gingerly lifting his head, blinking rapidly. "Marissa? Sorry. I mean, Sophie." He shifted in his seat and rubbed his neck and shoulder with his hand.

She scowled. "Of course it's Sophie," she said matter-of-factly. Internally, she walled off any remaining shards of sadness from before.

"Give me a moment," he said, running a hand over his face.

She felt her ire rise, masking her fear. "That wasn't funny, Daniel. Don't ever do that again." She meant it. Not just the sheer ludicrous fact that he claimed to speak for a dead monk, but the anguish. She couldn't bear that anguish.

"If all this pissed you off that much, I'll make sure to avoid doing it again."

She couldn't tell whether he was serious or mocking her. "Don't mess with me."

"Hmmm . . . if looks could kill," he murmured.

"And that's exactly what I'll do to you if you ever pull that again."

He flung his hands up in a gesture of peace. "I'm sorry, Sophie. I don't mean to laugh."

"You just had a conversation with a ghost. And you're laughing at me?" She placed herself directly in front of him, fists on hips, eyes slitted.

"Trying not to."

She looked him up and down. She sensed he was not one bit afraid of her temper. Deep down, she also knew he would never purposefully play with her emotions. "You mean to tell me this was for real?"

"So, you *do* believe I spoke to Michael. You believe what he said." His expression turned serious.

She shrugged her shoulders and sighed heavily.

"Come on." Daniel stood. "You heard what he said. You saw him, too, didn't you?" He leaned forward, his face inches from hers, and gripped her shoulders.

He smelled of musk and vanilla and sandalwood. His nearness, his touch, caught her off guard. Her already quivering muscles now felt heated by the blaze flaring in her belly. She fought to regain her anger. Even neutrality would do just fine about now. Daniel must have felt something too, because he dropped his hands as if they'd touched fire and stared, first at his palms, then at her face. She felt his soft exhale across her cheek. She lifted her fingers to the spot where his breath touched her.

"So, Michael and Marissa could be real?" she asked softly. She stepped back, away from Daniel, and waited for an answer.

His eyes didn't waver from hers. She was struck by how blue they were and the tenderness alive in them. She took another step back and willed the lava flow in her blood to cool. *It's only the rush of adrenaline*, she told herself.

The momentary glimpse of tenderness clouded over, and Daniel tore his gaze from hers. He thrust his hands in the pockets of his corduroy's. His jaw tightened as he spoke, "I came out here to sort through my thoughts, about being able to see ghosts again. I came back here specifically because this is where I have seen *him* most frequently." He looked up, searched her face, his eyes pleading with her not to resist the inexplicable. Nor to deny what she'd experienced.

Sophie chewed the inside of her cheek. He wanted her to trust what had just happened, but she needed to get as far away from him as possible. There was too much confusion in her body's response to his nearness. Too much grief remained lodged in her chest from the encounter with Michael—whoever or whatever he was. Hallucination or prank. Her logical mind just didn't want to believe any of this, regardless of her experiences to the contrary, but her wall of stubborn resistance was teetering. She had to leave now or she would do something completely rash. Like agree there was really such a thing as ghosts. Particularly, a ghost named Michael. Or maybe, even more foolishly, she'd grab Daniel and beg him to hold her. Even better, kiss her. *That's it*, she scolded herself, *no more of this*. She spun around, intending to bolt up the stone steps and out of the chapel. But Daniel grabbed her elbow.

"Wait. We can verify all of this. Well, hopefully we can. But even if we can't, I know what I felt when Michael mentioned Marissa."

Sophie froze. Either they were both imagining things or the ghost's story was real. She didn't like either option. She shook her arm free.

He grabbed her other arm. "You felt something, too, didn't you?" he demanded. When she didn't answer, he said, "Sophie, listen. It's okay. All of this seems strange, maybe even crazy, but we both felt something happen here. It's okay. Look, I believe he's real. At least we can be in this together."

She stared at his mouth as he talked. Lips soft and full. She couldn't reply, she could only stare. If she didn't leave now, she was afraid what she would do. Either kiss him or punch him. She broke free of his grasp.

"I'm sorry. I can't do this." She ran up the stairs.

She stopped at the top, her body tense. She pushed against the churning in her gut and made a decision—the kind of decision she would make if she were back reporting on the front lines in Iraq or Palestine. The kind of decision that had once marked her as fearless. Or maybe irresponsible and foolish. She wouldn't run away from her fear. She'd face it full on, anguish and all.

She shuffled back down the steps and held his gaze. "All right. We'll talk about this."

Daniel smiled. His easy, lop-sided grin lit up his eyes and creased his dimples.

"Umm . . . first I have something weird to show you, back in my room. Some new information that, well, let's say, recently came my way. I need to corroborate a few things." She sighed and shook her head. "Maybe even compare them to what we just heard. From Michael? Meet me in half an hour. Meet me . . ."

"We can meet at the Abbey Lodge," Daniel said. "There's a private study on the first floor we can use."

Sophie nodded, not trusting herself to smile, or frown, or show any emotion whatsoever, lest it soften her earlier resolve to stay focused and strong. She darted back up the steps and headed for her B&B to pick up the bizarre papers she'd penned that afternoon.

Chapter 32

Glastonbury, England
Present Day

Sophie jogged the steep lane up Wearyall Hill, to the B&B to retrieve the handwritten pages from her desk where she'd left them. She took a brief moment to pause by her sink and splash cold water on her face. Patting it dry, she observed the dark circles under her eyes. Her uprooted sense of reality, her tired and hungry body, and her unexpected reaction to Daniel's nearness, had all left her feeling bruised and shattered.

Once she passed through the large oak door of the Abbey Lodge where she had arranged to meet Daniel, her determination and resolve strengthened. He was waiting for her in the expansive foyer, leaning against the mahogany stair rail, his satchel looped over one shoulder.

"Hello again," he drawled, eyes riveted on her.

Still uncomfortable with the feelings he, and Michael, had aroused at the Mary Chapel, she avoided the direct eye contact. Instead, she looked past him, up the staircase. A series of timeworn oil paintings lined the walls, all depicting several of the more illustrious abbots of the Glastonbury monastery, including the last abbot, the ill-fated Abbot Whiting. Her attention snapped back to Daniel when he held up a brown bag of Indian carryout. Her stomach growled at the aroma of spiced curry.

He studied her face for a moment in his disconcerting way, his gaze an almost tender caress.

"What?" she pushed aside a few strands of hair, tucking them behind her ear.

"Nothing," he said finally. "Barry is waiting for us with the key to the library room, and a thermos of coffee." He offered his crooked smile. "It looks like we both could use some caffeine."

She smirked. "Yeah, well I probably couldn't sleep even if I tried. Too wound up. Plus, I've got this to keep me up." She patted her canvas bag holding the pages she'd brought with her.

"Well then, onward," he said, motioning her forward. "Follow me."

He led her to the back wing of the lodge, past two large sitting rooms fashioned with luxuriant woolen rugs and cushy sofas, and down a well-lit hallway. At its end, in front of a thick mahogany door, stood Barry, softly whistling. A grandfather clock opposite the door chimed 8:00 p.m.

"Sophie, good to see you again," Barry said. He offered his hand. She gave him a quick hug instead, turning his forehead crimson but bringing a shy grin to his craggy face.

He took an ancient-looking barrel key out of his front shirt pocket, a swirl of brass in an ornate pattern. "Guests can use this library room on request, but I'll make sure no one bothers you tonight."

He fit the key bit into the lock and when it clicked open, he ushered them into a modest chamber lined with glass-covered bookcases along three walls. Sophie was glad for the privacy, but hesitated, suddenly loath to step into any new discovery lest it prove as unsettling as her unconscious writing bout or Michael's ghost. She set her jaw, called on the resolve she'd felt earlier, and strode deliberately through the doorway. A long oak table and chairs were the central focus of the room, with brocade armchairs positioned in each corner. The brown velvet drapes that curtained the lead-lined window smelled musty to her, and she sneezed.

Barry set the thermos on the table and switched on the table lamps, making the room feel cozier. He closed the door behind them, then pushed on a wall panel next to the nearest bookshelf. It rotated outwards, exposing a locked cabinet.

"We keep a few old books in here. Nothing we'd like visitors to bother with. I think you may find some more obscure information in them. They may help you with your article, Sophie."

"Barry to the rescue, again," she quipped. "It's always best for me to quote original sources. Thank you so much." She was surprised and genuinely grateful at her luck to peruse such unique resources.

He produced another smaller key. The metal handle was fashioned in the shape of a Vesica Pisces, the two interlocking circles she'd seen forged in wrought iron atop the Chalice Wellhead. The symbol triggered a slight jolt along her spine, just as it had when she'd first seen it above the wellspring. It felt familiar. Important. She had no idea why.

Opening the cabinet, Barry pulled a few dusty volumes out from their hiding place. One was a reproduction of Richard Warner's 1826 major study, *The History of the Abbey of Glaston*. Sophie gasped in delighted surprise.

"I wanted to show you this one in particular. This copy isn't quite antique as the original, but it's still a good resource and in rather good condition," he explained.

He pulled two more tomes chronicling the abbey's history and placed them on the table. She ran her fingers along the book's spines, relishing the research ahead of her. But the books had to wait a moment. Setting her bag down next to the fresh stack, she pulled out her papers. She was eager for Daniel to see them, even impatient, and didn't mind Barry's presence. In her gut, she somehow trusted him not to think her silly or crazy.

"Would you like to stay?" she asked Barry.

"For just a moment perhaps. If I can be of help," he added.

Daniel set his knapsack and the bag of food on the table and took the pages from her hand. He studied the first one while Barry returned the rotating wall panel to its original position.

"Where did these come from?" Daniel's eyes scanned the pages rapidly as he shuffled through them.

She took a deep breath, watching him closely. "I wrote them."

At his confused look, she continued. "I mean, I did *physically* write them, only I don't remember writing them. And it's not my handwriting. But I was the only one in my room at the time."

Barry nodded. "You say you don't remember writing anything? It's not such an uncommon thing here in Glastonbury. It's called automatic writing. The words come from the subconscious or, perhaps, the spiritual. Maybe even the supernatural."

Sophie rolled her eyes. "Supernatural? Barry, I swear this place attracts bizarre ideas. Like flies to honey."

"Do you have another explanation for these?" Daniel asked her, holding up the papers she'd given him.

She shrugged her shoulders. "I give in," she muttered.

Barry simply grinned, reminding her of *Alice in Wonderland*'s Cheshire cat.

Sophie's phone buzzed inside her bag. A text message from Sid. *'How's the abbey story shaping up?'* Perfect. How was she supposed to tell her editor that their attempt at restoring her credibility was resulting in ghostly encounters and something supernatural called automatic writing? Reporting any of this would only make her the laughing stock of the journalistic world all over again. She hesitated. Maybe what she really wanted, really needed was, yes, responsible journalism, but on her own terms.

Barry watched her in silence as she clicked off her phone, then he walked to the bookshelves across the room and pulled out a curious-looking volume. "You might find some answers within its covers," he said, handing it over to her. "It's time I go now." He swung around and left the room, quietly nudging the door shut behind him.

Still standing, Daniel was occupied with Sophie's pages, scouring one penned sheet after another, piling them face down on the long table once he'd examined them. "Sophie, this is exactly what that monk, Michael, told us at the chapel."

She bowed her head slightly and sighed. "I know."

So, Daniel confirmed it. And he didn't call her crazy. His validation lay like sunken treasure in her gut. Its heaviness didn't allow words to surface for her to discuss the pages after all, much as she'd intended to. She suddenly longed for the verbal jousting they'd engaged in since they met. Hell, she didn't know what she wanted anymore. Or what was real. Confusion, acceptance, and stubborn rebellion made for a crazy concoction in her mind.

"That's why I brought the pages for you to see. Can you give me just a little more time before we hash that out? Let me go through some of these books?"

To her relief, he nodded in agreement, buying her a bit more time to digest all the strange occurrences since she'd arrived in Glastonbury. She eyed the cover of the last book Barry had handed her. It was a thin volume, published posthumously the back cover revealed. The title read *Gate of Remembrance*. She sat down at the table. Daniel seated himself opposite, once more absorbed in the written work she'd brought.

Sophie contemplated the book. Touching it sent prickles up her arms. She scolded herself for being silly and set it aside. She picked up the older reference work instead and set it in front of her. Reaching into the bag of food, she grabbed a samosa from its plastic container and absently nibbled as she began to read.

After only an hour of research, she shook her head. "Bastard," she spat out.

Daniel's head shot up. "What did I do now?" he said grinning.

"Not you," she replied, not taking the playful bait. "King Henry the VIII."

"Thank goodness. Wasn't sure what I did this time."

She didn't laugh. Head lowered, her finger ran along the words on the pages of the reference books. "It's his religious reformation. There were eight hundred monasteries and nunneries in England when he began his reign. In the 1530s he had them all dissolved, turned out the monks and nuns, and absconded with the abbey's wealth."

"None left whatsoever?" Daniel asked, turning serious since Sophie refused to take notice of his quips.

"None. Nada. All in the name of *religious preference*. More like greed and lust." Her voice rose and sped up as it always did when she spotted injustice. "He wanted a divorce so he could marry Anne Boleyn. The Church wouldn't allow it, so he makes a new Church. Many people suffered because of his capricious whims. Not only in England, but abroad as well. The Reformation grew like wildfire and neighbors turned to enemies. What an idiot."

"I've always been interested in the Reformation, how it all started. It was such a turning point in history. Not only in England, but abroad."

"Here's an interesting detail," Sophie pointed to a page in her book. "Wow. Protestant dissidents actually invaded the bedchamber of the French King, Frances I, at Amboise. They put an anti-Catholic poster in his bedchamber..."

"That's some security breach."

"No kidding. Within nine months of that, King Henry's chief minister, Thomas Cromwell, began the process of taking over and dissolving England's abbeys. Things sure moved quick."

"I would have loved to be a fly on the wall when Cromwell's men came here to Glastonbury Abbey," Daniel said wistfully.

"Yeah. To see exactly how he did it. Scum."

He coughed lightly "We could ask Michael."

Sophie shook her head, put her hand up. "Whoa. Not that again. I said I need some time."

He reached across the table and rubbed her hand reassuringly. "It's all right. Take the time you need. It's been a rough day."

She felt her hand tingle at his touch and pulled back. Her body was betraying her with these surprising jolts of energy. Or maybe her body was trying to tell her something her mind kept fighting and suppressing. She swallowed down the swell of distress she'd just managed to quell by engrossing herself in the sane activity of research. Head down again, she returned to her books in silence, making sure her hands were under the table, away from Daniel's.

Three hours later, she rubbed her eyes and leaned against her chair, arching her back, stretching her aching muscles. Daniel looked up from a sketch he'd been penciling and drained his third cup of strong black coffee. He hadn't interrupted her research since he'd finished reading her penned pages. In his patient fashion, she knew he was waiting for her to ask for his opinion when she was ready.

The grandfather clock in the hall outside the library door chimed midnight. He raised his brows, the question unspoken but understood.

"No, I'm not leaving just yet," she said. "These books validate and embellish my earlier research. To get information from original sources is fantastic." She paused. "I still have this last book to go through. Then I promise we'll talk about the pages I brought. Okay?" She opened the cover to the book Barry handed her earlier. Looking at the title, *Gates of Remembrance*, caused another shockwave to quiver up her arms. "Damn," she mumbled.

"I'll be here waiting," he said.

She took a deep breath to calm herself. "Thanks for being understanding with me. What are you working on?"

He came around the table to sit beside her, sketchpad in hand. "It's an image of Michael."

"Oh," she gingerly accepted the pad from his hands. The face looking back at her resembled the one Daniel had painted that morning in the abbey grounds, only this sketch exhibited much clearer detail.

"You're not going to faint again, are you?" he asked, watching her closely.

"Absolutely not," she snapped. She wasn't going to admit she felt light-headed just looking at the drawing.

Michael's sketched face disturbed her in the same way his ghostly words had at the Mary Chapel. She somehow knew that face. Intimately. The eyes held an uncanny depth. The smile was gentle, yet sad. A crooked smile accentuated by dimples. His tawny hair wasn't cut in the usual fashion of a monk of the sixteenth century, but instead, curled past his ears.

"I know his hair isn't tonsured. But that's how he appears to me," Daniel said, as if reading her thoughts.

"Of course he's not tonsured. He should never have been a monk." Sophie looked up, clapped a hand over her mouth. "I don't know why I said that." She shoved the sketch back toward him.

She turned to the piles of her handwritten pages that lay scattered on the table where Daniel left them.

"I swear those pages are taunting me," she said.

"Or pleading with you."

"All right, all right. Enough. Let me get through this last book, then we'll talk about them."

She skimmed over the introduction of *Gates of Remembrance* and concentrated on reading. Daniel flipped the sheets of his sketchpad to a fresh leaf and began a new drawing.

Sophie read the most interesting and strange findings aloud to him as he sketched. She learned that the book's author, Frederick Bligh Bond, had been an early twentieth-century archeologist and expert in ecclesiastical architecture, hired to help uncover some of the abbey's obscure history. She also discovered Mr. Bond relied on paranormal means to actually locate excavations on the abbey grounds. He continued working that way for over a decade.

Briefly suspending her focused reading, she told Daniel, "Bligh Bond was eventually dismissed from the project for his unorthodox and unusual activity." She glanced up, feeling smug. "Of course he was. Paranormal methods are a ludicrous excuse for genuine research."

He arched his brows.

"Well, he published his reports anyway. He said the abbey was the longest church building in England," she said.

"Nothing odd about that."

"No, but he reckoned there was some sort of occult significance to the length of the church and the way it lined up with other parts of the building. Something to do with the architecture intentionally built to connect with what he called a '*universal mind*.'"

He leaned his elbows on the table. "Universal mind sounds like Carl Jung. He's well respected."

"Yeah, I guess. But Bond said he tapped into this universal mind, pushed aside the veils of time and space, and then communicated . . . wait . . . he communicated . . ." Her voice trembled as she reread the last paragraph. "He communicated with the medieval monks of the abbey to acquire his information." She swayed on her chair. "Much of the time it was through automatic writing."

Daniel reached for her hand again. Sophie knew he meant to comfort her, but she pulled her hand back, afraid of feeling the enigmatic connection with him.

She stilled, staring at the next sentence in the book. "It says Bligh Bond's dig sites on the abbey grounds actually corroborated what the automatic writings had predicted."

"Aha." He held up a page of her notes. "So, you believe these now?"

Was it real? Could it be real? Pull yourself together, Sophie. She glowered at him. "You don't understand. I can never publish anything sourced from that damn automatic writing, can I? No one would believe me. It's not considered a credible source. Look what happened to Bligh Bond. Fired. I'd be ruined for good, just like him. My career is already on the line here."

The defiant phrase, *responsible journalism, but on my own terms,* popped into her thoughts again. She turned away so he wouldn't see the traitorous, frustrated, tear rolling down her cheek.

He reached out again, and this time managed to grasp her hand before she could pull back. "Sophie. Take this one step at a time. You've been given clues. Follow them through. Then worry about what to do with them next. Don't fight what's happening to you."

She knew he was referring to the paranormal experiences. She wondered if he also aimed his advice at the budding feelings between them. She turned back to him with a weak smile. "When did you get to be so wise?"

"Hard won, that wisdom."

She bobbed her head in understanding. Death and grief could do that to a person. He didn't let go of her hand and she didn't pull away. His touch surprisingly meant so much to her. Blue eyes searched hers for something she wasn't sure she was ready or able to give.

Gates of Remembrance slipped from her lap and fell to the floor with a loud thud. She bent down in her chair to retrieve it. Daniel knelt at the same time to recover it for her. She felt his face near hers, close and warm. Grabbing the book, she started to straighten herself. He still hadn't let go of her hand.

He lifted his other hand and tucked a strand of hair behind her ear. She found herself sliding gently down her chair to kneel, facing him. She couldn't have run away if she'd wanted to. And she didn't want to. She leaned forward, lifting her face to his. He met her with a kiss. For one unexpected moment, she felt her chaotic world restored to order. There was something right about how his lips felt on hers, his arms holding her against him, his hand stroking her back. The book slipped from her fingers, falling to the floor again. The thud startled her. She picked it up and held it up between them like a wall. A safe wall. What had she been thinking? She wasn't sure how to reset the panic button going off inside her.

"Damn book. You'd think it was alive," she said, forcing her tone to be light.

She could barely catch her breath. He didn't seem to be breathing very evenly either. She pulled her hand from his. Hers felt suddenly cold and empty.

"God, Daniel, I'm so sorry. That shouldn't have happened. I mean, I know you still miss your wife and all."

"What just happened was about you and me, Sophie."

"I just don't think either of us is in a good place for something like this."

His eyes betrayed his hurt, asking her to not run away from this, too. His voice was firm. "Something like this? You need to understand that I don't do anything unless I mean it."

They were still kneeling, and stared at each other for one long, silent moment. This was all too much, her emotions were flooded from the day's bizarre events, and now this intimacy with Daniel. She hung onto the table to help her stand.

"It's late. Maybe I . . . maybe I better get back to my B&B after all," she stammered.

This time he didn't try to stop her.

Chapter 33
England
Anno Domini 1535

The day was clear with no sign of rain as the de Boulle retinue passed from the woodlands to the grasslands. The third day of their overland trek to reach the narrow arm of the North Sea and their awaiting ship to France had been uneventful thus far.

Roger turned his horse to face the men, and held a hand up, gesturing for them to halt. "As we ride in the open, be yet again on guard."

"For what?" Philip cocked his head to one side, goading his brother on.

"Bandits, ye' little git," George said, mockingly.

"Bandits in the woods, outlaws on the roads. Is that all England has to offer? I much prefer Wales," Philip groaned, his perennial smile nullifying the complaint.

Roger faced his horse forward and announced over his shoulder, "If we remain on guard, there are enough trained soldiers in our party that any bandits brazen enough to attack can be skillfully dealt with."

"Ever the soldier. The leader. Not very much fun anymore," Philip whispered to Michael.

"Don't blame Roger. Blame England's high taxes and widespread unrest," Michael said.

"I know that. I listened when Master Ralph taught us as well, you know. Don't be condescending."

As usual, Michael took Philip's remarks in the congenial spirit they were intended. And as the retinue trudged forward, he fought to stay alert for any

255

surprise threats amidst his unrelenting thoughts of Marissa. Thoughts that made his groin come alive at the recurring image of her naked beside him, under the oak tree in Glastonbury a mere three days ago. He replayed the memory and smiled. He drew inspiration from her pledge of love, her bewitching eyes, the feeling of her in his arms, her legs entwined with his. He felt his body quicken yet again at the pleasure of all she taught him that night. The awe-inspiring way she brought him to an awareness of the Goddess within and around him. For he became truly divine when he was in her arms, when she embodied the Goddess as she had on Solstice Eve. He readjusted his position in his saddle and groaned silently for the sheer wanting of her.

Even Marissa's fury at his leaving for France, her demands he heed her warning to stay clear of the Glastonbury Abbey, only added to his longing for her. Her fiery nature invigorated him. He pictured their future life together when he returned. Days spent studying Avalon's exotic books, perhaps even writing books himself. Nights spent in unbridled passion with Marissa. Learning and living what their shared destiny entailed, for she hadn't the time to tell him what her vision had shown her before he'd needed to leave the village and rejoin his retinue. He wished he were with her right now. His eyes scanned the horizon and the grasslands, but his heart saw only Marissa.

The group rode on, and on Roger's orders, kept to the outskirts of the dense forests, riding their horses swiftly through open, grassy moors, and over the rolling hills of southern England. They kept to themselves and did not attract attention, only entering small villages when necessary to augment their supplies. They were now two day's ride from the watery channel between England and France, and the ship Roger had arranged to carry them across the water.

Whenever they set up camp in the dark and chill nighttime, Philip kept true to his word. As Michael had asked of him, his brother faithfully, perhaps a little too eagerly, poked him awake whenever he dreamt aloud or moaned in his sleep. Though his dreams were no longer haunted by a mysterious girl, his nightmares now exposed his agitation over his decision to be independent of his father's rules, and the discussion he would need to have with his Da' upon his return home. In return for his brother's nightly guard, Michael stopped the childhood habit of tousling Philip's hair in jest.

On their last night on the road, for they would reach their ship by late morning the next day, they once again set camp, and David began preparing the evening meal. The aroma of roasting hares, caught earlier in the day, made Michael's stomach rumble. He rested against an elm tree a short distance from the campfire. The knights sitting around laughed as they passed a flask of hard cider between them. Despite their rough ways, he'd grown close to these men, even sour-mannered George and patronizing David. In between their barbs, they'd shown him the ways of the road and helped him further hone his fighting skills with arrow and sword. He'd come to realize their jests stemmed from the camaraderie that ripens when soldiers quest together.

He held a small book in his hands, a volume Master Ralph had snuck into his pack before he left Mountain Manor. He touched the smooth vellum of the leather-bound tome, his fingers tracing the printed words inside. So far, there hadn't been time to read on this journey—not enough light to see the words in the dark once they'd stopped traveling for the day. But holding it was enough.

Philip strolled over, flask in hand, and held it out. Michael took a swig as his brother sat on the forest floor across from him.

"You're quiet tonight, brother," Philip remarked, taking back the flask.

"I've a lot on my mind."

Philip grinned and his eyes sparkled. "Solstice Eve?"

Michael felt his face heat. "Aye, there is that."

Since the night with Marissa, memories of his time as a boy in Avalon had returned. He'd shared recollections with Philip during the long hours riding side by side. How he'd felt bonded to her, even as a young lad when they'd first met by the lake. And the renewed promises they'd made during Solstice Eve, to be with each other forever. How it changed everything for him.

Philip squinted at him. "You've that look on your face again. No wonder the men tease you mercilessly." He punched Michael lightly on the arm and lay back on the twigs and grass, arms crossed under his head. "Me as well. I'm afraid my Solstice lass has wound her way into my heart."

"Really? You're not the sort to fall so quickly under a maiden's spell."

"This is no ordinary maiden." He turned his head to look at Michael. "She's beautiful, with golden hair and the palest blue eyes. And she's kind. Gentle."

"So, you've told me. Every day since we left Glastonbury."

"You know me too well. I won't have it. From now on, I'll keep my thoughts and feelings to myself," Philip said in mock hurt.

"You know you'll do no such thing. I'll be hearing more about her before the night is over."

Philip ducked his head in sheepish agreement. "You're right. But I have kept one thing to myself. I haven't mentioned her name, have I? I won't reveal it now since you chided me. It's something I'll treasure as my secret. Until we return that is. I mean to find her."

Michael somberly endeavored to smile. "That's something we both will do. Find our true loves upon our return."

Philip peered at him. "Why does that not bring joy to your face?"

"I will never be parted from Marissa again once we're back in Wales. It's not finding her that worries me."

Michael already knew his father's response if he were to approach him about bringing a heathen priestess to Mountain Manor's Christian estate to have their priest officiate a marriage ceremony. But he also now desired to live in Avalon, pursue his studies, become a learned man, and finally break away from his father's hold on him. Live life in his own way, as a scholar, not a soldier, no matter his father's surprise or disapproval. This was bound to enrage his father, and a roaring fight was sure to ensue. He had no wish to hurt or anger anyone, but he was confident of his life's choice now that he'd finally made it. It suited him, made him feel happy and fulfilled. He paused, unsure how to explain his concern to his high-spirited brother.

"There's another matter as well. It's just that . . . I'd rather have a book in my hand than a sword," he finally confessed.

"That's no secret, Michael."

"Perhaps not. But father will never allow it. I wish to study, perhaps even tutor, like Master Ralph."

Philip was silent for a moment. "You would forswear your inheritance, your home at Mountain Manor, for this?"

"Without a doubt in my mind. You and Roger can manage things quite well without me."

"You're right. Father will never allow it. He staunchly follows tradition." Philip spoke the truth Michael had wrestled with since he was a boy. He sat up and faced Michael, running his hand over his mouth and chin. "Wait. You aren't going to desert us, are you? Leave us during this enterprise to France?"

"Of course not." Michael's voice rose and he fought to keep it low, away from the ears of Roger. "Don't insult me. I would never dishonor our family name or myself. I am pledged to this undertaking. What I fear is that this soldier life will swallow me and crush my soul if I don't break away soon. God, Philip, there are so many more books I have yet to read. There are universities, monastic schools, and Avalon libraries filled with them."

"And you want to read them all."

"Yes. Is that horrible of me?"

"No. No, it's not." Philip reached out to place his hand on his brother's shoulder.

The gesture filled Michael with needed encouragement. "I fear Father will dash my dreams to bits, before I can do anything about them."

"I wish I could tell you differently."

"That's why my heart is heavy. Father has used my love and loyalty for family and Wales to barter away my studies until there is no time for anything but his agenda. Training me as a knight so I can protect our lands. Learning how to manage our estates. But I wish to pursue the life of a learned man and be with Marissa. Perhaps I could even be of use in that regard at Mountain Manor someday. There have been times, even now, when I don't know if I could bear father's disappointment. Or the consequences of his wrath. I fear that the life I aspire to will slip between my fingers if he continues to force his way on me."

"What will you do?"

Michael stared at his brother and through him, searching for the answers he sought. "I must act quickly and decisively once we return home."

Chapter 34
English Channel
1535 Anno Domini

Once they began boarding the seafaring carrack to sail for France, Michael sensed a gray mood settle on the men. He could only guess at the reasons why, but knew what lay heavy in his own mind as they journeyed ever closer to upcoming skirmishes and fighting potentially lethal battles in unfamiliar land. He sensed the unspoken pact of fighting side by side serving to bind the men together.

Quietly and perfunctorily, they all stowed their warhorses and packs below deck in the lower section of the hull. Amidst the activity, Michael heard none of the lighthearted jests he'd grown accustomed to in their earlier overland travels.

The ship's briny captain warned that while dangerous storms could arise, summertime was normally mild sailing weather. The seas indeed proved tranquil, and the animals and men were calmer because of it.

Despite the fair weather, once they'd set sail, Michael couldn't help but notice David's greenish pallor, how the normally robust soldier often leaned over the ship railing to heave. Theirs was only a short crossing with a planned landing after nightfall, but still, he felt sympathy for David's misery. Michael suffered none of the seasickness. Roger explained that living not far from the Irish Sea and traveling along the Welsh coast by boat with their father gave them stronger stomachs. While Michael was no stranger to the sea, he still gave it due respect. Since his near drowning in Avalon's lake, he had a healthy deference for any body of water.

Well into their sea travels, Michael settled himself on the aftmost deck and perched on a crude bench to oil his longbow with a mixture of wax, resin, and tallow. He had stripped down to his linen shirt and drawers, and was covered only by a thin tunic. His wool cloak lay rumpled in a pile at his side. Though the weather was cool, the sun shone bright above, and a film of sweat had already formed on his brow as he worked the congealed wax into the bow stave to keep it supple. The bow was six feet long, about as tall as he was, and he had to anchor it between his knees to hold it still as he waxed. Roger had passed by earlier, stopping briefly to admonish him to do his best to keep the oily mess from staining his clothes, reminding him, unnecessarily Michael thought, that they'd traveled light with only the bare minimum of attire other than their battle wear.

Philip approached soon afterwards, the usual impish grin lighting his face. Michael made room for his brother to sit beside him.

"Roger is tense again," Philip remarked, nodding his head to where their older brother stood talking with George several feet away.

Michael flicked a glance at Philip as he continued waxing his bow. "I suppose I would be anxious, too. Leading us into who knows what kind of trouble."

"Especially with an oaf like you in his band."

Michael elbowed his brother in the ribs, causing him to fall off the bench. Both laughed until they looked up to see Roger standing before them, arms crossed and shaking his head.

"Can never leave the two of you alone, can I?" Roger offered a hand to Philip, fighting for a straight face, and helped him to his feet. But his mirth died quickly, replaced by the all too familiar clenched jaw and tight-lipped expression.

Michael lay down his bow and cloth, waiting for whatever lecture Roger meant to give them.

"I'll be talking to all the men this evening, once we dock. Laying out the details of our plan. But there are some things the two of you need to know first. Things only we, as de Boulle brothers, must know."

Michael leaned his elbows on his knees and squinted up at his brother, who stood with the sun behind his back. Since they were on their way to ostensibly defend land and country, he figured it prudent to pay attention.

"All right then. First, know this. England has lost considerable territory in France. Our de Boulle properties are some of the few left in the southern portion. The lands our uncle maintains and protects."

"What do we care about England?" Philip asked. "We are Welsh. Cymry forever!" He raised his balled fist high into the air.

Roger frowned and gestured for him to calm his enthusiasm. "Yes, that is so. But there are rumors King Henry means to incorporate Wales into his English laws."

"Never!" Philip cried.

"I understand your enthusiasm, but hear me out. You must learn to temper your boisterous sentiments in favor of more subtle fact gathering. For now, at least. We must keep our eyes and ears open whilst we're in France. Listen for rumors and report them to me so we can sift out the facts from them. I mean for us to garner as much information as we can." Roger loosed his outer cloak, folded it, and laid it on the bench next to Michael.

"Why do we need to gather rumors and facts in France? Why not England?" Michael asked, picking up his own cloak from the deck and folding it as Roger had done.

"Because of the changing tide of religion and politics. Because we must always be aware of these things in order to best defend our Welsh lands and way of life."

Michael's thoughts drifted, anticipating a boring homily from Roger.

Roger locked his gaze with Michael's. "This is what you need to know. Listen to me as intently as you listen to Master Ralph. France's Catholic king has long tolerated anti-Catholic sentiments, but now the fervor of Protestant reform grows strong. King Frances will no longer be tolerant of this. These Protestant views flourish in England as well, especially with King Henry breaking ties with our Catholic Pope. Our King undermines our Catholic Church. All for his marital agendas, to assure a successor to his bloodline. He has claimed himself head of a new church—the Church of England, under his rule."

Philip asked, "How did he do that?"

Roger's face was solemn. "He had political puppets stirring up the people, poor village folk as well as landowners, in favor of his reform. The unrest will soon come to Wales as well, especially for those of us near the border. People will be riled up and start to act without reason. And once reason is lost, people often act out against those in positions of power, including landowners such as ourselves."

Philip's forehead creased and he stared at his hands, his jesting manner set aside. Roger let the information sink in, took a quick swig from a flask of watered-down ale he drew from his sash.

"What does King Henry's breach with Rome have to do with us? Why are we really here, Roger?" Michael asked, speaking aloud his sudden suspicion that something deeper was afoot for his father's men than his brother was letting on. The inkling felt leaden in his gut. It left his mouth dry.

"Some say the nobility, the land owners of Wales, will be strengthened under England's protection if Wales merges under England's rule. But Father and I say our system of nobility will only weaken under King Henry's control . . ."

"Weaken how?" Philip broke in.

"There are many of us who fear the King may take back Welsh lands and power on a whim if he centralizes his government. With the King no longer answerable to the Pope, those of us who remain Catholic are most at risk. We may be stripped of our legal powers over our estates. We may be forced to pay for protection from mercenaries since our time-honored system to compensate our loyal knights would no longer exist. The way of life for our men, who protect Mountain Manor out of loyalty, and those in estates like ours, are threatened. Change is brewing. More than brewing, it's boiling over."

Michael took in the sobering news, information his tutor had already warned him about. His respect for Roger grew at his clear grasp of the complexities of politics and how to play his role. Such matters were probably the reason his older brother had grown so serious in the last two years.

"Father has prepared me, schooled me in these winds of change. He does not like to give credence to anything but what has been in place for hundreds of years, the rules that have maintained our lands since we were first awarded them. But the neighboring nobles have convinced him of the upcoming danger and swayed his opinions. I fear I must agree. We need to be watchful, especially in France, who may yet be our greater threat."

"France the greater threat?" Philip asked.

Roger nodded. "As we speak, King Henry bolsters England's shoreline defenses in preparation for France's attack if the religious reformation gets out of hand and threatens to weaken England."

Michael was beginning to grasp the smoldering layers underneath King Henry's changing whims, and the profound impact his decisions would have across England and Wales. He saw how his father, and landowners like him, might begin to feel closed in on all sides, by both England and France.

Roger continued. "The situation now grows desperate. Last October, something happened here in France that has thrown kerosene on the fire of religious dissent. They are calling it the Affair of the Placards. Protestant dissenters put up anti-Catholic posters in public places. Large cities like Paris, Tours, Orleans."

Philip let out a low whistle. "The Protestants are serious."

Roger glanced behind his shoulder and leaned forward. "Yes, it's serious. King Francis is no longer conciliatory, he's no longer protecting the Protestants from the more extreme measures of the Parliament of Paris. It's said that some Protestant sympathizers have been burnt at the stake."

Michael interjected. "That seems extreme. But, Roger, we're Catholic. Will our lands here in France not be protected by the Catholic King and his Parliament?"

"Yes, we're under the French King's approval here. But I'm telling you that in France, provocative actions against the Catholics grow. The people are uprising against the nobles, and they're getting bolder. We're here to defend our family's French lands, and our uncle's lands as well, against such uprisings."

Philip furrowed his brow. "What happens if King Henry were to learn of our actions here? Because we're here to support the Catholic cause by protecting our Catholic lands from Protestant dissenters, will that not anger him and endanger our land ownership in Wales?"

Roger nodded his head and replied, "Exactly. Now you see the delicacy of what we are trying to do. Our family is not under the King's approval in England. We are Cymry. Welsh. *And* we're Catholic. We walk a fine line between our position in France and our position in Wales." Roger paused, eyes intense. "Our way of life is threatened, make no mistake about that. But if King Henry were to find out what Father and I have planned, the very action of us coming here to France . . ."

"Then why are we here? Is not the land we live on, the actual land we work and care for, more important than our faraway lands in France?" Michael asked. "I don't understand why we risk lives to assure our distant property in a fight that is not ours."

Roger's face turned red, a shade that meant he was barely controlling his ire. "It's not as simple as that. It all connects, trust me. We do run the risk King Henry finds out we fight Protestants here. I had to convince Father to let me come to France, to assess what's happening here, to our lands. Then to report my findings back to him. We may be able to stay under the notice of King Henry and save all of our lands, those in Wales and those here in France."

"Plus, we justly owe our uncle our protection and support," Philip added. "Is that not right, brother?"

Roger clapped him on the shoulder. "And that is all our men need know. France's unrest with these Protestant dissidents has reached our estate's borders on this side of the channel and we've come to protect that estate. The other underpinnings of this matter are for our family alone to deal with."

Michael pinched the bridge of his nose, forehead wrinkled in concentration. "So, we have Protestant dissidents who are against Catholic defenders, and Catholic defenders who are now supported by an alarmed King Francis who remains loyal to the Pope."

"Right. We have much to lose if we don't protect what we have, but we're still small enough in numbers not to garner the interest of either King if we act swiftly and assertively to defend our lands and assets."

"And in Wales?"

"In Wales there are only rumors of England taking over. For now. Until England formalizes its control and annexes it, we have breathing room. Time to plan. Time to see how we can best hold onto our traditions and allegiances. And our estates."

"And what happens when time runs out?" Philip asked.

Roger's frown grew deep. "If England incorporates Wales into the English legal system, we'll no longer be judicators over our own affairs at Mountain Manor. There will be sheriffs appointed to do that. Sheriffs who won't have our best interests at heart."

"Sheriffs who would not even know or understand our people," Michael added, feeling a surge of protective dread at the thought.

Roger shot him a sliver of a smile. "Now you understand. I told Father you have a natural and keen grasp on things."

Michael scowled. He wanted to understand, but didn't care to play the politics. Still, he cared for his family and the people of Mountain Manor.

"So, this is step one of *your* plan. Come to France, defend what is ours, and gauge France's role and influence with King Henry."

Philip finished his thought, "Then we can best decide how to behave and protect what's ours in England."

Roger crossed his arms over his chest and sighed. "Yes, now you understand."

"Why do you tell us this now?" Michael asked. "In truth, Roger."

Roger's gaze held fast. "Someone besides me needs to know of our intentions. In case something happens. To me. If it does, you would take over as heir apparent to Father's estates, Michael."

Michael pulled back as if he'd been punched in the stomach. Alarm surged, racing its way through his heart and lungs. Reality sunk in, and his world spun out of control. He couldn't lose his brother to battle. He loved him. Roger had always been part of his life. Moreover, what would this mean for his plans with Marissa?

Philip spoke up. "Nothing will happen to you, Roger."

Philip stood and clasped Roger's forearm. Roger returned the hold, linking them in brotherhood. Roger turned to Michael and offered the same gesture of camaraderie. Grim-lipped and muscles taut, Michael joined in.

Nevertheless, Michael's stomach clenched with the idea of the potential pitfalls of this vague plan they were to carry out. He felt the tides of the shifting politics draw him into their quicksand, sidelining his cherished plans with Marissa. He couldn't let that happen, but wasn't sure what to do. He didn't feel much like an innocent younger brother any longer.

Chapter 35

The Isle of Avalon
1535 C.E.

Night delivered the dawn. The golden glow fell upon the spring bubbling up at the foot of the gentle slope where the Halls of Avalon stood. Sitting on her knees, Marissa leaned forward and peered down into the gurgling waters of the Red Well. The sun climbed over the crest of the Tor, its rays spiraling across the water in slivers of light.

She rubbed her tired eyes. She had spent the night beside the well, her head resting on a low circle of boulders that rimmed the holy waters, seeking its comfort as she had done since she was a toddler first learning to link with the magic of the wellspring. She smoothed her robes, brushing off bits of grass and dirt. The others would be coming when the sun reached midday. Her mother was to lead the priestesses in the Autumn Equinox Ceremony, to honor the turn of the seasons—the time when day and night reigned equal in the sky.

Marissa reached down and trailed her hand in the cool spring waters. She sensed the ethereal presence of her ancestors surrounding her. She always felt them strongest here beside the well. They had revered this same spring, performed rituals alongside it, and used it as an earthly anchor to commune with the Goddess of the Stars and Sea, just as her priestess sisters would do today. Her ancestors radiated their tranquility and wisdom across time, but she couldn't let it in beyond the anguish that lay leaden in her stomach.

She desperately missed Michael. No one had heard from him for three months. He'd promised to return by summer's end. She despaired at what detained him, prayed it was not her worst fear—death in battle far from home.

A sudden compulsion to scry overcame her. To use the sacred water to discover Michael's whereabouts, yet again. She had to know he was safe, or at least alive. The well water provided the perfect medium, and there was still plenty of time before the others arrived.

She readied herself for the familiar, time-honored ritual. Hopefully, locating his soul in the Blessed Otherworld wouldn't be necessary. She focused her intention purely upon her beloved and called on the power of her priestess lineage, past and present. The power of her ancestors. She bowed to the Goddess of the Stars and the Sea and made her prayer.

> *Goddess, may I see true and clearly hear*
> *Heart to heart, bypass my fear*
> *Let me see*
> *Where Michael may be.*

She scooped a handful of Red Well water and poured it into the plain silver scrying bowl she had brought along with her. The water was tinged its usual faint red hue, a reminder that the waters of the earth flow through the Goddess's veins. Earth blood. The blood of the Goddess within the land of Avalon.

She stared into the still water and let her focus soften. Her vision blurred and she felt the tender hand of the Goddess, an ethereal brush upon her brow, aiding her scry. Deepening her trance with breath, she linked with the power deep in her womb-space and waited several moments, searching the water for signs. The sudden surge of prophecy rose from within her, passing through the caverns of her heart and ripening as it reached her throat, compelling her to speak aloud the words the scry inspired and demanded. Words she expelled in a wail.

> *You feel him in your heart and soul*
> *But does he come back to you?*
> *Not so!*
> *Fire, water, earth, and air.*
> *One will claim him.*
> *Much despair.*

"No!"

She scrambled to refocus. Leaned closer to stare into the water once more. She would will it to change its utterance. With vigilance she watched. Her heart battered against her chest, hands tight along the edges of the scrying bowl. Nothing new appeared in the still water, no other sounds emerged. No signs to give her hope against the bleak words.

"No," she repeated, this time in a fierce whisper. Shaking her head, her loose, dark hair fell about her face. If something had happened to Michael, she would know. His body had joined with hers on Summer Solstice Eve. Their ritual union had been made even more powerful by the love that had bound them since they were children when she'd saved him from death. She would know if he'd been hurt. She would feel it as he would. That was the way of true lovers. Especially those who'd experienced the profound touch of the Goddess during lovemaking.

Sobs lodged in her throat, clambering to be set loose. She would not allow them. To do so would be to give in to the feeling of doom. She bolstered her will to remain strong against the gloomy foretelling.

She'd nearly composed herself when the hint of a summer breeze caressed her neck, exuding the fragrance of ripening apples and sweet blossoms. It was the Faery touch of Shayla.

"I knew I'd find you here, dear friend." Her voice had grown melodious since Solstice Eve.

Marissa stood, hiding shaking hands amidst the folds of her silken robes. She would not speak of her divination. To speak it aloud would give it undeserved power. Instead, she looked deep into her friend's green eyes—a shade that reflected mossy rocks in a mountainside stream, and the feel of the wild Faery that grew stronger in her every day.

Her despair pressed her to ask. "How do you do it? How do you stay here, Shayla, when you love Folimot?"

Shayla arched one brow. "Do you wish me gone?"

Marissa wasn't sure whether Shayla jested, or if she'd unintentionally hurt her friend with the frank question. She could no longer read Shayla as she once had. "You know I want you beside me always. You're a true friend, and I trust you with all my heart, as I know Ciara does also."

A shadow passed over her forest-green eyes, then disappeared so swiftly Marissa wasn't sure she'd actually seen it.

"That is why I stay. For love of you and Ciara. And your mother Alianore, my High Priestess. Who is like a mother to me."

Marissa persisted. "I don't mean to prod an open wound. But it must be so difficult to be away from Folimot all he told you about your faery blood and your lifelong bond."

"I *will* go to him. But it must be in my own way." Shayla looked around her and her tone grew wistful. "Our holy well, the Avalon Halls behind it, the apple tree in our magic courtyard . . . as much as I want to be with Folimot, and as sincerely as I desire to meet my father, Avalon has always been my home. I am having a hard time saying goodbye to it and all the people I love."

Marissa considered their beloved home. She turned to view the land that bore the Goddess's mark. She saw the Goddess in Her holy Red Well, in the breasted knoll that gently sloped behind them, in the milky-white spring a short distance away, partner to the well. She lifted her eyes to the crest of the Tor beyond the spring, a reminder of the laws connecting heaven to earth. It was also a reminder of the parallel worlds, Avalon and the unseen realm of Faery who lived and danced and sang and loved beneath its base, in their invisible realm.

She understood why Shayla wavered. Marissa loved Avalon as well. Perhaps with a love even deeper than Shayla's, for she was of the holy line of High Priestesses. She would one day rule as such, would live and breathe as one with the holy well and the sacred land. But as much as she cherished her bloodline and her inheritance, right now, she wasn't sure she wouldn't trade it all away just to be with Michael, to see him safe.

After a few moments, she spoke. "It's undeniably difficult for you. And you show your strength by making it your own choice whether to stay or go. You're a true priestess who carries her sovereignty."

Shayla sighed. "Thank you for kind words. But I only truly delay the inevitable. There is no fighting Faery oaths and the bonds they create. One day I must go. And leave this home behind forever."

Marissa nodded. "I suppose if you'd conceived a child on Solstice, that day would have come sooner rather than later."

"Much sooner. Faery would not abide my hesitation if that were the case."

Marissa's eyes misted. Her worry for Michael kindled her frustration, which was starting to erupt. "There are days I wish I had conceived a child at Solstice. A babe to connect me with Michael. To help me bear this separation." Her hands pressed against her abdomen. "It feels so unjust. I wish it was me instead of Ciara who was pregnant."

Shayla bristled. Waves of dark green energy rolled off her. "Marissa, how could you say something so thoughtless?"

Marissa winced. Her friend had never spoken to her with such vehemence before. A swish of robes alerted her that someone had joined them. She turned to see her sister approach, and knew she'd been heard.

She faced her twin. "Oh, Ciara, I'm so sorry. I didn't mean you should not have conceived. Please forgive my rash words. I'm only feeling pity for myself today, nothing more."

Ciara glanced first at Shayla. "Calm yourself, my friend, it's all right. And you, dear sister, it's only your worry and despair speaking. Not your heart. I know you care for my unborn child and would never wish it away from me." She took both of Marissa's hands in her own.

Shayla took a step back and clutched her cloak tightly about her.

Marissa regarded her twin. Ciara was beautiful with the glow of pregnancy. Her breasts rounded, her blue eyes bright, her cheeks pink. All Marissa could do was wish the pregnancy had been hers. She couldn't help but feel she was selfish and didn't deserve her twin's forgiveness.

"By the Goddess, Shayla, you're right. I am thoughtless," Marissa said, her voice catching.

Shayla shook her head and pursed her lips. "No, I spoke harshly. Please just think before you speak. I worry your rash ways do offend."

Ciara smiled gently and caressed Marissa's cheek. "Dear Sister, you're torn apart not hearing from Michael. I'm sure all is well with him. Who knows the ways of politics in the realm of men? A thousand things might delay him."

Marissa gave her sister a weak smile. "You're too good for me. I can no more hide my anguish from you than I can turn the ocean tides." She placed Ciara's hand flat against her cheek and felt her sister suffuse her with sympathy, which only served to draw out the tears she'd tried so hard to quell.

"I'm sorry. I didn't mean to belabor my pain." Marissa wiped her eyes and cheeks with her sleeve and stepped into her sister's welcoming embrace, only to sob once more.

"There, there," she murmured. "He'll return soon. You'll see."

Marissa tilted her head back. She still would not give credence to her ominous scry. "I know he promised. I don't doubt his word, but I can't say I like this waiting."

"Ever my impatient sister," Ciara laughed softly. She released her embrace and sat on the ground, resting her hand protectively on her belly, though at three months pregnant her waist was still as slim as ever.

"Ah, but there's you and the babe to think about now. That at least brings us joy. I misspoke before. Truly, I'm happy for you."

Shayla interrupted, voice brusque, her eyes stern as she flitted her eyes from one twin to the other. "Ciara, have you not told Marissa yet?"

Ciara turned pale and swallowed hard. Shayla looked fixedly at Marissa.

"Told me what? What have you to tell me?" Marissa asked, sitting beside her sister. She motioned Shayla to join them, the same way they'd sat together since they were children.

Shayla remained standing. "Has she told you who the baby's father is?"

"Shayla, why do you bring this up now?" Ciara cried.

"Because she needs to know. She will be High Priestess one day. Enough coddling her. You deserve just as much consideration as she does."

Marissa stared up at her friend. "Shayla, whatever do you mean? What rankles you so?"

"His name is Philip. The baby's father," Shayla declared acidly.

"Philip? That's a nice enough name . . ." Marissa turned to Ciara, a puzzled look on her face.

"Philip," Shayla repeated. "*De Boulle.*" Her face was flushed and her eyes flashed. Ciara winced.

"Philip de Boulle? You mean Michael's brother? I don't understand. Why would you wish to keep that secret?" Marissa asked, turning to face her sister.

Ciara's lip trembled. "Oh, Marissa. I didn't wish to see you further upset."

"Why would I be upset?"

Shayla blurted out, "Because Ciara carries a de Boulle child. Finally she has *something* at least close to her heart's secret desire." She immediately covered her mouth with her hand.

Ciara's voice rose. "Shayla, please."

"Wait. What do you mean? Ciara's secret desire? What secret desire?"

Ciara spoke rapidly. "I didn't wish to upset you. I thought Philip being the father would only serve as a reminder that Michael was away still. I meant to tell you. It just became unimportant after a while. The important thing, as it has always been for us as priestesses, is that I'm indeed pregnant and I carry—"

"You carry the next in line to inherit the title of High Priestess," Marissa finished for her.

"Yes, there is that," Ciara said quietly.

Marissa straightened her back. "So, you told Shayla that Philip was a de Boulle but you didn't tell me." She paused before she added, "We've always told each other our secrets." With sadness in her voice she added, "Or we used to."

Ciara stole a glance at Shayla and shook her head to caution her from speaking further. "It's as I told you, Marissa. I didn't want to add to your pain."

"Why would I be upset that Philip is a de Boulle? It pleases me that we joined with brothers at Solstice. It's fitting." Marissa beamed with growing excitement. "Oh, Ciara, Michael told me about his brother, but I had no idea you chose each other."

Ciara remained quiet.

"I can't help asking." Marissa leaned in closer to her twin. "Wouldn't it be exciting if we loved men from the same family?"

Ciara flinched.

"Do you love him?"

Ciara looked at her twin with surprise. "Love him? No. I suppose I have a fond memory of him."

Shayla stepped closer and put her hand on Ciara's shoulder.

"Could you love him?" Marissa insisted.

Ciara looked down at the grass and thought for a moment. When she looked up again she said, "My heart might perhaps one day think of him as special."

"Then this is wonderful news. Think of it. We both love a de Boulle brother," Marissa rejoiced, smiling.

Shayla dropped her hand from Ciara's shoulder. "Yes, you certainly both do."

Ciara gasped, seemingly alarmed.

"Oh, Ciara, don't worry about that," Marissa said.

"Worry about what?" Ciara's eyes grew wide.

"Don't worry that you bear the first child to succeed after me."

Ciara let out a shaky breath. "Well then, all is well. I needn't have worried at all." She flicked a sideways glance at Shayla.

Shayla sighed heavily and knelt beside them, her green mantle trailing behind her. "I have been ill-humored. I am sorry."

A commanding voice interrupted them. Alianore stood a few feet away, arms across her chest, sapphire blue robes rippling in the breeze. In her knowing way, she regarded each of them in turn. "You three have all been troubled since Solstice. Each grappling with your own burden. Whatever it is, I do not like to see it make you ill-tempered toward each other. You have been close since you were babies. Do not take that for granted. It is a cherished blessing to share such love."

Marissa cast her eyes down at her hands. She wished yet again she would learn to reign in her heedless words and rash ways.

Alianore continued, her voice stern. "I do not know what distresses you, my daughters. I feel I am no longer privy to your inner secrets. But from what I have just heard, I caution you to choose what you say to each other with care. All but Ciara have spoken reprehensibly."

The accusation sliced through Marissa, reinforcing the sinking feeling in her stomach that her mother might think her unworthy to one day fulfill the role of High Priestess.

"Ciara and Marissa, prepare the grounds for the ritual." Alianore picked up a basket from behind her and handed it to the twins. Marissa saw it contained the silken blue cloths used to create an altar for the ritual, as well as purple violets, pink primroses, and the sacred talismans of their community, all wrapped in blue velvet. She leapt up to take the basket from her mother's hands.

"Shayla, I would speak to you in private," Alianore announced.

She turned on her heel, expecting her foster daughter to follow. Shayla rose and walked behind Alianore, looking back only once for support from her friends. Marissa watched them walk some distance up the slope. They headed for the giant apple tree in the center court of the Halls of Avalon. She absently sifted through the basket's contents, trying to focus on the task. She couldn't help but watch her mother and Shayla talking beside the tree.

Her heart fluttered wildly, knowing her mother's disappointment would bear upon her next.

Chapter 36

The Isle of Avalon
1535 C.E.

Shayla climbed the grassy slope behind the Red Well, following the determined footsteps of her High Priestess. Alianore did not look back, nor did she speak. It was not often Shayla had seen her foster-mother's wrath so provoked. She hated to think she was the source.

Once they reached the top of the knoll, the heavy wooden gates to the Courtyard of Avalon's Healing Halls rose before them. Alianore donned the hood of her robe, readying herself to engage in serious conversation. Their hooded heads represented the enveloping blessings of the Goddess, a call for Her compassionate wisdom to suffuse them through their discourse. Shayla swallowed thickly and followed suit, covering her head with her green mantle. Together they walked through the arched gateway into the courtyard where Avalon's Life Tree held sway. It bore its golden fruit, the revered apples of immortality, nectar of the Goddess.

Shayla felt the commanding presence of the central Apple Tree. It was said to be an ancient gift from Faery. Only a rare few in Avalon's world, priestesses who had passed the highest initiation could safely eat from it. To do otherwise would be too much for the body to bear. Its vitality made her skin tingle. It was only recently she was able to see its life force bubble up from the roots in undulating green spirals that traveled through trunk and branches, leaves and buds. Its kindred soul ignited hers, cleaving her to the mysterious ways of nature. She was no longer sure how much of her instinctual reaction to the Tree was from her Faery impulses or how much was from her priestess lineage. Today, the green beckoning made her heart ache.

The numerous Healing Halls encircling the sanctuary's central courtyard were busy as usual. She watched an Elder priestess walk from the Healing Hall of Earth to the Healing Hall of Water, carrying a silver cup and a large citrine gemstone. On the far side of the courtyard, a priestess tended to the many candles in niches along the walls, making sure their flames remained perpetually lit.

Alianore seated herself under the Tree's great boughs. A rain of perpetual creamy-white blossoms showered down as if to acknowledge the High Priestess. Shayla sank to her knees in front of her and bowed her head, her thoughts confused, her emotions still riding the waves of green effervescence the Tree exuded.

Alianore remained silent for several moments. Finally, she lifted Shayla's chin so their eyes met. Instead of the expected anger, Shayla found compassion in her gaze. And something else she couldn't name.

"Your Faery urges. They are getting harder to control, are they not, my daughter?"

Shayla felt her breath quicken. *She knew.* Tears filled her eyes. "Yes. Is it so apparent?"

"Do not forget, I have known you since you were a babe. You became like my own child after your mother died."

Shayla's words poured out in a tumble. "Though I love Folimot, every day I fight my compulsion to join Faery. I love my life here. I love you. It is a struggle and a choice I do not find easy."

Alianore sighed, dropped her hand to her lap, and searched Shayla's face. "I must tell you something, a promise I made to your mother. A vow that I cannot now, in good conscience, keep." She looked suddenly older, more fragile.

"What is it, my High Priestess?" Shayla's voice quivered.

Alianore's eyes grew distant. "I loved your mother. Kendra was my dearest friend."

Kendra. Shayla's heart beat in lonely rhythm for the birth mother she never knew but cherished nonetheless. Alianore had always made sure the stories of Kendra were told at table, her person praised, so Shayla would at least have memories of her mother to embrace and hold to.

"You know the story of how I helped birth you. Along with Vanora and two of our best midwives, we tended to your mother. With all our gifts, even with our Halls of Healing, we failed. Goddess knows we tried." Alianore's voice wavered with festered guilt. "What good are these gifts if they could not save the life of one who was so pure and good of heart? Your mother did not deserve to die."

Shayla bypassed formality and took Alianore's hands in hers, daughter to foster-mother. "I have always known you were not to blame. I know you did everything you could. If my mother could not be saved in Avalon, then there was no hope."

Returning from distant memory, Alianore caressed Shayla's cheek. "My heart grieves for her every time I see you. It is a balm to have you close." She sighed softly. "And it is a painful reminder."

Shayla gasped. "I cause you pain? Then perhaps I should leave."

"No," Alianore replied with authority. "That is not why I tell you this." She paused, adjusted her mantle, and sat up straight.

"I am about to break a promise I made to your mother at her deathbed. Weak as she was, she hugged you to her. There was such love in her voice, such adoration in her eyes as she looked at you. It was then she asked me, no, she obliged me, to agree to her dying wish. Understand, I would do anything for Kendra. As you would for Ciara or Marissa."

Shayla felt a guilt-ridden knot tighten in her chest at the thought of the forgetting spell she'd placed upon Michael.

The High Priestess continued. "Kendra told me how she had mated with a Faery man at the Summer Solstice. Not just any Faery. One of royal bloodline, as you are now aware. A Faery King who was beguiled by her innocence of heart, and she, enchanted by his regal dignity. Their attraction was undeniable, compelling them to join for the Solstice Ritual. Kendra told me she was so drawn to him that she found she could not help herself. She said your father felt the same. Still, they knew this one night would be their only. As it so often is for Summer Solstice."

Shayla was shocked to see her foster-mother with her mouth pursed and her jaw tight, fighting to compose her usual calm veneer.

Alianore took a moment to smooth her robes with hands that trembled. "After they joined together in the sacred union, the Faery King foretold your mother she had conceived that night. A baby of royal bloodline. He also told her that Faery would, of necessity, one day come to claim you as their own, as is Faery tradition for one of royal blood. Your mother believed that when that day came, she could convince him otherwise." She locked gazes with Shayla and leaned forward. "She truly believed that, based on the power of their mutual allurement, she could persuade the Faery King to concede you shelter in Avalon, shielded from this Faery claiming, even after your first Solstice Rituals."

Shayla backed away. "Wait. You mean my mother knew beforehand I would face this fate and yet she agreed to join with the Faery King? And then she assumed she could somehow stop it?"

"Kendra was told this *after* he sensed she had conceived you." Alianore's voice was both sharp and pleading. "Your mother never intended to die, Shayla. She thought she would always be here to watch over you and guide you. That is why she bade me promise to keep you shielded in her stead, so you could continue in the priestess tradition she herself could not. She treasured the heritage she passed onto you, wanted you to cherish it as well. She begged me to mentor you in our traditional ways. She begged me to not let Faery take you from us."

Shayla's breath was ragged, her chest tight. "Why did you never tell me this? You were a mother to me. I trusted you to be forthright with me, to give me the whole story, to not try to control me by omitting facts."

"It was your mother's wish to shield you. And, Faery Law or not, it was mine as well."

Fury surged through Shayla, forcing her to move, to stand. To forget it was her High Priestess she raged at. "In doing so, the two of you took away my choice. My freedom. Now look at me. You cursed me by your promise. My heart and my loyalties are torn beyond repair."

Tears swelled in Alianore's eyes. "Because you are a halfling, I am afraid that was always a likelihood, no matter what," she said softly.

Shayla fumed. "This is impossible for me. I am bound to Folimot in a way that haunts me night and day, but Avalon is home. Ciara and Marissa are my heart-sisters . . . wait. Is this why you were so upset when we snuck into the realm of Faery? Were you afraid for me? That I would be taken? Or choose not to return?"

Alianore nodded and looked down. "Marissa should never have convinced you to go. Even with Faery law allowing your upbringing here until your first Summer Solstice, I still feared you may never have returned."

"Marissa is headstrong and thoughtless. Because of her Ciara became deathly ill. And I grew forever restless, tormented. Brought to the Faery Realm too early, before my time, as the Lady Ravenna said. I should have been made aware right from the start of Faery's royal claim and my mother's wish to deny it." Shayla furrowed her brow. "Marissa did not know of your promise, did she?"

"No, she does not know. Nor does Ciara. It was Marissa's lack of sound judgment that persuaded you to go. It was indeed the contact with Faery that I feared. You were so young." Alianore's eyes pleaded. "I was afraid of losing you."

Shayla heard her adopted mother's loving concern, but only felt her High Priestess's control as a meddlesome thorn in her heart. "I repeat. You should have trusted me. Told me."

Alianore watched her closely. Shayla knew her eyes sparked, that her fury was a bristle to her foster-mother. She had to be alone, to think. She spun around to leave, not caring to ask for permission.

"Wait," Alianore commanded. "You are still a priestess, under my rule and my care. By my actions I may no longer deserve your love. But I deserve your respect."

Shayla turned back.

Alianore continued before she could speak. "I see your struggle. I know you are loyal to Avalon. I see how your Faery blood swells and your Faery nature grows. This restlessness, this battle inside you, it changes your disposition and makes you cross. I watched you with Marissa and Ciara by the Red Well just now. You have never been so bad-tempered with them before."

Shayla could not contain her spite, her feeling of being betrayed and lied to. "I do not care what you saw. You and my mother deepened this conundrum by not telling me. Yes, I love Avalon. But the Faery call is so strong." She buried her head in her hands. "I feel betrayed. Why? Why did you keep it from me?"

"We did what we thought best. We did what we did out of love."

Her words punctured Shayla. She understood the need to control and protect all too well. Wasn't she doing the same with Ciara? With the forgetting spell she had once cast? Doing what she could to protect her friend from the pain of Michael's unrequited love? But without her permission or knowledge.

Shayla's body shook with the realization. She lifted her face from her hands. Alianore and Kendra had tried to control her fate to protect her. Could she stop herself from doing the same with Ciara any more than her mother and High Priestess? Probably not. Still, the pain that had lodged in her heart had irreparably torn it.

She thought of Folimot's words. *Do not interfere in the affairs of humankind.* Her half-human heart didn't know if she could follow that edict. She glimpsed bright movement across the courtyard, beyond the open gate. Folimot's form shimmered in mossy translucence. Her heart hammered against her chest. She had not seen him since Solstice. He had given her time to make her choice, just as he had promised. Caught under her emotional waterfall of anger and guilt, the mere thought of him must have drawn him to her as surely as the moon summons the morning sun. She felt the familiar tug in her soul to follow him.

Alianore held out her hand. "As a High Priestess, I would not intrude upon your free will. But as your foster-mother who loves you, I cannot help but hope your choice be Avalon, despite the Faery law and calling." She blinked back tears. "I know I need to let you go. And you must make up your own mind."

Shayla tore her gaze from Folimot to look into her foster-mother's eyes. Her heart broke with love for Alianore and Avalon. They weren't so different, she, Kendra, and Alianore. She had done no better than them. They were all prompted by deep love to interfere, to try to control, to do things that shouldn't be done. Her rage dissipated. Guilt remained. She took her High Priestess's hand and kissed it as she choked back a sob.

"I love you like a mother. I will never forget. And I am sorry." Her decision made, Shayla released her hand. And ran to Folimot.

The High Priestess stood. "Wait! What shall I tell Ciara and Marissa?"

But Shayla had already passed through the courtyard and into Folimot's waiting arms. She gave Alianore one mournful backward glance as she closed the gate and then faded in a swirl of shimmering green.

Chapter 37

The Isle of Avalon
Autumn, 1535 C.E.

A hint of autumn chilled the air even as the morning sun rose higher. The apple trees in the orchard below Avalon's Healing Halls absorbed the sun's golden rays, their leaves echoing their own version of vivid gold and red. Marissa tightened her cloak around her shoulders and cast yet another worried glance up the knoll, towards the Life Tree. The tree's blossom-laden boughs loomed behind the closed gates that hid her mother and Shayla from view. Her muscles tensed in anticipation of the reprimand she was sure to receive once her mother was done speaking with Shayla.

She tilted her head from side to side and shrugged her shoulders, stretching them to release taut muscles. Despite her efforts to compose herself, she remained confused by Shayla's harsh comments and behavior, and concerned about her own thoughtlessness.

The Red Well beside her burbled noisily, as if trying to reclaim her attention. She turned back and caught Ciara's eye. Her sister waited quietly for her to return to their appointed task of setting up the altars for the Autumn Equinox Ritual. The basket holding the sacred implements lay at their feet. Marissa nodded and held out her hands to Ciara, who took them in hers. They closed their eyes, attuning themselves to the steady beat of their hearts and the embered heat in their bellies. Even with her sister's hands warm against hers, Marissa was keenly aware of Shayla's absence from their usual triad. It felt unbalanced, shifting her away from her focus and back into tension. Her heartbeat was not steady at all, and she could not ignite the fire in her womb, the core that normally connected her with her power and the wisdom of her lineage.

Whether it was Ciara's soothing influence, or the Goddess working through her twin, she felt a sudden warmth flow into her hands, a honeyed caress that trailed through her heart and belly. She gratefully followed that path back into communion. Both sisters slowed their breathing and sang the litany to invoke the Goddess of the Stars and the Sea in well-practiced harmony.

Goddess!
Great Mother will you hear me?
Hear me. Hear me calling to you.
Calling. Calling for your presence.

They repeated the simple song two more times. Through her inner vision, Marissa saw the swell of moonlit ocean waves under a starry sky. The Goddess emerged, trailing her usual swirls of silver and blue, walking the bright moon path that shone across the sea. Her blue cloak was strewn with thousands of nighttime stars. They glittered from her belly and tipped the ends of her night-black hair. More stars eddied in the earth's core, drumming the earth's heartbeat and singing the eternal refrain of the heavens and the celestial sky. Marissa felt the Goddess's blue mantle envelop her and Ciara, imbuing the area around the Red Well with a sense of peace she felt down to her bones. She was loved, soothed. Thankful tears wet her cheeks.

Once she was able to feel peace within her heart, alongside awareness of the outer world of sweet-scented meadow grass and bubbling spring, Marissa released her sister's hands. A bird twittered in the rowan tree branches close by. The holy spring sprayed fine droplets of water onto the hem of her skirts. She opened her eyes, feeling the Goddess infuse her and everything around her. Now ready to take on her duty to create the sacred space that would encircle, harmonize, and safeguard the priestesses in their upcoming ceremony, she eyed the sacred talismans in their basket, alive with magic that radiated palpable waves of warmth and luminosity.

She picked up the ancient, cherished necklace first. It was made of a strange metal no one could identify, wrapped in a soft material that had enigmatically endured for centuries. She ran her finger along the pendant's two interlocking circles whose intersection formed the sacrosanct shape of the Vesica Pisces, the sigil of their priestess lineage. Her finger's tingled and the sensation shot up her arms.

Ciara leaned into Marissa's side and the two of them chanted a simple blessing for the necklace, ending in a moment of silent reverence for its ancestral lore. The necklace had been handed down, High Priestess to High Priestess, from Avalon's very first priestess, Geodran. Geodran's story was recounted around the hearth fire every Winter Solstice—how she had travelled from the legendary land of Atlantis to Avalon, to share and preserve her culture's esoteric secrets. The necklace was their lasting treasure, unwrapped from its covering at every ritual to adorn the officiating High Priestess, the only one who could manage its power for the duration of their ceremonies. Marissa placed it atop the lip of the well, where it awaited Alianore's return.

In worshipful silence, she and Ciara began to cast their circle. Marissa intoned their intent and Ciara joined in as they both proceeded in a moon-wise direction around the holy Red Well.

> *We cast a circle of the Goddess's love.*
> *Rounded circle of no beginning and no end,*
> *The shape of the Great Mother's breast and the Great Mother's womb,*
> *that embraces us in balance and protection.*

As Marissa paced around the well, the circle's center point, she gauged the as yet invisible circumference to make sure they would create a circle wide enough to encompass all the priestesses who would attend the ceremony. When they finished their chant, she leaned over the basket of hallows to choose one to begin crafting the circle's boundaries. Four implements were to be placed along the edges of the circle, each to mark one of the four directions: a cup, a blade, a smoky mirror, and a silver bough. She picked up the cup and carefully removed it from its velvet wrapping.

She set the ornate silver cup, representing the grail vessel and cauldron of creation, in the direction West, steadying its wide base on the grass with a silken blue cloth. She glanced at the ocean waves cresting in the distance, far below the hill that sheltered the Red Well burbling behind her. Though the ritual hadn't yet begun, the powers flowing from the West surged into the circle. Still cupping the grail with her hands, Marissa sensed the primal ebb and flow of the star and sea tides, undulating waves that washed over her. She felt the power of regeneration, healing, and love swell her heart. The West was ready, awaiting official commencement.

She glanced behind her and noted Ciara held the dagger. A golden calcite gem adorned its sheath, reflecting the sunlight. Ciara placed the sanctified blade in the direction East on the circle, to represent the power of inspiration, the breath of life.

She heard Ciara whisper to the blade, *"Bring forth courage and acumen,"* before gently laying it on a yellow silken cloth on the grass.

Marissa chose to place the hallow of the North next, an obsidian mirror—the shield of death, rebirth, and transformation. She cradled it and aligned herself with its powers, felt it thrumming to the heartbeat of the deep earth, the element it represented.

She sat back and waited while Ciara positioned the silver apple bough to the South of the holy well. The bough's rod-like shape concentrated the fiery power of illumination, which would add focus to their ceremony's intent. Once the ritual began, the many silver bells attached to the bough would be rung to summon the Inner Realms of magic and mystery.

Ciara smoothed the red silk cloth under the bough and nodded to Marissa to complete the final step, placing the tallow pillar candle in the center of the newly formed sacred space, atop the well's rim. Marissa knelt to light the candle with her flint. She felt invisible hands upon hands touch her shoulders, feather light, and sensed the many ancestors who fanned out in an arc behind her. She felt the presence of every priestess who had ever lit a candle to the Goddess move through her actions to light this candle before her.

Once the flame burned high, the twins stepped back from the circle of arranged implements. Marissa felt prickles dance along her spine. Her belly ignited with the power of her womb-space, her source of creation, the locus of her ancestral wisdom. She closed her eyes a moment to adjust to the emerging swell in her chest, her heart, the place where the heavens and the earth danced in union. She wished the others would arrive soon as she was already losing herself to the spell the items were weaving in their communion with each other and with her.

After several moments spent in silence, Ciara whispered to her. "Mother is taking a long time with Shayla. I worry."

Marissa's fear of her mother's eventual reproof pulled her out of the trance. She inhaled sharply at the sudden shift. The resurrected dread lodged as a painful ball in her stomach. She was sure she would be rebuked for her thoughtless words and careless ways, cautioned to reign in her rash manner. Yet again. Nevertheless, her mother never humiliated her. Marissa always chastised herself enough. Alianore's counsel was wise and patient, meant to teach her. But it was a lesson that felt ever elusive, never overcome. Marissa's gut clenched further and her thoughts raced once more, shattering any calm or trance she had achieved. *Why do I fail to be considerate, to be gentle, like Ciara?* She lowered her head.

Ciara put her arm around Marissa's shoulders. Her twin had sensed her distress, as she often did, and her healing empathy perceived the source of it. "Marissa, don't. Don't blame yourself overmuch. If you turn to constant reproach, you'll censure away the wonderful parts of yourself, the parts that rouse people to enthusiasm. The parts that will lead others to follow you."

"But without wisdom and restraint I only seem to lead to disaster," Marissa said, voice filled with recrimination. "I've worked so hard to be trusted since the Faery Realm visit. What kind of demonstration of leadership was that?"

"That was a long time ago. You were but a child. Learn from it and use the lesson well. But it's past time for you to move forward from that memory." Ciara's voice was soft.

Marissa raised her head and studied her twin. It was Ciara who was blessed with patience, wisdom, and forbearance, not her. "You forgive too easily."

"Because I love and know you." She kissed Marissa's cheek and slid her arm though hers. "Now then, where is everyone?" she asked, looking around. "Especially Shayla. I missed her presence in preparing for the ritual."

"Yes, as did I. It was strange to do so without her. I don't think we ever have."

Ciara tidied a strand of Marissa's hair that had fallen across her cheek. "If twins could have a third, Shayla would be ours, would she not?" She smiled and slipped her hand into Marissa's.

Marissa nodded, feeling small next to Ciara with her gracious ways, and wondering again why Shayla had been so cross before. She regretted that she'd misspoke about Ciara's pregnancy, but that was for Ciara to forgive, and she had. Shayla had taken up the fight with a particular vengeance. It seemed very odd.

"There's Mother," Ciara exclaimed, pointing to the top of the knoll.

Alianore approached, hands clasped in front of her, head high, as befit a High Priestess. Marissa did not need to be the empath Ciara was to see she was shaken. She noted the red-rimmed eyes and pallor. Had her willful ways caused her mother's upset?

Ciara rushed to her side. "Mother! Whatever is the matter?"

Marissa's heart sped up. She scanned the knoll behind her mother, all the way to the Life Tree beyond the now open gates to the Healing Halls. "Where's Shayla?"

Her mother's mouth quivered, and she pulled it tight before answering, "I'm afraid Shayla will not be joining us for the Equinox Ritual."

"Is she ill?" Ciara asked.

Marissa swallowed back alarm.

"Shayla has made her choice."

Ciara gasped and put her hand to her mouth. "She what? Do you mean she . . ."

The question hung heavy before Alianore replied. "Yes. She has left Avalon."

Ciara sobbed behind her upraised hand. Alianore opened her arms to her daughters and embraced them, leaning her cheek first on Ciara's head, then Marissa's.

Ciara moaned. "She didn't say goodbye. Why did she leave us without giving us the chance to bid her farewell?"

Marissa felt a hole open in her heart, empty as a freshly dug grave. She stroked her sister's back. "We knew this day might come."

"How did she leave, Mother? Was she happy?"

"There is much you do not know, much I have to tell you." Marissa watched her mother's chin tremble. "There will be time for the telling. For now, we must preside over the ritual. Our dear ones are gathering as we speak. I will talk to you both in private afterward."

Marissa turned her head and saw the other priestesses approaching in groups of two's and three's, heading for the well. She pulled away from her mother and sister's embrace. Ciara took a deep breath. Alianore lifted her chin and stood tall. Marissa wiped her eyes and bent over the well lip to retrieve the talisman necklace. She resumed her duties with force of will, lifted the chain to Alianore's neck, reaching around to secure the clasp. She felt the magic of the necklace tease at her fingertips again. More acute was grief's effort to dredge the hole the startling news about Shayla had dug in her heart.

She whispered in her mother's ear. "I'm sorry for how I spoke to Ciara and Shayla this morning. I promise to mend my ways."

Alianore laid her hand atop Marissa's. "Rebuking you is not necessary."

"You're not angry with me?"

Alianore held her gaze. "I mourn Shayla. Any anger I may have felt is long gone."

Marissa nodded, her eyes working to hold back the hot sting of tears. "I do not wish to add to your sorrow."

Alianore looked straight ahead, tipping her head in acknowledgement to those who joined, as they tread quietly to encircle the Red Well. Marissa turned and knelt to bless the central candle. Her mother raised one arm to the heavens, the other pointing to the earth beneath their feet, and began the ritual invocations.

"We honor You, Goddess of the Stars and the Sea, You who presides in the heavens and in the earth, You who lives in our bodies and in our hearts . . ."

Marissa stood and took her place alongside Ciara in the circle. Despite the power being raised, Alianore's voice receded in the background as Marissa's thoughts consumed her attention. Shayla had been angry with her, had quarreled with her this morning. She wondered with an aching heart, *Have I done something to cause her to leave?*

Chapter 38

France
Autumn Anno Domini 1535

Lord Bernard de Boulle's Great Hall was filled with road-weary knights and their squires. Trestle tables accommodated Michael's father's soldiers and his Uncle Bernard's men. Sputtering torches hung from the walls, and the bright candles of overhead chandeliers dispelled the darkness, chasing shadows into the far corners. Minstrels sang a lively tune and servants carried in trays of venison stew.

Michael sat amongst his companions and leaned back in his chair, the sweet French wine already going to his head. *Odd drink*, he thought, swirling it around in his cup. The high notes of a lute brought his attention back to the Hall. He felt the vast room spin, much like the strong wine in his cup. He preferred his Welsh ales.

He'd spent the last three months on the road, combing the French countryside with his companions, defending estate borders and thwarting Protestant uprisings. Now they'd returned to his uncle's castle for a well-earned respite. *Shaved and bathed, they smelled all the better for it*, Michael mused as he chuckled to himself.

War gear and padded gambesons were laid aside for the night in exchange for clean tunics, hose, and short cloaks, but everyone kept their short daggers tucked inside their boots. His father's men wore practical garb. The French had their own peculiar sense of what made up men's attire. Their clothing had a pretentious flair his father's Welsh warriors lacked. More ornate, with the wealthier of them dressing in silks and satins to excess. He chuckled again, taking another gulp of wine.

"Slow down, lad," David laughed, clapping him on the shoulder. "Ye'll not be used to your uncle's vineyards and strong drink."

David was seated next to Michael and immediately returned to scooping venison stew from his wooden trencher. Philip was on the other side, eyeing his own wooden plate. Back home in their father's household they still used bread trenchers to portion food.

"Wine, David. The grape drink is called wine," George called out from across the table. "You big lout," he added in friendly insult.

The men at the table howled. Michael laughed with them and Philip joined in, his cheeks flushed and his words already slurring.

George, still grinning, added, "Besides, you're one to talk, David. You've spilled half your cup down your tunic."

The men roared and raised their goblets in cheer. Michael lifted his in return. He saluted the table of knights that had become brothers, mentors, and friends to him over the last few months.

He now knew more about fighting, offense, defense, and political parlay, than he'd ever thought possible. He'd grown adept at watching his back while keeping an eye out for his fellow soldiers. These were hard-won lessons garnered during campaigns throughout the French de Boulle estates and surrounding regions. Traveling and living on the road, he'd even come to endure the ever-itching lice and fleas, moldy hard tack, and weevil-infested bread.

He could now distinguish David's snores from George's, discriminate between Roger's truly bad moods and his standard tough exterior. He knew David would fart each night after dinner, and Ralph would scratch his crotch before turning over on his side to sleep. He never knew his father in the way he'd come to know these men. They were family.

Philip leaned in and stabbed a morsel of Michael's venison with his dagger, popping it in his mouth before Michael could steal it back.

"You've lost your manners, Philip," Michael chided, grinning.

"That's your fault," Philip countered. "You sit and think all night. If you don't eat your meal, you forfeit it."

The dinner set before them smelled savory, steam still rising from potatoes, turnips, and leeks nestled in cream. His stomach growled. It was better than their travel fare by far. He shoved in a mouthful of stew and chewed. After soaking up the last of the drippings with bread, he realized the food hadn't stopped the wine's heady effects. He stared into his cup and startled when images of the skirmishes he'd fought flashed across the garnet surface of the claret. He frowned.

He turned to his brother with a sudden sense of maudlin despair. "I sicken of fighting. Never liked it. Never will." The words felt thick on his tongue.

"What's that you say?" George called across the table from him. "Do you think any of us really like fighting?" He spread his arms to indicate the knights seated around the hall.

"Yes, I do," Michael answered.

"Well, you're wrong," George's weary grin told the truth of it. George relished a knight's life, but the man had no family, no one to return home to.

"I don't mind it," Philip said, flipping a grape into the air and catching it in his mouth. "Long as I come out alive." He beamed as he chewed, challenging Michael's pensive mood with his liveliness.

"Oaf," Michael replied, but still had to laugh as his brother pulled the short dagger from his boot, slashing it this way and that through the air in mock bravado.

David hunched forward and belched. "Just for ruining my mood, Michael . . . or trying to, mind you, because you haven't succeeded," he began, eyeing the servant girl bringing in the next course of fish steamed in pungent herbs, "but just for trying to, I'm assigning you to early morning training. Lance and sword, followed by bow and arrow."

"Argh," Michael groaned. Were there two of David's face wavering before his eyes? "But we're going home two days hence. No need to practice any longer."

"Doesn't mean you don't need to train. Then maybe one day you will finally make a good soldier." He winked and the men laughed.

Michael pretended offense. He stood, swayed, and latched onto the back of his chair to steady himself. Couldn't lose his dignity now. Though these men wouldn't consider his joining in their drunken fun a loss of dignity at all.

The room spun as he tried to focus on the toasts shouted from the head table. Roger sat beside their uncle, up on the dais facing the rows of tables in the Hall. Above the din of laughter and music his Uncle Bernard called out a salute.

"Vive la France!" his uncle roared, goblet held high in his broad hand and firm-muscled arm, despite his middling years. Then he repeated for his Welsh brethren, "To France!"

The response erupted around the hall. "Hear, hear!"

"To my loyal knights," his uncle declared. He then nodded to the table of Welshmen, "And to our cousins from Wales." When the yelling died down, he added, "To the men who fought by our side and fell, protecting what we hold true."

The last toast sobered everyone, and the hall fell silent. Michael picked up the flagon of wine to refill his cup. Wine sloshed in his goblet and the red wine seemed to turn to red blood. Battle-shed blood. He hung his head and stared down at the tiled flooring, seeing the faces of his uncle's lost men—Hugo, Jerome, and Lucas—in his mind. The border patrols and skirmishes had refined his skills at arms, but at a grisly cost. The fighting had not been heavy, and Roger told him they could count themselves fortunate their losses numbered only those three. But amidst the close-knit group, those three had been their friends and brothers-in-arms, whose deaths left behind widows and fatherless children.

Michael's uncle nodded to the musicians seated in the corner. The harpist began a slow lament accompanied by a clear, high voice, a song composed to honor the fallen and their knightly deeds.

Some men stared into their cups while others wiped their eyes. Michael considered the Welsh companions sitting at his table, relieved the tune mourned none of them. Bile rose in his mouth from too much wine, or possibly the memory of too much fighting, he wasn't sure.

He watched David, chin lowered to his bulky chest. And pious George, hands clasped in prayer for the dead. He knew he wasn't nearly as seasoned as these two, his father's most trusted knights, or even as hardened as most of the soldiers around the hall, but he'd already had his fill of fighting. He welcomed the upcoming return home. He had honored his father's wishes, had become a soldier his father could be proud of, and fulfilled his obligation to family and land. Three months of skirmishing had proven he belonged to the company of knights. But there remained a part of him that didn't truly fit.

The bard's song ended. Bernard de Boulle raised one last cup into the silence, an effort to rally morale. "To King and Pope."

"To King and Pope," came the united response.

His uncle clapped his beefy hands once and the minstrel holding a lute began strumming a spirited melody. The sweet notes of a flute soon accompanied him, then the harpist joined in. Their music washed the sorrow from the hall, refilling it with the boisterous cheer of soldiers celebrating the good fortune of being alive yet another day.

Michael's hand slipped from the chair that supported him and he pitched forward, nearly landing on his meal. "I need fresh air."

"You need to retch, lad," George said.

"I just need fresh air," Michael insisted, feeling his stomach roil.

"He needs Marissa," Philip jested.

Michael's smile faltered. His brother had come too close to the truth. The men all knew of his love for the woman. Months of shared road travel did not leave room to keep such secrets.

"We could all do with a missus," another of his party cried, adding to the raucous laughter.

Michael twisted around, clapped his hand over his mouth, and raced for the door, knocking into a man on his way out. The smell of leather and sweat, horse and fear, clung to the man, adding to the churning in Michael's stomach. Michael grunted. The man marched past him without a backward glance.

He crossed the courtyard and headed behind the stables. It was dark, the moon a mere sliver of light. He bent over the stubbled grass and gagged. He hoped it would calm his queasy stomach and clear his head. Unpleasant as it felt, it still wasn't as bad as what happened after his first real sword fight. After that clash, involving rioting Protestant peasants—really no match for soldiers, but still armed and incited to slay the Catholic bourgeois—Michael had surveyed the carnage with dismay. As skilled as he'd become, his first kill hadn't left him feeling proud. It sickened him. David had strode to his side to lead him behind the nearby bushes, holding his head as he heaved, not once, but three times, as if the retching would expel the torment. He remembered David patting his back, telling him how he'd pissed his pants the first time he'd killed a man.

Michael wiped his mouth with the back of his hand and stood. The night air was chilly. He fastened his cloak and looked up at the stars in the clear night sky. Marissa would be looking at the same stars, watching the same waning moon trace its nighttime path. He longed for her, to feel her kiss, to run his hands through her raven hair and gaze into her amber eyes. He yearned to be away from these intricate plots and plans and the need to be ever vigilant. There had to be a better way. He didn't know what that would be. He was no longer a naïve lad reading about the affairs of history with Master Ralph and his many books.

But those very books had already stirred his views. He considered ideas and philosophies ancient and new: notions of how land ownership could be distributed so that the many did not suffer for the few in wealth and power. His father ran his estates so that no one wanted for anything. Every family was taken care of.

But the King's rule, Henry's England, was another matter. There seemed no personal concern for the people, for the families who toiled and struggled. The King's rule extended into Wales now, and his rule demanded the people switch their religious loyalties. To devote themselves to a new and different church, one controlled by the King himself. It seemed an empty and ill-omened tribute, for the Welsh were ever independent and loyal to their Catholic faith. Religious differences were only brewing uncalled-for hatred between neighbors and friends. And abroad, where he battled here in France, the call for religious change was rampant. Michael did not understand how a man could be expected to switch his faith as easily as changing a cloak, nor how these religious loyalties could lead to such divisive fighting. He scowled. He was a soldier, soon to become knighted. He still didn't think much like a knight.

Cries of anger reached him from the distant hall.

"For King and Pope," echoed out the door. This time the tone was more inciting than celebratory.

The music stopped mid-tune. He staggered back to the hall to see what had happened. Men were shouting, their arms raised with fisted hands. Roger and his uncle stood behind the head table, leaning close in conversation with the same man Michael had bumped into when he'd left the hall moments earlier.

Philip met him before he reached the table. "I was coming for you," he said. His brother's flushed face was a mixture of wine and zeal.

"What happened?" Michael asked as Philip led him back to their table.

"There's been a messenger from King Frances' court. It seems our duty here is not over after all. I'm afraid we will not be leaving for home in two days."

David caught Michael's eye. The gruff knight added, "The King has called for support. The Protestant riots in Paris grow. He has commanded all of his nobles to provide him with soldiers. He wants these insurgents crushed. For good."

Lord Bernard raised his head and bellowed, "Make ready. We leave at sunrise."

$\mathcal{C}$hapter 39

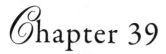

France
Autumn Anno Domini 1535

Grey clouds shrouded the sky and drizzled chilly autumn rain on the company of soldiers. Michael reckoned they numbered some one hundred strong between his uncle's French knights and his father's Welshmen. They rode in silence, single file along a narrow muddy road barely lit by the dawn. In their second day of travel, they were now a mere half-day's journey from Paris, on their way to the King's aid.

Ground fog snaked up the destrier's fetlocks as they cantered down the lane. The warhorses raised their hooves high, as if trying to gallop above the low-lying mist. Robins piped animated morning calls, and the rain splashed on fallen oak leaves scattered across the ground and surrounding forest floor. Michael kept his hood up and head down, watching the water pool and trickle off his cloak. The news that their departure back to Wales had been delayed was more biting than the cold air. He yawned and shook himself alert. He'd slept poorly last night.

When the hard gallop of a horse riding toward them broke through the patter of rain, he lifted his head. He tensed, then recognized the markings on the leather armor bearing his Uncle Bernard's family crest. The rider was Gilbert, sent ahead as a scout. Hugo, his uncle's skilled field marshal, raised a hand and the long trail of men slowed their horses to a stop.

While Gilbert conferred with Hugo and Roger, the party waited. Someone behind Michael coughed. Up ahead, George sniffled from the damp air and wiped his nose across his sleeve. Michael's horse whinnied and pranced back, splashing into a puddle. He laid a soothing hand on his destrier's withers and whispered, "Calm now."

As his hand slid off to the side, he cocked his head and peered into the dark oak forest bordering the muddy road. The robins' song had changed. They twittered in a rapid, high-pitched sequence. The hairs on Michael's arms rose with their new cry. Robins back home in Wales only made this call when alarmed. He drew himself tall in his saddle, muscles taut, eyes scanning the trees. He noticed others doing the same. Men's hands fingered the pommels of their swords. Archers reached for their bows. Word was sent back quickly, man-to-man, in hushed tones. There was trouble ahead. Much sooner than expected. Much closer than anticipated.

They were exposed on the road. The oak forest would hide only so many and would hinder them if pursued or attacked. Philip pulled his steed next to Michael's, catching his eye. His brother clasped his gloved hand and offered an encouraging smile. George trotted his charger in front of the them and David took position behind, ringing them, according to Roger's orders. The designated positions for an imminent skirmish—Roger's way of protecting his inexperienced brothers. The horses encircling them gamboled in place, sensing their riders' tension.

A shout rang out further up the road. More voices joined. Horse hooves, hundreds of them, rumbled faintly ahead, the sound swelling to a thunder as the enemy approached. An ambush.

Rasping steel filled the air, the scrape of swords pulled from scabbards. Michael pulled his own sword out and up, waiting. Hugo called out orders, pointing to where he wanted men to station themselves.

The troops immediately obeyed, scrambling to their defensive positions. Some led their horses into the woods, swords and shields up, readied for retaliatory attack. Others hurriedly climbed trees, setting arrows to bows for a concealed offensive strike from the high branches. Roger charged his horse to the rear lines and lead the remaining men back a few furlongs, to the meadow they'd just crossed. Michael figured Hugo's plan to return men to the meadow would give them the necessary space to fight, in addition to keeping their back route open so there'd be no chance of being trapped in the woods.

Michael's charger snorted and he turned him round, galloping towards the meadow with the others in his band. Wind pushed his hood back. The rain fell harder. There was no longer birdsong, only galloping hooves and the echoes of shouts somewhere behind. Once they reached the meadow, they closed ranks. Philip once again beside him, George and David forward and behind.

They waited only moments. Assailants who'd made it through the first line of defense raced out of the woods and hurtled toward them. Michael's first thought was, *There's so many.* He braced his sword arm, suddenly realizing the skirmishes he'd previously been part of had mostly been a show of defense with no mass bloodshed. They had fought against small numbers of largely untrained protesters. The knights racing toward them now were chain-mailed men-at-arms prepared for heavy battle. They carried the banners of the noblemen's houses who defied France's Catholic King and had reformed their faith to proclaim Protestantism as their new religion. No rioting peasants here. He felt the soldiers around him tense as one, then release that tension into united action, storming forward to meet their opponents.

He cast a quick glance at Philip, who returned it with a nod and a serious set to his mouth. With a roar they surged forward. Michael met the eyes of his enemy through their silver helmet slits. Shields up. Parry, lunge, strike. He could hear the words in his mind as he executed them. He used all the tactics he'd learned in training. With Philip at his back, he narrowed his concentration on each warrior who appeared before him, zealous to take his life.

His destrier obeyed the tight grip of his thighs, immediately knowing where to turn, when to charge. He released momentary control only to let the battle horse rear up and beat down men who had fallen to the muddy ground before they could rise again to hack at his legs or horse.

Battle cries pealed out. Horses jarring, men shouting . . . or groaning. Hugo and Roger called out orders in quick succession, background harmony to the fray. Maces whirled around him, swords clashed, crows cawed in overhead circles, eager to taste death's blood.

Parry, lunge, strike. Arrows hissed by his head in search of soft flesh. Shredded skin and hard bone collected under the scrape of his sword. Shields up. Shrieks of battle-lust. Cries of pain, of death, of dying. He scowled. No glory abided in this fight of religious allegiance. Only bloodshed and butchery, feast for the crows.

The Goddess's tears showered rain over them all.

Michael raised his shield, blocked a hit coming at him from the side. He slashed his sword down with all his power, roaring, screaming. He spun in his saddle and plunged his sword into the next man, this time avoiding looking into the eyes behind the helmet slits. His steel rang hard on armor and leather. Driving again, he knocked the man to the ground, where a horse's hooves trampled him into the earth.

He continued to plunge through the horde of armored bodies before him, exchanging one opponent for the next, lunging to drive his sword into an abdomen, a chest, or a neck. The metallic smell of blood and the salt of sweat saturated the air. He also smelled fear. Slaughter was all the eye could see in every direction. He had to keep on.

There were two men on him now. David rushed in and took one on while Michael fought the other. His bones shook with the pounding of a sword on his shield. His arms ached but he drove on. Rivulets of sweat coursed down his back and trickled down his forehead under his helmet. He panted with exertion.

"Behind you!" George shouted.

Michael twisted around, confused. His position was clear of attack. Then he saw it. Off to his side, a mace whirred above Philip's head. George lifted his sword, catching the mace mid-air, but it twisted round the blade, hitting him in the shoulder. Michael watched as George was thrown back in his saddle with the force of it. He rode in closer, shielding George until the knight either regained balance or fell off his horse.

Seeing a man injured but still on horseback lured a swarm of enemy soldiers. The one who'd injured George dropped his mace and charged Philip. David nodded to Michael, and their unspoken understanding launched into immediate action. Lunge, strike. Michael shielded the recovering George with the bulk of his steed and a wide swing of his sword while David bolted towards Philip. George snarled and shouted, and from the corner of his vision, Michael saw him raise a sword. He breathed in relief. George would be all right.

David was already at Philip's side, his blade lifted in defense. Michael heard a shout, and the familiar voice caused his heart to miss a beat. *Philip.*

His own scream tore from his throat. Philip was down, blood spurting from a gash in his neck. Michael was off his horse in an instant. He ducked under the whirl of an attacking sword and a defensive lunge wielded by David, to kneel by his brother's side.

Philip gagged and spit up blood.

"You'll be all right, brother. You'll be all right," Michael repeated again and again, pressing a palm over Philip's neck. Blood seeped between his fingers. He couldn't stop the pulsing stream. Tears swam before his eyes and his heart clenched, his breath seized.

Philip gaped at Michael, his blue eyes starting to glaze over.

"Ciara." He choked the words out in a soft rush.

"What?" Michael leaned close, grabbing Philip's hand tight in his.

"Her . . . name . . . is Ciara." His words burbled.

Comprehension dawned. Ciara was Philip's lover, the woman he wouldn't name, wanting to keep her identity as his own private treasure. Ciara. *Marissa's twin.*

Michael felt hot tears overflow and stream down his cheeks. "Stay strong, Philip. We'll have a double wedding. You and Ciara next to me and Marissa."

"Tell Ciara . . . I love . . . her." He clutched a faded blue ribbon.

Michael recognized Ciara's token. Philip had carried it with him since the Solstice.

"You will tell her yourself," Michael insisted.

"Love . . . you . . . brother," Philip gurgled. His chest shuddered.

Michael felt his hand go limp, letting loose the blue ribbon. He watched in horror as blood trickled out the corner of Philip's mouth. His brother's eyes stared at him without seeing. The ribbon fluttered away in a strong gust of wind.

"Get up," came the shout. "Now!" Roger's voice was urgent.

He looked up to see his older brother, his horse prancing nervously beneath him. Roger's eyes were wet and reddened, but his mouth was firm. He threw a tortured glance at Philip before setting upon a soldier seeking to take advantage.

Michael's breath came ragged, his limbs froze, his soul cleaved. Looking back down, he cried, "Wake up, Philip! Wake up!"

Somewhere, David grunted. Roger again yelled, "Get up," while fighting mere feet away.

Michael clung to Philip's hand.

Horse hooves tramped beside him. David's horse to his left, other horse and riders a blur. A glint of silver cut across Roger's armor, and his brother's muffled cry rose above the din.

"Behind you, lad!" David cried, his voice roaring with exertion.

Michael felt the blow first, hadn't seen it coming. A sword tip jarred his ribs, then slashed deeper, followed by a bash to his head.

He fell forward, slowly—eyes on Philip, hands still grasping his brother's, his vision clouding, his life force seeping. He fell across his younger brother, protecting him from further ravage, though it didn't matter now. His brother's body crimson. His brother's body still warm.

He heard Roger shout, "No!" before he saw only darkness.

Chapter 40

Glastonbury, England
Present Day

Daniel had wanted to walk Sophie home from the Glastonbury Abbey Library. It was late, he'd said, and drunks and drugged-up young people would be about town. Sophie didn't let him. Kissing him in the library had opened Pandora's box. She didn't know how to close it again. Being with Daniel this late at night wasn't something she wished to tempt herself with in the midst of the strange events of the last few days and her confusion about it all.

She'd left him in the library and set off, taking the long way around town, needing to walk the pavement, needing the fresh air, and using the darkness of night to veil her unease. It had been a long day. Ghosts and dead monks communicating with her and Daniel. Ethereal choirs only she could hear singing on the abbey grounds. The way Daniel's lips tasted. Sweet and promising. *Oh crap*, she thought. She hitched her briefcase higher on her shoulder and quickened her steps.

Once she arrived at her room, all she wanted was the escape of sleep. She threw her bag in the corner and ran an arm along her desk, swiping everything on it to the floor in one furious crash. That felt better. God, now she was getting a headache.

A text message softly pinged from her phone, catching her attention. It was from her editor, Sid. *Not now*, she thought, and ignored it while she slid off her shoes, pants, and sweater, and pulled on an old T-shirt to sleep in. Then her phone rang. Pushing it away, she slipped into bed and pulled the duvet up under her chin. It rang again.

"Dammit," she hissed. Daniel's name glowed on the screen. She picked up, knowing he wouldn't leave her to sleep until she answered.

"Just wanted to make sure you got back okay," he said. "I was worried."

It had been a long time since anyone worried about her. Since she had allowed anyone to worry about her.

"Yes, I'm okay. I walked around a bit to clear my head. I was just getting into bed."

She felt herself soften, suddenly wishing he was there with her. She rubbed the words from her mouth with her hand so she wouldn't say them. She couldn't afford the complication of Daniel right now.

"Lonely, are you?"

She imagined him grinning, with his lop-sided smile. "Tease," she said, unable to stop herself from flirting back.

"I can help," he offered gently.

Visions surfaced, visions of Daniel in this bed, caressing her in places that hadn't been touched in a long time. And even deeper than the physical sensations, him sweeping aside the dusty corners of her heart. She ached. "I have to go. I'm tired. Goodnight," she said hurriedly.

Too brusque. No wonder no one has touched you in so long. Well, the few one-night stands didn't really count, they never eased her deep longing. This was different. Daniel was different.

"Wait!" she said.

He'd already disconnected.

She laid her phone down on the bedside table just as it rang again. Her heart thumped as she answered.

"Daniel. I'm sorry." She lowered her voice. "You're right. It's a big bed. Come over." There, she said it before she could think about taking it back.

"Well, I don't know how big the bed is, but Daniel's going to have his hands full." Sid's laughter rang across the line.

Sophie bolted upright, heat flaming up her neck and searing across her cheeks. She put her head in her hand and hurriedly changed the subject. "What do you want, Sid? I was just going to sleep."

"Didn't sound like it to me," he replied, still chuckling.

"It's none of your business," she barked. "Why are you calling me so late?"

"Late? More like early. It's 5:00 a.m. your time."

"Jesus. No wonder I'm beat. Spent the whole night researching."

"Is that all?"

"Sid, I swear I'm hanging up if you don't tell me why you're calling."

"Okay, okay." She could tell he was trying to stifle more laughter. "I want to see how the story is coming along. We have an inquiry from the *Chronicle*. They want someone to cover the president's tour in the Middle East. They were putting out feelers. Seeing if you're back on your game again."

She scowled. "I never left the game. They should know that."

"Sophie, we don't need to go over that again. I just wanted to know if the assignment is almost done there. The guys from the *Chronicle* hinted that if your Glastonbury story flew, they would consider hiring you on their overseas correspondent team. On loan from me, obviously," he added.

"I only need a few more days," she said, her spirits rising immeasurably.

Writing the Glastonbury commemoration article would be a piece of cake. She just had to make sure she cut out all the supernatural fluff. Real or unreal, it would never be accepted in the world of journalistic reporting she was so close to reentering. It would destroy her chances to work for the *Chronicle's* correspondence team. Or any other legitimate press assignments.

"Great, kid. Send me what you've got and I'll make sure you're on the right track."

Sophie bristled. "Since when do you edit my pieces?"

"Since you got yourself into this latest mess. Since your career is on the line. You want my help getting back in the game with the real players? Then do as I say. Let me help you. Send me what you've got."

She sighed. He was right. She *needed* his help to claw her way back to the top. Her talent was reporting and writing—his was making the right connections and getting the right assignments.

"Okay. You got it. Tomorrow. I mean today. I'm going to sleep now."

"I want it by 5:00 p.m., New York time, Sophie. These boys don't wait."

"Plenty of time. You'll have it by then, boss."

"You're going to make it. Don't worry. You'll be a credible reporter again soon."

"Thanks, Sid," she replied. And meant it.

She clicked off her phone with a heavy sigh. No more ghosts. Or choirs. Or pleading dead monks. She couldn't afford to go off on this fantasy tangent. Most of all, no more foolish romantic daydreams. No more Daniel.

A light knock on the door woke Sophie up. The sun was bright, shining through her curtains and traveling across the flowered patterns on the duvet. She groaned and pulled the covers over her head. The knock came again, still faint.

"Sophie? Are you there? The innkeeper said you didn't come down for breakfast."

Daniel.

"Go away," she muttered.

She heard him laugh. "We were scheduled to meet. To go over your storyline and my photos together. First draft and all? You know, our Glastonbury assignment?" he said, his voice teasing.

He pushed the door open halfway and peered inside.

"What the hell?" Sophie shouted.

She shot out of bed, disheveled, half asleep, looked for a robe that wasn't there. Too late. He'd already seen her. Her T-shirt and bikini underwear were all that stood between them. She swallowed slowly, saw the desire flash in his eyes. He looked away and held out a coffee cup. She reached for her blankets to pull them around her, then grabbed the proffered drink.

"Sorry." His voice was husky.

"Oh for heaven's sake, you can look now. I'm covered."

They stared into each other's eyes for one tremulous moment. She summoned all her strength to stop herself from dropping the blankets and devouring him. She wasn't sure what he was thinking but could guess by his imploring eyes and tight jawline that he desired her as well. She finally tore her eyes from him and turned her back. If she looked at him much longer, all her earlier resolve would fly out the bedroom window.

"I can't meet right now. I have some rewrites to do."

He coughed. "That's what I thought we were going to do together. Mock up our piece, text and photos combined."

She turned back, avoiding his stare. "My piece needs some work. On my own."

"I see."

Silence hung between them.

"Does this have anything to do with last night?"

"No." She'd answered too quickly. Damn him, he wasn't going to let it go. "I mean, yes."

She looked up, pleading. "I can't, Daniel . . ."

He nodded, barely masking his disappointment.

"It's not you," she said, and moaned. Oh God, not that lame excuse.

She squared her shoulders, shook off the tender feelings he evoked. "Thanks for the coffee." She took a sip and sighed. "I have to work on my piece on my own for a bit. My editor wants to look it over." She flicked a glance at her bedside clock. She had eight hours to write it. More than enough time.

"Your editor wants to see your first *draft*?"

"Yeah. By 5:00 p.m. his time. He's just trying to help. He has a major assignment waiting for me and he wants to make sure I'm ready for it. Long story. I've got to do things his way. You and I can get by on our first draft without coordinating the photos."

Daniel studied her. "All right," he said with resignation. "Mrs. Henderson wanted to see our progress today. What should I tell her?"

Sophie exhaled the breath she hadn't realized she'd been holding. "Tell her we'll meet her at three this afternoon."

"And Barry had a message as well. He wants us to meet him at 9:00 p.m. on the abbey grounds."

"Nine o'clock. Why then?" She couldn't help her curiosity.

"He wants to use all the daylight he can to do some planting. Then the grounds are closed for the evening. He didn't say exactly what he wanted." His tone had turned formal and stiff. "Just that it was important."

His reserved, professional tone hurt her heart. "No ghost hunting, I hope," she said lightly.

He shrugged. "What shall I tell him?"

Sophie hesitated. Maybe there was no harm in seeing what Barry was up to. She really liked the old man, eccentricities and all.

"Okay. Nine at the Abbey House back gate."

Daniel turned to leave. "Write the story you really want to write, Sophie." He turned back to face her again. "And I'm not sorry about last evening. I don't think you are, either."

Chapter 41

Glastonbury, England
Present Day

Late afternoon crowds were beginning to thin in the small abbey museum outside Mrs. Henderson's office door when Sophie rushed in, three minutes late for their meeting. The curator sat behind her desk, glasses perched on the end of her nose. Her eyes glared over the rim, reminding Sophie of a bird of prey. Daniel was already seated. He looked up as she entered, arched one eyebrow, and grinned. *Damn his dimple*, she thought. She laid the draft of her commemorative piece on the desk and slid it across. It was the same piece she'd just e-mailed to Sid, as promised.

Daniel leaned back in his chair and spoke as Mrs. Henderson reached for the folder. "Naturally, my photos will align with Sophie's reporting and compliment her angle. I'm also including photos of the unexplained apparitions that appear at dusk around the Lady Chapel. And my painting of the abbey in flames will be featured on the celebration day platform."

Sophie whipped around and Mrs. Henderson's head shot up at the same time. "What?" they said in unison.

The curator's hand stopped short of the folder containing Sophie's piece.

"I thought I made it clear I wanted none of that New Age drivel in your report. The abbey's commemoration and fund-raiser is important to me, to the whole board. To the entire town. Ms. Morrison, I thought I could count on your professionalism and reputation," she said tersely.

"I assure you, you'll find no such nonsense in *my* piece. Go ahead and look for yourself." Sophie pointed to the folder lying on the desk between them. She cast Daniel a scathing look. What was he up to?

Mrs. Henderson continued. "I thought you were above listening to such foolishness. Both of you. You came so highly recommended. Who have you been talking to? Certainly not reliable and professional people, I assume." She looked around them to make sure no one outside her open door was nearby listening. "You've encountered something unusual on the abbey grounds?" she asked with a penetrating glare.

"No," Sophie said.

"Yes," Daniel said.

"Well, don't dwell on it."

"We can't deny what we've seen," Daniel insisted.

"Daniel, stop it." Sophie's face was flushed. "No, we haven't seen anything unusual, Mrs. Henderson. My report is factual and professional. Exactly what you asked for."

"Sure, we've encountered nothing, if you don't want to count a persistent ghost or an invisible singing choir that no one but you can hear," Daniel scoffed under his breath.

Sophie shot him another wilting look. Mrs. Henderson watched them with her bird-like stare for a moment, then picked up the folder and said in an official tone, "Glastonbury might have a reputation for being a town of mystery and lore, but the abbey is a respectable historic site. Such silliness has no place in our commemoration."

"You have nothing to worry about," Sophie assured her.

"It better be what we hired you for. Or your editor will hear from me personally."

"Just read my piece," Sophie snapped. She rose from her chair. "I'll have the final article to you in two days."

"Oh? That's earlier than you originally proposed," Mrs. Henderson said, opening the folder.

"I find I don't need more time." Sophie's tone was clipped. "Until then." She stalked out of the office.

Striding out, she heard Daniel say, "You'll have to excuse her, Mrs. Henderson. She was up quite late last night. Researching."

His chair scraped against the tiled floor and his footsteps sounded behind Sophie. He followed her. Once outside, she turned on him.

"What do you think you were you doing in there?"

"Trying to get you to admit the truth."

"Daniel!" She sputtered, took a breath, and lowered her voice. "You could have cost me my career. This piece is crucial to me. I have to get this right or I lose my credibility. No one in journalism will trust me again."

"So you've told me."

"Then why did you do that?"

"It seemed to me you've been barking up the wrong tree. Going about this all wrong," Daniel replied.

She had to get away from him. His blue eyes sparked. With concern. With unspent passion. Damn him.

She pointed a finger at him. He didn't back down as most people did when she was furious. "How dare you interfere. It's none of your business. Who do you think you are? How dare you think you know what I want!"

"But I do, Sophie. More than you realize. Maybe your career trouble isn't about getting you to go back to the same reporting jobs. Maybe it's meant to point you in another direction."

Cold fury stormed through her body, a tempest of sleet and snow, its icy edges filling her voice. She wouldn't let him ruin her career. "Don't you ever compromise me again. I don't care what you think you know about me. You don't get to intrude just because you kissed me."

Swift-moving emotions flitted across his face. Shock. Hurt. "I seem to remember you kissing me back." The hurt in his eyes was quickly replaced by an amused smile.

Sophie turned and fled across the broad expanse of the abbey grounds. She wanted to be anywhere but in Daniel's company.

Chapter 42

Glastonbury, England
Present Day

Sophie stormed off, heading for the cover of the cider orchards on the abbey grounds. Who did Daniel think he was? Cheeky. No one had ever stood in her way and she wasn't going to let him ruin her carefully strategized career plans.

She stalked across loamy ground sprinkled with the white petals of fallen apple blossoms. She kicked at them and they rose in a perfumed cloud, settling back down to cover the soil. All around her, the gnarled apple trees lined up in neat rows, their sheltering green leaves and promise of sweet fruit emanating nature's magic. Her fuming temper began to subside in the presence of the trees' soothing charm. Still, disconcerting flashes of the last few days' events ran through her mind. Communicating with dead monks and the music of indiscernible choirs only she could hear was enough to mess with anyone's head.

Movement at the other end of the orchard caught her attention. Barry was pushing a wheelbarrow across the apple grove, heading toward the duck pond. He was a welcome distraction, exuding his normal calm. He lifted a hand in greeting.

"Will I see you later tonight?" he called out.

She felt caught off guard. She adored Barry, but this invite meant she'd have to face Daniel, and she didn't feel ready so soon after that last argument. Barry smiled, waiting for her answer.

No, she wouldn't take out her frustrations on this kind man. Besides, facing Daniel again might be easier in the buffering company of Barry. "Yes, see you then," she replied, waving back.

He continued walking, wheelbarrow creaking in front of him. Leaning against the nearest apple tree, she slid down to the ground, her back supported by the trunk. She folded her comfy sweatshirt to sit on and exhaled slowly, exhausted from lack of sleep, her conflicting feelings for Daniel, and all the crazy things she'd recently seen and heard. How was she supposed to make sense of it all? It wasn't possible to neatly analyze or compartmentalize any of it. Everything swirled through her awareness, even her body, in squalls of confusion. She worried about her career, trying not to overthink things, trying not to feel so lost. She hoped the fragrant apple trees might help soothe her.

At first she was still too worked up to let them. She watched their leaves quiver in the warm summer breeze and sniffed the honeyed air, its fragrance intensifying as late afternoon grew to early evening. Furry caterpillars inched across twigs, and ants scurried over the grass. She closed her eyes, and in that place between dozing and wakefulness, thought she heard gentle chiming. Abruptly, she opened her eyes and sat up straight.

"No. No more singing or chanting No more mysterious sounds."

Swirls of luminescent blue and silver eddied around her in a fluttering caress. She put her head in her hands, blotting out whatever it was that shouldn't be there. A pervasive peace enveloped her, something she hadn't felt in a very long time, if ever. A woman's voice whispered on the breeze.

"Beloved daughter. You are safe."

Sophie kept her eyes closed. Maybe whatever this was would go away. But when she fought against it, she encountered only sweet tenderness. Part of her craved the serenity, the comfort. Another part feared it, believing it couldn't be real. Oh, but it felt so good. So right. What was happening? Who spoke to her? Something familiar yet lost to her beckoned her to remember. She felt as if she'd somehow come home. Tears streamed down her cheeks. It was so beautiful. Too beautiful.

Images of women holding candles in procession around a gurgling wellspring flooded her mind. Elegant turquoise robes swirled around their ankles. Silver starlight and the distant sound of lapping ocean waves accompanied them. A full moon shone brightly overhead, its glow reflecting in the well water, shining silver on blades of grass, leaves of hawthorn, and the apple trees growing beside the well. The women chanted softly. Prayerfully. Sophie found herself swaying with the rhythm of their song. Saw herself standing amongst them. Becoming one with them. Did she recognize herself wearing one of the silken robes? Singing with them? Raising reverent arms to the moon?

A repeated phrase in the chant grew louder: "Goddess of the Stars and the Sea."

The images flickered and faded, leaving behind the deep emotions they elicited. Devotion, peace. A sweet aching, yearning. She opened her eyes, heart pounding, her skin clammy. Who were these women? Where were they? *When* were they? Why was she part of whatever they were doing? Her mind fought a tug-of-war, pushing away the strange elusive memories and at the same time clinging to them. The swirls of blue and silver receded.

"It is all right to remember who you are. I am yours and you are mine, my ancient priestess," the sweet voice said in parting.

"Wait." Sophie reached out but grasped only air.

Her tears turned to sobs. The voice touched a buried part deep inside her heart and soul. For the hundredth time since arriving in Glastonbury, she asked herself if she was going crazy.

Wiping her eyes, she decided she had to cling to something real and tangible or she was certain she *would* lose her mind. She looked around. Midsummer daylight lingered in place of the luminous silver and blue swirls. Eventually, shafts of sunlight turned from gold to orange as early evening aged into twilight. The mellowed sunlight chased the dancing tree shade. *There is nothing supernatural in this apple orchard.* No mysterious choir song, no praying women, no ghosts. She slowed her heaving breath and touched the earth, the white petals, the rough tree bark—beginning to trust in the world, the real world, once more. It was a dream, that was all. She'd hardly slept last night, and it was catching up to her. She had to dismiss all these strange experiences if she was to be considered for the new assignment Sid claimed was waiting for her.

When twilight cast its final glow, turning the orchard into a burnished version of its daytime splendor, she stretched and stood. The trees shimmered in subdued greens and browns. She felt a little shaky but was convinced she'd merely dozed and fantasized. A beautiful dream. She checked the time on her cell phone. Close to nine o'clock. Thank God, no messages from Sid. Or Daniel. Slowly, she walked the path to the cedar tree to meet him and Barry.

They were waiting for her, seated on a bench, heads close together, chuckling about something. Barry, still in his work dungarees and striped shirt, and Daniel, in jeans and a roughed-up T-shirt that matched his hair. He looked up as she approached and smiled at her. She sighed, glad Barry was there as a buffer. The evening was still balmy, so she busied herself by stuffing her sweatshirt into her satchel. It was a good cover to hide her shaking hands.

"Enjoying our heat wave?" Barry grinned.

Daniel made room for her on the bench. She seated herself instead on the low-lying cedar bough next to it. "I still don't understand why you Brits consider eighty degrees a heat wave," she said, keeping her tone light.

The two men laughed.

"Have you eaten?" Barry asked.

"I forgot," she admitted sheepishly.

"I have the perfect snack. Picked them this morning. Surprised you didn't pluck a few while you were out there in the orchard all afternoon."

She flinched at the memory of her too realistic dream and the tender voice calling her *priestess*. Daniel raised an eyebrow, but she ignored him. Barry offered two ripened apples, handing one to each of them.

"I suppose I was preoccupied," she said, giving Daniel a sideways glance.

She bit into her apple and juice dribbled down her chin. "This has to be the best apple I've ever tasted," she said, wiping her chin with the back of one hand.

Barry beamed. "I'm steward of the apple orchard. The secret to good apples is in talking to the trees. Touching their trunks, their souls."

Sophie looked up in surprise.

"And good organic fertilizer, without question," he added with a wink.

She couldn't be annoyed at his eccentric ways, but she couldn't help feeling he was somehow teasing her. Daniel leaned back and watched her as he chewed.

The groundskeeper pulled out two bottles of water, Chalice Well water by the look of the red tinge and sediment on the bottom of the bottle. He handed one each to Daniel and Sophie.

"Best water around. Good for the body. Good for the spirit." He smiled at Sophie again.

She decided to focus on her apple, sure now that Barry's words held cryptic messages meant just for her.

"And how is your research, Sophie?" he asked.

Daniel coughed on a bite of apple and slugged down some water from his bottle. She looked away.

"It's going well. I e-mailed a first draft to my editor today," she answered in a tone that sounded too bright, even to her.

Barry nodded. "I hope the books I gave you helped."

"Yes, thank you. You've been so kind." She let her affection for him seep into her voice.

"Well, there are some things the reference works won't tell you. Oh, there are many books out there that will talk about the hidden secrets of our abbey, but nothing like that is kept in the museum collection."

"What kind of secrets?" Daniel asked.

Sophie wanted to lob her apple core straight at him. This conversation was going in the exact direction she didn't want. She took in a deep breath, recalling the practical solidity of the orchard with its strong trunks, green leaves, and ripening fruit. Normalcy. After recalling that bit of earthy sustenance, she could handle this one discussion, couldn't she?

"Yes, secrets," Barry replied, his eyes lighting up as he warmed to the topic. "Well, for one, there are Dion Fortune's works."

"Who's that?" Daniel asked, throwing his apple core to a squirrel, who seized it and ran up a nearby cedar.

Sophie watched him closely. Were the two men trying to purposefully provoke her with this talk of secrets? Daniel's face remained neutral, no teasing smirk. And Barry was the picture of sincerity.

Barry continued. "Dion Fortune was a famous and respected British occultist, as well as a psychologist, teacher, and mystic. She maintained a home and teaching center at the foot of the Glastonbury Tor in the early to mid-1900's." He pointed to the foot of the Tor where that old house still stood, privately owned and used as a B&B. "I met her when I was a very young boy. A fascinating person. You know, it was Dion who spearheaded the efforts to offset Hitler's WWII invasion plans of England with the use of magic and meditation."

Daniel nodded. "I've heard that." He glanced at Sophie. "In the research I did this afternoon. I read she united many of England's mystical Lodges and spiritual circles for that cause."

She watched the two of them, her gaze traveling back and forth between them.

"Indeed. Now you're getting it," Barry said. He caught Sophie's eye. "And Dion was a priestess of the Goddess. A Moon and Sea priestess. Even wrote novels about it." He kept his eye steady on hers.

She startled at the word "priestess," jerking her head up and nearly dropping her apple.

Barry continued. "And there's one more thing about her that relates to the Glastonbury Abbey, actually."

Well, that's finally more relevant, Sophie thought. She couldn't even guess where he was heading with his talk about this Dion Fortune person.

"Dion Fortune was a contemporary of Frederick Bligh Bond."

Her heartbeat quickened. Bligh Bond was the abbey's archeologist she'd read about last evening. The one whose findings had been so disconcerting. He'd reported paranormal sightings similar to her and Daniel's at the abbey. And he'd been fired from the abbey's archeology project for his reports.

"Dion Fortune claimed she had similar experiences to Bligh Bond's. She saw, and more importantly, she said she talked to the ghosts of Glastonbury Abbey's dead monks."

Sophie's throat went dry. *Not this again.* Barry still held her gaze, his countenance keeping her from straying from surprise into anger.

"Come on," he said, offering his hand. "Let's walk over to the abbey ruins. I want to show you something."

She hesitated, fearing she'd hear the unseen choir again. But he kept his hand out and his smile welcoming, offering her what seemed to be a safe haven. She took his hand and he looped it through his arm. Daniel peeked at her from Barry's other side, giving her a swift smile. As they walked, approaching the ruins from the back—the east end—Barry kept up the conversation.

"Glastonbury Abbey was the greatest medieval abbey in England. And the richest . . ."

Although he was talking about things she already knew, Sophie kept her focus on Barry. She refused to look at Daniel.

"The St. Mary's Chapel was the site of the first Christian church in England, built by the uncle of Jesus himself, Joseph of Arimathea. Joseph brought the chalice of the last supper with him to England, the cruet that held the blood and sweat of Jesus. You visited the St. Mary Chapel together, Daniel tells me." Barry patted her hand.

He didn't stop to hear her answer. She wouldn't have spoken about it anyway. That was where Daniel had seen the apparition of Michael and claimed he had communicated with him.

"Anyway, I'm sure you've noticed there are cruets carved beside a cross in the gateway to the Abbey Retreat House where Daniel is lodging. One gold cruet, one silver. Symbolizing the alchemical marriage."

"The what?" she asked. She'd noticed the carving but hadn't understood its meaning.

"The ancient alchemists spoke of the sacred marriage. Where body and spirit unite."

"Sounds a bit esoteric," Daniel said.

"Oh, it is. It's a common enough theme in all religions, Christian and Pagan included. But what is really relevant to you, to your research and to the abbey, is the carving of a dragon close by the cross and cruets."

Sophie recalled seeing the stone carved dragon when she'd first entered the gateway, a few days ago now.

"The dragon carving has a specific symbolism. It means 'dragons below.' It's referring to the two dragon lines or serpent lines. They are the two earth energy ley lines that converge in the abbey ruins. These ley lines are thought of as natural electromagnetic power centers." He stopped walking. "Here we are. This is where those very ley lines unite."

Ley lines? Questions formed in Sophie's mind, her skepticism casually taking over. But she waited to ask them, letting Barry lead the way. He'd brought them to the eastern section of the ruined abbey, a spot open to the sky. Mere remnants of the glorious stone walls remained. A distance ahead of them were the famous abbey archways, at the transept that bisected what was once the cathedral's nave. What remained of the two arches were two lofty fragments that curved high toward the heavens but were broken in the middle, disjointed, reaching for each other, but just short of connecting.

To Sophie's right was a roped-off section with a sign indicating what had been the location of the abbey's 'High Altar'. Close by was an area bearing another sign designating the burial site of the renowned King Arthur and his wife, Queen Guinevere.

She sighed, unable to keep her skepticism at bay any longer. "Barry, I'm sorry, but energy lines? It sounds so New Age. Why are you telling us this?"

"You'll see. As I said, the ley lines are earth-power channels. They underlie many sacred sites around the world. Here in England, specifically right here at the abbey, we have a confluence of two of these earth energies. We call them the Mary and St. Michael lines, because their qualities are seen as feminine and masculine respectively. They meet their full polarity, right here." Barry pointed to the ground between the High Altar and the tomb site.

He looked at Daniel and Sophie. "This is where the ley lines meet. A sacred marriage of sorts, combining the Mary and Michael lines. The monks of Glastonbury must have known that, because that's where they chose to inter Arthur and Guinevere's graves. And this is where they put their abbey's High Altar."

Sophie gently pulled her hand from Barry's. "I'm sorry. I respect you. I just don't believe in this kind of thing."

Daniel interjected. "I was just talking to the Gothic Image bookstore owner about Glastonbury this afternoon while I perused his stock. He made a point of mentioning this." He leaned around Barry to glance at Sophie. "He told me that archeologists acknowledge these lines, but they don't offer an explanation for their existence. He said occultists believe there is power centered where the ley lines converge."

"Still doesn't make me believe."

Barry patted Sophie's hand again in reassurance. "I didn't bring you here to believe or not believe. I brought you to this spot to experience it. It's part of the abbey as surely as any chronological history."

He walked to a specific point between the altar and the tombs. It looked like a patch of innocuous grassy lawn to Sophie. Dusk had darkened into night, and bright stars punctuated the sky while a full moon painted everything around them in its silver glow.

"Stand here. Feel for yourself," Barry said.

She stepped back. "Barry, I just don't want to do this."

"Afraid?" Daniel asked.

She bristled. "No . . . I mean, of course I am. Too many weird things have happened to me on these grounds. I don't need any more craziness."

Barry stood still, eyes closed, a slight smile on his lips. The craggy lines of his face diminished. He let out a slow breath, opened his eyes, and held out his hand. "I promise there's nothing to be afraid of. I would never let you come to harm. You may want to prove to yourself, yay or nay, that ley lines are something that can be experienced. Or not." He shrugged his shoulders.

Daniel moved to stand beside Barry. He, too, held out his hand.

Sophie chewed her lip, decided it would be better to face this and prove to herself it was nothing. Nothing. Just like her dream earlier in the orchard. She needed it to be merely wishful thinking on Barry's part. Besides, if she backed off now, Daniel would think her a coward. Despite her confusion about all the strange things happening to her, she would think herself a coward as well if she didn't do this. She'd faced *real* danger on foreign assignments abroad. She grabbed Barry's hand and stood beside him.

"Close your eyes," he instructed. "Ground yourself, just like those apple trees in the orchard today. With their roots deep down in the earth."

Sophie hid her sneer behind closed eyes. Already it felt ludicrous, but she'd face it for Barry's sake at least. She did as instructed, imagining the apple trees she'd sat under all afternoon—feeling their rough bark and gnarled roots, imagining those roots seeking the depth of the nourishing black soil beneath them. Roots searching for sustenance, for the life force of water and earth.

"Good," he said. "Now extend your awareness even deeper into the earth beneath you. Use the tree roots to bring you down. Just feel. Sense with your body. Feel your sensations."

She grinned when she felt nothing. It verified her sanity. How silly this all was. She exhaled loudly and waited. Still nothing. Barry's warmth pulsed in her hand. He was such a kind man. Too bad he got involved in such nonsense. She waited some more out of respect. Her mind began to wander. At first to mundane things: the sweet taste of apple that still lingered in her mouth, the nuts and raisins she'd snack on when this was over. The feel of Daniel's lips on hers. *Stop it*, she chided herself.

"Keep focus. Keep sensing," Barry encouraged.

She willfully pulled her attention back to the tree roots and gave it another try. Imagined traveling along the roots as he had suggested. Nothing again. She was about to give up, about to tell him this just didn't work for her, when she felt a surge of warmth shoot up her feet, through her legs and into her lower belly. She opened her eyes in surprise. Barry and Daniel had theirs closed. She closed hers again as well.

Tingling bolts of sensation coursed from the ground, spiraling up her calves, into her abdomen, and back down again. A circuit of warmth. If she could give it a color, she'd say it felt green. She had no other word for this tree root vitality. Then she noticed a deeper pulsing. *Thrump, thrump.* The sound morphed into a chorus of vibrating beats and pulsations.

She was fixed to the spot she stood upon, drawn into the pulsing. Something else surged up her limbs, something different from the original pulse. Something vigorous. It filled her entire body, this push and pull of energy. She felt like she'd plugged into an electric socket, been shocked, but also grounded with the pulsing energy. Like she was lit up from the inside with a vitality that surged and undulated. Coils of sensation spiraled and intertwined in her belly and along her spine.

"Okay, Barry, you win. Something is happening," she whispered.

When she opened her eyes, it was Daniel's hand that grasped hers. Barry was nowhere to be seen.

Chapter 43

Glastonbury, England
Present Day

Sophie wanted to yank her hand from Daniel's. *Keep away from him.* The warning rolled through her hazy mind. *If you go down this road called Daniel, there'll be no turning back.*

She didn't let go of his hand. It was as if she'd been holding his hand for centuries. It was then she realized he was no longer wearing his wedding ring.

Her body still thrummed to the slow and steady beat of the earth, with undercurrents of spark and fire. Barry had told her she was sensing the Michael ley line. Yet, something else had emerged as well in this peculiar spot between the High Altar and the king and queen's grave. It coursed through her body in a spiraling dance of energy. This was a different beat rising into her. Barry had called it the Mary ley line. Uniting with the Michael line's fiery undercurrent, this line thumped in a lighter fashion, drawing Sophie down into herself, to the places that actually did want to hold Daniel's hand. And so much more.

She turned to face him. He opened his eyes and looked into hers, his blue eyes dark, smoky. He lifted her hand to his lips and slowly kissed each finger. Her breath hitched and she watched her hand tremble before taking a step back, in what felt like liquid slow motion. Still, she did not let go of his hand.

"Where's Barry?" she murmured.

"I don't know." His voice was husky. It flowed over her like sun-warmed honey.

She took another step back. With their hands still interlaced, Daniel was pulled toward her. "What's happening?" This time her voice was a whisper.

She wasn't afraid. Wasn't angry. Just confused. Her thoughts cleared the further away she stepped from where the two ley lines converged. A part of her yearned for the intertwining sensations that the grassy earthen spot conjured in her body. The lush vitality. When Daniel came closer, she felt the vigor flow again, without either of them standing directly on the lay line juncture.

He leaned in. Something broke open inside her and spilled a torrent of withheld love. Love she'd pushed away and suppressed for years. The years she'd spent following her career, encased in a bubble of ambition and compulsive desire to succeed as a journalist. No, that wasn't entirely it. This was more like suppressed love she'd carried tenderly for centuries, pocketed in a secret place within her. Waiting for . . . waiting for the man standing before her now. She didn't know how she knew that, but it caused her heart to ache, this great love.

Before she could stop herself, she raised her hand to touch Daniel's face. She couldn't begin to describe to him what she felt. Her touch was all she could offer.

She saw everything she was feeling reflected in his gaze.

"I thought I'd never be able to love anyone else after Laura died. After my baby died," he began.

She swallowed thickly. Put a finger on his lip. "Shh," she said as she drew him to her.

He kissed her in a way she'd never been kissed before. Deep and intimate, awakening her heart and stirring her soul. She felt the inevitability of this. Of them together. Her caution melted into a stream of hope. It surprised and delighted her. She could no longer argue or deny. Daniel held her newfound trust in his caring arms as he pulled her to his chest.

He drew her gently onto the grassy ground. They undressed each other slowly. She, cherishing each stroke of his hands. He, caressing her every movement. She desired him with a deep, primal longing.

"Marissa," he sighed.

She didn't correct him. She wasn't startled or surprised. Some part of her knew he was right. She was indeed Sophie, but in this moment, she *was* also the priestess called Marissa. And he was the Michael to her Marissa.

They touched and joined and loved by the light of the stars and the silver rays of the full moon. It was Summer Solstice, and the earth took their joining into her fecund belly. The ley lines throbbed with each moan of pleasure, accepting their loving as an ancient, holy offering.

Afterward, Daniel and Sophie lay together on the soft spot of grass on the abbey grounds, finally fulfilled. As if the past five centuries had held its breath, waiting for this moment of remembrance and reunion.

Chapter 44

Southern France
Anno Domini 1535

Michael sucked in rasping swallows of air, struggling to breathe. The battle surged around him. He lay across Philip's body like a human shield, cradling his brother's head in the crook of his elbow. Through a haze of searing pain, he inched his fingers across Philip's face, the familiar blue eyes now glazed over. He closed the eyelids, covering the unbearable vacant stare. Bile rose, burning his throat and mouth.

"I hope God loves you as much as I do," Michael whispered, lowering his head to the ground.

His cheek pressed against the sodden earth, wet with rain, with tears. With blood. Every breath he took, he felt Philip's body grow colder beneath him. With every beat of his heart, wild grief filled him to overflowing, pummeling his chest for release.

Pain lanced across his ribs and torso and pierced through his shoulder. He shivered uncontrollably. Lifting his head again, he searched for any of the knights who'd been riding at his side when they fell prey to the surprise attack. Where was Roger? David? George? Fingers clutched his arm, then let go. Peering down the length of his body, he found Sir David to be a mere hand span away, lying on his back, sword and shield scattered at his feet in a puddle of rain.

"Ye'll be all right, lad. Stubborn as you are." David's voice was weak.

Michael found it difficult to reply. He forced air from his lungs to generate words. "You, too."

The sounds of fighting in the near distance engulfed him in a shroud of brutality. The battle had moved farther across the field, yet still close enough for him to hear the harsh grating of sword against shield and armor. Flesh and bone. Every blow he heard made him wince.

The rain came down harder. It washed over the blood seeping from David's side. David lifted his arm and put his palm over his torn tunic, raised his bloodied hand and examined it, his face unable to hide his dismay.

"Oh, hell." After a moment, he lifted his eyes to Michael. "I tried my best, lad. To save your brother I mean. Philip was brave."

Michael nodded through tears that now ran freely as the rain. He mustered strength to reply. "Thank you, David."

"For what?" David had closed his eyes but opened them again to look at Michael.

"Everything."

The two fell silent. Michael turned his head away. From David's bloody wound. From clank of blade on shield. From the whinnying shriek of wounded horses.

"Well, me' wife will surely have something to say about this sad mess," David said, eyeing his bloody gash once more.

Michael forced himself to look at his friend's wound. Entrails spilled through the torn fabric of the tunic. He swallowed back alarm. "How bad is it?"

"Acht. 'Tis nothing in the life of a warrior." David coughed, and blood trickled out the corner of his mouth.

Sudden movement behind David stole Michael's attention. Roger fighting. He watched his brother raise his sword overhead. An enemy soldier advanced stealthily behind him. Michael screamed a warning. His cry was lost amidst the shouts of soldiers, and the ceaseless clash of metal on metal. Roger turned and ducked, but the enemy's sword caught him, slicing deep into his thigh. He fell. George, fighting at his side, blocked the second blow, impaling the enemy with his blade.

Michael struggled to rise, to get to Roger. Pain threw him back down without mercy. Back down atop Philip. Back down into an expanding pool of blood. His vision blurred, and Philip and Roger, David and George, and clang of sword and shield receded, growing fainter, until he was only aware of a pitch-black emptiness. He drifted in the black nothingness. Time slowed and sound hushed.

An image pierced the emptiness. A face dear beyond measure.

"Marissa," he cried. He thought he reached out to touch her raven-black hair and stroke her face, but he wasn't sure.

Her eyes focused on him, pinning him with love, willing him to hang onto life. He longed to hold her in his arms, to kiss her, but her face dissolved until there was nothing but pitch-black once more. His heart stripped hollow without her.

He heard himself groan. Cold rain showered his head and crawled down his neck, the sky crying along with him over the loss of life. A horse neighed and snorted. Michael fell back down into the blackness, floating, until he noticed glimmering stars riding a night sky. A streak of silver and blue pierced the dark and a vast and beautiful Lady appeared. It was the same Lady he'd seen when he almost died in Avalon's lake as a boy. He'd never forgotten Her serene face. She was crowned with stars and caped in flowing robes of midnight blue. She was fiery as the blazing stars around Her, and bright as their frosty silver light. Her Presence soothed his barren heart. For a brief moment, peace edged out anguish.

"My beloved son," She whispered.

Her words were a mother's caress. So like his own dear mother's touch on his brow, comforting and filled with nurturing love. But more. So much more flowed from the Lady.

"Am I dead?" he asked.

"Nearly," She replied gently.

He choked back a sob, his chest leaden with sorrow for the lifetime he'd lose with Marissa.

"And Philip?" he asked. He already knew. He wanted to hear it from Her.

"He has returned to me."

The sob tore free from his throat. "Can you bring him back? Take me instead?"

"It was his time. It is not yours." Her voice was both loving and firm.

He persisted. "Why? He was too young. He loved someone as well. He loved Ciara."

She did not answer. Invisible arms embraced him. He did not know how long he cried for the brother he cherished, the life cut short. His thoughts eventually returned to Marissa.

"If it is not my time, does that mean I will live? And return to Marissa?" he asked, daring to hope.

"Your destiny is yet to be fulfilled."

Michael searched the velvet black sky surrounding Her, following the shining pattern of the stars with his eyes.

"My destiny is to be with Marissa," he replied, wondering what other destiny there could possibly be for him.

"The stars foretell a larger fate for you," She said, as if reading his thoughts.

"What could hold more promise than loving Marissa?"

"Don't you see, my dear one?" The Goddess answered in an impassioned voice. "*I* am your destiny. I have called you and you have answered."

"I answered?"

"You have sought Me your whole life. When you nearly drowned. When you trusted Avalon's priestesses to heal you. When you fell in love, made love, with Marissa. When you searched your cherished books for the answers to the mysteries of life. When you raised your voice against the atrocities of war. I have been there throughout it all. It is I you seek within everything you long for."

Michael's mind raced, grasping to understand. His heart wrenched open. Closed in on itself. Opened again.

She continued. "I am calling you to safeguard something you were born to protect."

What could She possibly want him to protect? Roger's life? Marissa's? His father and their Welsh estates against the English Crown? No. Surely She wouldn't ask him to protect lands in return for life.

Again, She answered his thoughts. "You are to be devoted to Me."

He struggled to understand. The priest had taught him that God was an all-loving Father. Not a beautiful Lady. But this Lady was unmistakably a deity. *Creatress*. His body trembled with the knowing.

She exhaled softly, blowing warmth into his limbs, relief over his wounds, air into his lungs. Her breath was sweet and rose scented. "I am Goddess. The Goddess of the Stars and the Sea."

He let out a rattled breath. Marissa had spoken of Her, the Mother of Creation that she and her priestesses revered in Avalon. What did devotion to the Goddess mean for him? He certainly could not become a priestess of Avalon.

"What do you want from me? What am I to do?" When his father's priest spoke of devotion, he'd always referred to the Church. "Am I to offer my devotion to the Church?"

Her smile ignited the night sky with the light of a thousand stars. "It is not to the Roman Church, but to the Glastonbury Abbey you must give your devotion. You will find Me there. You will find truth and peace. You are to save and protect Me there."

His thoughts were riddled with more questions. How could he—a trained soldier, not a priest—protect Her? Protect Her from what? Maybe he could bargain. Would She give something in return for devotion to Her? "Will You save Roger from harm? And David and George?" he asked.

"I cannot if it is their time to return to Me."

"Wait! Please. Save them and I will devote myself to You."

"I do not trade lives for devotion. Devotion must come freely," She answered tenderly.

"But how do I find You in an abbey? What does that mean? And what about Marissa? We're to marry. I promised her to never set foot in that abbey."

"Your destiny is always your choice, Michael. But the clarity, the peace you seek, can be found in Glastonbury Abbey."

"Why *that* abbey? Can't it be another?"

"What you were born to protect can only be found at the Glastonbury Abbey," She repeated. "The sacred land the abbey is built upon, its elevated arches, its chapels, and High Altar. The men who sing in perpetual choir. They all carry a deep and ancient secret."

"I don't understand." He felt more hot tears stream down his face, pooling in the mud beneath him. He didn't know exactly what She wanted him to do, but he sensed raw truth in this destiny She spoke of. Something about it resounded deep in his bones.He had a yet unknown mission. It competed with his need for Marissa.

His vision grew dim, and cold clutched him in its grasp once more. What if he was indeed dying, though the Goddess assured him he was not? If he died, there'd definitely be no lifetime with Marissa. He recalled her passionate touch. Felt her love even now coax him back into the realm of life, much as she had done when he was a boy saved from drowning. He clung to the thought of returning home to her. Of loving her. He wanted her with an aching desire that coursed through his battered body.

"You have to understand. I must be with Marissa. Nothing matters without her."

She captured his gaze, Her eyes awakening his soul.

"If you are meant to be with Marissa, you will be."

His hope blazed but was soon doused. He knew if he devoted himself to Glastonbury Abbey, if he agreed to this request that inexplicably resonated with his soul, if he became a monk—a celibate monk, as all abbeys required—then the life he envisioned with Marissa could never be.

But if he lived and agreed to fulfill this unknown destiny as a monk, he might at least catch glimpses of Marissa in Glastonbury even if he couldn't be with her. Still, mere sightings of her would never be enough. How could he forsake her?

"You ask much," he said.

"And I give much."

Michael fell silent.

"Trust in this destiny of yours."

The images of Philip dying, Roger fighting and falling, reemerged. At the very least, he would ask her again to save his brother. "If it's too late to save Philip, will you protect Roger, keep him safe in this battle, if I willingly do as you request?"

She sighed, the feeling of it like the soft summer breeze flowing through the hawthorn trees of Glastonbury, massaging his pain with Her love. "Answer my call willingly. Pledge yourself to the abbey."

"Then you will save Roger?"

He saw the compassion in her eyes, in the tear that glistened and spilled over onto Her cheek.

She sighed. "Your prayer is already answered."

"Thank you," he whispered.

His heart raced and his soul warred. He had promised Marissa his love. That love would never change. But his heart also felt such unexpected longing for the peace and truth he sensed in the Goddess's offer. It beckoned him with a future, which although unknown, was one that his soul recognized. His life would have a larger purpose beyond fighting and killing as a soldier. Moreover, Roger would remain safe. Roger would be spared.

He knew what his choice had to be. His heart cracked and broke for the life that would never come to pass with Marissa. He'd have to break yet another promise to her: the vow he'd made to never come close to Glastonbury's Abbey. He prayed she would one day understand and forgive him. Could he ever forgive himself?

His voice caught. "I will devote myself to You. To the Glastonbury Abbey. And Roger will be safe."

Suddenly, Michael felt the excruciating throb of his wounds penetrate his awareness within the pitch-black void. Someone yelled. George's rough voice.

"Quick. Grab him and get him out of here."

Other men shouted, their voices coming closer. Strong arms lifted him and threw him face down onto a horse. He cried out in agony. The Goddess swathed him in Her midnight blue mantle. In the night sky, with its silver stars, She embraced him in her velvet womb until he mercifully sank back down into a dreamless void.

Chapter 45

France
1535 Anno Domini

Michael woke to his own cry. Excruciating pain seared down his shoulder and traveled across his middle. Warm blankets and soft linens—though far better to lie on than the cold, wet earth—did nothing to stop the agony. Footsteps bustled across stone floors, and muffled voices competed with the drum of his heartbeat in his ears. His body throbbed with each pulse.

When he finally opened his eyes, a tonsured monk, with cowl pulled back, hovered over him. The man was elderly, with white wispy hair and rheumy brown eyes that reflected kindness.

"Ah. He awakens," the monk said, in English heavily accented with French.

Roger leaned in, blond hair matted with blood. A broad grin creased his face. "You're safe now. You're in a Benedictine Monastery. Still in France. Abbot Etienne has been kind enough to offer us shelter. You'll heal here." His voice choked and his jaw muscles clenched.

George stood behind him, hands clasped together in either prayer or anguish, Michael couldn't be sure. He wondered how bad his injuries were and if he was dying. When another wave of pain washed over him, a part of him wished he would.

He tried to form words. His tongue felt thick, his lips dry, throat parched. Another monk, a younger, heavy-set man, lifted a mug of warm liquid to Michael's mouth. It smelled pungent, but he swallowed, sputtered, and carefully took some more. Nausea overpowered him.

"Try to drink it all," the younger monk encouraged. "It will help."

Michael choked down the rest of the brew. He looked behind the monk to Roger. "Philip?" The name squeaked out in a tight whisper.

Roger's eyes glistened. "Field Marshall Gilbert, Sir Hugo, and the rest of our uncle's men brought him back to Uncle Bernard's manor to be buried on family ground." He lowered his head. "David, too, I'm afraid. We'll honor them together when you're well and able to travel."

The younger monk exchanged a covert glance with Abbot Etienne and mumbled, "They think he can travel?"

The abbot's face remained impassive. Roger slid onto the chair beside Michael's pallet and clasped his hand tightly.

Michael's thoughts scrambled, one over the other. Dear Philip's fate he'd known. But David, too? The indestructible knight? He felt their loss knot up inside his chest. Too much. He let himself fall back into the nothingness.

When he woke next, the younger monk was wiping his brow with herb-infused water scented with lavender. He wondered how much time had passed.

"It is good. It has been a long three days, but your fever finally breaks. And your wounds—they are deep, but I think they will mend if we can offset infection." The monk patted his shoulder and continued to talk in a low, soothing tone. "I am Brother Claude. How do you feel? Your brother worries, he comes to visit you often. As does Sir George. We treated Roger's leg wound and he recovers well so far."

Brother Claude continued to sponge the wet cloth over Michael's brow and face. Michael's body felt bruised, battered, but he forced himself to slide a cautious hand down each arm. Moved his feet an inch or so. Testing. Realizing he still had all his limbs, he sighed in relief.

"You were dealt a serious injury. Do you feel dizzy? Sick to your stomach?"

Michael nodded. The monk gathered a tincture from the bedside table and put a few bitter drops onto Michael's tongue. The distant sound of chants and prayers, dogs barking, the monk's conversation, all receded to background noise, then he heard nothing more as he succumbed to regenerative sleep.

When the abbey bells woke him the next day, Brother Claude was, again, at his bedside. "It is Prime."

Michael must have looked confused, for the monk explained, "Our third set of early morning prayers. When you are well enough for me to leave you, I will attend, but today is not that day. God understands when there are those in need. I will pray at your bedside as I work."

He adeptly unwrapped the linen cloths binding Michael's stomach, chest, and shoulder. Michael's eyes widened. The gash that ran from his shoulder, across his chest, and down to his belly was deep. It oozed blood and clear liquid.

"See here," Brother Claude said, pointing along the line of the laceration, "There are no red spots, no odorous discharge. I have used herbs to keep your wound clean and sewed it together myself. Our abbey is known for its healing ways and herb gardens, you know. Many come to us for help. You are lucky you were nearby when you fell in battle."

Michael dipped into slumber yet again, dreamless since his fever had subsided. When he woke hours later, the healer was still tending him. Noticing Michael had opened his eyes, Brother Claude began to tell him about the monastery gardens, how the birds and jackrabbits nibbled the courgettes and herbs, and especially the lettuces. Michael rubbed his brow. By God, this monk liked to talk. Nevertheless, it was these conversations that kept Michael from falling into the deep depression of inactivity and grief while he slogged through the arduous process of healing.

For weeks the monk stayed by his side, doctoring his bodily wounds, except during the divine prayer hours that punctuated the abbey's day routine. The treatments and herbs, the simple routine and rituals of administering them, brought up boyhood memories of Avalon's Healing Sanctuary and how Elyn, Ciara, and Shayla, even Marissa, had tended to his care while he recovered. Though Elyn's remedies had seemed more magical and mystical, there were still many similarities to this gradual convalescence.

Each morning, Brother Claude named the herbs he gave to Michael, though Michael already recognized them by their scent and shape despite their foreign names. His manor's wise-woman, Mistress Helen back in Wales, had taught him well. He liked the camphor-like smell of the French lavender best. It relaxed him and cleansed his more minor cuts and scrapes. Just as he'd done with Avalon's healer, Elyn, he learned practical medicinal skills by observing

Brother Claude macerate garden herbs with mortar and pestle before mixing them into tinctures and unguents. Michael watched quietly and didn't talk much, preferring to nurse the wounds of his soul in private. The excruciating memory of the battle that killed his brother and Sir David repeatedly flashed in his mind, morning and night—causing him to tremble, to jump at the slightest noise, to sweat as his heart raced in grief and horror. Still, through it all, like a welcoming homing beacon, he never forgot his vows. To the Goddess. To Marissa.

His private agony deepened one week later, the evening Roger and George arrived to tell him they would be leaving for Uncle Bernard de Boulle's service again, leaving him at the monastery to mend. He tried to bolt upright in bed, but pain shoved him back down.

"Why must you go?" he asked, trying not to sound weak or sullen.

Roger closed his eyes, grim-lipped. He sat on the bed next to Michael. "My leg is well healed now. You're finally out of danger and on your way to regaining your own strength and health." He paused. "Uncle Bernard still needs us."

Fear shot through Michael's chest. He turned his head to the wall. "Stay safe," he murmured.

With gritted teeth, he turned back, locking eyes with Roger. "I mean it. Stay safe," he added, his tone vehement.

His brother nodded and stood.

Roger and George's departure early the next morning left Michael feeling lost without their tether of brotherly and soldierly kinship. He turned to the infirmary monk for the missing companionship. Brother Claude listened as Michael spoke of Philip, their bond, the stories of their youth together in Wales. He even bore witness to Michael's recounting of the horror and killing on the battlefield. The healer gave him soothing brews if he cried out in his sleep, and smiled alongside him as he spoke of his love for Marissa. Michael's loneliness abated with their developing friendship. What did not abate was his sense of powerlessness. Guilt. He couldn't bring Philip back. Why did his brother die, and not him? Fear for Roger and David and all his comrades consumed him.

One morning, as Brother Claude laid fresh strips of linen on his shoulder wound, he advised Michael to speak with Abbot Etienne.

"Why?" Michael asked, holding down one end of the bandage as his attendant tied it in place.

"I help heal your wounds. They were serious but you heal well, as if God sent his angels to nurse you. But God works most powerfully through our abbot to tend the wounds of the soul."

Michael felt a fresh surge of grief well up inside his chest. He thought of Marissa. Philip. Sir David. Even the early loss of his mother came to mind. And the unknown men and boys who stared unseeing up to the heavens on a bloody battlefield. Their faces haunted him, their images mercilessly surfacing, unbidden. They all competed for space in his heart, pushing it to its breaking point yet again. Would it never end? So many people had, and would continue, to lose brothers, friends, husbands, and fathers. He cried out and lowered his head so Brother Claude would not see the tears of his unremitting anguish. The comforting hand on his shoulder told him the monk was very much aware of the state of his heart. Michael wondered what the monk would say if he told him he believed a beautiful Goddess now watched over him.

"No amount of herbs can relieve the injury to your soul. Speak to our abbot. When you are ready."

Michael pulled away, hiding his thoughts and feelings within, running from the suffering of a battered soul that bled these anguished memories. But he couldn't truly hide. Especially during his increasingly nightmarish slumber where vivid images of carnage, crimson entrails and body parts, swords and unnecessary deaths, besieged him until he woke screaming, trembling, drenched in his own tormented sweat. The sedating herbal chamomilla and hops brews couldn't touch what haunted him.

It wasn't until two weeks later, when he was able to stand and limp about his small, sparse dormitory cell in the infirmary, growing both in vigor and restlessness, that he finally met up with the abbot. He had craved the warmth of the sun on his face that day, wanted to smell the fresh air, even if it was late autumn with crisp mornings and fallen brown leaves. He left his cell to venture outside for the first time. The glare of the sun hurt his eyes after weeks in dim lighting, as his cell only had a single, small window slit.

Lifting his hand above his eyes to shield himself from the brightness, he tipped his face to the sky, soaking up the warmth. Once adjusted to the sunlight, he hobbled beyond the dormitory building and infirmary that housed him. Up ahead was the refectory hall and adjoining kitchen, where the smells of baking bread wafted onto the grounds. The abbey cathedral was beyond and to his left, its two transepts spreading their wings out at right angles to the nave. Partially built into the rock outcropping of the mountain behind it, the cathedral's spires and arches were carved with saints and angels, dedicated to the glory of God.

Strangely, even amidst the carvings, icons, and saintly statues of the cathedral, it was the luminous face and star-song voice of the Goddess Michael had come to know on the battlefield that filled his awareness. A divine, loving Presence. The only force so far that could, albeit fleetingly, penetrate his brittle heart. Like a raindrop of golden ambrosia, it peeked through the thick clouds of his torment. Not for the first time, he wondered how he could sustain this feeling of reprieve and grace.

Hearing the low murmur of solitary prayers, he turned and spotted the elderly Abbot Etienne sitting on a bench in front of the refectory, beside a fragrant plot of rosemary and thyme. The abbot raised his head and smiled at him, his cheeks creasing in deep folds. Unclasping his hands from prayer, he patted the stone bench beside him, gesturing for Michael to join.

Michael obliged and sat, leaning his back against the cool stone of the refectory wall. Neither spoke for a long time. A quiet calm emanated from the older man, surprising Michael that it briefly eased his sorrow and momentarily banished the demons of grief and war horror. It was a gentle succor like he'd sometimes felt from the Goddess.

Abbot Etienne finally addressed him. "You are gaining strength."

"Yes, Father. Brother Claude is gifted in the healing arts."

"Our good brother mentioned you, too, have an interest in the healing arts."

"I do." Michael found himself inexplicably drawn to tell the man about his life. "My father calls upon a local peasant, Mistress Helen, who knows the herbs of our land. She taught me as a child. Provided me with bundles of remedials for the wounded on the battlefield . . ." Michael choked on the last word.

Abbot Etienne watched him, training his patient eyes on Michael's face. "Brother Claude also tells me you have had visions."

In all the time with his healer, Michael was sure he had never mentioned his battlefield vision of the Goddess. How did Brother Claude know?

"What visions?" Michael asked cautiously.

The abbot spoke gently. "He said you called out to a Goddess in your delirium the first few days you were here."

The warring of Michael's soul came to the fore, ripe to be pacified, to be cleansed. His confessions spilled out.

"I have soldiered and killed. Though I grew to cherish my brothers-in-arms, I hated every moment of fighting and battle." He thought he'd expunged some of his guilt and remorse in his conversations with the younger monk. But what came forth in the abbot's presence flowed from an even deeper source, now open and exposed, a gaping chasm that threatened to swallow him if he didn't immediately tell everything he'd quelled inside.

Abbot Etienne remained silent, staring straight ahead, giving him time for the full telling. His presence served as a holy witness that embraced Michael in a mystical cocoon of mercy and absolution. Michael poured out his dilemmas: his father's aspirations for him to be a knight, despite his desire for the learned life; his need to please his father; his love for Marissa, and their promise of a life together.

He raised his hands in frustration. "I am ready to pursue my own life. It does mean confronting my father. Gerard de Boulle is an obstinate man, not prone to negotiation or reconciliation. He'll be furious."

"But that is not what bothers you so."

Michael lowered his hands to his lap and shook his head. "No, it is not. I've learned to accept my father's judgment of me. But this excursion into a knight's life has left me . . . broken. I will no longer prove myself to my father. I will *choose* a different life."

"And what will that life be?"

"Well, therein lies my dilemma. The learned life, a life like Master Ralph's, my tutor back in Wales, suits my desires. And in that life, Marissa and I could find happiness together." He stopped. His stomach clenched, not from the battle wound, but from the unwelcome tug-of-war that had lodged there. "I love Marissa beyond anything I could have imagined."

"That is a noble love, a noble path in life," the abbot replied.

"Yes." Michael exhaled, trying to release the qualms that gripped his gut. "But I vowed to the . . . to the Goddess. In a vision, on the battlefield as I lay wounded. A vow of devotion to Her. In the Glastonbury Abbey no less. I don't understand it at all, but I promised myself to Her. It's a vow I willingly gave. It feels right, blessed," he admitted. He rubbed his hand over his face. His newly found vow of devotion to the Goddess and Glastonbury Abbey would, of necessity, take the place of the life he'd envisioned and planned with his dear priestess. He turned to face the abbot.

The older man smiled and his eyes shone. "Ah, yes. The Goddess."

Michael sat up straight. "You are not surprised? You know of the Goddess? How? You're of the Church of Rome. With its Holy Father and God of vengeance and mercy."

Abbot Etienne shifted in his seat to face Michael. "It's all Divinity, my son."

Michael's heart pounded.

After a moment, the abbot patted his hand. "Here in the Languedoc region of France, we know very well the face of God called the Goddess."

A seed of joy coursed through Michael's body. These words validated his experience. Still, as Master Ralph taught him, a reasoning mind should pursue all matters with further questions.

"But how? That is not the teaching of the Church in Wales or England." Michael grunted. "Even the reformist King Henry, who now calls himself the head of the Church of England, does not speak of a Goddess."

The abbot raised one brow. "Perhaps not. Still, She is as real as God. You don't have to take my word for it. You have had your own experience."

Michael nodded. "Twice she has visited me. The first time as a boy when I nearly drowned. The second, as I told you, when I lay injured in battle."

"Then that is all the proof you need."

Michael answered slowly at first. "Yes, I feel the purpose She calls me to." His inescapable grief shifted to anger. "Still, as much as I want to honor Her, devote myself to Her, She asks me to give up my beloved, Marissa."

The abbot tilted his head. "Does She?"

The question landed like a blow to Michael's stomach, piercing his doubts, conjuring further questions. "Of course! The Church, the Benedictine Order of Glastonbury Abbey, they demand celibacy." The words died on Michael's lips as the abbot shrugged his shoulders.

The bells of noontime Sext prayers chimed in the background. The abbot rose. "I must go for midday prayer before I nap."

"But, what about this celibacy? Is it not so?"

He looked at Michael. "Yes, the Benedictine Order requires celibacy. But as to your fate with your Marissa? Perhaps it is not in the way or in the timing you envision, but . . . ." He smiled compassionately. "If it is meant to be, it will be."

Chapter 46

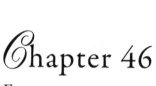

France
Anno Domini 1535

Winter came early to France, and it came hard. Cold frosted the air and ice covered the roads of the Languedoc region. The sea between England and France churned with freezing brutality. Travel was impossible, leaving Michael no choice but to further gain strength while a guest at the abbey. It was a good thing, for his body needed time to fully heal. His soul even more.

During those five months of winter, his shoulder and abdomen eventually mended, and he regained full use of his shield arm. The thick scars faded from red to white, but the memories of how he came to bear them remained inflamed.

For the first three of those arduous months, his nights were filled with uncontrollable tears and trembling. Shadow images flitted through his waking moments—daymare scenes of laying atop Philip's cooling corpse, David's mortal combat wound and their last battlefield conversation, bloodied limbs and the severed heads of men he knew and those he didn't. Hours of staring vacantly out his room's window slit were punctuated with episodes of uncapped rage where he exhausted himself pounding his fists on the unyielding stone wall of his dormitory cell.

"Why? Damn it all! Why?" he'd shout before collapsing on the bed, or sometimes the floor, where Brother Claude would find him crumpled and dazed.

Interspersed with the unbidden battle images were moments of longing for his dear Marissa. Her dark eyes, the tender touch of her hands, her soft body shared freely with him alone, her fierce spirit, and her whispers of promised love. He fought within himself, a battle of devotion to her against his newfound commitment to a destiny he knew was bigger than them both.

He could almost hear her voice telling him their love was a worthy destiny in itself. But he always came back to the same impasse, no matter how he yearned for her. The same Goddess Marissa was devoted to had come to him. The Goddess had spared Roger. She had brought purpose, even peace, to his battered soul. And he'd vowed to be Hers.

Messages came through a network of riders to the abbey nearly weekly, bringing news of his brother and George and the rest of their men. Roger visited him twice during those five wintry months, telling him how he and the men carried out Uncle Bernard's campaign to support King Francis I's order to tamp down the Reformist resistance. Michael, though mending, was still too weak to rejoin them. If given the opportunity when he grew strong again, he wasn't sure he would do so.

Abbot Etienne visited Michael daily. The abbot invited him to read from the monastery's well-stocked library until he healed well enough to tend the herbal gardens and assist Brother Claude in the infirmary. When he'd fully regained his vitality, he was asked to help tutor the boys from local noble families, much like Master Ralph had tutored him.

Even so, there was that part of his beleaguered soul that at first no one could touch. No one but the Goddess, with Her devoted nurturance, tended that festering wound. He prayed to Her in Chapel. He pleaded for Her healing compassion as he walked the verdant monastery grounds or weeded the prolific gardens. Her love enveloped him, and he came to feel Her presence more and more throughout his daily life.

Once his body healed, Abbot Etienne's patient counsel helped him endure his tormented battle memories. The abbot seemed to appear at his most fraught moments, those times when he stopped whatever he was doing to hold his head in his hands, fighting to push away the haunting images of death and gore, straining to keep his shuddering and tears at bay. He didn't want anyone to see him in those tortuous moments. But inevitably, the abbot would find him and rest his hand on Michael's shoulder, whispering, "Remain open to God's ever-present, healing love." Michael swore the grace of God flowed directly through the man.

Reluctantly at first, painstakingly, slowly, Michael allowed the monks and students into his heart, much like the warm-spirited lad he once was. They became the safe harbor in the storm of his soul tides. He came to understand that the Goddess worked Her grace through these very people.

Finally, at spring's thaw, he began to experience the undeniable peace that came from participating in a monastic life. Peace that settled into the far corners of his heart, flushing out the red-raw shadows, much like his bodily healing had faded his scarlet battle wounds. He found a purpose-filled life upholding service to God and to those who came to the abbey doors asking for healing. Not that Michael didn't appreciate the nature of the service knights like his brother and Sir George offered to protect and maintain order. But his soul relished the contemplative and learned life he'd always truly longed for.

He found a measure of reconciliation to the warring inside him and grew content. Perhaps for the first time in his life. One early spring morning, Abbot Etienne came upon him sitting on the very bench in front of the refectory where they had first conversed five months ago. The same two pots of rosemary and thyme were just beginning to flower, and the air was rich with their spicy pungency.

The abbot sighed heavily as he sat beside Michael, and he rubbed his hip before he leaned his walking stick against the bench. They sat in companionable silence. Michael scanned the bushes and trees for the morning doves he heard cooing, a smile on his face.

Abbot Etienne broke their quiet. He patted Michael's knee and said, "A peaceful life we have here, is it not?"

Michael chuckled. "It is. Once my heart healed enough to embrace it."

The abbot eyed him, arching one brow. "And has it? Has your heart finally found the peace it craves?"

Michael leaned his head against the stone wall behind him. "A measure of peace, yes." He allowed himself a moment of thought before he continued. "I'm now certain I will not return to the soldiering life." He turned his head to catch the abbot's gaze. "Not because of fear, or shirking from pain or duty, mind you."

"Of course not."

"It's because I have, indeed, with your and Brother Claude's help, soothed the terrors of my memories. Now I can make a clear choice within my heart."

He sighed. "My decision to leave the soldier's life feels freeing—freeing from my father's hold on me, from a misplaced sense of duty. I choose my own destiny." Michael looked into the abbot's eyes. "I serve the Goddess now."

Abbot Etienne smiled, joy crinkling the lines around his eyes. "And She serves your heart. She always has."

Michael's journey home didn't come until late spring, when the seas could once more safely bear him, Roger, George, and the remaining five knights of his father's retinue, back to Wales. Back to the keening of his father once he learned of Philip's death. Back to the fury and disapproval when he learned of Michael's choice to join the Glastonbury Abbey.

"Why?" Gerard de Boulle shouted when Michael told him of his decision.

Gerard was older, his hair grown more gray in the ten months his sons had been abroad. Yet he still held himself tall, cutting a noble figure in front of the hearth in his manor's great hall on his Welsh estates.

The servants eyed one another, knowing their master's temper well. Slowly and quietly, each backed out of the hall, leaving Gerard and his middle son to their quarrel. Only Roger remained, sitting behind the long oak trestle that served as their meal board.

"Why do you have to become a *monk*?" his father repeated, his voice just under a roar.

While he now felt sure of his decision, Michael could never explain the reasons to his father. Gerard didn't have the capacity to understand motives that did not involve acquiring or protecting property and people.

"Father, I've never dishonored you . . ."

Gerard interrupted. "You're trained to be a knight. Like your brother Roger."

"Like my brother Philip . . ."

Gerard raised his hand to strike. He stopped himself midair.

"Not fair, brother," Roger interrupted. "Tell Father your reasons, but do not further pierce his grief."

Michael lowered his eyes. His father always brought out the worst in him. *No more*, he promised himself.

Roger continued. "And Father, please, hear Michael out. I've come to know he has good reasons for his choice. I've seen him on the field. He fights well, boldly, and with honor. The men include him as one of their own. Be proud of him. But even you have always known of his desire to learn, to teach, to read."

A blue vein bulged on Gerard's forehead and his eyes sparked. "If you insist on the learned life, you will teach here in Wales, like Master Ralph. Why become a monk? You have a responsibility to carry on the de Boulle line, especially now that . . ." His voice cracked, and his sentence trailed off.

Michael's eyes glistened at the reference to his brother's death. "Roger will one day bring you an heir. The life I choose as an ecclesiastic is no shame for a nobleman's son. Especially a second son as myself. Be pleased, Father. I've found my calling and I've become man enough to answer it."

Gerard's face reddened and he pounded his fist on the table, scattering the bowls and trenches from the morning meal to the floor. Michael watched the chipped pottery and rivulets of goat milk seep into the rushes before he answered. He offered his father the only justification he might understand.

"I felt God's calling, Father. After Philip died, while I lay for those many months healing my wounds at the French monastery, I felt God's call." Gerard would never comprehend it was actually the Goddess who bid him to Her service. "On the battlefield, while I lay wounded next to Philip's dead body, I prayed to God to spare Roger. He answered that prayer. I owe Him my devotion."

Gerard sighed and his arms fell limp to his side. He nodded but stalked from the room, giving neither blessing nor denial. Michael would have left the family estates either way but had hoped for his father's acceptance at least. Even that would have been satisfying, for he knew a blessing was something his father would never give.

Roger approached him, grasping him by the shoulders. "I'll sorely miss you, brother. I cannot help but ask one final time. You're sure about your choice to leave us?"

"I am sure," Michael replied, his voice choking back grief.

"Then I give you a brother's blessings and hope it will suffice. Say your goodbyes to George and the men. They're your brothers now as well, no matter where you go or what you do."

Michael felt the truth of his brother's words. "Roger, I . . ."

"Acht. There's nothing more to say. Father will come around. I'll see to it." He held out his arm and clasped Michael to his chest. Michael held his brother.

Maybe for the last time. "You're a fine soldier, Michael. And you'll make a fine monk." Roger stepped back. "You will always have a home in Mountain Manor. Do not forget us."

"My heart salutes our brotherhood. You. Philip. To the happy days of our youth," Michael declared proudly, though his voice cracked.

Late that same morning, on an unusually clear and bright day for springtime in Wales, he gathered his few belongings and his warmest cloak and packed them in his travel satchel. He also packed the plain brown robes he had worn at the monastery in France. He would put them on after he began his trek, for he did not wish to further provoke his father. His sack readied, he carried it to the stables and tied it to his horse's saddle. The horse was a fine chestnut gelding with a steady disposition, perfect for travel. He then crossed to the opposite stall and approached his destrier. He would leave his warhorse at the manor, having no need of him at the abbey. Scratching the stallion behind one ear, he murmured, "Thank you, boy. You were loyal and brave."

The horse whinnied and bobbed its head, nudging Michael's shoulder. He stroked the warhorse's neck, then turned back to lead the gelding out to the courtyard to make his farewells to the entourage of soldiers and squires gathered around. He received many a hearty pat on the back, and an embrace from George who told him, "You're a good soldier. David was proud of ye'. So am I. Blessed be your journey, lad."

Philip and David's absence lent poignancy to his leave-taking. His father's absence even more so. Although he was sure his father watched from behind the window slit in the manor's solar. He felt Gerard's eyes on him and turned around. Though he could not see his father, he bowed to him.

Once mounted on his horse, he touched the leather pouch on his belt, assuring its contents. It contained his letter of introduction to Glastonbury Abbey, written by Abbot Etienne and endorsed by his father's priest. Urging his horse forward, he rode off, a mere two days after he'd returned to Wales. He headed for Glastonbury Abbey, just as the Goddess had entreated.

Chapter 47
The Isle of Avalon
1536 C.E.

Marissa could hear its voice, a solitary crane gliding across the surface of Avalon's lake, its cry a forlorn echo inside the shrouding mist. She took a step closer to the shore, into the impenetrable wall of fog enclosing Avalon, blanching its morning light. The white mist beaded on her arms and hair, moist droplets joining with the tears that carried her sorrow. Every dawn she had walked these borders, passing through the apple orchards and oak avenues to stand beside the lake. Longing for Michael's return as she had since last Summer Solstice, when she'd lain with him before he'd left for France. She wrapped her arms around her middle as if to comfort her yearning, and kept a hopeful vigil, her faith lingering on Glastonbury's opposite shore.

This spring morning, Avalon's magical barrier felt more imprisoning than protective. Though a foggy wall separated her world from Michael's, it could never barricade her love, nor did it dampen her abiding desire to share her life with him. When he returned, *for surely he would*, she told herself, she would bid him again to join her in Avalon, as other priestess consorts had done for millennia. She asked herself for the thousandth time why he hadn't yet joined her here as they'd ardently planned. Especially after he'd claimed that he wanted no soldierly vocation after fulfilling his family duties in France. She daydreamed how they would spend their days: he with his cherished books, learning and teaching, and she, in acquiring wisdom on how to best rule Avalon. And their nights . . . their nights would be spent in passion and holy joining in the ways of the Goddess. The mere thought of those nights heated her belly. She needed Michael's touch as much as she needed his heart.

But it had been nearly a full year cycle and he had not yet returned. Her arms tightened around herself and she continued to gaze into the mists and through them, using her second sight. Trying to sense Michael, where he was, why he hadn't come back. Willing him to come to her. Fighting the lure to give up. She couldn't. He would return. He had to.

An orange and blue kingfisher rose from the rushes to fly low over the water, its rattle-like song piercing the veiled cocoon. Sighing, Marissa told herself tomorrow would be another day for hope to be reborn. She turned, smoothing her robes and wiping her tears, readying herself to make her way back home. Readying herself to move on with her life, but secretly nurturing the seed of hope within her heart.

Michael wiped the perspiration from his brow with one sleeve. It was warm and humid for spring, and the early morning sun promised a heated day. As he trotted his horse around the bend of the well-travelled Glastonbury road, the ridge of Wearyall Hill rose on his right. Atop the hill, an ancient thorn tree—which legend asserted was planted by Jesus's uncle, Joseph of Arimathea—bore a dazzling white bloom. A short distance down the road to the east, the Tor rose up to touch the dawn sky. Its conical shape, topped with tower ruins, caused him to stop a moment and ponder its bewitching essence.

He patted his horse's neck, soothing him as he gazed up at the Tor. Marissa had once told him that Gwyn ap Nudd, the King of Faery, presided under the Tor. Sir David had also spoken of the Faery King last summer when their company passed through Glastonbury on the way to France. While setting up camp, David had regaled the men with country folk tales of the Faery King's nightly hunt to gather the souls of the dead. As the soldiers sat listening, entranced, the devoutly Christian Sir George fervently made the sign of the cross to offset any lingering Faery magic. Recalling the laughter of the other men at Sir George's superstitious ways, Michael smiled, grateful he could now find fond memories of his time soldiering, even amidst the agonizing ones. He lifted his reins and nudged his mount onward.

In the valley below the Tor, between Wearyall Hill and the knoll that sheltered Chalice Well, Michael spotted Glastonbury Abbey. The abbey had its own brand of enchantment with its elegant spires and towering arches. But it wasn't the magnificent architecture on which Michael's attention lingered. It was Avalon's lake he regarded, its waters lapping the shoreline beneath the Chalice Well. The lake reminded him of his first meeting with Marissa. How, even at his young age, he'd loved her from the moment he saw her.

The deep forest beside the lake was where they'd reunited last Summer Solstice. He spurred his horse on at a gallop to reach the lake's shore. Dismounting, he gazed into the shadowy depths of the forest that held his passionate recollections. Reaching up slowly, he pulled the cowl off his head, the monk's hood, part of the robes given to him by Abbot Etienne to properly present himself before Abbot Whiting at the Glastonbury Abbey. He stepped down to the shore, his heart doubling in beat.

"Marissa," he called softly. For a moment he thought he could feel her. Maybe it was merely the strong memories of the spot. "Marissa, I'm back. We must speak. Please, come to me."

He wished for her to emerge from the veils of Avalon. To hear his story. To consider his apologies. He was sure his beckoning could reach her across the lake's barrier with the strength of his intent. Of his love. She was an Avalon priestess. Surely, she could feel his pleading from the opposite shore.

He waited before he spoke again. "So much has happened. There's so much to tell you." He hesitated. "I've answered a calling bigger than myself. A vow to the Goddess. The Goddess you taught me about."

His thoughts jumbled. His decision had seemed so firm, so clear, to follow the Goddess's directive and become a monk. Now that he was so close to Marissa, something in him hesitated. He'd thought he left his ardent desire for a life with her back across the ocean in France. He realized now, in his heart, he could never truly exile the future he'd once, and still, held dear. He'd stand by his decision to dedicate his life to the Goddess, but a war within him raged.

He paused again, waiting in desperation for her to part the fog and cross the lake to him so he could tell her everything, tell her what he could only share in person. He again spoke into the mists, fearing the news would both infuriate and devastate her. "I'm pledged to the monk's life. At . . . at Glastonbury Abbey."

Michael lowered his head, fighting the ache in his heart he knew would never leave, even when he one day took his vows.

"Forgive me, Marissa," he whispered. "I will always love you."

Closing his eyes, he reached for solace in prayer to the Goddess. He pleaded his heart would return to the peace he'd known the last few months at the French monastery. He prayed for Marissa's happiness and well-being. He prayed for her understanding.

"Marissa!" he cried. He had to be the one to tell her of his decision before he entered the abbey. Had to see in her eyes that she might someday forgive him. And maybe one day even bless him for his decision.

A short distance away, in a realm parallel but far deeper than the world of man or even that of the priestesses of Avalon, the halfling Shayla also lingered beside the lake, amazed and puzzled by what she saw. She watched Michael from her vantage point within the land of Faery, screened from the world of man as well as the realm of Avalon, as all Faery were unless they chose to be seen.

Sensing the deepening sorrow of her sister-friend, Marissa, Shayla's heart had called her to the lakeshore. She dismounted her horse, and Folimot alighted to stand beside her. Although she had recently fully crossed over into the land and life of Faery, her human heart would always bear love for her dear ones of Avalon. She was forever bound to them through that love, and since her leave-taking, had found she often could sense their more intense sorrows and joys. Folimot put his arm around her shoulder, watching her carefully.

"Michael returns," she said, pointing across the lake. "Marissa does not yet realize it."

Following Shayla's gaze, Folimot stared fixedly at the young man. Her lover had told her how he had visited the soldier's camp last summer, when Michael inadvertently summoned Faery by carving a pipe from a hawthorn branch to play tunes for his company of warriors.

"But, oh, take notice." She peered more intently. "Michael wears the garb and tonsure of a monk. A monk! I do not believe it! So now he rejects Marissa."

"Rejects?"

"Yes," she said, protective instincts making her voice fierce. She turned to face her lover. "He has forsworn his love. Turned to the Church. But why?" She shook her head. "If I'd known he might one day choose the vocation of a monk, I would not have put him under the forgetting spell when we were children."

Folimot caressed her cheek. "Ah, but if you had never asked for that forgetting spell as you sat beside the hawthorn tree those many years ago, you would not have met me that same day."

Her eyes glowed with tenderness. "That is true, my love. And perhaps I would not be here with you now if not for that meeting."

"Nay, I have always watched over you. We were bound from birth," he reminded her, clasping her hand in his. "And now you make ready to finally meet your father, and fully claim this life that is your heritage."

He gathered Shayla in his arms and kissed her sweetly. She returned his kiss and laid her head on his chest. "Marissa pines for Michael. I know Ciara secretly does as well. I feel them both. Should I warn them he has returned?" She lifted her head to search his eyes for answers.

He put his finger under her chin and spoke gently but firmly. "My beloved. You are in the Faery realm now. Remember, we do not interfere in the affairs of the human world."

She lowered her head and sighed. "Folimot, my heart is half human. It will never forget the love I bear Marissa. Even more so, Ciara. She has always needed me more." She shook her head. "Michael's presence will only break their hearts again. Marissa's heart because he is now a monk and cannot be hers, and Ciara, because Michael was never hers to begin with. His presence only brings them sorrow."

Folimot peered through the barriers that separated Faery from human, to where Michael stood on the shore. "Shayla, it is time for them to determine their own destinies."

"But I would spare them pain."

"It cannot be your decision, my love."

She frowned. "I am given the gift to feel them, to sense them. I am allowed to visit them when I choose. I have to help them somehow. Besides, I miss them. After we ride to meet my father, I will pay them a visit in Avalon." She pondered a moment. "But maybe I will not tell them Michael is in Glastonbury after all. It will not be by my words that they learn of his dooming presence. I will shield them that much at least. That's the least I can do for them. For Ciara."

Folimot became quiet, his arm around her waist. He gazed softly into the distance of the Faery forest behind them.

Shayla turned her head into his shoulder. Her voice was low when she spoke. "Oh, Folimot. I am just like my mother. And my foster-mother Alianore. Both tried to protect me from pain when they made the choices they did on my behalf. They loved me as much as I love my priestess sisters. And look what anger and sadness their control and interference wrought in me. I am doing the same as them, am I not?" When he remained silent, she nodded and continued. "I am. And I can no more help myself than they could." She swallowed and bit back tears.

Folimot turned to her and kissed the top of her head. Offering his hand, he said, "Come. Let us leave them to their fate. And take you to yours. I hear his approach. Your father awaits you."

From Avalon's shoreline, Marissa lifted her head. She felt a strong breeze suddenly graze her bare arm, and she ran her hand over the spot. Something tugged at her awareness, her womb-space flared, and her second-sight sharpened. She turned around to cast one last glance across the lake toward Glastonbury's shore. There stood the figure of the man she'd waited for these long ten months. She heard him call her name through the veils. With a racing heart, she lifted her arms to begin the magical crossing invocation. Her beloved had finally returned! Her tears ran freely again, though now from joy. She hurriedly spoke the first words of the incantation to part the mists.

"By the name and the magic of Avalon . . ."

Smiling, she imagined how it would feel when she ran into his arms and kissed him.

Something about him made her stop. His odd manner of dress compelled her to look closer. The plain brown robes, the wooden cross hanging around his neck. His hair was shorn, cut in a tonsure! She put a hand over her mouth, lest she scream aloud her shock.

Unsure what to do, she lowered her arms and watched him make his way through the stand of birch trees, through the tall reeds, to the spot where she'd saved him from drowning seven years ago. It was not with joy that he greeted the place. She could feel him. Lost, confused. But why?

She watched him sit down on the grassy shore. The lake banked with reeds that moved in concert with the wind. An ancient gnarled oak grew there, beside a silver birch, their mingled branches covering Michael in shade. She sucked in a breath again when the length of his brown robes caught the dappled sunlight. Yes, they were indeed the plain robes of a monk. Had he forgotten her? His promise to her? No. Surely she had not been forgotten. He would explain. All would be well. He had returned after all. Come back to her at last!

She jumped aboard Avalon's ever-awaiting barge, raising her arms once more to part the veils between the two worlds, the words of the invocation spilling forth in a rush. As the barge silently glided forward, the familiar suction-like feeling pulled at her middle, drawing her through the mists towards Glastonbury's shore. She nearly retched from the intentionally swift transport. She shoved down her nausea and clambered onto shore.

Michael jumped up, dropping the cross he held against his chest.

"Marissa," he whispered. "At last."

She ran to him, threw her arms around his neck, holding him tight. His heart raced beneath his robes. Her mouth found his, warm and pliant. Suddenly he stilled and pulled away.

"What is it?" she asked.

He swallowed uncomfortably, stood taller. "There's so much to tell you." He closed his eyes for a moment. "Look at me, Marissa. Look at what I'm wearing."

She took a step back. Her heart refused to beat in rhythm. "I see the robes," she said, her voice flat.

"I've changed. Everything has changed." His eyes held sorrow.

"You no longer love me?"

"Yes! I mean, yes, I love you . . ."

"Then that's all that matters." She moved toward him, and, again, he stepped back. "Michael?"

"You need to understand. This wasn't my intention. We were ambushed. In France. I bargained with fate. Philip was . . . Philip was gone. Roger was hurt. So, I bargained . . ."

Marissa watched his face contort in grief. "I'm so sorry," she said gently.

"I'm a monk," he blurted out.

She waited.

"I didn't set out to become one."

"But you did. You are," she said, anger erupting, or was it grief she felt engulfing her words.

"Let me explain."

"Yes, please do." Her voice was sharp now. "What does it mean? For us?" She needed to hear him say the words that would determine her heart's fate, but dreaded them as well.

He looked down. "I'm to be a monk, at the Glastonbury Abbey."

The wind, the birdsong, the lake lapping on the shoreline, all funneled into a tornado of sound that roared in her ears.

"Glastonbury Abbey . . ." Her breath hitched as she fought back tears. "How could you? You promised me you'd never set foot in that abbey. You knew about my vision. You told me you believed me."

He absorbed her anger, unflinching. "You should be angry with me. But please, let me tell you how it happened."

She glared at him, crossing her arms over her chest.

Michael met her stony gaze. "I'm now a member of the Dominican brotherhood. A . . . celibate monk."

She felt the blood drain from her face. Of course. Christian monks were bound by the rule of celibacy. His admission speared her heart. "Our promise to be with each other? Did you ever mean it?" she asked quietly.

"Yes."

She shook her head, confused. "Then why? And especially *that* abbey."

He took two steps forward, grabbed her arms, and pulled her to him.

She pounded his chest in a blazing eruption of fury. "Don't touch me! What you did is unforgiveable! I didn't understand why you didn't return to me. I sometimes feared you'd died. I never imagined *this*." She could feel her rage turning to something else in her gut. She fought it. She would not give into this binding passion for him. Looking up, she saw it, too, reflected in his eyes. He turned away with a moan. "Tell me. Tell me why." She demanded, fighting to hold in the passion that, she knew with a sickening feeling, could only now be rebuked.

"Sit. I will tell you," he said, his voice husky, pointing to the oak tree.

"No." She didn't trust herself not to rail against fate, or worse, plead with him to hold her.

"All right." He stood straight and looked directly at her. "I nearly died. I lay for hours on the battle field, my chest slit open, my head bashed in by a sword hilt."

She gasped and her demeanor softened.

"She appeared to me. The beautiful Lady who was with me when I nearly drowned as a boy. I made a vow to Her . . . Mother Mary . . . the Goddess."

Marissa's breathing grew quiet and her heated rage began to wane. She held herself tight, her knotted muscles reining in her despair.

"I prayed if She saved Roger, I would do whatever She bid. Dedicate my life to her."

Marissa shook her head. "The Goddess would not demand such a price. And She would never require you to sacrifice our love, our pleasure with each other."

Michael lifted his palm, his eyes pleading with her to understand. "Roger was spared. I recuperated at a French abbey. I found peace from the torment of my battle memories. Our Lady came to me again. Asked me to trust Her and make a choice. For Her. For the abbey. I didn't want to, but something inside me knew I had to. I promised Her."

Marissa's words flowed in a torrent. "And you also made promises to me. About us. About staying away from the abbey. What of those promises?"

He closed his eyes. When he opened them again, grief and resolve clouded his expression. "I know I promised you. I can't be with you and also follow the Goddess's behest. Not as a monk in the Catholic Church." He rubbed his hand over his face. "Believe me, it's killing me inside to deny us a life together. Please understand that my promise to the Goddess is an even higher calling."

"Michael, your destiny is with me. We have a shared destiny. You've felt it as well, and She confirmed it in a vision. If you live in that abbey, it will be your ruin. I've seen it. I've told you."

"It's what She asks of me."

"You've abandoned . . . us."

He sighed heavily, his voice filled with anguish. "Marissa, you of all people must understand the power and demands of the Goddess's call, even if the call is cryptic or unclear."

Marissa's shoulders dropped. Her hands unclenched and fell limp to her side. "That's the only thing I do understand."

His confession about the Goddess's bidding had cooled her anger. Her body shuddered and a lament slowly rose from her. She had lost him. He had done the unthinkable—joined the ranks of monks who obeyed the laws of the Christian God and vows of celibacy. At Glastonbury Abbey no less.

"Our shared destiny? What of that?" she asked, her voice low.

"I have no idea what that means for us now," he replied, his eyes begging her forbearance. "The Goddess will undoubtedly show us the way,"

"The Goddess will show us the way?" He'd rejected her and the life together they had promised each other. Yet all she still wanted to do was run her fingers through what was left of his curly, tawny hair, kiss him, hold him, and beseech him to return with her. But how could she fight what the Goddess asked of him?

She raised her eyes to watch a pair of cranes swiftly rise from the lake, then gradually disappear into the enclosing mists. She wished the two of them could follow the birds in flight, free from the constraints of their life paths, free to rise above and leave behind the misty shrouds of impossible freedom that would soon separate them once more.

She bunched her robes in her hands. She could see in Michael's eyes, in his actions, that he longed for her as much as she did him. But he had so clearly stated his choice. A choice requested by the Goddess. How could she ask him to deny that? Yet, how could she bear a life without him? Nodding her head, she turned to leave.

"Marissa. Please," he stepped forward, reaching for her.

She would not turn around, though her heart and body longed to.

"I hope one day you will understand, one day you will forgive me."

She wasn't sure if she was angrier with him for making his choice or with the Goddess for demanding it of him. She choked back a sob. She, of all people, the future High Priestess of Avalon, should know the call of the Goddess to be something divine, something powerful and not to be ignored. But why? Why this?

Without looking back, she ran toward the lapping waters of the lake. Imploring the mists to take her back to Avalon. She would rely on them to keep steady her resolve to let Michael go.

Like Michael's choice, the veil would now keep them apart.

Chapter 48

The Isle of Avalon
1536 C.E.

"Push!" Elyn ordered.

Ciara bore down, her face contorted in wrinkled exertion. She clutched the arms of the birthing chair and screamed. Finally, her tight belly softened with the end of the latest contraction. She laid back against her mother, who was seated and holding her from behind. Alianore wrapped her arms around so that her daughter's back rested against her chest, providing bodily support in the short spaces of rest between pushing.

Ciara groaned and reached weakly for Marissa's hand.

"I don't know if I can do this anymore," she murmured, eyes closed and skin pale.

Marissa held her hand, noting the dark circles under her sister's eyes, and how limp her sister's body became when her belly wasn't tight. She had been in labor for over a day. Marissa chewed on her lower lip, raising her gaze to Elyn. The healer didn't look up. Instead, she placed the palms of her hands over the distended belly, moving them around to assess the baby's position. Marissa could almost feel the baby's movements as if it were her own hands assessing. She held her breath, sensing the baby's struggle to be born. Quelling her alarm, she tightened her hold on Ciara's hand, and with her free hand, wiped her sister's forehead with a cool, damp cloth.

"Your baby is close to crowning," Elyn said. "Stay strong. It's nearly done."

Marissa whispered a silent prayer. Ciara was two weeks overdue, which she knew added to the healer's concern.

Elyn reached for a tincture bottle on the bedside table and opened it. "Here, take some more of this. It's the raspberry leaf tincture, but I've added a bit of blue cohosh. The two combined will help your contractions be more efficient."

Ciara opened her mouth to let Elyn drip the dark pink liquid into it.

"I've also added more skullcap to help you with the pain."

Ciara raised grateful eyes to the healer, mouthing, "Thank you," before she closed them again.

Frowning, Elyn bent down to mop up a pool of blood under Ciara. Remembering the basics of midwifery taught to every priestess, no matter what apprenticeship they belonged to, Marissa knew enough to realize bleeding was normal. Or, in Ciara's state, it might signal the baby's distress. She watched Elyn assess her sister's belly once again, hands moving slowly, eyes closed. She could almost hear Elyn's thoughts. *This baby had better come soon.* The healer massaged the uterus, pressing on the abdomen to help the contractions and halt the bleeding.

"Lie back more against your mother," Elyn ordered.

Late morning sunlight beamed through the healing lodge window onto Alianore's back and shone over Ciara, highlighting how pallid her skin was. Alianore brushed Ciara's damp hair from her forehead. "It won't be long now, my darling."

She tilted her head to look up at her mother. "Is the baby going to be okay?"

"There, there," Vanora, kneeling at their side, said in a soothing tone. "You are going to deliver a fine, healthy baby."

Marissa wondered if her sister presaged something going amiss, or if she was simply voicing what concerned all birthing mothers.

Vanora held onto Ciara's left arm and Marissa moved to brace her sister under the right arm. Ciara grunted, then screamed again with the onset of the next contraction, still clutching Marissa's hand.

Elyn reached for the wooden box beside her and lifted the lid to reveal several vials of precious oils she had been using on Ciara's belly since she first went into labor. Marissa watched her once again choose sweet-scented jasmine. She rubbed it on Ciara's belly to help strengthen contractions and speed up delivery. The fruity-smelling helichrysum was the next oil selected, chosen for the first time since the labor began. She dabbed it just outside the birth canal. *To prevent tearing and swelling*, Marissa noted to herself. A pungent brew of healing herbs, to be used for tissue healing and to decrease swelling of the vulva, sat cooling on the hearth, ready to use once the baby was born. Elyn had prepared the mixture herself, combining calendula with meadowsweet and feverfew, and boiling them together to form a yellow-orange paste for poulticing.

"Squat now," she instructed, as she unfolded clean birthing linens underneath Ciara.

Vanora and Marissa helped Ciara sit forward, and supported her once she settled her legs into a squatting position. Elyn knelt in front, her expression a mixture of eagerness and concern.

"Once the baby's head shows itself, things will move swiftly," she said.

Ciara wailed. "By the Goddess, I can't take this any longer. This baby is never going to be born."

"I know, my sweet. But soon you will hold your babe in your arms and all the pain will be forgotten," Alianore said.

The pain would be forgotten? Without thinking, Marissa snorted skeptically, which earned her a disapproving look from Vanora.

She covered her mouth. "I'm sorry," she mouthed.

She didn't wish to upset Ciara, but she wasn't so sure she believed what her mother said to be true. This certainly wasn't the first birth she had attended. In addition to rudimentary midwifery training, all the priestesses, young and old, converged in the birthing room once a baby crowned, to bless and sing the child into the world. But her twin looked on the brink of unbearable exhaustion, more so than any other birthing mother Marissa had witnessed.

She glanced over at their mother. Alianore's expression remained calm, but Marissa saw the concern mirrored in her eyes. The whole ordeal might be the natural course of things, but Marissa was growing increasingly frightened for the mother-to-be. She didn't know if it was because this was her twin sister screaming in pain, or because the amount of blood between Ciara's legs was an indication that something was truly wrong.

She turned to Elyn once more, to see if the healer was as concerned as she was. There were frown lines on her forehead, but there were always deep frown lines there. If Elyn was worried, she was masking it well, perhaps for Ciara's sake.

Marissa rubbed her sister's back in the brief resting phase between contractions, recalling how she had once longed to be pregnant like her twin.

She had been greatly disappointed when her blood courses began after the last Summer Solstice, for she had wanted to bear a child with Michael and give her lineage progeny. It would have been wonderful to love an infant that was part of him, especially since he was now a monk and lost to her in that way. Perhaps it would have filled the cavernous hole carved deep within her heart after their argument and parting a few days ago at the lake. Any envy she might have had over Ciara's pregnancy was slowly vanishing over this arduous progression of her sister's labor.

Marissa pushed a damp tendril of hair off Ciara's forehead, swallowing down her grief. There would be time enough in life for her to bear a child. Perhaps more than one. The stab that pierced her heart was that it would never be with Michael.

She sighed heavily. Michael's precipitous appearance as a nearly drowned boy had changed their lives seven years ago. It had wrought brooding tension between her and her sister. Although that unnamable tension had mended with time, Marissa was always aware of the scar-laden rift it left behind. Watching her sister now bear down with all the strength she had remaining, hearing her scream, made her yearn to bridge that rift and make things between them whole again.

Still, nothing had ever broken their instinctual physical bond as twins. Marissa was beginning to feel a modicum of her sister's birthing pains as Ciara grew weaker. It shot through her womb in synch with the latest contraction, causing her to want to double over and scream along with her sister. She had to remain calm for her. Maybe this sharing of the birthing pain would help her twin deliver faster. She found herself taking the short, panting breaths Elyn had suggested, right along with Ciara.

"You're doing fine, my dear sister," she murmured into Ciara's ear. She glanced at the blood-stained linens. In her mind she added a silent prayer, *Please don't die on me.* She steadied her grip under Ciara's arm. It wouldn't do to have her twin sense her fear.

Ciara began breathing quickly again, exhaling in short puffs.

"Good," Elyn affirmed, peering between the spread legs. "The baby crowns."

Marissa picked up the relief in the healer's voice. With this reassuring sign, her own womb-space relaxed. With no more sympathy pain, her breathing calmed, her worry eased.

Alianore began the slow serenade that signaled the other priestesses to enter the healing lodge. They had been waiting outside for hours, and once they were signaled, they filed in quietly, sitting in a wide circle around the birthing mother. Each held a rose and a glowing candle. Joining in song, they welcomed the newest member of their priestess lineage.

May the Goddess bless your eyes to see only beauty.
May She bless your mouth to speak wisely.
May She bless your ears to hear truth.
May She bless your hands to provide comfort.

Still squatting, Ciara screamed as she pushed down. Once the contraction had subsided, Marissa took a fresh strip of linen, dipped it in the basin of cool water, and wiped the perspiration from her sister's forehead.

Elyn encouraged her, brightly stating, "Soon, my dear!" She sprinkled holy Red Well water on the birthing linen and over Ciara's birth canal.

The priestesses carried on their birthing song.

May She bless your legs to carry you with dignity.
May She bless your back to help you stand strong.
May laughter and joy number your days.

After the next contraction, the healer announced, "I see the baby's head!"

The priestesses chanted louder. Marissa and a few others added harmony to the song, making its melody rich and dulcet.

"And here comes the shoulder!"

May She bless your heart to be loving
May She bless your mind to be quick.

Marissa hadn't realized she was crying until she saw wet tears fall on her sister's shoulder. Whether they were from her anguish over losing Michael or simple joy for Ciara, she wasn't sure, but she couldn't stifle them either way. The baby's birth had released every floodgate in her heart.

"Ah, the baby arrives!" Elyn proclaimed as the babe finally slid out, its pink face creased with taking in the first breath, tiny fists punching the air. Soft tawny hair.

The priestesses continued to sing, now humming melody without words, waiting to hear the baby's sex to determine the next part of the birthing song.

Elyn's cry of, "It's a boy," was followed by the strong wailing of Ciara's newborn son.

Ciara collapsed backward, sobbing. Alianore and all the others present had tears as well. Marissa leaned forward to help Elyn remove the heavily blood-stained birthing sheets.

"Is this normal?" Marissa asked in a low whisper, pointing to the scarlet cloth in her hands.

Elyn shook her head and whispered her reply. "Sometimes. But she seems fine. We will keep close watch."

Marissa's heart clenched. All previous reassurance she'd felt evaporated. To add to her concern, she couldn't sense anything with her second sight. Perhaps she was too close to her sister, and carried too much fear, or was it sorrow, within her to allow prophecy to emerge. If something was terribly wrong, Elyn would be frantically working to help Ciara, she reasoned. Elyn would not hide the fact if her twin was in imminent danger.

The healer patted Marissa on the shoulder before she stood. In her official role as birthing attendant, Elyn asked, "And what shall you name this new babe of our lineage?"

Without hesitation, Ciara answered, "He shall be called Michael."

Marissa gasped, the sound of it concealed by the next line of the birthing song, but Ciara noticed. She turned wide-eyed to Marissa.

The priestesses sang.

> *Young Michael we welcome you into the world.*
> *You are daughter to Ciara,*
> *grand-daughter of High Priestess Alianore.*
> *Child of our lineage.*
> *May your life be blessed.*
> *You are loved and cherished.*

"Marissa," Ciara whispered, motioning with her hand for her twin to come closer.

Marissa was unable to speak. Why would she name her child Michael? She leaned in to hear her sister's explanation.

Ciara's words came out haltingly. "I only meant the name to honor our childhood friend. To celebrate the good times, not to reinforce your sorrow. Not to cause you pain."

Marissa nodded dazedly, but she saw something else in Ciara's eyes. Heard something else behind the words. And she finally came to realize something for the first time. The knowledge punched her stomach hard and bruised her already battered heart.

Her sister was in love with Michael.

Marissa sat back on her heels, numb. She watched in a haze while Elyn cut and tied the baby's cord. The pungent scent of myrrh oil filled the room as it was rubbed on the umbilical stump so it would dry in speedy time. Elyn held the baby high for all to see before she laid him on Ciara's chest. She then massaged Ciara's womb again, this time to help expel the afterbirth while little Michael rooted for his mother's breast.

After the expulsion of the afterbirth, Marissa caught Elyn's eye. The healer nodded her assurance that all would be well. She whispered reassurance to Marissa, "Just to be sure the bleeding stops, I'll brew some shepherd's purse tea for Ciara to drink after the ritual."

Marissa nodded, half listening, the revelation about Ciara's feelings for Michael still disorienting.

The singing continued softly as the priestesses processed out of the healing lodge, taking their candles, but leaving the roses scattered around Ciara and her newborn. Marissa stared at her sister. All these years her twin had kept this secret. Marissa had been too self-absorbed to notice. All during the pregnancy Marissa had believed it was Philip that Ciara pined for.

Why had she never seen this before? Her own grief doubled with the newfound knowledge.

Chapter 49
Glastonbury, England
Present Day

Sophie woke with a start. The night air was mild and her body was still warm from making love with Daniel. She must have dozed off. He held her in his arms, the soft grass of the abbey grounds cushioning them. Their legs were intertwined, their clothes scattered about.

Her back grew chilled and goose bumps formed on her arms despite the temperate night. She tilted her head back. The full moon made it easy to see the outlines of the markers for the historical location of the abbey's High Altar and King Arthur's grave. The arched transept ruins framed the nighttime stars.

Her attention returned to Daniel when she sensed him watching her, a gentle smile playing on his lips. His eyes reflected the tenderness she felt for him, making her forget the light chill creeping over her skin. He delicately swept her stray hair from her cheeks. With his thumb, he traced the course of her drying tears down to her neck. She hadn't realized she had cried. His touch reignited the stirrings in her belly that told her she wanted him again. He kissed her and she moaned low in her throat, and was about to offer herself up once more when he placed his fingertips on her lips.

"I think we need to get dressed," he whispered.

"Really?" she asked, surprised. She nibbled his lip.

"Believe me, I would rather lay here with you. But I feel a visitor approaching."

"What the hell?" Sophie jumped up, grabbing her blouse and holding it against her. She didn't see anyone and shot Daniel a puzzled look.

"Sophie, don't be upset. His back is to us, and he's waiting over there, beyond the Edgar Chapel ruins." He pointed down the long and narrow grassy space that had once been the abbey's nave.

"Who's there? I thought Barry said no one was allowed on the grounds past closing."

"I'm afraid this person doesn't go by the same time standards we do."

She was putting her arms into her blouse when realization dawned. "Oh."

She finished dressing and enjoyed watching Daniel do the same. She'd want more of him later, after this . . . this *encounter*, for she now recognized that her chilled skin felt the same as it did when she first met Michael's ghost in the Lady Chapel the previous evening. Though she couldn't see him, she knew it was Michael who waited for them. She sighed, resigned to the fact that she and Daniel would soon be talking to the dead monk's ghost, again.

Once dressed, Daniel pulled her to him. Holding her, he asked, "Are you okay with this?"

"With making love to you? Yes. Let's do that again, shall we?" She nuzzled his neck provocatively. "Am I okay with talking to a ghost?" She shrugged. "I won't fight what's staring me in the face any longer. Even if a part of me still thinks I must be crazy."

He smiled and clasped her hand. She shivered. Whether from the throbbing his touch induced or facing another conversation with a dead monk, she wasn't sure. It made no difference. She was going to march straight into loving Daniel. Straight into accepting Michael. She wasn't going to look back now, no matter who tried to talk her out of it. That included herself.

She straightened her shoulders and waited for Daniel to take the lead. She couldn't see where Michael was standing and wouldn't be able hear what he had to say directly anyway. Daniel would translate his words as he had done previously. She looked up at her lover and winked. Daniel chuckled and led her across the lawn to the grassy spot beside the Lady Chapel, where the original wattle hut dedicated to Mother Mary had once been built.

Sophie frowned and looked back at the Edgar Chapel where Daniel had first indicated Michael was waiting.

"He moved. He wants to meet us at this spot. Another powerful spot, he says," Daniel explained. Still gripping her hand, his gaze grew unfocused and he canted his head to the side. "He's pleased for us."

Sophie smirked. "There has to be more to his existence than cheering on our affair."

Daniel turned to her. "Affair?" he asked, eyebrows lifted in mock surprise.

She chewed on her cheek but looked directly in his eyes. "It's more than an affair," she admitted. "Right?" she added, with a hint of hesitation that even she heard.

"I do believe so," he said, locking eyes.

"All right then." She turned to face where she thought Michael would be standing. "Let's see what Michael wants."

Daniel shook his head and chuckled again. Then his expression turned serious. He leaned forward, apparently listening. "He pleads with us to tell his story."

"I thought he told us that last night. Ask him what he wants us to say." Without her previous skepticism, Sophie's curiosity was truly piqued.

"He can hear you when you speak. You can talk to him directly. There are two stories. The first is about him and Marissa, his beloved priestess. He says it's also about . . . us."

She realized that while she might not be able to hear or see Michael, she could certainly feel his emotions. A wave of grief washed over her, making her chest heavy. She glanced over at Daniel. His brows were furrowed and his breath came quickly. So, he felt it too, she surmised. The feelings clung, as if Michael wanted to imprint his tragedy.

"What happened to them?" she whispered.

Daniel paused. "He'll tell us. But the most important thing is that . . . is that we've made things right between them." He looked over at her, his lips parted, eyes lit with understanding.

Confused at first, her heart began to race once she grasped the truth. "Do you mean what I think you mean?"

He nodded, more to Michael than to Sophie's question. "Yes. Your soul is Marissa's soul."

"And yours is Michael's?" Her breath caught and she searched Daniel's face, not sure what she was looking for with this new information. "But how can that be? His ghost is here now."

He shook his head. "I don't understand the logic of it. Something to do with the spiral of time and space. But he's here to make sure things are righted between them. Us. And that the truth is told."

She felt her knees weaken and she clung to his arm. "It's confusing." She put her fingers on her temple. "I'm getting a headache."

"I think we need to sit down, because there's more."

They both eased themselves onto the grass. Sophie felt the solid ground beneath her, glad for it, as she felt the power of their conversation with Michael taxing her stamina. Taking a deep breath, she steadied herself for the rest.

Daniel spoke slowly, repeating the words as Michael told him. She watched him, as well as the space before them, hoping she'd see something of Michael. She didn't.

"He says he and Marissa loved each other deeply. From the time they met as children. But they were torn apart."

Sophie interrupted. A deep, almost cellular recognition dawned on her. "Torn apart. Yes." Something in her heart tightened in remembered despair. She began to cry. "How?"

His expression somber, Daniel reached for her hand again, pausing before he spoke. "I don't understand all of what he has to say about Marissa because now he's moving on to the story of events as he and the monks of Glastonbury Abbey lived them. In September of 1539. He's talking fast. He's eager because we're finally listening. Listening together."

Lightly squeezing Sophie's hand, Daniel listened and relayed what happened to Michael during his time at the Glastonbury Abbey in 1539 A.D. During the time when King Henry's men, under the leadership of his chief Minister, the Protestant Reformist Thomas Cromwell, rode in and claimed the abbey for the King.

Chapter 50

The Isle of Avalon
September, 1539 C.E.

"I want to do this," Ciara said, an uncharacteristically determined look on her face.

Marissa stood at the other end of the sitting room in their mother's lodge, arms folded across her chest, matching her sister's stubbornness. It was raining outside, and the humid air wafted in through the windows and open door. Her mother walked over and closed them, not wanting the argument to be heard by everyone in the priestess community, although they would know of it soon anyway.

Ciara's toddler son chortled in the corner of the room, amused by a wooden toy horse. Marissa loved baby Michael almost as fiercely as his mother. And she'd loved her sister since they'd shared their mother's womb, despite the rift her jealousy had caused between them when they were twelve years old. And despite the knowledge that Ciara loved *her* Michael. But this request of Ciara's made her uncomfortable. She couldn't say why, but she didn't have a good feeling about it at all.

"I want Philip to see his son," Ciara repeated.

Marissa's body tingled and her head hurt with another surge of intuition. She huffed out a long exhale, her foresight warring with her twin's plea. She'd been initiated into her Seership apprenticeship, so she was well aware of the signs her body emitted when foreknowledge was given to her. Even so, she'd been familiar with these signs before her training, when others doubted her abilities and judged her as impulsive.

"Think about this, my daughter. There are many good reasons to oppose this request of yours," Alianore replied. "Firstly, it is not our tradition to do this. Secondly, Michael is only two years old. Too young to leave Avalon and be fostered in a brotherhood of the Goddess's priests, even if you wanted that. Do you want that as well?" She had returned to the high-backed wooden chair at the head of her oaken dining table. She sat up straight with her hands folded in front of her.

Marissa marveled at how her mother remained calm in the face of her sister's adamance. No matter how she practiced that serene demeanor, she never felt as composed as her mother appeared.

"I do not wish for my child to be fostered. Yet, I mean."

Alianore raised one eyebrow. Ciara leaned down as Michael toddled over holding a large black beetle in his chubby fingers. He giggled and opened his mouth, but Ciara grabbed it before he could swallow it. She handed him a wooden spoon and small pot to bang on instead, which earned her a wide, toothy grin from her son.

Marissa shook her head and smiled down at him. He would raise quite a racket with his wooden spoon, but she didn't mind. It was her darling nephew.

"Help me to understand. If not fosterage, then what exactly do you wish from this visit?" Alianore pressed.

"I only wish for Philip to meet his son."

"I remind you, again, that is not our custom," Alianore insisted.

"I know, Mother, and I mean no disrespect. Truly." Ciara's voice was tame, but she remained resolute.

Marissa interrupted, patience worn by the to and fro-ing. "What is it you really hope for?" She hoped her tone sounded calm, like her mother's, not like the turbulence she felt inside from her warning intuition vying with the strange request.

Ciara looked up at her; their eyes locked. "I have thought long on this, sister. Philip deserves this."

Marissa rubbed her forehead. The head pain that came with her prophetic foreknowledge was growing. She wondered if her personal feelings countering this request clouded her intuition. She didn't want more reminders of Michael's rejection by showing up at his family's door. It would be yet another reminder that they were no longer a pair. Ciara must know such a trip, such a reminder of Michael, would only resurrect pain for her. She hadn't seen nor heard from him since they'd last spoken on the shores of Avalon's lake two years ago.

In her mind's eye, she could still picture him in his monk's robes with his Christian cross and tonsured hair. Oh, she had certainly sensed him since that day. He had gone to the lake's shore many times, always wearing those plain brown robes and that cross around his neck. She'd not gone to meet him, much as she'd yearned to. What was there left to say between them? He had made a difficult choice, and it did not include a life together. The pain of his decision felt too much for her to bear.

Indeed, she understood the Goddess's calling and Michael's vow to be in Her service because she, too, had a calling as a priestess, made even stronger by the ties of her bloodline. Still, the reasoning never stopped the familiar stab to her heart. She pushed her sorrow down yet again. It never eased, this longing for him, though he had abandoned their promises to be together. He'd chosen a life of celibacy, a life that could never be shared with her. A path that turned aside their love and betrayed his trust in her portent that he should never step foot in Glastonbury Abbey.

Now Ciara wanted to insert their family into Michael's family? Introduce themselves and share baby Michael with his paternal father?

"What if Philip's family wants to be a continuing part of little Michael's life? What if they want to claim the child for their own? You know how important sons are in the world of men," Marissa asked. These possibilities shred her heart. In addition to all the reasons her grief dredged up, she still had that unnamed niggling telling her something was not right about this meeting her twin proposed.

Ciara did not look away when she spoke next. "Michael was a special part of our childhood. A dear friend to us all. And his brother holds a place in my heart as well."

"Do you wish to name Philip your consort? Invite him into your life?" Alianore asked. "That would mean he'd most likely come to live here in Avalon with you. Is that what you desire?"

Marissa winced. That was exactly what she and Michael had planned for their own future, almost two years ago.

Ciara fingered the hem of her tunic. "A consort? Perhaps. If he wants me."

Marissa watched her sister. Ciara was not being entirely truthful. When had they stopped being honest with each other? She suddenly wondered how much Ciara's unrequited love for Michael entered into this appeal. Marissa read her sister's reasoning without her having to state it, and the realization stole her breath and softened her heart. Ciara wanted Philip to fill the hole in her heart left by Michael's unreciprocated love. She desperately wished her sister to find some measure of contentment. But could she ignore this bad feeling in the pit of her stomach?

Ciara sighed. "I just wish to link with this family that has entered our lives. There has to be a reason Michael came to us. A reason I joined with Philip on Summer Solstice out of all the lads I could have laid with. A reason why I bore his son." She looked down, adding faintly. "And perhaps I am lonely."

"*Lonely*?" Marissa's words burst from her without thinking. "Why? You have all of us, our whole community. You have a son." Oh. She suddenly understood. She felt the vacancy Michael left within her like a hollow pit in her core. Could Ciara be feeling that as well? She felt her heart clench again. This hellbent request *should* persuade her to seek out Michael and speak to him just once more. Much as Ciara had always advised and encouraged. She just couldn't bring herself to do so. To feel his certain rejection again would only deepen her already bottomless sorrow. She stiffened against the ache in her chest, not wanting her anguish to cloud her premonitions or obstruct her twin's happiness. She put her hands to her head. The pain of this furtive premonition was now making her feel dizzy.

"Please listen to me. I have a bad feeling about this," Marissa whispered.

Ciara lowered her eyes, but spoke clearly. "I don't wish to cause you further unhappiness. But this isn't your decision."

Marissa let her arms fall to her side and turned to her mother. "I've had no visions, no dreams to base this warning on. Only my intuition."

Alianore reached across the table and grasped Ciara's hands in hers. "Daughter. You have heard Marissa's counsel. If you do not trust it, then feel into the wisdom of your own intuition before you make any rash decisions."

Ciara interrupted, her eyes cloudy with unshed tears. "Marissa, please don't make this harder for me. I do trust you. But I truly wish to do this. I need to do this."

Marissa felt her sorrow double with the striking pain of her twin's heartache. Ciara was dealing with grief in her own way. Hoping to find a resolution. She slowly nodded. "Possibly I am wrong." The relief in Ciara's eyes pushed aside any misgivings about the proposed trip.

Alianore's gaze traveled between the twins. She sighed. "If we do this, if we travel so Philip can meet his son, perhaps we could also visit the priests in Northern Wales. Introduce baby Michael to them. Arrange for his year of fostering when he is of an older, more appropriate age for learning the ways of the brotherhood of the Goddess."

Ciara rose from her chair to wrap her arms around her mother. "Thank you. I know this is the right thing to do." She turned to face Marissa, holding out her arms to embrace her twin.

Marissa held her sister, burying the bad feeling in her belly—suppressing it alongside the personal discomfort of forging a link with Michael's family when the two of them would never be together.

Alianore spoke, as if reading her thoughts. "It might be wise for you to remain here in Avalon, Marissa. It will give you the opportunity to test the robes of being a High Priestess. Vanora can counsel you as needed."

Grateful for having a good excuse to remain behind, she readily agreed. "Yes, Mother. Though the day of my leadership is far in the future, practice can only help me." She truly meant that. Perhaps it would hone her patience. Mostly, it would prevent her from having to tear open the wound of her lover's rebuff.

"Then I suppose it is settled. We will hire two lads from the village, those two who apprentice with Leif the blacksmith, to accompany us on the road to Wales."

Ciara's brow creased. "But why, Mother? We have never done so before when we've needed to travel."

Alianore bent to lift her grandson onto her lap. She tweaked his nose and kissed him tenderly on the head. "Two women and a baby are vulnerable traveling this distance alone in these times. News of the outer world filters into Avalon. There is much unrest with this worldly King Henry. If it is true that he forces his religion onto his people, if it is true his men are confiscating the abbeys' and the Church's wealth, then there will be turmoil. And when there is turmoil, men do rash things."

An icy finger crept up Marissa's back. "Surely this King has no such power to seize the abbeys. Especially not Glastonbury Abbey. It's the strongest in England."

"That is precisely why he would set his sights on it. But, do not fret. The affairs of the world are not our concern, my dear. We are here to hold a candle in the darkness and aid the injured and dying, as always. We do what is needed from behind our mists." She handed Michael over to his mother.

Worry creased Ciara's brow. "Do you really think travel will be dangerous?" she asked, hugging her son tightly. He squirmed.

"For a priestess, travel outside the veils has always held risk. Being a woman, no doubt, but more so, women with powers demonized by Christianity," Alianore continued bluntly. "Traveling afar without protection, we could be attacked, raped, or judged and burned as witches. That is why we rarely venture beyond our mists except to the Glastonbury village on holy days. We will prepare ourselves well and use reasonable caution. Tell me. Knowing this, do you still wish to make this journey?"

Ciara chewed her lip. "Yes. Please. We will take all good precautions."

"Mama! I hungry," Michael cried, pulling on a strand of her hair.

Marissa reached to offer him a piece of an apple they had cut up for him earlier.

His little hand grasped the fruit. "Aunt 'rissa.' He smiled at her and gnawed on the apple.

Marissa fought her tears. She subdued her fears and grief, for the sake of her sister. But doubt simmered in her gut, and she began to question squelching her intuition. She wondered how wise it was, and how she could ever rule as High Priestess, if she ignored the counsel of her own soul?

Chapter 51

Glastonbury Abbey
September, Anno Domini 1539

Michael tied a leather belt around his brown tunic and stepped out into the drafty dormitory hall that housed the Glastonbury Abbey monks. Reaching behind him, he gently closed the door to his sparse bedroom and joined the silent group of brethren as they made their way to Matins, their middle of the night prayers. Once outside, the moon lit the way with a silver glow, negating the need for candles. The prayers of those already kneeling in St. Edgars Chapel inside the abbey church rang clear. It was the song of the perpetual choir. The Benedictine monks alternated turns singing to maintain their eternal offering to the glory of God, a soulful reminder of their Creator's Omniscient Presence.

Michael trudged down the nave, trying not to yawn or rub his weary eyes in front of his fellow monks. He chided himself—he should be used to rising at 2:00 a.m. after three years of practice. Turning left, he entered the St. Edgars Chapel and knelt, ready to take up the chant. The songs washed over him, the refrains both soothing and refreshing. He forgot his tiredness.

After their hour of devotion, the monks filed out of the chapel and back into the night, heading toward their beds once more, until they would rise again for Prime prayers at dawn. The period after Prime was Michael's favorite. It was his opportunity to study in the great Glastonbury Abbey Library before he broke fast. After that, he would return to library duties or help with the gardening chores in the vast orchards and vegetable beds. The library stimulated his ever-curious mind, and the greenery relieved his soul and soothed his inconsolable heart. He'd given up much to follow the Goddess's edict. He'd given up Marissa, though he carried her always in his heart. He didn't begrudge his choice. That didn't mean he didn't also suffer with it.

On this early morning in late summer, he entered the library after Prime prayers and came upon Brother Gregory. The monk was twenty years his senior, but had a youthful vitality and outgoing personality that drew Michael to him. His humor and wit reminded him of Philip.

"Brother Michael, good morn'!" Brother Gregory whispered heartily as he clapped him on the back. "I bid you to come with me to the outer study rooms where we can talk."

Michael followed him eagerly, always glad for his companionship. They'd spent many mornings before breaking their fast debating Church theology or comparing studious notes. Michael had learned much from his friend and always found the books he recommended to be invigorating.

Brother Gregory sat down at one of the several oak tables that lined the outer study room. Michael joined him, noting they were alone.

"You look serious today. Is there something on your mind?" Michael asked.

The other monk looked around the room and back at its entrance before he pulled a small book from the pocket of his robes. He gently laid the well-worn volume between them.

Michael eyed the ornate leather cover. "Ah, another recommended reading?"

Brother Gregory ran his fingers across the binding with reverence. "It is time."

"Time? For what?" Michael sat up straight in his chair.

Brother Gregory gripped Michael's forearm. "We have watched you these last three years. Noted your progress. Your abilities."

"I hope Abbot Whiting is pleased with me?"

"Do not fret," his friend chuckled. "This is not about evaluating how fit you are to take your final vows." His face grew serious. "There are things I wish to tell you. Things that may surprise you."

Michael folded his hands on the table and looked directly into Gregory's eyes. "Then I wish to hear these things."

Brother Gregory nodded and slid the small tome across the table but kept his hand rested atop it. "This is a precious volume. It bears the words of a special apostle to our Lord Jesus Christ."

"The words of Peter, the Rock of the Church?"

"No."

Michael waited for him to continue.

"These are the teachings of Mary. Here we call her the Magdalene."

Michael cocked his head to the side, surprised. "You mean Mary the repentant prostitute?"

Brother Gregory shook his head. His brown eyes, already shining with wisdom and compassion, grew more luminous. "No. Mary, the Apostle of the apostles. Here we revere her as the wife of Jesus the Christ."

"Wait . . . wife? Jesus had no wife. He was celibate."

"Hmm. Yes, the Church does tell us so. Our legends, our hidden stories, tell another tale. Of her exile, with the two other Marys of Jesus' discipleship, and their child. A daughter named Sarah."

"Is that not a heretical view?" Michael whispered, leaning forward.

Brother Gregory chuckled softly. "Perhaps so. But some of us here at the abbey still honor that tradition. Not as openly as in centuries prior, mind you. Many burned at the stake for that view, a large number in France, in the Montségur siege for example. Others were branded as heretics in other areas of France. We are a clandestine group, those of us who uphold the belief of a married Jesus."

Michael shook his head. "I am confused. But I do seem to recall Abbot Etienne speaking to me of Mary Magdalene during my recuperation in France."

"I would assume their abbey upholds Mary's teachings since they live in the region of France where she preached."

"She preached?" Michael tried to remember if he'd ever come across any of her homilies in all of his research.

"In France." Gregory paused for emphasis. "And also, here in Glastonbury."

"How do we know she preached?"

Brother Gregory opened the book. "We have recorded here the Gospel of Mary. It was rejected for the canonical Gospels the Holy Church holds to be the only truth. But we know they aren't the only holy Gospels."

Michael leaned forward, his focus intense, interest burning in his mind.

Brother Gregory pointed at a page in the book, quoting, "*Peter said to Mary, Sister, we know that the Savior loved you more than the rest of woman.*" He looked up at Michael before he continued pointing and reading. "*But if the Savior made her worthy, who are you indeed to reject her? Surely the Savior knows her very well."* Then, he read, *"He who has a mind to understand, let him understand . . ."*

Michael help up his hand. "These are all quotes from Mary Magdalene? From a Gospel written by *her*?"

Gregory nodded, shutting the book and sliding it back toward him.

"Why would these be excluded from our well-known book of Gospels?"

The monk shook his head sorrowfully. "As I said, politics. Those who had power eventually ostracized Mary Magdalene because she was a woman. Because she was powerful in her own right. The same reasons the Goddess is not revered today, but is forgotten and marginalized. Even demonized."

"Then who was Mary Magdalene, really? Why is she so important that her word is preserved secretly, her message confiscated and hidden?"

"She was Jesus's special Adept, as well as his wife. His marriage partner, despite what the Church teaches or what it upholds about its vows of celibacy."

Michael looked down, studying the book and becoming aware of a delicate tingling in his fingertips as he traced its ornamental lettering. Somehow, while the news surprised him, he found he could easily believe it.

"Women are not evil, as many churchmen state," Michael said.

"No, they are not," Brother Gregory replied, watching him.

Michael continued his line of critical thinking as Master Ralph had taught him years ago. The priestesses of Avalon were compassionate and wise. And yes, powerful. He could see how that would threaten the clergy.

He'd experienced a sacred female presence, had seen the Lady come to him both times before he nearly died. She was the ethereal Presence that he deemed *Divine Goddess*. The one who bid him to devote himself to Her service.

His brow creased with new understanding. *Maybe this is why the Goddess told me to dedicate myself to Her. To come here.* To learn of this secret gospel of Mary Magdalene. Based on what Brother Gregory had just told him, his mind traveled down another path. He had known of the Goddess through his association with the priestesses of Avalon. Through his dear Marissa. His head snapped up. His mouth fell open as realization dawned.

"Celibacy. It is one of the three vows of a Benedictine monk," he said slowly. "Obedience, stability, and conversion to the monastic way of life. A life that includes celibacy."

Brother Gregory nodded, watching him intently. "Yes. Those are the *Benedictine* vows."

"I came here to fulfill my vow to a Goddess who implored me to serve Her through the Glastonbury Abbey. I bound myself to Her, though the vows required me to become a monk."

"These vows are sacred. But they are the outer form of our religious order at this abbey. There is a deeper, secret Order. It is that which I speak of now. Through this sacred book I place in your hands to read."

"But, it's all been for nothing then. All for nothing." Michael rose, letting his chair fall behind him. The sound reverberated around the empty study room. He began to pace, rubbing his chin.

Gregory leaned back in his chair, folding his hands on his lap.

"Don't you see?" Michael pleaded, coming to stand before him.

Brother Gregory met Michael's frenzied gaze with his own steady one. "I know this knowledge can be a shock. That is why those of us privy to it bring others into the fold slowly and gently. We need to be careful. We need to be sure to include only those who can truly align with what the Church would call heresy. That is why we have watched you closely. We believe you are one such man."

"No, that's not it. Mary Magdalene being Jeshua's wife, preaching His Word. I understand that. I believe that could be true. No, it is indeed true. I feel it." Michael's words tumbled over one another. "I feel it here." He covered his heart with his hand.

"Go on," his friend said, patience in his tone.

"No one told me this before. I know you have your reasons. But I've wasted three years."

Gregory raised one brow.

Michael turned to the wall and pounded it with his fist. Not once, but thrice. He leaned his arm against the wall and laid his head against it. "I've forsaken my dear Marissa because of a Benedictine vow. A vow that is a lie."

Chapter 52

Glastonbury
September, Anno Domini 1539

Michael heard the outer study door open, admitting two elder Brothers into its haven. With a tight jaw he nodded a silent greeting, lowering his eyes so as not to betray the fury burning his soul. He was glad they had arrived, for it stopped him from aiming that rage against his good friend Gregory. But it did not stop his anger at the one who had brought him to the abbey in the first place. The one who'd deceived him from the start. The Goddess.

"I need to go," he hissed.

Brother Gregory rose from the library table to join him.

"No. I need to be alone," Michael insisted, louder than he intended.

The two elder monks glanced at him in surprise. Brother Gregory raised his hand in a gesture to reassure them all was well. They nodded and seated themselves with books in hand.

Michael strode out the library door, looking around the vast abbey grounds for something to throw, something to hit. For the first time since coming to the abbey, he missed his sword. He kept it in his room, in the chest beside the bed. A silent reminder of his choices, of the life and family he'd left behind.

He never imagined he would use it again, never really wanted to, but it called to him now, and he answered the irresistible lure. He hastened to his room, to the sword, not caring that Gregory followed behind. He didn't care who saw him, didn't care what the consequences would be from the outburst. *To hell with them all,* he thought, as he raised the chest lid and retrieved the sword. The other monk caught up with him and paused in the doorway.

Michael tied the scabbard onto his waist. It felt good. Even in his rage, that feeling surprised him. He abhorred what swords had done to his brother and friends. Loathed using a sword in favor of reason and diplomacy. None of that mattered now. He needed to feel it slice through the air. Needed its primal power. Needed it to shred his fury and grief to pieces.

"What are you doing, Michael?" Gregory asked when he saw the sword laying against his hip.

Michael strode past him and out the door without answering. His friend followed again, to the cover of nearby oak and rowan trees. Michael pulled out the weapon and gripped its handle. Heat flowed down his arms and burst through his hands. He wielded the sword with parry and blow and slash. He had no visible opponent, only raw anguish, and the air around him to slice through.

"You betrayed me!" he screamed to the Goddess, repeatedly, with every sword stroke.

Thirty minutes later, he fell to his knees and slumped forward, spent. "I am so sorry, Marissa," he whispered.

Rivulets of perspiration ran down his neck and back, and his chest heaved. The sword lay on the ground by his side. Turning his head, he stared at it with unseeing eyes.

Brother Gregory had silently watched the tirade from a distance. Pushing away from the oak tree he was leaning against, he walked over to the younger monk. Standing behind him, he laid his hands on his shoulders.

Michael shrugged the hands off. Gregory knelt beside him. A black raven landed on an oak branch above and eyed the two monks with a sideward stare. Michael looked up, blinking, as the bird's form came into focus. The branch bowed under the large bird's weight.

"Raven," he murmured. "Bird of desolation. Harbinger of death."

"Also, the messenger bird of prophecy."

Michael lowered his gaze and stared hard at Gregory. His voice was tight when he spoke. "No. Symbol of desolation. Don't you see? I broke her heart. I broke mine. I broke my promise to love her as only a man can."

"You must have had good reason," Gregory said, kindness in his tone.

Michael lowered his head. "The Goddess told me it was not my time to die. She was so beautiful. So loving." Tears began to course down his cheeks—he didn't even feel them. The raven cawed. His companion remained quiet.

He raked a hand through his hair. "I made another promise as well. My lover had a vision. She's a prophetess. It was important I believed her when she felt no one else did. I broke my promise to never go inside the walls of Glastonbury Abbey."

The monk's eyes widened. "Who is this love of yours? This prophetess?"

"Her name is Marissa."

"Ah, yes. Marissa," Gregory repeated tenderly.

Michael's head snapped up. "What? Do you know her? How do you know her?"

Gregory exhaled slowly and sat back on his feet. "She's a priestess of Avalon."

"Yes. And you're a Christian monk of the abbey. How would you know her?"

His eyes softened. "I've known Marissa, and her twin Ciara, since they were babes. I know their mother, the High Priestess Alianore, as well. They're friends of mine. I'm caretaker to the priestesses when they step through Avalon's veils and journey to Glastonbury to participate in the village's seasonal celebrations. I make sure they're safe to come and go, to perform their rites as priestesses of the Goddess without interference from the local Christian priests or anyone who might wish to cause them harm."

"Why you? A monk?"

"Many of the Glastonbury villagers still believe in the old traditions. I may be a Christian monk, yet I, and my secret group, uphold our villagers in their desire to observe the old ways. It's our conviction that it does no harm to their Christian faith."

Michael studied him. "But you watch over Marissa and Ciara especially?" he probed, speaking from a sudden hunch.

"Yes, Ciara and Marissa especially."

"And why is that?"

Gregory held his gaze. "You see, I was born in this village. As a lad, before I turned to the abbey, I once participated in the Summer Solstice rites." He paused, settling back, cross-legged. "With Alianore."

"Hold on. You're Marissa's father?" It was more statement than question.

Gregory nodded.

"What happened after that?"

"My true calling was to become a monk."

Michael persisted. "And what of Alianore and your babies?"

Gregory answered with a gentle smile. "I was infatuated with Alianore once. As a young man experiencing my first Summer Solstice celebration, she was my goddess. She taught me how to venerate a woman and find the divine in lovemaking. We both recognized we were never destined to be together. The lads of the village all know that any child a priestess births from partaking in the Solstice rituals is to be raised in Avalon. Those babies are claimed by the priestesses, by the Goddess. I have not lain with Alianore since that time. But it's been my special privilege to call her a dear friend. And to watch over the twins when I can, whenever they enter into our world."

"Have you broken the vows of celibacy since you became a monk?"

"No. By choice, not by requirement."

Michael lifted his hand, palm forward. "Wait. Not by requirement? More to the point—you never bothered to tell me this?"

"Why would I have had need to, Michael? I knew nothing of you and Marissa. You never declared your love for her, or even revealed you knew her before today. You've kept your secrets to yourself, even while in close friendship with me," the older man replied, his manner calm and patient.

Michael's lips set in a grim line. "Why did you not tell me about this group of yours sooner? Why did you not tell me about the deception of celibacy?" His voice rose; he pounded his fist on the ground. "Celibacy is a lie."

"We needed to test you, to see if you could align with our hidden tradition. Celibacy is the Church's official decree, and as such, our abbey follows that dictate. But not all. In our small group there are some monks who do not."

"Why did you wait so long?"

"It was imperative we made sure you were someone who could help us. One whom we could trust to keep secret the knowledge of our clandestine group. The stakes are high. We needed time to discern the measure of your character."

The soldier in Michael rose up again. Part of him wanted to punch the monk, punch anything. He wanted to hurt him for keeping him from Marissa. His fingers itched for his sword. *God help me.* He leaned forward, palms on the earth and head bowed, breathing heavily. Battling his urge to strike out. *This is not who I am.* He kicked the sword away from him. The raven swooped down and landed beside it.

Beneath the heated rage, there was a part of him that knew better than to blame his friend. Knew better than to blame the Goddess. It was his decision after all, his soul that had answered the divine bidding to come to the abbey. But damn this secret group for concealing this vital piece, for hiding the whole truth. Celibacy was a lie. Knowing so would have made all the difference. The deception had changed everything. It had ruined lives.

He sat up on his heels, his arms shaking from the effort to control himself. The others had to know what this had cost him. "The Goddess came to me in death."

Gregory listened. Michael felt his friend's compassion. He snubbed the sympathy. Tears began to course down his cheeks, but he didn't care. The sun rose above the trees and shone into the forest clearing, ringing him in its warm, bright rays. He was blinded by the light and covered his eyes.

After a moment, he continued haltingly. "Twice She came to me. A beautiful Presence. The first time when I nearly drowned in Avalon's lake. Marissa saved me." His hands balled into fists and he locked his eyes on his companion's. "The last time was on the battlefield. My brother Philip was dead. His blood all over me. My older brother, Roger, had fallen." His voice trailed off.

He stared into the surrounding woodland, feeling his chest constrict. Anguish vied with bloodlust. The raven hopped closer.

"Go on," Gregory said gently, after several moments of silence.

Michael faced Gregory, searching the monk's face. "The Goddess asked me to devote myself to Her. Said She had a mission for me. I agreed to Her mysterious mission. Even if She had not saved Roger, I know I would have promised Her anything. She was . . . She was . . ."

"God."

"Yes," Michael whispered.

The feeling of loss washed over him. His hands fell limp to his side. Breath lodged in his chest. The only release was the torrent of sobs. Gregory laid his hand on his arm.

Michael's words carried his anguish. "She asked me to do something I had promised Marissa I would never do. She asked me to come to Glastonbury Abbey. I argued. I told Her I would go anywhere but this abbey. I had given Her my devotion, dedicated myself to Her. Wasn't that enough? Why did She insist on me becoming a monk, of all things, and *here* of all places?" He swiped away tears. "By promising Her, I believed I had to abandon my dear

Marissa. My betrayal turned her from me. Because I believed that to become a monk meant to vow chastity."

His anger reignited, and he twisted away. "How could this be? It's a falsehood. The Benedictine vow of celibacy is a lie."

Brother Gregory watched him with an expression of compassion on his face. Michael stared at the raven preening itself a mere few feet away. He sighed heavily.

"But you know something?" Michael shook his head sorrowfully. "Devotion to the Goddess was a calling that beckoned my soul in a way I simply could not deny. She said it was important that I be here at this abbey, and no other. So I came here and became a monk, as She asked." A harsh laugh broke from his lips. "But why, Brother Gregory? Why, when all along this vow of celibacy was a tainted lie? I could have done Her bidding, been a monk but not forsaken Marissa all this time. She said nothing to make me believe otherwise. The Goddess deceived me."

Brother Gregory tightened his grip on Michael's arm. "Listen to me, my friend. Perhaps I might have told you of all of this sooner, about Jeshua and Magdalene. About their sacred union. We had to wait until such time as we were certain you could handle this and that you might even be open to this tradition that is considered heretical by the Church. This knowledge is of great magnitude. However, know this—your Goddess did not deceive or betray you. There is indeed an important mission, and I believe it's why She guided you here to our abbey."

Michael straightened. "What important mission?"

"First, there's more I need to tell you."

Michael's voice rose. "*More?*"

Chapter 53

Glastonbury
September, Anno Domini 1539

A red squirrel scurried past Michael and scampered up a gnarly oak trunk across the glen, far from the raven still settled alongside the cast-off sword. Brother Gregory cast a quick glance around the woodland clearing. When reassured they were still alone in the dell, he reached under his cloak and brought out an object wrapped in linen cloth. He unwrapped the plain covering to reveal a simple wooden bowl, polished from years of handling. He held it out to Michael. It smelled of olivewood and resinous desert trees.

Michael took it in his hands. "What is this?" A surge of energy shot up his arms, nearly knocking the bowl from his grasp. Looking up at his friend in surprise, he steadied his grip.

The bowl emanated peace, a honeyed balm to his rigid muscles and taut nerves. He sensed the wooden bowl begin to link its essence to the oak trees surrounding him in the glade. His body quickened. His legs tingled, feeling almost as if they could sprout sinuous tree roots and penetrate the moist earth beneath him. Inside, he surged both icy and hot, the sensation rushing out the top of his head like outstretched tree branches reaching for the sun.

Visions rose in his mind's eye as he held the bowl. Images of red roses and lush gardens filled with exotic flowers. A couple embracing. The lilt of children's laughter. Friends sharing bread and wine. In his inner mind, he felt the gentle caress of a sea breeze and heard the song of silver starlight ring in his ears.

Love swelled in his heart and caressed his ravaged soul. The bowl shone silver in his hands. The sudden yearning to cradle it to his chest, to protect it, revere it, rose up in him. Although anger still smoldered low in his gut, he was now able to clear his mind to listen to his friend's explanation.

Gregory watched him and nodded. "I thought so," he said. "You see, legend has it that those who are meant to protect the bowl will sense its magic and bring the bowl to life. You've just brought it to life. See how it glows?" he asked, pointing.

"Well, there's definitely magic in this bowl." Michael was not afraid of magic. Marissa had taught him to never be afraid of magic that opens one's heart. "But I still don't know what this bowl is. Or what it has to do with me."

The sun had traveled in an arc overhead, heating the glen and summoning the greening scent of grass and fern and musky, damp earth. Gregory took his time removing his over-cloak before he answered. Michael fidgeted, feeling impatient.

Gregory set the garment aside and rested his hands on his knees. "It's a special chalice of sorts. A cauldron."

Michael's heart raced. "A chalice? Do you mean like the Chalice of our Lord? The Chalice of the Last Supper?"

"Yes," the older monk replied, smoothing his robes with his palms before he went on. "More importantly, it was originally the cauldron of the Goddess. A special bowl much older than Jeshua, the Last Supper, or Christianity. Older than old. From a time when people understood that trees and flowers, animals, ocean, and sky, were all sacred. It's the bowl of birth and rebirth. The vessel of regeneration. It is the Creation Bowl."

Despite his raw emotions, Michael's curiosity was piqued. "Back home in Wales we have the old tales we call the Mabinogian. These stories speak of such a magical vessel."

"Yes. The ancient Celtic cauldron of creation. When the gods walked the earth, the Great Mother was worshipped as the womb of creation. The cauldron of birth. For our secret Brotherhood at the abbey, this bowl represents Her Creatrix womb, and more. Mary Magdalene herself brought this bowl here to the abbey. She came to preach the true Christianity: Jeshua's message of love, both divine and human, where union between a man and woman is a blessed act."

Michael winced at the reminder of what he'd forsaken with Marissa. He swore he would soon right that mistake. First, he had questions that must be answered if he was ever to cool his simmering resentment. "Why this bowl?"

"Having this bowl at the Last Supper was not coincidence. This ancient holy object has been passed down from early times when the Goddess was revered as the womb of creation. Some of our group claim the bowl was given to humankind as a gift from the Faery race. To remind us that holiness lives within the earth and her creatures. As such, it's a magical talisman."

"Do you believe the Faery exist?" Michael asked.

Gregory shrugged. "Superstitious fear shrouds their existence today, though they were very real to our ancestors."

The wind whispered through the trees and the raven drew closer, its eye trained on Michael. "I once knew one of the Faery kind. Her name is Shayla. Foster-sister to Marissa and Ciara. And a talented healer. But I suppose you also know her."

Brother Gregory nodded. "I do." He gazed longingly at the wooden bowl. "The bowl has proved enchanted, no matter its origins. Whoever holds it finds peace. Solace. It's meant to open the heart— a healing force."

Though Michael could feel magic enveloping him in that golden solace, he held the feeling at bay. He wasn't ready to exonerate the monk or the Goddess for their part in keeping him from Marissa.

Gregory shifted his legs to the side. "The bowl is the symbol of the Magdalene and the tradition we are protecting for an age when the tale of Jeshua and Mary Magdalene can be remembered and celebrated in safety, not punished as heresy."

As he listened, Michael rubbed his thumb along the rim of the olivewood bowl. The sound of a thousand silver stars rose in pitch in his inner senses. The love in his heart expanded throughout his chest, encompassing his body in warmth.

He couldn't help the awe in his whispered words. "So this bowl was brought to the abbey by Mary Magdalene. Why is it held in such secrecy? Exactly what tradition are you protecting?"

"We protect the true mystical Christianity." The monk's voice took on a reverent tone. He gestured to the bowl. "It's a symbolic message of the reality of the Goddess. And of sacred union. The bowl is an object that represents what we cherish and guard for posterity."

"A wooden bowl does all this?"

Gregory offered a slight smile. "We cannot overtly tell the story of Goddess veneration, or more importantly, of the union between a man and woman being a divine act. We'd be labeled, and punished, as heretics. As such, this truth could die with us, or be expunged by the Church forever. We have to hide this tradition in a meaningful symbol, so the truth can be recognized and carried forward. The Creation Bowl, symbol of the cauldron or the chalice, is an object to remind us of that sacred truth. It's also a reliquary of that power. It is a sacred vessel containing the power of the Goddess's divine love. The power to catalyze compassion where and when it is needed."

Michael cocked his head, squinting his eyes, knowing Gregory read the uncertainty in his expression.

His companion continued. "Think on this, Michael. Mary Magdalene is the living cauldron, a woman who gave birth to Jeshua's children. These children are the fruit of their sacred union. Knowledge of their love, their union, their children, and their children's children, would be considered heretical, and sure to elicit the Church's repudiation. This knowledge has indeed already suffered the Church's suppression, as well as her military vengeance."

Nodding his head, Michael grew thoughtful. "Abbot Etienne did speak of massacres in France. At Béziers, Carcassonne, Montségur. Areas where thousands deemed heretical for their beliefs lost their lives."

"Yes. And our beliefs are considered unorthodox as well. If Mary Magdalene's womb embodies the cauldron of life, she is a holy embodiment of the Goddess. The love and union she shared with Jeshua can be found right within Christianity's Gospels. The secret Gospels in particular. The Gospel of Mary, for one. Unlike what the Church teaches—more like what the Church has hidden."

Michael sifted the words in his mind, testing their validity, sensing the truth behind the tale.

He watched as Gregory's eyes grew impassioned. "This sacred bowl keeps our inner tradition and our hope alive. It reminds us there is a Goddess, and that She is the other half of God. The bowl is a reminder of Her when the world has forgotten."

Michael placed the bowl on the ground between them and took a moment to let the interpretations soak in. He clearly recalled how Marissa and the other Avalon priestesses spoke reverentially of the Goddess. He remembered how peaceful he felt when he encountered Her, on the brink of near death both times. Still, at this moment, he felt his soul's undeniable response to Her bidding. How his soul continually longed for Her presence once he'd devoted himself to Her. Though it felt a lifetime ago, he would never forget how Marissa had lovingly shown him the inherent divinity during their joining on Summer Solstice.

"This could change everything within the Church. In the Christian world." Michael studied the bowl once more. "Does it not glow for you when you hold it?"

"It once did. But its glow is diminishing for me. It needs a new protector. It's time for a new guardian. The bowl is in danger. King Henry's men are dissolving the abbeys of England and confiscating their relics and wealth."

"Yes, Abbot Whiting informed us all. But the abbot feels sure the King's men would never touch Glastonbury Abbey. It's the most powerful and wealthiest of all of them." He paused as realization set in. "Oh. Of course."

Gregory nodded. "Yes, undoubtedly the king will want the wealthiest for his own. The abbot's faith is boundless, but the king's men are certainly coming to Glastonbury. They must never get their hands on this object. It is holy to us, and magical in its own right."

"They would not understand, and it would be called heretical. Maybe destroyed?"

"Possibly." The monk's gaze was pointed, his words passionate. "They can't know this bowl represents all of the hidden truth within Christianity. They can't discover that it passes that truth along in symbolic form, hidden from the casual eye, but understood by those who can interpret its message. The Creation Bowl must be safeguarded to preserve that truth."

"Why can it not be revealed to the world now? Why merely safeguard it when its help is greatly needed now?"

Brother Gregory shook his head. "The world isn't ready to receive its message and its power. The prophecies surrounding the bowl show it to be a relic whose time has not yet ripened. A power not accepted or revered is no power at all. If the bowl's message and power is not received, no matter how freely given, the gift is wasted."

Michael bobbed his head in understanding.

"At some point in the future, when the time is right, humankind will once more be able to recognize and acknowledge this bowl and the truth it represents. Someday, humankind will be able to feel the bowl's magic, its power to deeply heal and open the heart. A power that can then be used to mend the evils of that future world. Until that time, we must safeguard it."

Michael eyed the bowl with new appreciation.

Gregory's tone grew low. "This is where you're needed. We chose you because you're young, hale, and strong. The Brotherhood of the Creation Bowl believes you to be someone who values peace and is devoted to the Goddess, and it's an advantage that you're already within the Church's ranks." He chuckled. "Also, well trained in use of the sword, as attested to earlier."

Heat rose up Michael's neck.

"Sword strength can be a good thing. It means you can also physically protect and defend this treasure."

Ah, my sword training might finally be put to good use, Michael thought.

"But it's not our personal choice that determines who the next guardian is. The sacred bowl chooses. And by its response to you today, it affirms my suspicions that it has chosen you."

"Hold on. Am I worthy of this?" Michael asked. He nudged the bowl toward Gregory.

The monk slid the bowl back to Michael. "It matters not what you think about yourself. This cauldron chose you. As we believed it might. But more importantly, from what you've just told me, the Goddess Herself chose you. This mission is what She asked of you on the battlefield."

"You mean . . . ?" he hesitated, the puzzle pieces of the Goddess's bidding beginning to fall into place.

"Yes. This undertaking is why you have come to Glastonbury Abbey," Brother Gregory affirmed.

Despite all he'd just heard, all he'd just felt by merely touching the Creation Bowl, Michael still clung to a vestige of bitterness, or was it grief, for the lost time with Marissa. "Why should I do this when I've been betrayed?"

"Because, my friend, it appears this is your destiny."

Michael stood and began pacing the small clearing. The raven hopped backwards as he tramped by.

"Destiny? I'm not sure about that."

"Then you do it because you promised the Goddess."

"But She still deceived me." He stopped and stood before Gregory, arms folded across his chest. "I came here on Her request, believing the vow of celibacy was a necessary part of my monkhood. Her ways are deceitful."

"No. But Her ways might be mysterious."

"I'm trying to make sense of all this." He sat back down again, running his hand down his face.

"You cannot think or rationalize your way through God's ways, Michael. You can only trust. With your heart."

His agitation stilled at his friend's words. An unnamed pressure in his chest released. His soul exhaled. Perhaps Gregory was right. Maybe this was his destiny. Maybe it was indeed why the Goddess had insisted he become a monk at Glastonbury Abbey. Her bidding no longer seemed a cryptic riddle. Was he truly meant to help preserve the knowledge of the Goddess and Her tradition—a tradition of birth and regeneration, a tradition of sacred union, symbolized and carried in this simple wooden bowl laying on the ground before him?

Everything began to click into place in his mind. His vow to the Goddess. His and Marissa's sense of a shared destiny. Wait. Marissa had said she was going to tell him of her vision about their destiny when they were together on Solstice those three years ago. She never did. They hadn't time then. That shared future must have something to do with this Creation Bowl. But how? And what part did Marissa play? Exactly what part did he play? More important to him in this moment, he still could not fathom why he had to go through the torture of abandoning her to the falsehood of celibacy. He had to know more about this clandestine group that held such secret knowledge.

"Does Abbot Whiting embrace this tradition? Who is this group you say has watched me?"

"No, the abbot, and most of the Brothers at our abbey, abide by the Church's official rules. We're but a small, clandestine group within our Benedictine order. We're called the Brotherhood of the Creation Bowl, and we meet covertly. You might say we are the hidden abbey. There are eleven of us. You will meet the rest if you agree to the task at hand."

The lingering anger warred with Michael's growing sense of purpose. With his gut churning, purpose nevertheless won the upper hand. "What is it I must do?" he asked.

Gregory beamed, then leaned forward, his expression turning somber. "We already have it planned. You're to leave by cover of night, taking the bowl with you. There are men along the route who will aid you. The bowl is to go to the northern mountains of Wales, out of the reach of the king and his men. There is a holy place there, a hidden cloister of those dedicated to Our Lady, the Goddess." He chuckled. "I met these Brothers once. They are more Druid than Christian monk. More importantly, they are true of heart and intent. You are to transport the bowl to their safekeeping. You must leave within the week. Our messengers tell us that is all the time we have before the king's men arrive here."

"I'm far from at peace that the truth has been hidden from me all this time. But I accepted this task when I accepted the Goddess's bidding, so I'll do as you ask. I'll bring this bowl to the cloister in Wales. However, there's one very important thing I must do first."

Brother Gregory raised his brows in question.

Clutching the bowl, Michael stood. "I will see Marissa before I go. I must make things right between us."

Chapter 54
Wales
September, Anno Domini 1539

Alianore and Ciara rode their mares side by side through the flat, clay vales of southwest England on their way to Wales, to the home of Philip de Boulle. Little Michael rested securely strapped to Ciara's chest. He'd spent most of the trip asleep. Having just suckled as the party rode, he slept soundly, oblivious to the chirping birdsong prevalent in these parts, a natural melody that delighted Alianore. The rough pasture was sweet-smelling, and it added to her pleasure.

She turned, shading her eyes from the bright summer sun to wave to Matthew, one of the three Glastonbury village lads, a brawny young man who volunteered to help guard the small party as they traveled. She had a hunch the youth was secretly interested in Ciara, but he hadn't approached her daughter in any of the Summer Solstice rituals they both took part in the last few years. So she kept her mother's intuition to herself. Besides, Ciara had expressed keen interest in Philip de Boulle and, other than her cursory kind nature, hadn't taken notice of Matthew. Alianore turned as the blacksmith's sons, Jack and Humphrey, rode toward her from their forward flank.

Jack bowed his head deferentially before he spoke. She suppressed a smile. Long ago, the boy's father had once been a Summer Solstice lover of hers, and the man still retained his awe at the presence of the Goddess he'd experienced at their joining. Married with a family of his own now, he'd taught his son Jack to maintain the respect he still nurtured.

"My Lady, once we pass through these chalk and limestone downlands, we'll skirt the Bristol Channel and enter forested acreage. We can rest for the evening then, well under protective cover."

"Thank you, Jack." She turned her attention to Humphrey. "I assume the way proves clear? Your scouting was successful?"

"Yes, my Lady. I've spoken to other travelers. Unrest is reported in England, thievery and bandits, but we're a large enough party to deter most threats. And Jack, Matthew, and I will safeguard your passage into Wales, you can be assured," he answered, pride in his voice.

"We're grateful to you," Ciara said, which earned a deep flush from both young men.

Alianore knew her daughter had no idea how her beauty affected the lads. *Just as well,* she mused. The kindness in her daughter's heart, and her skills as a healer, far outweighed even her lovely and fair features. For Ciara's sake, Alianore hoped this Philip of hers would feel the same way.

The young men took up their protective positions once more.

Ciara huffed out a sigh and adjusted her kirtle. "This long skirt is roomy and comfortable, but *Fie*, my fitted bodice is not. I keep fearing I'll leak milk into its constraining folds."

"It is worse for you because of that. I, too, prefer our loose, silken robes, but we do what we must. To wear our normal attire outside the boundaries of Avalon or Glastonbury is to invite trouble. Besides, we will appear much more acceptable to your Philip's Christian household dressed in the manner they are accustomed to."

Ciara nodded and pointed to the forest line in the distance. "Not too far, I hope."

Alianore breathed a sigh of relief two days later when they spotted their destination, Mountain Manor, atop a tall knoll straight ahead. The light and shadow of sun and racing clouds gave the land a dappled, intriguing look.

"This is a lovely vale, Ciara," she said, inhaling the earthy smell of meadow grass and the fragrant scent of wild red campion and yellow daffodils. "A beautiful place for Philip to have grown up, I would imagine."

"Yes," Ciara murmured, chewing her lip.

Alianore leaned across the gap between their horses to pat her daughter's shoulder. "You will get answers soon. You will have the opportunity to speak with Philip and see if he desires to become your consort as you hope. At the very least, you will have your wish—he will meet the fruit of his union with you from those three summers past. His son, our precious little Michael."

"Thank you, Mother, for allowing me this trip. For coming with me."

Alianore smiled lovingly at her sweet daughter. She knew very well this trip was also part of Ciara's healing for the loss of her unrequited love for Michael. A loss her daughter held close even after so many years, and despite Michael and Marissa's professed, if unfulfilled, love. She would grant this daughter of hers anything to see her get on with her life with an open heart. She secretly hoped Philip would be the salve Ciara needed.

As they neared the manor home, a rider approached from the pasturelands in the north. The three Glastonbury boys closed ranks around the two women. Alianore held up her hand to them. "There is no danger from this rider."

The young men fell back a few feet but remained close. As the rider approached, she heard her daughter's sharp intake of breath and understood why. The man had the same blue eyes and smile Michael did, and though his hair was much darker than Michael's tawny mane, there was no doubt they were brothers.

"This is Philip?" Alianore asked.

"No," Ciara whispered. "It must be the older brother he spoke of. Roger."

Roger cantered over to them and reined in his horse as he neared. "Welcome to Mountain Manor. I am Roger de Boulle." He cocked his head, furrowing his brows. Staring at Ciara, he added, "Have I had the pleasure of your acquaintance?"

Ciara blushed. "Perhaps. I know your brother, Philip."

Roger glanced at the small bundle across Ciara's lap. Little Michael chose that moment to awaken.

"Mama, are we done riding the horse?" he asked, yawning and rubbing his eyes.

His mother held him close, cradling him in her arms. "I am called Ciara, and this is my mother, Alianore."

Realization dawned in Roger's eyes, followed by an emotion quickly guarded. Alianore noted it with curiosity. Before she could introduce her party and explain their visit, the eldest son of Gerard de Boulle gestured widely toward the manor home.

"I think it best you come inside with me. Refresh yourselves. And we will talk."

Alianore felt her stomach tighten. Something was wrong and she couldn't pinpoint it. But something was definitely wrong.

Chapter 55
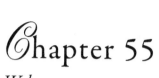

Wales
September, Anno Domini 1539

Once inside the manor's manicured courtyard, Roger ordered the stable hands to care for the horses and sent the kitchen maid to tell the cook to prepare a hearty meal fit for guests.

Turning to the three young men escorting the two priestesses, Roger said, "The kitchen is that way. You'll find our cook happy to feed hungry lads such as yourselves. Tell her I sent you."

While the offer of a hearty meal earned an appreciative nod from Jack and Humphrey, who immediately followed the maid to the kitchen scullery, their third guard, Matthew, remained behind and stepped beside Alianore. "I'd like to remain with my lady."

Ciara smiled kindly, placing her hand atop his arm. "These are good people. They're my son's family. There's no need for concern."

Matthew frowned but joined the others anyway, looking over his shoulder as he walked to the kitchen. Alianore was about to apologize for the over-protectiveness but realized Roger hadn't noticed, enthralled as he was with her grandson.

He gingerly reached out to little Michael, who was peering curiously from behind his mother. "You say Michael is his name?" His voice caught.

"Who is he, Mama?" Michael asked boldly, stepping out from behind his mother's skirts.

"My name is Roger, my little man. I suppose I'm your uncle. You have the same name as my brother." He bent to the toddler's level. "We miss Michael greatly," He said, looking up at Ciara.

"As do we," she replied wistfully. "I mean, especially my sister," she added quickly.

Roger stood. "Of course. Marissa. Michael spoke often of her on our journey to France, and in the monastery as he recuperated."

"You mean before he chose the ecclesiastical path, forsaking her," Ciara retorted curtly.

Alianore intervened, surprised at her daughter's rudeness. "But we are not here to discuss that, are we? We are here so Philip may meet his son. To introduce young Michael to his Welsh family." She eyed Ciara, not sure why she would risk provoking Philip's family. Had her unrequited love for Michael turned her bitter? That wasn't in her daughter's nature. Before the Faery curse that is.

Something clouded Roger's features at the mention of Philip's name. He swiftly hid the raw emotion, his face now impassive, and smiled. Alianore noted the smile was forced.

He gestured to the great hall door saying, "Come. Eat. Let us get to know each other."

She and Ciara entered the manor's great hall behind him, young Michael abandoning his mother's skirts to trail close by Roger's heels. Late morning sun streamed through the many windows. The warmth of the sunlight enhanced the scent of lavender strewn over the rushes. An enormous hearth with a lit fire was situated at the far end of the hall, and roomy wooden chairs were set before it. Behind the chairs was a long wooden table with a stack of rolled-up scrolls piled at one end. Under the table, a long-haired wolfhound lifted his head at the intrusion on his nap. When he noticed the newcomers, he padded his way across the room to stand beside Roger, tail wagging. His massive head reached the man's waist.

Roger faced the women. "I must speak with you privately. First. Before you meet my father. He should be here by the time the meal is served. Father and I were to meet with our priest to plan the baptism of the babies from our village. It is a holy ceremony followed by a large festival." He brightened slightly. "Perhaps Michael can be baptized as well?"

Ciara picked up her son and held him tight. Before she could protest, Roger stammered, "I'm so sorry. I forget you're priestesses of Avalon. Not Christian. Excuse my bad manners."

His sincerity touched Alianore but didn't obscure the feelings she sensed permeating the great hall. This was a manor house of respectable fortune and prosperity, yet it was not a happy home. Grief hung in the air. Unhealed heartache and burden. She shuddered with the overriding sensation as it traveled up her back and settled at the base of her neck.

Roger pulled two chairs from the table. "Please, sit. We need to talk."

An elderly man—obviously his father, with the same clear blue eyes— entered the great hall from a side corridor.

Roger visibly tensed. "Father, you're early."

The man leaned on a wooden cane as he limped toward them. Alianore's intuition easily perceived this was once a virile man, now wracked with illness and misery. The feelings he emanated broke her heart. But it was the man walking beside him that stoked her caution. His malicious glare incited her to instinctively extend an invisible ring of magical protection around her daughter, grandson, and herself.

This other man was about the same age as the head of the de Boulle's, and wore the black robes and dangling wooden cross necklet of a Christian priest. His balding head and sharp nose accentuated sunken eyes. Alianore sorted through her impressions, not sensing an immediate threat. Still, the priest reeked of fear, manipulation, and control. The invisible protection that had sprung up prompted Ciara to glance her way, cocking her eyebrow, aware of the circle. Alianore kept her eyes trained on the two men before her, shaking her head nearly imperceptibly to let her daughter know not to speak up. She would handle this, whatever *this* was.

Roger strode to his father, grabbing his elbow and guiding him to a chair at the table. "We have surprise visitors, Father." He looked warily at Alianore and Ciara.

The priest frowned. "As we entered, I heard something disturbing. Did I hear you say these two women are *priestesses*?" he asked, directing his question to Roger and ignoring the women.

Roger disregarded the question. "Alianore, Ciara, meet my father, Gerard de Boulle. And this is his priest, Fr. Timothy." He put a hand on his father's shoulder. "Father . . . meet your grandson." He paused before adding, "Michael."

Gerard's head shot up. "Is he yours, Roger?" His voice was strong, belying his frail bodily countenance.

"No, Father. He is Philip's son."

The statement brought an overbearing silence to the room.

"Mama," young Michael whimpered, hiding in the folds of his mother's skirts.

Alianore interjected. "We come in friendship. As family." She held her hands out, palms up, in a gesture of peace.

Ciara took Michael's hand and stepped forward, smiling sweetly. "I've come to speak to Philip. To have him meet his son. Will you kindly bring him to us, please?"

Gerard gave a strangled cry and his face turned red, then ashen.

"Can you not see you're upsetting him?" Fr. Timothy cried. He went to his lord's side and patted his back. Gerard waved the priest aside and dropped his head into his hands.

Alianore watched him, shocked at his reaction. Ciara turned to Roger, puzzlement on her face. "What is wrong?"

Gerard raised his head. "You cannot meet Philip," he bellowed.

"Why would you deny my daughter and your grandson that?" Alianore asked softly.

He pounded his fist on the table, shaking the scrolls to the floor. "Because," he shouted. "Philip is dead!"

Ciara cried out. Covering her mouth, she took a step back. "No. It can't be."

Roger closed his eyes momentarily. When he opened them, his lips were set in a tight line. "Fr. Timothy, please escort my father to his bed quarters. Stay with him until I come. Give him some of the tincture medicine from his bedside table."

Fr. Timothy glowered at Ciara. "This is your fault. You did this," he muttered.

Alianore stepped forward, placing her arm around her daughter's shoulder. Roger watched the two men leave the hall before he turned back to face them. Michael pulled on his mother's skirts. "Mama? Please no cry," he said, patting her leg with a chubby hand.

Roger knelt beside him. "Well now, little man. How would you like to pet my dog, Sebastian? He's very friendly." He gave a low whistle and the hound loped over. Roger lifted the toddler's hand gently and placed it on the dog's side, allowing Michael to pat its shaggy hair. Michael's eyes opened wide. Sebastian turned and licked his hand, winning him over.

"Nice doggy. Big doggy," he cooed, his attention consumed.

Roger turned to Ciara. "I'm so sorry. I meant to tell you before you met my father."

"It is not your fault. There is no good way to impart such news as this," Alianore interrupted. She glanced sideways at her daughter, noting how pale she'd become.

"How?" Ciara asked. "How did he die?" Her mouth quivered.

Roger took her hand. "He died in battle. In France. The same battle that claimed his life severely injured Michael. He was hurt trying to save Philip."

She pulled her hand from Roger's and turned into her mother's embrace. Burying her head in her shoulder, she sobbed.

Alianore rubbed a palm up and down Ciara's back. Looking over her daughter's head, she watched Roger. She sensed he was a good man. A caring man. Much like Michael. If Philip had been anything like his two brothers, he would have been a good consort for her daughter. Her heart broke for this daughter of hers, twice denied love.

She lifted her chin and spoke. "It has been a long trip. And such hard news to bear. I am sorry you and your father have had to suffer the heartache of losing a brother and son."

Roger dipped his head to her briefly, in appreciation for her sympathy. "It has been difficult. My brothers and I were very close." He swallowed hard. "But it's my father who shoulders the greater burden. Sending his sons off to battle, losing one to death, and one to a faraway monastery. Without my mother here to cushion his grief, with only Fr. Timothy and me to console him . . . I'm afraid he's not the gracious man he once was."

Alianore nodded her understanding, the information validating the intuition she'd sensed upon entering the household.

Ciara pulled away from her mother and wiped her tears. "There's no need for you to apologize. You've been very kind and hospitable."

Spine straight and head held high, Alianore looked to Roger "I think it best we rest now, if that is possible."

"Certainly. Let me show you to our guest quarters. I'll have refreshments brought to you as well."

Ciara held out her hand to Michael. "Come, my darling."

The hound was licking his hand. Michael pouted. "I want to stay with Sebastian."

"I suppose Sebastian can tag along to your room, for now," Roger said.

Michael stretched his arms up to his uncle, wanting to be picked up.

Roger's eyes brightened and he reached down. "Would you like a ride on my shoulders, little man?"

"Yes, please," came the squealed response.

Alianore fidgeted on the bench beside the lone window in their bower. She gazed out the window, then back into the room. The walls were bare of the faded tapestries that decorated the great hall, but the room was clean, with a blazing fire in the hearth and a large featherbed.

Michael had long ago fallen asleep on its plush sheets after playing with Sebastian and Roger for hours. Late evening's shadows now shaded the room, a grey hue that matched the atmosphere of the manor home.

Although they had eventually supped with Roger, with Gerard glaringly absent, Ciara had eaten little, so Roger had a tray of bread and cheese brought up for her should her appetite return. The food lay untouched on the table by the fireplace. Ciara lay curled beside her son, having dozed off while settling him to sleep. The melancholy of the de Boulle household settled over Alianore like a shroud; she craved fresh air.

She pulled a brown kirtle from the bottom of her clothing bag. It would do, for she would simply be stepping out to walk amongst the fragrant kitchen gardens she'd spotted when they'd first arrived. Pulling the kirtle over her chemise, she topped it with a long woolen mantle to keep the chill of the late evening at bay. Tiptoeing across the room, so as not to awaken her daughter and grandson, she grabbed a heel of bread from the food tray on her way out. She unlatched the large wooden door to the bower, letting it close quietly behind her.

She made her way down the hall to the dark winding staircase, surprised the torches were not lit for the guests' benefit. Still, as a trained priestess, her sense of her surroundings was keen. She was about to enter the great hall when she heard voices raised in agitation. She peeked around the corner to find Gerard and his priest conversing. Lord de Boulle sat before a dying fire, wine goblet in hand.

Their harsh whispers stopped her. Pulling her cloak tightly about her, she slid back into the shadows of the stairwell, unsure whether to make her presence known. The next words spoken made her decision for her.

"How can I do what you advise?" Gerard asked Fr. Timothy, his words slurred, the wine decanter beside him half empty.

"It's easy, it's God's will. They are witches."

"They are priestesses," Gerard responded in a surly tone.

"One and the same. They do not worship the one true God." Fr. Timothy sneered. "They're heathen. Sinful."

The venom behind the accusations struck Alianore as if she'd been punched in the stomach. She reeled and caught her breath.

Gerard stared into his goblet, his head lolling forward. Fr. Timothy poured the rest of the decanter into Gerard's glass.

"Think on it, my lord. They may appear beautiful, but it's only an illusion." He licked his lips. "They're demons. Do you wish your grandchild to be raised by such vile creatures?"

"Of course not," the other man answered. He tilted his goblet, draining it.

"That's right, my lord. This is the godly thing to do. Save your grandson's soul while you can."

Alianore stashed the heel of bread she'd been clutching in her pocket, and quietly stepped closer, hardly believing this sordid conversation, desperately needing to hear its conclusion. She'd trusted her party would be safe once they reached the manor home. As it turned out, the danger was not traveling the unguarded roads. The true danger lay in the minds of men such as Fr. Timothy and those with weak character who would listen and believe the lies that came from the priest's lips. Perhaps Marissa had been right. Perhaps she and Ciara should never have traveled outside of Avalon. The High Priestess Rhianna had put the protective mantle of invisibility around Avalon centuries ago for good reason.

Gerard hiccupped and wiped tears from his eyes. "Anna, what would you have me do?" he enquired, looking up to the heavens as if to search for the face of his beloved wife, before turning his bleary-eyed gaze to the priest. "I wish my sons were here. All of them. They would tell me what to do. I don't feel all that well. I must consult with Roger."

Fr. Timothy stood tall. "You must be strong, my lord. Strong as you once were, and strong as I know you can still be. This decision must come from you. You're the ruler of this house. I'm your spiritual advisor. To save your soul, and the soul of your grandson, I advise that you must do what God would want. You must be the one to save your grandson before these heathen priestesses taint him. Before your household is fouled by their ruinous ways." The priest's voice, while still low, hissed with fevered passion.

Gerard dropped his goblet onto his lap where the dregs of crimson wine stained his tunic. With heavy lidded eyes, he searched the priest's face. "You're right. You're always right, always at my side, always wise." He patted the priest's hand. "What would I do without your moral advice?"

Fr. Timothy made the sign of the cross in the air before him. "You will do God's will then? Keep your grandson here? And rid the world of these unholy women?"

Lord de Boulle's head had already lolled to his chest. "Save my grandson. Make it so." His words ended in a wine-induced, soft snore.

Alianore quietly backed up and raced up the stairwell to the room, her mind spinning, plans already forming to save her daughter and grandson. They needed to get out of the manor house. Now.

Chapter 56

Wales
September, Anno Domini 1539

Nighttime shadow gripped the guest quarters, the candles having long ago burned down to their nibs. Alianore tiptoed swiftly across the room and bent over the bed to whisper sharply in her daughter's ear. "Get up, my dear. Now. Quietly."

She was glad Ciara had fallen asleep with her clothes on. It would save them precious time, time they needed to make their escape. Morning light, mercifully still a few hours away, would be too late to leave.

When she didn't stir, Alianore spoke again, softly, so as not to waken Michael, thanking the Goddess he was such a sound sleeper. "We are in danger. We must leave."

"What? Why?" Ciara rubbed her eyes.

Normally ever calm, Alianore felt an unusual rise of panic, even anger, making her heart thump and her body tremble. Her family was threatened. Her community so very far away. Who knew what extent Fr. Timothy would go to in order to carry out his narrow-minded plan? Avalonian magic would only protect Ciara and Michael so far, and perhaps not against the mortal danger she sensed the priest posed. In the natural order of things, if death was coming, there would be no easy way to stop it. Her magic was by no means weak, but the natural order of fate was stronger.

It didn't take many words of explanation before Ciara was up, alert, and wrapping Michael in blankets to carry in her arms. Alianore grabbed their two sack bundles. Peering down the hall corridor outside their bower room for signs of anyone still up and about, she gestured for her daughter to follow behind her and descend the stairwell leading to the great room. There was no other way. They had to cross through the huge hall in order to exit the manor home. She heaved a sigh of relief when they found the room free of the priest. Gerard slumped snoring in his chair, but they could easily pass by him in his drunken, probably drug-induced stupor.

Little Michael moaned and the two women stopped short, eyes meeting in alarm. But he immediately snuggled into his mother's chest again and continued sleeping.

They slipped out the front door and entered the courtyard. The hound Sebastian bounded toward them, sensing his new tiny friend, tail wagging. Before he could bark, Alianore remembered the bread heel stashed in her pocket. She bent down and offered the bread, dropping it to the ground. She was rewarded with a generous lick before the dog lowered his head to retrieve the treat.

The small party headed for the stables. Their travel guards, the three young men from Glastonbury, would be sleeping there, along with their horses. In her mind, she formed a clear picture of her chestnut beauty Belle, as well as the other horses in the party, being quickly saddled and ready for a hasty retreat. *Make it so*, she whispered.

She stopped, startled. The stable door stood wide open when it ought to have been closed and locked. Entering cautiously, her breath caught in her chest when she saw the empty partitions where Belle and the other visiting horses should have been kept.

Ciara looked around wildly. "Where are the horses? Mother . . . the horses?" she whispered.

Alianore squeezed her daughter's shoulder, and put a finger to her lips, gesturing for silence. Ciara nodded. They quietly made their way past the vacant stalls, searching for their men, not wanting to awaken the livery boys sleeping in the upper loft.

"Our men?" Ciara mouthed silently.

Alianore shook her head and shrugged her shoulders. Michael whimpered, picking up on his mother's panic. "Shh, my darling. We're playing a game. A game of hide and seek," Ciara whispered.

The tiny face peeked above the blankets, eyes wide. He squealed, looking behind his mother's shoulder. Alianore spun around to find Roger. Her arm shot out to shield her daughter and grandson.

Roger halted, raising his hands in the air. "It's all right. I mean to get you out of here."

Alianore pierced his mind with her second sight, a priestess power of sensing a person's true motives. No time for subtleties when the lives of her family were in danger. Roger looked up, startled, as if sensing something. She detected no malice therein and quickly withdrew her intrusion into his mind.

Eyes still on the High Priestess, Roger said, "Come. Quickly and quietly. Your men are out back, saddling your horses."

Roger led Alianore and her family through the dark stables into the pasture behind the building.

"How did you know? How did you know about Fr. Timothy's plan?" she asked him.

With interlocking hands, he lifted Alianore's foot into her stirrups, helping her to swiftly hoist herself upon the readied Belle before he answered.

"I learned of it from Mistress Helen. She's been the local village's wise woman since before my father was born. She caught Fr. Timothy rifling through her herbal storage cabinets. He made up some excuse and left hastily, but she saw that her hidden store of hemlock and arsenic had been tampered with. She reported the incident to me."

Reins in hand, she looked down at Roger from atop her mare. "He meant to poison us?" The fiend. Still, poisoned food or water she could have magically discerned.

"I don't know all of the priest's plans, but I discovered enough to realize I needed to lead you away from here under cover of night. Tonight. I don't trust his overzealous fanaticism. Nor his hold over my father."

"We'll have you out of here before any harm comes to you or yours, my lady," Matthew declared, speedily loading packs onto her horse. Jake and Humphrey hurriedly finished saddling the other horses.

"Could I have a boost up, please?" Ciara asked. Matthew and Roger both hurried over, Roger arriving first. Matthew frowned but held out his arms to hold Michael so Ciara could mount.

Before Roger boosted her up, he said, "I'm truly sorry for your heartbreak. I wish things might have turned out differently." He searched her face.

She looked down. Roger gently took her hand. "I would have gladly made sure you and little Michael had a welcoming home."

Ciara let out a small gasp. Before she could speak, he kissed her hand lightly. She wrenched it away. He quickly hoisted her atop the horse. Her lips stayed pursed tight. Matthew held little Michael up so she could seat him in front of her. Roger eyed the toddler with sad longing.

Alianore interrupted the uneasy exchange. "Matthew, please allow Michael's uncle to hold him once more."

Matthew transferred Michael to Roger's arms. He tousled the toddler's hair. "You be a good lad for your mother. Protect her well."

"Yes, Uncle Roger," the child gurgled with newfound adoration in his blue eyes.

"Well then," Roger said. He pulled a necklace with a gold medallion from around his neck. Engraved on the medallion was the de Boulle family crest—a white horse pawing the air beside a great oak tree. He placed it around his nephew's neck, where it hung down to his rounded belly. "This is to remember your father, Philip. And me, your Uncle Roger."

Michael clutched the medallion in his tiny hand. He looked at Roger solemnly, unexpectedly pledging in his toddler voice with words far beyond his years, "I will remember my father. I will remember my uncle."

Roger looked up at Ciara one last time, dashed hope in his expression. She stared straight ahead.

He turned to Alianore. "Change of plans. I'll lead you through the swiftest passage to our Welsh borders and accompany you safely home before I fare thee well." In a commanding voice, he said. "We leave. Now." He mounted his steed, urging the horse forward with his knees and a pat to its hindquarters.

The party formed behind him, and at his word, swiftly rode off. Matthew and Jake galloped on either side of Ciara, while Humphrey jockeyed his horse to Alianore's side. She had visibly relaxed once they realized they had bypassed danger.

They had barely started their journey through the pasture, hadn't even reached the tree line of the surrounding woods, when a shout splintered the night air.

"There they are! Don't let them escape!" Fr. Timothy's voice shrieked.

"Ride forward," Roger roared, as he turned his mount and rode back, his hand up in a halting gesture to stop whatever pursuit was about to ensue. A line of six Mountain Manor soldiers stood behind the priest, arrows notched and ready. His anger flared. Surely, his men would not resort to such violence against women and a child. And without his orders!

He yelled above the priest's orders. "No. Stand down your arrows. By whose authority do you do this? I command you to stop."

"We follow your father's commands," one of the men answered.

The livery boys, awakened from sleep in the loft above the stables, had clambered down the ladders and were running out into the yard, adding their cries of surprise to the melee.

"I order you now to stop." Roger barked, knowing his brothers-in-arms would ultimately obey him over his father Gerard. "Sir George, I *order* you," he bellowed at his second-in-command.

George plucked his arrow from its quiver and rested his longbow beside him, a look of utter confusion on his face. "We were told these were your father's emergency orders, and yours as well, my lord!"

"No! I never gave such orders. Stand down!" Roger repeated.

Fr. Timothy shoved past the soldiers, screeching. "The lord of this manor is still Gerard de Boulle and he commands you to stop those women from leaving. It is God's will. God's orders. The highest directive!"

The soldiers looked from Roger to the priest, who was spewing threats of God's punishment upon them all should they disobey. Amidst the ruckus they obeyed Roger, and, following Sir George's example, lay down their weapons. Fr. Timothy swiftly bent, grabbing the nearest longbow, and with a fevered cry, let loose one lone arrow before Sir George tackled him to the ground. Roger felt it whiz by his head. Damn the man!

Not caring it was his father's Christian priest, he raised his fist, cursing the man, when he heard the unmistakable thump of arrow piercing flesh. The priest's errant arrow had surprisingly found a target. Roger turned in horror. The escaping party was riding hard toward the forested border.

Still astride her galloping horse, Alianore slumped to the side.

Chapter 57

The Isle of Avalon
September, Anno Domini 1539

The sun shone bright in Avalon and the clouds were few and soft, yet Marissa still shivered. She lifted her head high while allowing her tears to fall. She couldn't stop them anyway. *A priestess is never ashamed to feel,* she heard her mother say, as if Alianore continued mentoring her as she always had. *Honor all your feelings and they will always lead you back to love.* Marissa's chest clenched in a spasm of grief.

She squared her shoulders as she headed the procession of her priestess community to circle the towering apple tree in the courtyard of Avalon's Healing Sanctuary. In honor of her mother, each woman paused to leave an offering at the base of the tree—a stone, a ribbon tied to a branch, a homemade charm—all given in homage for the passing of their beloved High Priestess.

She palmed the garnet ring Roger de Boulle had given her the previous day. He'd accompanied Ciara's small group from Wales all the way to Glastonbury's lakeshore, where he formally delivered her mother's shrouded, still form into Avalon's care. His face had been tight when he handed over Alianore's body, remorse etching his darkly circled eyes, guilt edging his words as he told her it was his father's priest who'd committed this heinous act. Although he wasn't the one to shoot the lethal arrow, he clearly felt responsible for Alianore's murder. The lavish garnet ring he'd offered as his humble gift, saying he knew it could never recompense what had happened, but he would do whatever Ciara and Marissa wished to try and make up for it.

Grief-stricken from her mother's demise, shocked by Michael's brother's presence, Marissa had said there was no more Roger could do. She thanked him for his gracious gift and for accompanying her sister and nephew home. The entire short time he was in her presence, she had fought back tears, struggled to keep her breath even and her heart from racing. How closely he resembled Michael. His eyes, his mannerisms. Reminding her yet again of her own despair over being abandoned for monkhood. Now, with trembling hands, she placed the garnet ring with the other offerings.

Ciara watched her sister lay the ring upon the fallen petals under the apple tree. "Roger tried to visit Michael at the abbey," she whispered in her ear.

Marissa swallowed around the lump in her throat.

Ciara continued, her voice gentle. "Michael was otherwise occupied outside the abbey, so he didn't have the chance to see him. Brother Gregory sent word to give us Roger's farewell, saying he needed to return to Wales straightaway to take care of his father and all the turmoil back at their manor home. You have been so busy with preparations, so I waited to tell you."

"I think he wanted to see you again, Ciara," Marissa replied frankly. This was no time to mince words. What should be spoken, must be spoken.

She had noticed the way Roger looked at Ciara when the group arrived. Fondly, hopefully. Her sister had returned his overtures by coldly ignoring him.

Her twin's eyes hardened. "Then he'll wait for naught, for I won't change my mind. I'm done with loving men. It never ends well."

Marissa reached for her hand. "Ciara, please don't become bitter."

Ciara pushed away her sister's hands and looked her in the eye. "That's like me telling you to not grieve over Michael."

Marissa gasped, feeling the slap of her words.

"I'm sorry," Ciara said, putting her head in her hands. "Mother's death. This whole trip. You were right. I should have listened to you and never insisted she travel to Wales with me." She turned into Marissa's open arms and sobbed, clinging to her.

Marissa knew that nothing she could say or do would erase Ciara's self-reproach. Because of her own guilt over the Faery Realm misadventure of their childhood, she knew only too well how the remorse could eat away at her, putrefying inside. Never had she wished that kind of guilt on her dear twin.

Her tears flowed with her sister's. The other priestesses patted them tenderly as they walked past to gather beside Vanora, their glances and gestures expressing their own grief, but also their understanding of how deeply Alianore's daughters mourned. While Marissa's tears streamed for her mother, they also flowed for Michael. For Ciara and her hardening heart. For all that paled in Avalon's world with Alianore's death.

The Healing Sanctuary's wooden gates squeaked as Vanora pushed them open, ushering the priestesses to head toward the Red Well. Marissa spent another moment embracing her twin, letting her tears run dry. Then she wiped her eyes with her sleeve, and holding hands, the two joined the other priestesses beside the holy well.

She feigned a composed expression, much as she'd observed her mother do over the years when taking on the mantle of leadership. Letting her gaze roam over the faces raised expectantly to her. Tomorrow, as successor, she would be officially installed as Avalon's newest High Priestess. But today, as Alianore's eldest daughter, she was to preside over her mother's funerary rites. While she always knew her day of leadership would eventually come, and she'd spent her life preparing for the eventual transfer of power, she'd always imagined the timing to be much farther in the future.

Exhaling softly, she turned to the wellspring, leaned over, and dipped the silver cup always kept beside it into the gurgling water. After taking the first sip, she passed it around the circle for all to partake of the holy water. The healing waters washed over her sorrow, softening its edges, but not quite reaching the deep pit of her grief. She closed her eyes and silently prayed for strength to continue.

Once every woman had drunk from the spring, she led them down the rounded hill, walking the grassy paths she knew by heart. The group spread across Avalon's orchards, the sweet fragrance of apple blossoms filling the air. The cacophony of whispered prayers from the bereaved priestesses echoed around the orchard. Marissa could hardly listen for her anguish, wanting to cover her ears with her hands. But she kept her hands clasped in front of her and her gaze ahead. *Keep going,* she commanded herself.

She gestured for the women to proceed. Passing through an opening in the prolific hawthorn hedges, they were met with the heady perfume of the rose garden. Her mother's favorite spot. Each priestess stopped to pick two roses for the ritual, one white and one red. She steered them next into the woodlands, filled with wildling plants and gigantic oak trees. Normally a peaceful refuge, their greening vitality did not comfort her this morning.

The group slowly made their way to their destination, the shore of Avalon's lake. Marissa felt her legs become more leaden with each step closer to the lake. The wailing of the community rose in pitch. Alianore's body had been prepared for their arrival. She lay in stately repose, in a coffer atop a wooden platform beside the shore, dressed in white, hands folded on her chest, golden hair garlanded with lilies, the lake softly lapping behind her. Barinthus, the Ferryman of Death, stood guard, a silent sentinel—his head hooded, his face hidden as always. His barge moored on the shoreline behind him.

The priestesses each placed a red rose beside the body, then positioned themselves around it. Vanora stood to Marissa's right, Ciara to her left. She felt fortified by their presence and hoped it would tame her nerves. Her stomach lurched at the thought of how she might console these women, what inspiration she could offer these priestesses who'd converged to honor their own, to send Alianore of Avalon to complete her death journey. She hoped she could emulate her mother's poised demeanor and gentle wisdom, and felt relieved knowing Vanora would help if she floundered with the many details of the parting ritual.

A crane flew overhead, sign of the Goddess. Marissa watched the soft white blur of its beating wings as it made its way to join a group of other cranes clustered together on the lake. She tried not to think about Michael on the opposite shore, in Glastonbury.

She returned her attention to the funerary rites. The priestesses strung the white roses they had picked into garlands and hung them along the boat's sides. They readied the frankincense and myrrh resin Vanora procured from a special pouch, blending it and placing a pinch to burn in the tiny brazier on the barge—all in the tradition befitting a High Priestess's passing.

Marissa plucked a gold coin from the purse tied to her belt and offered it to Barinthus. The ferryman reached out to accept the traditional token in exchange for his immortal service and pocketed it in the deep folds of his cape. He picked up his lantern, fastened atop a long pole, and held it high above his head. Pointing two fingers at it, the lamp lit, ready to light the way for him to usher Alianore's body through the mists and out to sea. Then beyond the ninth wave, the magical access to the golden shores of the Otherworld, for her soul.

Marissa smoothed her robes and reached out her hand to grasp Ciara's. She squeezed tight, sending a silent message of reassurance to her twin. Or perhaps, hoping to receive reassurance herself.

Vanora leaned in to whisper in her ear. "It is time for you to introduce the ritual prayers."

At this, Marissa nodded and rested her eyes on the six pairs of snowy-white cranes floating beside the barge, admiring their grace. She licked her lips, preparing for speech. Her pounding heart confessed she was terrified. She wasn't ready. It was too soon. She wasn't good enough. They didn't believe in her. She was play-acting. But she had no choice. She must step into this role. Into her destiny.

"I'm ready," she said, hoping the lie would convince herself.

She turned and raised her hands, palms up, to address the gathering of priestesses assembled at the shoreline. Exhaling slowly, she poured her concentration into her womb-space as she'd always been taught, the potent gateway to her power. She waited until she felt the familiar surge, a bold golden flow of energy coursing through her. Her soul kindled. She was grateful when, finally, the right words of comfort, the prayers of invocation, began to flow.

Eyes closed, she led her community first in toning and chanting. The crystalline music of the heavenly stars paired with the deep hum of the earth's pulse and flowed through the sacred chant, energizing the crowd of priestesses. When the songs ended, she recited the ritual prayers.

"We send you off with love, our High Priestess. May the hands of the Goddess guide you. May the wings of the angels on both heaven and earth carry you over the crest of the ninth wave and onto the golden shores of the Otherworld. The Goddess will embrace you and accompany you to the altar of Her heart where you will sing Her praises and drink from Her golden nectar until it is time for you to be reborn again."

Marissa paused and opened her eyes, sensing an interruption in the flow of energy pulsating through the crowd. Priestesses stepped aside as a path cleared in the throng, parting participants right and left. A young woman emerged to kneel before her. A second surprise visitor. Shayla.

Resplendent in her Faery aura, silver white hair flowed loosely down her back. Her green mantle caught the lake's breeze as if afloat. If Marissa hadn't known Shayla so intimately for most of her life, she might not have recognized her. It had been a few years in Avalon time, perhaps only a few months in the Faery Realm, since she'd seen her. The shift to Faery had blossomed elegantly within her childhood friend.

"I am sorry I am late. I came as soon as I received the message." Shayla's vibrant green eyes were tear-rimmed. She looked up at Marissa before turning to Ciara. "I am so sorry for your loss. Our loss."

Marissa held out her hand and helped Shayla rise. There would be time for them to grieve together in private, to console each other in the way only sisters brought up together could. For now, she would welcome her long-lost friend into the funerary ritual.

"Join us on the barge," she said.

Vanora gasped her disapproval. "Shayla is no longer a priestess."

Marissa directed her reply to the Elder with as much authority as she could muster. "Shayla is like a daughter to my mother. She still is, and always will be, an honored priestess. She will join us. My mother would have wanted it this way."

"Thank you, Marissa," Shayla said softly. With a graceful wave of her hand, her green mantle faded and was replaced by one of cornflower blue, to offset Ciara's turquoise robes and Marissa's royal blue adornments, to represent the colors of the Goddess of the Stars and the Sea.

"Let us proceed," Marissa said.

Barinthus fitted his lantern into its niche on the barge's prow. He turned to Marissa, bowed, then gently picked up Alianore's body in his arms and carried her onto the ferry. Once he rested her onto the center platform, the three young women stepped onto the barge. They formed a semicircle at the prow while Vanora boarded last, to take up the post at the rear of the boat. Marissa stood tall, ready to see her mother off on this segment of her death journey. The priestesses on shore held candles to symbolically light Alianore's way, and the flames glowed brilliant even in daytime's light. The women stepped forward to scatter red rose petals as Barinthus poled the barge from the shore.

Prayers were called out from those remaining on shore. "Blessings as you travel to the sea of the Mother. When you crest the ninth wave, we bid you fare thee well and Goddess blessed."

Their litany floated on the water's breeze as the barge glided over the lake, the sound of the prayers fading the further they drifted from shore. The barge traveled on of its own volition, the water silently parting before its prow. It wasn't long before Marissa sighted two cliffs in the distance. The tall precipices faced each other with a narrowed inlet of water flowing out to sea between them. The stone peaks glowed in the sun's rays. She shaded her eyes with her hands, blinking at the outline of the rocky crags. They were carved and shaped like two female sentries, in flowing robes, with crowns on their heads and swords in hand. The keepers of this threshold to the sea.

As the barge entered the passageway between the twin cliffs, she felt the wild sea beyond thrum in her veins. Ahead of them, she heard the bark of seals as they sunned themselves on weathered rocks protruding from the ocean spray. Further out, a pod of dolphins spiraled in and out of the water, squeaking and clicking playfully, one swimming beside the barge in greeting. A solitary whale spewed water from its blowhole before leaping up, its massive form landing with a splash for show. It was as though the sea creatures put on a special appearance just to honor her mother.

Marissa cupped a hand around her ear and listened closely. She could make out the mournful cries of a selkie, even the siren song of a mermaid. The mermaid's glittering turquoise tail flashed on the ocean surface before dipping below.

She cast a sorrowful glance at her mother, lying in the center of the barge. The dance of life went on, though her heart wanted to stubbornly stop time to mourn.

With a whispered, secret command, Barinthus slowed his barge and poled it toward a shallow cove off to the side. Four horses awaited the priestesses for their journey back to Avalon. Before the four of them disembarked, Marissa leaned over to kiss her mother's forehead one last time.

With a lingering glance, she turned away, leaving Alianore's body with Barinthus, to cross over the ninth wave and send her on to her golden resting place.

Chapter 58

The Isle of Avalon
September, Anno Domini 1539

The remainder of Alianore's funeral day turned overcast, the usual golden sunlight of Avalon unusually obscured by clouds. Their shadows, along with early twilight's muffled light, matched Marissa's gloomy disposition. Tomorrow would bring her first official day as Avalon's High Priestess. Her installment ceremony would precede the traditional centennial council meeting—an assembly where the priestesses discuss and evaluate the continuance of Avalon's concealing mists. The Elders considered canceling the meeting, but decided against it, stating Alianore would want things to continue as normally as possible.

Marissa couldn't help but be anxious, even concerned. At tomorrow's twilight gathering, she would begin her role as Avalon's newest leader in earnest. Would her community trust her? Would the Elders, would Vanora, believe in her? Had she proven herself worthy of their respect?

She sat beside the Red Well, trying to gather strength from its holy waters, relying on it as priestesses had done for eons before her. She longed for a vision, for a message from the Goddess. She prayed for clear direction and guidance. Thus preoccupied, she startled when Shayla quietly approached, only the swish of her silken green mantle giving away her presence.

"You have become stealth incarnate," Marissa teased. She gazed up at her friend, who lifted the gossamer robes and sat beside her on the grass, as they had often done as children.

Marissa sighed. "You were always beautiful, but you exude such elegance now. Such ethereal grace." She smiled sadly. "Do you have some to spare? I could use some grace and charm. More so, wisdom and faith."

Shayla's mouth twitched slightly, and she sighed. They both looked towards the distant plains, watching the thick white marine mists roll and undulate.

"Alianore was like a mother to me," she said softly.

"I know."

"Things are so different for us all now."

Raking a hand through her dark hair, Marissa turned to her friend. "I have the gift of prophecy, but I never saw us living apart. Or Ciara turning bitter."

Shayla cast a sideways glance. "I thought you, Ciara, and I would be together forever," she said, her voice full of longing.

"Me, too." Marissa slid an arm lightly over Shayla's shoulder. Another moment went by before she spoke again. "I never saw myself so alone."

"Alone?" The lilting Faery voice rose sharply.

"That's how I feel."

"With your whole community beside you? You know nothing of being alone." Face flushed, Shayla furiously shook her head, her tone riled. "You have not changed!"

"What do you mean?" Marissa asked, wary.

"You still sulk. And think only of yourself."

Leaping up, Marissa held her stomach as if she'd been physically punched by her friend's words.

"Shayla! I feel incapable of the task before me." She raised her hands to her chest. "Plus, my mother, who is dear to you as well, has just died. How can you not allow me my grief?"

Shayla stood as well. Her eyes sparked. "Grief is not what upsets you so." Sorrow and anger clouded her face.

"What? Why would you say that? What makes you so upset with me?" Anger quickly replaced Marissa's shock at the caustic words. They burned in her gut.

Shayla puffed out a sharp exhale. "I dare to say that because I know you. You are concerned about meeting the council's approval as High Priestess. Whether they will trust you. You do not even trust yourself!"

The truth stung. Marissa balled her fists. "You're being *insolent*!"

Shayla did not stop at the rebuke. "And, in addition, you are more concerned about yourself than any of the other priestesses. They are grieving and scared as well. Especially Ciara."

All Marissa's unspoken fears and doubts spilled over into unbidden tears, coursing hot down her cheeks faster than she could swipe them away. "You think you know me? You truly believe I don't care?" Her voice rose, harsh and loud.

Shayla interrupted. "I do know you. Too well. Do you know what your sister goes through? Her child's father, Philip, is dead. Her mother's death is a guilty burden she carries in her heart. And her overriding love for Michael . . ."

"No! You will not speak of Michael. He is *my* great loss. You will not speak to me this way. When did you become so cruel? We once loved each other as soul sisters and friends. Your accusations are untrue. And I'm well aware of all these things you speak of."

Taking a step closer, Shayla spoke slowly, disapproval icing her words. "Being aware and having compassionate empathy are two different things."

Marissa's heaving breaths, the blood rushing in her ears, all came to an abrupt standstill.

"My Faery blood may not harbor emotions, but I still have more empathy than you, despite being only half human." Shayla rubbed her temples with her fingertips. "I have loved you as a sister all my life. I have also watched your self-centered actions hurt those around you. Especially Ciara. My heart breaks from it." Eyes glistening, she pointed at Marissa's chest. "You are of Alianore's lineage. Find the compassionate wisdom of your heart. Before it is too late."

Marissa's mouth opened but no words issued. Her anger, grief, and self-pity rose in a pounding crescendo within her chest, then were swallowed in a tidal wave of sudden understanding. When the startling realization dawned, it pierced her heart. She dropped her fisted hands limply to her sides.

Studying the change in demeanor, Shayla said with a woeful smile, "Now, maybe, you see."

Marissa could only stare at her Faery friend. Her whole body trembled. Shayla's words had slit her heart open in one swift slash. Her fears began to unexpectedly dissolve into an ocean of gold, deep within. It was a slow, warm trickle, a swelling sensation that both surprised and awed her.

Her friend nodded. "*Now* you might be ready to learn to lead." She turned to leave.

"Wait," Marissa whispered, unable to speak louder.

Shayla stopped, turning only her head to the side. Marissa saw that her eyes watered and her chin trembled, but no tears flowed.

Marissa didn't know what to say. She could hardly begin to comprehend what was tumultuously shifting inside her. She was both furious with, and grateful to Shayla. But the words did not come. She slid to her knees.

Her Faery friend continued to walk away, down the sloping hill. She headed toward the forest of hawthorn trees and her beloved Folimot who waited for her, on the glimmering border of the Faery land. She stepped into her blood-borne realm and disappeared from human sight.

Folimot guided Shayla into his embrace, laying his chin atop her head. "I am sorry about Alianore."

"As am I." She wrapped her arms around his waist. "Marissa allowed me to take my place on the funerary barge."

"Wise and gracious of her."

She looked up sharply. "She is neither. Yet. But hopefully I have cracked the barriers to that wisdom and compassion."

Folimot leaned back. "What have you done this time? What interference have you brought upon that poor girl?"

She drew him close again, savoring the feel of him. "I only said what I should have told her years ago."

He waited for her to continue.

"I waited too long to say the things I have longed to say. It came out cruel." Now the tears escaped and slid down her cheeks. "But I think harsh words, the brutal truth, were the only things that would break open her heart and allow the wisdom I hope she carries deep within her to come forth."

He shook his head with a tender smile. "Sometimes I am not sure if you are interfering where you should not, or if you are wise."

He wiped her tears with his thumb.

"But I have indeed interfered elsewhere," she confessed.

"Not interfering is a Faery lesson you are making quite difficult for yourself." He lifted her chin. "There is more to tell me?"

She chewed her lip. "It is about Michael."

His forehead creased in puzzlement.

"When I began to cross over into the realm of Avalon for the funerary rites, I passed through the world of men and encountered Michael by Avalon's lake. He was agitated, pacing. Calling for Marissa."

"I thought what was between them was over. That he'd chosen the Christian abbey and lifestyle of a celibate monk. Pity, though. I remember meeting him as a younger lad. He was carving a flute from a hawthorn branch. He was so full of vitality. And love for Marissa."

Shayla tilted her head in agreement. "He was. He still does. Love Marissa, that is. Apparently, he has had a drastic change of heart. He wants her back." She gazed into the shimmering green of the hawthorn forest behind Folimot. "Will Marissa and Ciara ever be rid of the heartbreak he causes? My forgetting spell from years ago did not hold. Whenever he is around, with even the memory of him, one or the other of my friends suffers. Ever since he came into our lives, Ciara and Marissa suffer because of this man," she said with vehemence.

Folimot slanted his eyes, appraising her. "What did you do?"

She shook her head. "Nothing. That's just it."

He smiled. "Good. You did not interfere?"

"I would not say that . . . you see, he was worried that he had not been able to contact Marissa. He has been calling her from the distant shores of the lake, calling to her across the border of the Avalon mists."

"Would she not have sensed him calling her across the veils if their love is that strong?"

"With Alianore's death and her new role as High Priestess, I am sure the connection was obscured for her."

"Go on."

"Michael and I talked." Shayla stared into the greenwood once more, recalling their conversation.

Folimot held her and waited.

Licking her lips, she continued. "Michael told me that he had to talk to Marissa. He said it was vitally important. Urgent. And asked if I would give her the message to come to the lake and meet him."

He exhaled slowly. "I know this is hard for you, but mark my words: No good ever comes from Faery intervening in the affairs of man. That is why we hold to that guideline."

"I know, dear Folimot. But which is the interference? To convey Michael's message? Or to not convey the message."

When he did not answer, she continued. "I made my choice. To protect Marissa. To protect Ciara. As always. Nothing good comes from his presence, no matter how good he may be."

Folimot squinted down at her, searching Shayla's face.

She closed her eyes. "I did not give Marissa the message.

Chapter 59

The Isle of Avalon
September, Anno Domini 1539

Moon rays sheathed the immense apple tree in the central courtyard of Avalon's Healing Sanctuary with a silver glow. Normally bustling with activity, the sanctuary had quieted after nightfall. Healing apprentices murmured reassuring words of consolation to those convalescing, replacing the daytime chatter and commotion of washing linens, gathering herbs, medicine making, and general cleaning. The ill slept, restfully or not, in their beds within the infirmary wing.

Softly undulating chants could be heard coming from the Toning Hall, housed in the east wing of the Avalon citadel. The dulcet tones permeated the sanctuary, the magical hymns designed to promote recovery and regeneration. Deep in the innermost rooms of this sanctuary, nine priestesses held a silent vigil. The Nine tended a perpetually lit flame that represented sacred life-force, kept ablaze in an ancient brass tripod in the shape of a cauldron, or bowl, symbol of the Goddess's regenerative womb.

In the northern wing, deep within the Halls of Prophecy, Marissa lay curled on her side on the hard, earthen floor, clasping her knees to her chest.

"Goddess, please help me," she whispered into the darkened room.

Alone in the Hall, it had been hours since her argument with Shayla. After their exchange, she had raced up the hill from the Red Well, frantic, past the sanctuary's apple tree, through the labyrinth of Healing Halls, and on to the Divination Cave, seeking relief and guidance.

The cave's stone walls, some thick with moss, some streaked with veins of crystal and gems, enveloped her like a womb. Yet Marissa's heart remained forlorn.

At first, the argument seemed to catalyze an upwelling of insights and fragile filaments of wisdom, but that brief glimpse of understanding was short-lived. Now she felt only shame smothering her heart like a rough wool blanket that scratched to bleeding.

Shayla's biting words haunted her, repeating in her mind, spurring endless tears.

You are more concerned about yourself than others.

She cradled her head in her hands, hiding her blotchy face. "Goddess, help me to see where I'm selfish and harsh. Where I'm insensitive towards others."

The Divination Cave's rock walls seemed to sprout watchful eyes, piercing her soul with their appraisal.

She remembered how obstinate she had been three years ago, in the face of Michael telling her of his mission from the Goddess. How she wished she'd responded differently back then. Maybe some sort of compromise would have gone a long way toward reconciliation, and they could have avoided being apart these last three years. She sobbed harder, dwelling on the lost possibilities.

You do not even trust yourself.

Could Shayla be right? Marissa concentrated, forcing herself to probe the bruised core of her self-doubt and hidden insecurities. The numerous instances when she'd acted impetuously, without thought to the consequences. Sitting up, she wrapped her arms around her middle, slowly rocking forward and back, as if to soothe herself. How often had she acted solely to gain the approval she desperately believed would erase the stain of guilt living inside her after the curse of the Faery Realm? She could feel doubt binding her heart, cinching it tight like a knotted rope, leaving her unfit and undeserving. How could compassion or wisdom ever break through that?

More accusations resounded in her mind.

Being well aware and having compassionate empathy are two different things, Marissa.

Was her heart really that cold? While her feeling of guilt was by no means new, she realized with a fresh pang how much her selfish impulsiveness had hurt Ciara and Shayla when she'd cajoled them into breaking the rules.

It also hurt to recall how she'd spurned her twin after assuming she and Michael were in love and keeping it a secret from her.

She covered her mouth with her hand as she reflected on always taking her dear friend Shayla's presence for granted, until she left for her Faery home.

Alone in the dark, she felt naked. Bared.

Shayla's last indictment echoed in her mind.

Find the compassionate wisdom of your heart. Before it is too late.

Before it is too late. Before it is too late . . .

Panic held a clamp over her face so she could hardly breathe. Marissa choked on her sobs and beat the floor with her fists. "I'm to be High Priestess. I must be worthy of the role *now*!" She stopped when she realized her hands were scraped red and raw.

Her heart felt cracked and bleeding, much like the tiny red drops on her scratched, raw palms. Broken by Michael's rejection, torn asunder by her mother's murder, filled with dread at the bitter change in Ciara, and crushed by Shayla's brutal honesty.

Now, in the darkened cave, she only felt empty, a hollowed reed cast to and fro on the hot winds of shame. Her sobs ran dry. No more tears, no more moisture. She stared, unseeing, into the darkness.

The Divination Cave grew suddenly fragrant with the perfume of fully blossomed roses. Marissa grew dizzy with the heady scent. A soft caress swept along her cheek as eddies of silver and blue iridescence swirled around her. Tingling raced along her spine. Her belly, her womb-space, heated. Sure signs she was about to have a vision. The Goddess of the Stars and Sea had heard her anguish, had come to answer her plea.

"I am here, my daughter." The Goddess's voice sang the song of a thousand stars, resounding gently against the cavern walls.

"Where have You been? Please tell me what to do," Marissa pleaded.

"Have you forgotten that I am always with you? Always here to guide you?"

"I feel so lost," Marissa whispered.

"Take my hand and let Me help you."

Reaching out, Marissa felt slight pressure in the palm of her hand. The Goddess's touch. Ah, she relished the feel of Her presence. Like the fecund, rich black soil, always ready to transform her suffering.

"Such horrible things have happened. To Mother. To Ciara. And my own suffering, my longing for Michael. I long for my mother now as well, and the friends I've lost from my own temper, my selfishness. And now I'm High Priestess. I beg you, tell me how to walk this path before me."

There was a lull, and Marissa thought maybe the Goddess would not answer. She swallowed thickly. Maybe she was no longer worthy of an answer.

Finally, the Goddess's voice rose again, filling the space, reverberating inside her mind and deep into her bones. "How do you navigate your life path? You must go straight into your path, into your pain, to go through it. Go with your heart open and filled with love. Only then can you become strong. Most of all, when your heart is open, you grow in compassion."

Marissa couldn't help but ask, "Keep my heart open? How? There's too much pain."

A breeze passed through the cave, the breath of the Goddess. "Place your heart in My heart. Then yours will guide you through anything."

Hands still pressing into the gritty earth, Marissa chewed on her bottom lip, contemplating. "And what about wisdom?"

The celestial voice rose and fell with the cadence of an ocean wave. "Wisdom will come from your heart and knowing it well. Your strength comes from your love. Wisdom and strength grow like flowers from the fertile soil of an open, honest heart."

Marissa sat up, eager. "If I can keep my heart open, then I will be wise? Like my mother? Wise enough to lead?"

"Leading comes from a patient and loving heart. Wisdom without compassion is meaningless. Remember, love, or yearning for love, is the reason behind everything. Love can always be found around and within you. Find it and you find Me."

Marissa picked at the earthen floor. "I'm not sure I understand."

A tender gust of wind, soft as a kiss, whispered across her skin. Still, her grief felt inconsolable, her doubts too numerous to fend off. "How narrow my vision is. Shayla is right. Is what she says true? Am I selfish? Do I lack compassion?"

She had certainly always felt selfish around Ciara. Not because she was a bad person. She wasn't. But because she felt she could never measure up to that depth of innocence and kindness.

"Go gently, My daughter. Easier on yourself. Recognize the power of your loving heart."

"Does that mean I *am* compassionate?"

"Yes. More than you know."

"If I'm compassionate, then why do I cause suffering in others?" Marissa hesitated, feeling the answers emerge from within. "Oh," she gasped, her eyes widening. "Of course. It's more about me being headstrong, isn't it? It's not that I lack compassion, but I've always been told I'm impetuous."

A lilting sound Marissa could only say resembled gentle laughter echoed through the cave, a light balm to her self-examination.

"So, I *am* right?"

"Find the strengths within your faults," the Goddess advised.

Marissa pondered this. "What *are* the strengths in my faults?" she murmured to herself. At the moment, she could find none. She lowered her eyes. "How do I fix my own broken heart?"

"Bring your suffering to the altar of *My* heart."

"The altar of Your heart? Where is that?" Uncertain, she scrutinized the silver and blue luminescence that eddied around her.

Deep, vast silence ensued. She quieted her breathing. Within the stillness, she heard the steady beat of her heart. Or was it the heart of the Goddess? Or the pulse of the earth? The heartbeats resounded through the cave. If she listened carefully, with her inner senses, she could feel her heart beat in synchrony with the heart of the Goddess. She felt stronger within that harmony. The merging of her heart with the Goddess's swelled in her chest. Here, in her heart, was the altar the Goddess spoke of, the ineffable place where she could offer her questions and sorrow and find answers and solace, wisdom and strength. Hope.

She drank in the vitality of this sacred altar deep inside her chest, like a pilgrim thirsty for an everlasting wellspring. Her own temple, her own power. Her own wisdom. She was complete already. She memorized the sensations of body warmth, flowing breath, beating heart, for they were the breadcrumb trails that would lead her to return here. She dug until she found the golden jewel, the nectar of love that lay inside her. Encompassing it, she took up residence there.

"There's so much more I want to ask you. So much more to understand."

"I have told you all you will ever need," the Goddess said, on a breath of scented roses and fresh sea air.

The whirling iridescence began to fade, the scent of roses diminished.

"Wait! Don't go!" Marissa called out.

Silence prevailed. At first she panicked. Then, carefully, followed the breadcrumb sensations she'd just memorized and returned to that fertile place inside where she could cull her wisdom and compassion. She would use it to direct her actions as High Priestess. As friend. As sister. As lover.

Lover. Her heart skipped and raced, and she brought her hands to her chest. Still enthroned within her sacred heart, she recognized a sensation that was not anxiety for tomorrow's officiating of the centennial council meeting, nor was it anticipation for her installment ceremony. This was different, something prescient. Her sacred heart was giving her a message. She waited.

Finally, in inner vision, she saw him. Michael. She heard his familiar voice. Calling her, imploring. He was standing on the distant shores of Avalon's lake.

Waiting for her.

Chapter 60

The Isle of Avalon
September, Anno Domini 1539

Marissa jumped up and grabbed her cloak. She raced out the Divination Cave and along the corridors of the citadel, hastily donning the cape and fastening its brooch as she ran. With light feet, she sped through the courtyard and down the green hill, past the gurgling Red Well. Bathed in full moon's light, the Healing Sanctuary rose shimmering behind her. Her prescient vision propelled her forward. To the shores of Avalon's lake.

As she reached the bottom of the knoll and neared the adjacent darkened grove, Ciara stepped from the shadows of a willow tree. "Marissa?"

Struggling to slow down, Marissa paused, breathless, surprised to see her twin. "You're up late. Are you all right?"

"Yes." Ciara looked down, wrapping her arms around her waist. "No."

Marissa ached to reach her destination. But the dark circles under her twin's eyes, the trembling of her voice, stopped her. She put an arm around her. That was all it took to start her sister's soft sobbing. She held her twin tightly, another part of her feeling the pull of Michael's call.

Lifting her head, Ciara brushed at her tears. "Nothing will ever be right again." Her voice sounded deadened.

Alarmed, Marissa gripped her sister's shoulders. "I know it seems so. Until moments ago, I too felt lost."

"What changed?" No hope reflected in her eyes.

"The Goddess spoke to me. I asked Her for guidance, and She came."

"What did She say?"

"She told me to always keep my heart open, to stay present in it no matter what. Call for her. She will aid you as well."

"I hear nothing when I plea. Nothing but accusations."

Heart thudding with eagerness to reach Michael, Marissa's feet and hands nearly betrayed her, fidgeting in preparation to run to him. But here was her womb-mate, begging her for solace.

Tenderly, she held her sister against her chest once more, saying kindly, "You once told me to release my feelings of guilt into Her hands. Can I offer you the same counsel?"

Blond hair fell over Ciara's cheeks as she shook her head. "This is different. It's Mother's death I speak of. I'm accountable."

Marissa knew better than to offer rational arguments. Telling her it was not her fault would not help in this moment. She enclosed Ciara's hands within her own.

Tilting her head, her twin's brow creased. "Why were you running?"

"I had a vision. Of Michael. He calls to me." She searched her sister's eyes, hoping she would not find pain at the mention of his name. It was not to be so. Her expression still hardened with the pain of her unrequited love.

"How do you know your vision is true?" Ciara's voice had turned to steel.

"I know it in my heart," Marissa said softly. She felt Michael tugging at her, pulling her to him even now. She restrained the urge to take off running once more.

Ciara pulled away from her arms. "You won't find your fulfillment in love with a man." Reaching into her robes, she pulled out a letter, handing it to Marissa.

"What's this?"

"It comes from Roger. He sent it by messenger after leaving Glastonbury. He plans to return but had to deal with Fr. Timothy first, have the priest arrested and punished for . . . for . . ." A lone tear coursed down her cheek.

"What more does the letter say?" Marissa kept her tone gentle.

"He offers marriage. To be my consort. A father to my son."

"Ciara, does this please you?"

Abruptly, Ciara snatched the letter back and crumpled it. "Does it please me you ask?" Her voice was shrill. She tore the letter in two and threw it to the ground. "Certainly not. His family's priest killed my mother. His father is beastly." Rancor lined her words. "Am I to go through all three de Boulle brothers searching for true love? I think not."

The air around her went cold as Marissa's heart sank. She studied her sister's face. Gone was the sweet innocence, the joyful countenance her twin had carried most of her life. All she saw now was resentment drawn in the downturn of her lips, in the newly formed lines across her forehead, in the hard set of her jaw.

"I wrote him back already. I told him not to come."

Marissa reached out to tuck a wisp of Ciara's stray flaxen hair, but her twin backed away. "Oh, by the Goddess, I know the pain of lost love. Ciara, no priestess ever *needs* a man in order to practice her art. But love can be a balm for the heart, a comforting reason to rise in the morning and greet the day."

Ciara thrust her hands up in the space between them. "Stop. I can't listen to this. Would those words have eased your suffering when you thought Michael was lost to you?" Her eyes bored through Marissa. "I love my son. With all my heart. I love my fellow priestesses. I love you. And Shayla, and Vanora." Her voice turned hard again. "But I will never love a man again. It brings nothing but suffering."

Not knowing how to answer, how to pierce Ciara's bitterness, Marissa said nothing.

"Go." Ciara waved her hand.

Marissa felt the dismissal stab her heart.

"Do not shirk your duties tomorrow because of Michael," her sister added.

Marissa felt her body stiffen. She wanted to slash back with a biting rebuttal for such words, but kept her tongue in check. Her sister was broken hearted. Anger would only add fuel to the fire. Ciara turned to leave. Marissa reached for her, grabbing her arm. Her twin stopped but did not turn around.

"I'm so sorry. I love you, Ciara."

Head down, Ciara nodded but continued walking, melting into the shadows of the surrounding trees. Marissa watched her walk away, chest heavy with the weight of her sister's sorrow, knowing she could not take it from her but wishing she could nevertheless. She raised her face to the moon, letting it bathe her in its silver balm. Then she heard her name.

"Marissa." It was Michael's voice resonating from across the misty veil, clear, pleading. Still waiting. She held onto hope for her lover. This time, she would go straight to him.

Chapter 61

Glastonbury
September, Anno Domini 1539

It felt like a painstaking eternity to reach Michael. Marissa approached Avalon's border, breathless from running, muscles trembling in anticipation. With the full moon shining encouragement overhead, she bunched her robes in her hands, lifting them high as she raced along the shoreline—Michael's voice her homing beacon. She sensed him on the opposite shore, Glastonbury's side of the lake, straight across from where she now stopped to catch her breath. Her heart raced wildly, thrashing against her chest like a caged bird.

She found one of her community's small boats moored beside the lake and clambered aboard. Lifting the paddles, her palms damp with excitement, she pushed forward. Laying her oars back down inside the boat, she let it silently glide along the lake's surface, propelled by its own magic. Once she'd reached the lake's midpoint, she stood and hurriedly spoke the invocation to part the mists between her world and the world of man, her voice eager.

> *By the name and the magic of Avalon.*
> *I call upon the curtain shielding Avalon.*
> *Oh, you white mists . . .*

Shortly, she reached the opposite shore and disembarked, parting the tall, thick reeds in search of Michael. She spotted him a few feet down the shoreline, facing the lake. His tawny hair still styled in a monk's tonsure, the shadow of an unshaven beard on his cheek and chin. She noted his muscled arms, evident even beneath the clothing. Her eyes widened. He did not wear the black robes of the Benedictine monk, but instead, sported plain brown breeches and hose, with a belted over-tunic. Her breath stopped at the sight of him. How had she gone so long without him? She prayed he had called her to reconcile. Not to break her heart in two once more.

Sensing her, Michael turned. Marissa stepped closer, slowly, gauging his response. Wanting to run to him. When she was an arms-length away, she saw the longing in his eyes, the yearning that matched her own.

"I was wrong. So wrong," he whispered. His eyes pleaded with her. "Can you forgive me?"

She thought he deserved a tongue lashing, that he ought to at least listen to the suffering his relinquishment had caused her. But the grief that had besieged her heart, the anger that had boiled at his betrayal in joining the Church, slowed to a simmer and vanished. He was back. Her love belonged to her once more.

He opened his arms to envelop her and she leaned into his embrace. Dipping his head, he kissed her tentatively, his mouth testing her response. At first she was restrained, but relaxed quickly and yielded, at home again in his arms.

His face nuzzled her hair. "I don't deserve you," he murmured.

Chuckling, she leaned back. "So you're saying you'll appreciate me, appreciate us, and never leave again? Hold to the promise we made as children?"

His expression was solemn. "I will never again leave you."

She sighed. "Then all is well."

Marissa took his hand. The reasons for his change of heart, the details of how they would move forward together, could be worked out later. For now, she led him to the nearest copse of hawthorn trees. The rich exuberance of the nightingale's warble floated down from the overhead branches. Once in their private, forested enfoldment, she undressed him, one button at a time, her eyes never leaving his. He unclasped the brooch on her cape, let it fall, and slid her robes over her shoulders. She sensed the moon smiling on them, in pearly illumination of the Goddess's gift of sensual earthly pleasure.

The celestial glow laid latticework shadows across his chest and shoulders, and over her breast and belly. Using his cloak as a blanket over the woodland mulch, he gently laid her down. Her parched heart was sated by his warm body, his scent of mint and musk. She drank in the sight of his familiar muscles and tanned skin, the birthmark on his chest. She ran her hands along the thick scar she'd never seen, a puckered red line running from his shoulder across his abdomen.

He kissed her neck, her shoulder, buried his head in her hair once more. "I've missed you. All of you."

When he lowered his mouth to her breast, she let out a small moan of pleasure, aching with her need for him.

After a long moment, he looked up at her, eyes smoky. "You must know . . . throughout everything we've endured, I clung to the memory of your smile, the color of your eyes, your long black hair." He lifted a silky handful, letting it slide through his fingers. "My heart forever memorized the way you look when you're happy. A small smile, like now. I know well the blaze in your eyes when you're angry or upset—hands on your hips, your chin jutting out in stubborn defiance." He kissed her again, exploring her mouth with his tongue and murmured, "I never lost the memory of the fire when you're roused. The scent of our lovemaking." Pausing, he cupped her chin. "You're my heart, Marissa. My soul."

She felt him warm against her and her tears flowed from his confession. This was all she'd needed to know. She pulled him on top of her, wrapped her legs around his waist, and grasped his shoulders.

"I want you forever," she whispered.

Her need was almost more than she could bear. His hands cupped her buttocks and he kissed her deeply once more. She arched her back to meet him and pure joy thrummed in her heated pleasure to his body fitting hers. Her sacred heart expanded outward, touching his. She heard the gasp of recognition as she embodied the magic of the Goddess for him in their lovemaking.

The nighttime stars still glimmered overhead once they had taken their fill of each other. Michael rose up on one elbow and studied Marissa from head to toe, his fingers lightly tracing her curves.

She wanted him yet again, but her questions begged to be answered. "Tell me, why now? Why have you waited until now to return to me?"

He held out a hand to grasp hers. The familiar tingle raced up her arm, the same feeling she had when he'd first held her hand those many years ago as children.

Stilling his other hand's caresses, he cleared his throat and captured her gaze. "I've been told something critical. To me, to us, to the world. It's about the original Christianity. When I learned of it, I realized the mistake I'd made."

She couldn't imagine what this had to do with him returning to *her*. She must have looked confused, because he paused and smiled.

"Bear with me. This revelation is about Mary Magdalene and Jeshua's marriage and their love," he began. "Brother Gregory told me all the hidden truth of it. About the early Christian mystical teachings of sacred union, and how these teachings have been suppressed but remain treasured in a secret sect within the Church. Within a secret group I'm now part of, called the Brotherhood of the Creation Bowl."

She took a sharp breath, reminded of her vision about the Creation Bowl three years ago. About their shared destiny. The vision she'd never had the chance to share with him. Once he finished with his own telling, she'd relate it to him, finally.

Michael paused, shaking his head, eyes ablaze. "I lost three years with you because I adhered to the Benedictine rule of chastity. King Henry even threatened punishment to all holy houses if we didn't follow his six Articles of Faith, one of which distinctly reinforces the canon of celibacy."

Marissa noticed how tightly set his jaw was. "I believed it was something I needed to consent to as part of becoming a monk, as part of my mission given to me by the Goddess." He touched her lips with his fingers and laid his hand to rest on her belly. "You know how much I thought I had to do this. Answer the Goddess's calling, I mean. Because She saved Roger. Because I promised Her." His voice was filled with his zest, and his anguish, in dedicating himself to the Goddess.

Marissa ran her fingers along his tense jawline and softly said, "Yes. I know." Remembering her insights in the Divination Cave, she felt her heart accept his words better this time when he conveyed the Goddess's mission. However, she still didn't understand this rule of celibacy.

"But this vow of celibacy? Avalon's Goddess has always taught about the holiness of sacred union. That it's a holiness within each of us, and also between lovers. We've experienced it together."

"I understand that now. I wish I'd come to these conclusions sooner. That's why I beg your forgiveness." He searched her face for the understanding he dared hope she would offer.

With a slight nod of her head, she placed her hands on his chest. "I should have fought harder to help you see this truth three years ago, on this very shore where we parted. Instead, I only felt betrayed and angry." She sighed heavily. "But that's now an old argument. It's healing now."

"Truly?" he asked.

"Truly, yes. But there's much I have to tell you as well."

He lifted his fingers and outlined her lips, her chin, her breasts. She lost herself in their body's passion once more, relishing their fiery joining, feeling him full inside her, hardly believing they were in each other's arms again.

Once they sated themselves, they lay back, her head tucked comfortably against his shoulder. The moon was still bright, the forest quiet, holding them in a private cocoon. Marissa looked past him to contemplate the white trumpet blooms of the evening blossoming moonflower that lent its sweet scent to the forest enclosure, taking a moment to recollect the many things she had to tell him.

"Brace yourself," she began.

Chapter 62

The Isle of Avalon
September, Anno Domini 1539

Michael turned his head to look at Marissa, eyes questioning.

"I'll be straight forward," she said.

He smiled. "I've never known you not to be."

With a grin, she poked him lightly on the arm. "All right, here it is. Ciara has a baby. A boy. Conceived in the same Summer Solstice rituals when we first lay together." She waited for his reaction.

Michael sat up. "But she laid with Philip." His voice choked when realization dawned. "Philip's son?"

"Yes, Philip's son." She sat up as well, bending her knees beneath her and facing her lover. "Recently, Ciara and my mother visited Mountain Manor in Wales."

"Whatever for?" The disgust in his tone evident, his voice angry. "I've told you how my father is."

Tears began to form in Marissa's eyes. "Ciara wanted Philip to see their son," she said slowly. "She wanted to reunite with your brother."

"Philip would have loved that." Closing his eyes, Michael leaned his head back.

"Roger told them Philip had died."

She saw the way his body tensed. His hands moved to cover the thick scar on his torso, his eyes revealing the painful wound his heart bore over his brother's demise.

His voice was urgent. "I wanted to tell you about Philip that day by the lake when I first returned. But everything happened so fast. We fought. You were so angry."

"More shocked . . . and hurt."

His broad shoulders sagged as he nodded and sighed. "I tried to save him," he said, his voice raw. "Philip was dead before I could do anything. So much blood. So much carnage that day. For no reason. All because one man preaches a different facet of God than another man's version."

She listened as he relayed the full story of how he had been wounded, and his subsequent recuperation in body and mind at the French abbey. He filled in the gaps he hadn't told her on the lake shore three years ago, when he first announced to her his decision to become a monk. His body shuddered with the telling. Leaning in, she held him until he stopped shaking.

Now there was more for her to disclose. So much more. "Michael, there is another piece of the story you must hear," she said, sitting back on her heels.

"More?"

She continued, slowly forming her words. "Whilst at Mountain Manor, your father's priest, Fr. Timothy . . . he . . . he murdered my mother."

Sweeping her into his arms, he held her against his chest, murmuring, "No. Oh, no."

Once her tears had run dry, yet again, Michael jumped up, hands fisted.

"She was killed and betrayed in my own family's household!" he yelled. Reaching down, he grabbed a stone and hurled it into the woods. Then paced, clenching and unclenching his fists.

He turned to her. "Where was Roger in all of this?" he demanded.

"He was helping them escape Mountain Manor. My mother was killed on horseback as they rode away."

Hands still quaking with rage, Michael squatted in front of her. "I'm so sorry, Marissa. I loved your mother as well."

"Roger brought Mother's body back to us."

"Roger was here? Why didn't he come to me?"

She shook her head. "Brother Gregory sent a message saying Roger tried to visit you, but evidently you were not at the abbey—"

He exhaled heavily. "Of course. That must have been when I left the grounds, upset over Brother Gregory's revelations. I needed time alone to think." He reached for her. "I'm so sorry my family did this to your mother. To you."

They held each other as their grief poured out through more tears, their embrace buffering the blows of loved ones lost. They clutched each other tightly, as if their clinging could fix the broken pieces of their lives.

"How did everything come to this?" he murmured.

Releasing her from the tight embrace, he stood and held out his hand for her to rise. In mutual silence, they dressed, picking up robes and cloak, tunic and breeches, and donning them.

Marissa broke the silence. "Later this morning is my official investiture as High Priestess."

"And you're anxious."

Chest tight, she nodded. "Yes, you know me well. But I also feel emboldened by my visitation from the Goddess."

Michael stopped tying his belt to listen. She told him of Shayla's visit to Avalon and their subsequent argument. About her desperate retreat to the Divination Cave, where she was visited by the Goddess and received healing counsel. Then how she'd heard his voice calling to her from across the veil.

He interrupted. "Wait. Do you mean Shayla didn't relay my message to you?"

"What message?"

"She passed me on her journey to Avalon. I asked her to tell you I had to see you. That it was crucial."

Her heart sank. "Shayla withheld your message? Why would she do that?" Incredulous at her friend's omission, she felt the heaviness in her heart swiftly ignite into rage. She might never have known Michael waited for her had she not gone to the Divination Cave and cleared her mind enough to be able to hear his urgent plea.

When she looked up, Michael's face was flushed, his eyes steely. "My father's treachery. Shayla's betrayal. Even the Goddess deceiving me into unwarranted celibacy. Why?" His voice choked in fury and grief.

Her anger matched his, roiling in her gut. She put her hands on her hips, but suddenly stilled. The Goddess's counsel forced its way into her awareness.

In a tranquil tone, she repeated the guidance aloud. "Keep your heart open. Stay in your heart no matter what."

He stopped pacing. "What did you say?"

"It's what the Goddess told me to always do." She dropped her focus inside herself and quickly followed the inner path back to her sacred heart, felt its golden beat, and asked it to remain open. To hold it all. Her love. And her anger.

"I'm so angry, but I think the Goddess meant that our hearts can contain both love *and* anger. Maybe one day it will alchemically transform how furious I am at Shayla's betrayal. Maybe not today, but one day."

Michael watched her with a questioning eye. "I suppose you can only ask her why she didn't give you my message when you see her again."

"That's wise, but I know not where our friendship stands after our argument," Marissa said quietly.

With a grunt of assent, he looked down at his hands. After a moment, he said, "There's one more confession, one more matter to discuss."

"What is it now?" She held her breath.

His eyes flickered between her and the ground. "I have one task I must accomplish. Before you and I plan our future together."

She let out the breath. He had used the word *future*. So, there was a future together, no more forsaking each other.

"What is this task?" she asked, feeling sudden trepidation chill her.

"I'm to bring a holy relic, a sacred bowl to safekeeping in the hands of a monastery in Wales."

"A bowl?" Marissa gasped.

"Yes," he said. "A wooden bowl. It's a special talisman, having a mysterious, healing effect on those who hold it. Particularly me, apparently, marking me as its current guardian."

She nodded vigorously. "The Goddess showed me a sacred bowl in a vision. Three years ago. She told me it had to do with our shared destiny. It was a simple wooden bowl. She called it Her Creation Bowl."

She paused when Michael blew out a breath. "She showed you this in your vision?" His voice grew excited and he clutched her hands in his. "That's exactly what Brother Gregory showed me. A wooden bowl he calls the Creation Bowl."

"Yes. It sounds very much like the holy cauldron of my priestess tradition. For us, it is a symbol of the Goddess's regenerative womb and ever-renewing soul," she confirmed.

"Yes! Gregory said it was the lost symbol of the Goddess and the container of Her loving power. And that it's also a reminder to include the Divine Mother within Christianity. He said that's why it must be preserved, so the Mother in

God will not be forgotten. He said it catalyzes compassion. But why did you never tell me of your vision?"

"I meant to. I was going to tell you when we were together that Summer Solstice but we hadn't the time. If you remember, we parted under duress." She laid her hand over his.

"I wonder why the Goddess gave you this vision."

"She said it had to do with our shared destiny. The destiny we've sensed since we first met."

Squinting, Michael's eyes implored hers. "But what does it mean? What are we to do together?"

"I don't have that answer." She felt heat in her belly, her womb-space. "But it feels important. I suppose She'll reveal that when the time is right. That's the way of the Goddess."

He rubbed the bridge of his nose, thinking. "The King has defamed the monasteries and their clergy, accusing them of being corrupt. He has proclaimed his Reformation as the new religion of England."

A chill crawled up Marissa's spine.

"There are substantial rumors that King Henry's men will come to seize Glastonbury Abbey as they've done with others. His representatives will confiscate its treasures," he said.

"You think they'll take the bowl? It's not gold, or silver. Will they think it valuable?"

"This bowl is not worth gold, but it's priceless in the hidden tradition of the abbey and the faith of Mary Magdalene and Jeshua. We can't take the chance they'll seize it."

Her womb-space blazed stronger. She clutched Michael. Her vision swam and her eyes glazed over. In her mind's eye, she saw fire licking at the Glastonbury Abbey walls. The vision that had so terrified her as a child, that same vision that had driven her to make Michael promise to never set foot inside the abbey, repeated itself in mesmeric detail. She moaned and slumped forward into his arms.

"When do you leave on this mission?" she murmured into the folds of his tunic.

"This morning."

"Look at me," she said, raising her head and locking eyes. "Remember my vision about the abbey," she demanded.

"I remember."

"You know my visions to be true. Believe me. Take the bowl and leave today. Today! Promise me," she insisted, her voice panic-stricken.

"I will, I will. I promise," he replied, clutching her to him until she calmed.

Her head rested against his chest, and she heard the reassuring sound of his heartbeat. Alive and strong.

"Goddess, may this danger pass," she whispered.

"As soon as I return, we'll make our life together. No more delays. I'm forever yours, Marissa."

"I'll come with you. To deliver this special bowl."

"No, it's dangerous. I would have you here, safe."

"But I sense this must be our shared destiny. I need to come with you."

Marissa was about to return the promise of her forever love when screams in the distance pierced the forest grove. The screams and shouts of men. Many men.

Chapter 63

Glastonbury
September, Anno Domini 1539

Michael spun around and angled his head. Listening. Behind him. Ahead. To his right. "The screams. I think they're coming from the direction of the abbey." He waved his hand toward the pink hue of a rising sun.

Marissa gasped and scrambled for the rest of her clothes, a half second behind him. She noted the force of habit that made him reach for his waist, where, as a soldier, a sword and scabbard would have been sheathed.

"Stay here," he ordered.

"No! Why?"

"If it's the abbey . . . Gregory may need me. It may not be safe." His muscles were pulled taut, ready to leap into action.

"I'm going with you," she said, hitching up her robes to run faster.

He bent over to pull on his boots. "I can't take care of you if you come," he said, straightening.

"I promise to stay hidden in the trees."

Face red, he grabbed her by her shoulders. "There's no time to quarrel." He quickly kissed her on the mouth. "I love you."

Turning, he raced through the woodland toward the sounds of screaming. Marissa took off behind him. Even with her robes held high off the ground, Michael's years of battlefield training proved him a much faster runner. Still, she followed.

Her robe caught on a branch and she paused only long enough to yank it free, tearing it. She stilled, senses on alert. Forest wildlife had grown eerily quiet around her, with no birdsong to greet the dawn. Only the sound of men's yells. She coughed. Acrid smoke curled around the tree line up ahead—the land bordering the abbey grounds. The sky above was smudged a murky yellow-and-orange hue. It glowed against the predawn sky. Her gut clenched, and an uncontrollable dread filled her. It couldn't be. Snatches of her childhood vision resurfaced, the red and orange tongues of flames.

She rushed forward, keeping her eye on Michael, now a few yards ahead. After passing near the village edge, he took the path to the right. Toward the abbey.

Losing sight of him, she scanned the trees for his brown tunic.

"Michael!" she cried. She raced ahead, finally spotting him.

A few yards away, he turned and put his index finger to his lips, gesturing for her to remain quiet. The edge of the woods was up ahead, no more than thirty feet from them. She caught up to his crouching form, hidden behind a great oak, and dropped to her knees beside him.

Her gaze followed his. The abbey stood magnificent beyond the forest boundary. But smoke enveloped its spiraling arches. When she dropped her eyes and saw the mayhem scattered across the manicured grounds, she had to cover her mouth to stop from screaming, or cursing. Soldiers, carrying the king's flag. Soldiers on horseback, everywhere. Shouting. Shoving. Striking the monks who tried to flee. The monks' panic and fear, the soldier's malicious intent, all assailed Marissa's empathic senses. She tried taking steadying breaths. Her heart still pounded, sounding to her as loud as the horses' thundering hooves.

The two lovers inched forward, to the forest's edge, yet still under cover of tree and shrub. They stooped low, not wanting to be discovered. Marissa clung to Michael's arm, watching some of the older monks cower against the outer walls of the monastery, their black robes disheveled, hands clasped together. Others ran for cover from soldiers with upraised swords. A large group of monks clutched buckets of water, passing them along in a ragged line from the central well to a side chapel on the western side of the cathedral, where billowing yellow flames raged.

Frantically, she pointed to the fiery inferno, the smoke thickest there. Horror sickened her stomach. Her vision. It was real. It was happening.

"The St. Edgar's Chapel," he said.

His practiced eye scanned the chaos. She was sure he noted strategic details only a trained soldier could. He gestured straight ahead of them, in the direction of the rose gardens adjoining the Mary Chapel. Two men stood in front of the chapel in heated discussion, hands gesticulating wildly and voices raised.

"That elderly man, the one in church vestments. That's Abbot Whiting, my abbot."

Dread sinking her stomach like a weight, her gaze followed to where Michael pointed. The abbot stood grim faced. But didn't cower. A sudden flash of him passed through her. His garments covered in blood, his head and bowels separated from his body.

"Michael! He's in danger," she hissed.

He nodded, tight-lipped.

The abbot raised his hand, palm forward, in a defiant gesture. Marissa heard him speak. "I don't care if you're an official commissary. I'm loyal to the Pope in Rome. Not your Thomas Cromwell."

She shivered when she heard the name. "Who's Cromwell?"

"A fanatic. The one who's organizes the abbeys' destruction and overtaking. Displacing and slaughtering the monks."

She looked down when she felt his arm tense. Hands fisted, his expression was grim. His eyes flicked from one section of the abbey to another. Assessing. His mind formulating his best move.

"Michael, what are you planning?" she asked, alarm raising goose bumps along her skin.

He gave a quick shake of his head and didn't answer. Her stomach clenched.

The abbot, white of hair, with solemn countenance, turned to survey the chaos. He waved away the commissioner by his side and limped toward the burning Edgar chapel, leaning on his walking stick.

Cromwell's representative, a middle-aged man of some wealth—by the cloth of his brocade tunic and quality of his hose—turned to issue an order to the soldiers under his command.

"Gather all the treasures you can. Leave the monks in peace," he bellowed.

Marissa winced at his insincere tone, worried for the helpless Brothers.

"They're mercenaries," Michael said, indicating the soldiers not attired in the English redcoat uniform. "More deadly," he muttered under his breath.

"Why is that?"

"They're soldiers for hire. Less likely to care."

Five soldiers closest to the commissioner dismounted their horses. Michael and Marissa cautiously inched forward, hoping to hear the conversation.

One soldier brazenly countered the commissioner's order. "We'll be as peaceful as the monks who receive us. And so far, they do not receive us nicely."

The commissioner gave a dismissive wave. "Then take by force what is rightfully the king's."

Abbot Whiting also raised his voice, giving his own command to the Brothers under his leadership. "Keep peace. Comply with the king's men. That's my order."

A cry rose from a young acolyte amidst the monks. "My abbot, they steal our relics. We must protect them. It is our duty."

A soldier stomped over to the young monk and struck him on the jaw. Michael flinched and lurched forward.

Marissa grabbed his arm, trying to pull him back. "You can't fight all of them."

"Those men over there," he said, pointing to three monks huddled together. "They're of the secret order."

"Michael, don't go to them. Those flames! They're just like in my vision!"

"I won't leave them to flounder. I'm sworn to protect the Creation Bowl."

He regarded the three monks warily. His eyes turned steely when two soldiers approached the men, knocking them down in quick succession, leaving them motionless on the ground after searching their robes.

"This won't end well. Please believe me," Marissa pleaded.

Out of the corner of her eye, she saw Brother Gregory surreptitiously duck inside the lower level crypt of the Mary Chapel.

Michael saw it too. "Gregory. I'm sure he goes to guard the bowl."

"Then let him do his job," she implored.

"I'm the only one amongst them trained to fight. I must help to protect it."

"You gave me your word."

Turning to look into her eyes, he stroked a hand through her hair. "I'll come back. Trust me."

She shook her head, terror nearly choking her. "Listen to my warnings. Please. Don't go."

"I'm sorry, Marissa. I couldn't live with myself if I didn't help protect it. And them."

"Then I'll go too. And die with you."

"What? No!" He grabbed her. "I will *not* put you in danger."

Heart pounding, she stared stubbornly into his eyes. She tried to rise, but another pair of strong arms restrained her from behind. She screamed and a hand covered her mouth. An iridescent green mantle covered the arms confining her.

Shayla nodded to Michael. "Go. I will keep her here."

He hesitated only briefly. "I must leave." He gave Marissa a swift kiss on the forehead. "I'll return."

Without a second glance, he sprang forward and hastened toward the Mary Chapel. Marissa kicked Shayla's leg. She removed her hand from Marissa's mouth, but held tighter.

"Let me go!" Marissa hissed. "How dare you."

"Not until you quiet down."

She shoved against the Faery. "Why are you here?"

"If you promise to hold still, I will tell you."

"Don't stop me from following Michael. I'm warning you!" Marissa snapped.

By the Goddess, Shayla had grown strong in the Faery Realm. The two panted with the exertion of their struggle. Fear for Michael coursed through Marissa's body, fueling her resilience, and she had nearly pulled free when Shayla spoke, her tone firm.

"Be reasonable, Marissa," she said. "A woman, a priestess dressed like you, on Christian grounds? You would be captured or killed. Or worse."

Marissa stopped struggling, hating that Shayla was right. She twisted around to face her. "Why are you here?"

Her friend sighed. "I came back for your installment ceremony. This commotion, and your presence amidst it, diverted my travels." She looked down, relinquishing her grip on the priestess's arm. "In truth, I came to apologize to you for my harsh words yesterday."

Marissa flicked a panicked gaze toward the Mary Chapel, shaking Shayla off. "I don't have time for this. He needs me."

She parted the bushes, intent on watching Michael's every move. Stooped behind a hedgerow, he looked back and forth, checking for safe crossing over to the Mary Chapel. If she saw he needed help, she would go to him, no matter what.

Shayla knelt beside her, pulling on the sleeve of her robe to demand her attention. "You cannot put yourself in danger. You are now our High Priestess. You are indispensable. Your priestesses need you. They could not bear to lose another High Priestess upon the heels of your mother."

"I can't desert him." Frustrated, Marissa swiped at her tears. "My vision . . ."

Shayla eyed her critically, but didn't make any moves to further restrain her, only nodded in approval when she didn't try to bolt away. Marissa watched Michael dart from the hedgerow to scuttle behind one bush to the next, always crouching low. Finally, he reached the Mary Chapel and bypassed its upper-level entranceway to scramble down the lower crypt stairway Brother Gregory had used. Once inside, she could no longer see her lover, but no one had noticed him enter as far as she could tell.

She turned her focus to the flames, farther down the nave of the main cathedral, praying they would be kept in check. Their fiery tongues licked at two of the northern facing basilica windows, and the heat exploded the colored stained glass. Both women gasped at the shattering blast. The flames burst through the window frames with long scorching fingers. A few monks passed along buckets of water in a frenzied attempt to douse the spreading fire. The king's soldiers laughed as they overturned and emptied the buckets.

She whipped around, back to watching the Mary Chapel, mere yards away from the tree cover. There was no one near the chapel, and she heard no sound from within. Her heart thumped so hard that her body rocked in its rhythm. Her hand gripped the low branch of the oak tree that concealed her, her muscles twitching with the desire to run to Michael's side.

Sudden movement broke out on the grounds near the nave, not far from the fire. Two of the king's soldiers tied the abbot's hands behind his back and were leading him towards the cloister. Abbot Whiting held his head high as a soldier kicked his legs from behind, forcing him to his knees.

"Peaceful? Fie!" murmured Marissa. His being treated as a prisoner worried her as much as it angered her.

Focusing again on the chapel straight ahead, she whispered to her companion, "Shayla, use your Faery senses. Do you hear anything within that chapel?"

Shayla cocked her head to listen.

Before she had time to report anything, two soldiers converged in front of the Mary Chapel entrance. The first soldier had come from the direction of the cloisters beyond the abbey. Marissa held her hands over her racing heart. The second man had emerged from the chapel's lower-level crypt, gold candlesticks and sacred tabernacle in hand. He pointed behind him, back inside the crypt, whereby the first soldier nodded agreement to some unspoken plan. The soldier carrying the pilfered items strode away, shoving the riches into a cloth bag, while the other soldier climbed down into the crypt where Michael had entered only moments ago.

Marissa screamed.

Chapter 64

Glastonbury
September, Anno Domini 1539

Shayla lunged for Marissa, but her friend proved too swift—gone before she could grab hold of her.

"Marissa, no!" she cried.

The Mary Chapel crypt emanated danger. Malice. She rose, to follow and drag her High Priestess back to safety within the forest cover, when her enhanced hearing caught snatches of a conversation. Within the chapel crypt. The malicious force behind the words pummeled her stomach with an energetic force. Dizzy and nauseated, she fell back against the concealing oak tree. Gathering her breath, she made ready once more to call Marissa back. Or, Goddess help her, to run inside and somehow assist her friend. She wasn't sure what she could do to help, but she had to try. She had to interfere. Maybe use Faery magic?

All movement around her suddenly abated. The chill of northern frost and the scent of snow dusted pine boughs hung heavy in the air. Through suction force, she was pulled into another place, a timeless place. She recognized Faery magic. Strong Faery magic.

Stunned, she watched snow settle on her green mantle. The Northern Faery Realm. It could mean only one thing. "Father?" she whispered.

King Laighlon, ruler of the Northern Faery Realm, extended his strong hand. Shayla kissed it and looked up into emerald green eyes, their color so like her own. Her father stood tall, his long black hair and silken beard tinged silver. His dark green cape swelled around him, though there was no breeze.

Though she'd met him once before with Folimot, the official introduction had been devoid of any time alone together. She felt unexpectedly shy. With her heart beating wildly, she wondered why he had brought her to him. Especially now when Marissa needed her help.

Laighlon answered her unspoken question. "You will interfere." His voice rumbled throughout the snowy forest. He sighed a blustery, cold wind that shook the snow from the boughs. "I have sensed your despair, daughter."

Shayla composed herself, smoothing her countenance to hide her thoughts and raw emotions from him, wanting to present the dispassionate demeanor her Faery-born father surely expected from her.

On the outbreath, he closed his eyes. Her hands fell to her sides. She sensed him reading her soul, as if he parted the curtains cloaking her private heart and exposed her torment and grief. She couldn't move, frozen in place by his enchantment. No place to hide from his commanding scrutiny.

He read the threads of her thoughts and emotions like the needle that traced the embroidery patterns she used to stitch in Avalon. She swallowed with a dry throat once her father found the source of her anguish. He saw how she felt she never truly belonged—in the realm of Avalon, nor the realm of Faery, since both flowed through her blood.

Desperately, she tried to push the painful emotions away, not wanting to feel nor reveal them, but her efforts were useless. She began to silently cry, longing for her father's understanding. Not wanting him to find her weak or flawed.

Laighlon probed further, casting a scrutinizing torchlight onto her soul, the heat of it almost unbearable. There, he found her despair at watching her two childhood friends' torment over the tawny-haired Michael, the lad who forever disrupted their lives and divided their friendship. He detected her disappointment and guilt over her unsuccessful attempts to remedy her friends' grief with her reckless memory-erasing spell, cast to prevent Michael from returning.

Her father let out an almost imperceptible gasp when he uncovered her early memories of Kendra, her mother, his one-time human lover. But he continued to search deeper, baring her grief at losing Alianore, the foster-mother she dearly loved. How heavy her chest felt when her father discovered the deep cavern within her where she felt so alone, even with the love of the man he'd arranged to watch over her, her guardian and lover Folimot.

But more than anything, she knew by his sudden frown that he'd found her deepest secret: her remorse at the consequences of her interference in Marissa and Michael's love. The forgetting spell she'd cast over Michael's memories. Never supporting Marissa in her relationship with him, and never talking things through with Ciara. Not notifying Marissa of his return when he'd asked it of her. She hung her head. She'd meddled with their fate. She'd . . . interfered.

King Laighlon opened his eyes. "You are confused. Heartbroken outside the Faery Realm."

Shayla nodded, chin quivering.

"You see why Faery do not interfere in the fate of humankind," he said, more statement than question.

Her heart writhed and cinched with the shame of trying to keep the two lovers apart. She had always told herself she had done these things to help Ciara. To help Marissa. Her father's scrutiny exposed her true motivations to be much more selfish. She ached with the loss of the closeness the three of them had once shared.

Her father's voice was throaty, like the wind whistling around a forested mountain and through the caverns beneath it. "Decide if you wish to be with Folimot—if you wish to be with me."

"I do," Shayla cried.

He pierced her with his emerald gaze. "I had wished to spare you this pain, this tearing of your soul. One foot in the world of man, the other in Faery. Now you must choose. If you are Faery, be Faery. If you are human priestess, go back. You cannot be both."

With her Father's blunt words, her heart ached anew. She had already chosen to be with Folimot. But was it her exclusive and forever choice? How could she abandon her friends? How could she deny one half of her nature for the other? The one side, the wild greening world of Faery. The other, the emotional riches of her human half. Albeit, the human half that came with suffering and guilt.

He held out a strong hand and helped her stand. "Choose now," he repeated. "Choose for good."

Shayla's breath caught. Her stomach cinched, trying to gird the uncertainty and guilt that had lodged there for so long.

Tenderness flicked across her father's eyes. "Come to your true forever home, daughter."

She squeezed her eyes shut, putting her hands over her ears to block out what she heard happening inside the Mary Chapel. The chapel where Marissa now headed. The ultimate consequences of Shayla's interference lay within the shadowed stone walls of that crypt. Quieting her sobs, she took her father's hand.

"I have done enough harm. I will come with you, Father. For good."

Chapter 65

Glastonbury Abbey
September, Anno Domini 1539

Michael steadied his breath, focusing his mind in the disciplined manner his brother Roger and Sir David had taught him. With stealth, he approached the Mary Chapel, confident he advanced within unnoticed. He chose the small stairwell that led into the basement crypt, the same entryway he'd seen Brother Gregory use. Peering down the steps to make sure no one was climbing up, he swiftly and quietly descended the wide steps into the dim vault. A soldier carrying two golden candlesticks strode down the long nave toward the steps he'd just descended. Ducking under the staircase, Michael pressed his back against the shadowed walls. Luckily, the soldier exited without noticing his presence, and he cautiously stepped out from his cover, breathing easier.

As his eyes adjusted to the shadows, he scanned the spacious crypt for Brother Gregory. Grunting, moans, and muffled whimpers came from the main entrance, the stairwell that ascended to the upper level of the chapel, only a short distance from the crypt entryway he'd used. He moved toward the noise. Approaching the rising staircase slowly, he followed the muffled sounds. Beneath the second chapel stairwell, he discovered another soldier, breeches around his knees, grasping the buttocks of a half-naked young monk. The young monk was crying.

The soldier punched the monk's face. "Be quiet or I'll go find your friend and do him again."

Michael recognized the younger man. Geoffrey. The lad had joined the abbey two months ago. The soldier was too preoccupied to notice Michael creeping

449

up behind him. He slung his arm around the soldier's neck and twisted it in the opposite direction with his other hand. A maneuver he'd learned while in France. The soldier's neck snapped with a cracking sound. The man fell to the ground, pants still twined below his waist. Brother Geoffrey dropped to his knees, hands over his face, weeping. Michael gently lifted him by the shoulder.

"Run and hide," he told the lad. "In the cloister. Better yet, in the woods. You'll find a lady there with long black hair dressed in silken robes. She'll help you."

"Brother Gregory," Geoffrey whispered between sobs. He pointed to the far end of the crypt, toward its stone altar.

Alarm clenching his heart, Michael spun around. He didn't see anything in the deeply shadowed crypt.

"Behind the altar," Geoffrey said nervously, pulling up his breeches.

"Leave Brother Gregory to me. Go!"

Geoffrey clambered up the steps to the crypt exit. Swiftly, Michael leaned down, grabbed the dead soldier's sword from its scabbard, and raced to the wide alcove that housed the chapel's stone altar. He found Brother Gregory sitting on the marbled floor, slumped against the wall behind the consecrated slab of stone. His eyes were clouded, and his hand gripped his left side, covered in crimson.

Laying the sword on the ground alongside the monk, Michael knelt beside his friend.

"I'm here, Gregory."

He didn't need to lift the monk's hand from his side to know the wound was lethal. "Who did this?"

Brother Gregory blinked, struggling to keep Michael in focus. "I tried to get the Creation Bowl. I fought the soldier. Best as I could." He coughed and a trail of blood trickled down his chin.

"Don't worry about the soldiers now. None of them are in the crypt any longer."

"Get the bowl," Gregory whispered, so low now that Michael had to lean in to hear. "Behind that stone to the left." He raised one shaking finger, trying to point.

"I'll take care of it. But I need to tend to you first," Michael said, wiping the blood from the corner of the man's mouth with the end of his tunic.

Gregory shook his head almost imperceptibly. "No. I know what I face, and I will soon be in the glory of God." His voice was raspy. He gulped for air. "But the bowl . . . take the bowl and leave. It's imperative . . ."

"The fire can't reach these stone walls," Michael reassured him.

Gregory coughed weakly. "Don't let them find it."

Michael gripped his friend's shoulders. "I won't. Find your peace knowing I'll deliver the sacred bowl to safety."

He stood and strode to the back of the alcove. "Somewhere here?" he asked, standing before the rough-hewn masonry. He turned when there was no reply.

The injured man nodded weakly. Michael moved his hands over the wall, looking for the precise stone that sheltered the wooden bowl. One stone felt looser than the others when he pushed it. He dug his fingers into the mortar cracks and tugged. The stone hardly budged. He pulled with more force, ejecting the stone from its housing. He reached into the deep niche behind, fingers searching. Finding a large piece of cloth, he stroked the course linen, brushing something enfolded within. He recognized the jolt of sensation from the one previous time he had held the bowl. Warm, pulsating. Pulling out the linen covering, he unfolded it. Inside, the Creation Bowl appeared to glow and hum, just as it had done for him before.

"Ahh. Good." Brother Gregory's voice rattled.

Michael returned to his friend's side, but the familiar brown eyes were glazed over, staring vacantly. He swallowed back a surge of grief. For now. With a steady hand, he put his palm over Gregory's eyes, closing his eyelids, as he'd once done with Philip's.

"God be with you, my friend." He lifted two fingers and made the sign of the cross in the air above Gregory's head and the circular sign of the Goddess over his heart.

He was gently folding Gregory's hands over his chest and offering prayers when the hairs on the back of his neck hackled. He stiffened. With his warrior's sense, he knew someone quietly approached from behind. Ever so slowly, he inched his hand toward the sword lying beside his dead friend and gripped its hilt in preparation for an upswing. The boots of his attacker slid quietly down the central aisle of the crypt. Michael bent his head as if he hadn't noticed. He shoved the bowl under Brother Gregory's legs, then listened carefully, waiting for just the right moment.

Daybreak's first light streamed through a small slatted window high up on the nave wall. Michael cast a furtive glance backwards at the shadow thrown against the opposite wall. The soldier's helmet was a vague outline that allowed him to calculate his attacker's stealthy advance. He waited, his body taut and alert.

Now, he thought.

He jumped up and spun around in one fluid motion. He raised the sword and sliced the soldier's sword arm. The man dropped his weapon. Michael retracted his to thrust into the attacker's abdomen. The soldier clutched his stomach and dropped to the floor, gurgling frothy blood.

The man's body spasmed, then lay still. Michael knelt and bent over him, checking for breathing. The soldier's hand still clutched a dagger unsheathed from his belt. Michael barely glimpsed the glint of steel from the corner of his eye as the soldier raised his hand for one final thrust, stabbing the knife into his chest. Michael felt it twist inside him. Dropping his hand, the soldier convulsed, and died.

Michael slumped alongside him, hand across his chest, fighting for air. He heard a woman's scream. Marissa raced from the far end of the long nave. The chill of the stone floor beneath him began to seep into his bones.

"No," he murmured, "I'm so sorry, Marissa. I never meant to leave you again." He sputtered blood. Damn, he could not seem to catch air.

She cradled his head in her lap, caressing his face, smoothing his hair. "Shh. Save your strength. I'll get you to Avalon's Healing Halls."

"I'll always love you, Marissa. Even in death."

She nodded quickly, biting her lip.

He coughed up more blood. "I'll find you again. Someday, somehow, we'll be together."

"Yes, my sweet."

He had to say more, before he could no longer speak. "The bowl . . . under Gregory's robes. Bring it to Wales for me. Will you do that?"

Marissa choked on her tears. "Yes. I promise. I'll finish your task for you."

He studied her face, her beautiful amber eyes. He saw her as he'd first seen her years ago—a young impetuous girl who'd saved him from drowning. The captivating young girl who held him in her lap just like this, her raven-black hair like a private enveloping curtain.

He lifted a hand, reaching for that silky black hair, needing to touch it one more time. "If you're not Faery, then who are you?" he asked, as he'd asked once before, those many years ago.

She smiled, though her tears washed over his face. "Nay, I'm not Faery. I'm Marissa. I'm a priestess. A priestess of Avalon."

"Ahh," he whispered. "A priestess. My dear priestess." His blue eyes darkened.

His hand fell to the floor. Marissa intertwined her hand in his. He felt the familiar touch that rejuvenated his heart, just as it had done the very first time she'd clasped his hand as a boy.

"The Lady is here. She's so beautiful . . ." His voice reflected his awe. "My dearest priestess. My love." Michael let out his final breath.

Chapter 66

The Isle of Avalon
September, 1539 C.E.

"Michael has been dead nearly a minute."

The message was barely a whisper, nearly soundless, like the delicate leaves that fall from an autumn-tinged oak tree. The muted words wafted through Ciara's inner senses, an augury waiting to be discovered.

She cocked her head, nearly but not quite grasping the telepathic trail. Still tired after a restless night's sleep, she yawned and absently patted her son's back as he sat in his raised chair at the dining table, rubbing his eyes with chubby fists. She had deliberately awakened early in order to get a head start on her responsibilities. The details of the many tasks she needed to accomplish this day for Marissa's installment ceremony filled her mind, taking up full residence with singular focus.

Preoccupied with making plans, she absently opened windows to the fresh morning air. The scent of dewy grass and purple morning glories filled the kitchen. Early morning sunlight filtered through the birch trees just outside the cottage, banishing the room's nighttime shadows. She snuffed out the candles on the great oaken table, no longer needing their light. Michael's morning porridge began to form small bubbles in its pot over the cooking fire. She stirred the gruel, hoping her son would eat this early in the morning.

Spooning the porridge into a bowl for her little one, she mentally rehearsed her specific duties once more. She was to preside over decorating the altars, arranging the candles, flowers, shells, and ceremonial gems and crystals.

The cauldron that would hold the central flame for their sacred circle needed setting up. It would be her job to tend it throughout the ceremony. She also needed to help Marissa go over the schedule particulars for the centennial priestess meeting to follow. The meeting was an all-important tradition in Avalon, and she wanted to make sure everything went according to plan. Their community would gather to discuss whether to retain the veils shielding Avalon. She sighed away the ache in her heart. These jobs were the tasks she would have arranged for her mother—had Alianore still been alive.

She drizzled honey onto little Michael's porridge. He squealed in delight and licked his lips.

"Yum," he said, giving one of his dazzling toothy smiles.

Her heart melted for the thousandth time. She reached for just a few drops more honey and her hand stopped midair. Strands of the elusive message drifted once more along the edge of her awareness, begging for her clairvoyant attention. Now loudly demanding it. Her vision blurred and became unfocused. She stared vacantly, seeing with her inner eyes, listening with her inner ears.

"Michael has been dead nearly a minute."

Ciara gasped, her breath strangled in her chest.

"Mama?" The toddler pulled on her sleeve. "Mama?" His face puckered, readying to cry.

Vanora burst through the front door, breathless. "Ciara! Have you seen the vision? Marissa needs us. It's Michael. He . . ."

Ciara blinked, finishing Vanora's sentence, pushing the words past the shock squeezing her heart. "He's dead."

"Mama! Crying?" her son asked, his tug on her sleeve urgent this time.

She reached for him, hugged him close, choking back sobs. "I'm so sorry. It's your Uncle Michael's time to join your father in the Otherworld, my sweet boy."

Little Michael nodded sagely, his blue eyes big and round. He reached around his neck and lifted off the chain he'd worn since Roger had given it to him. The chain with the de Boulle emblem of a horse reared up beside an oak tree carved into its gold metal. He rubbed it with his tiny thumbs, then handed it to his mother. "For Uncle Michael. For him and Da' now."

Marissa pulled her hood over her head. The night was clear, the moon luminous, lighting her path to the Red Well. She wiped an errant tear, feeling hollow, her heart stripped bare. Her mother and her dearest Michael. Gone.

She needed the well's sustenance before she faced the morning's installment ceremony for her role as the new High Priestess. More importantly, she needed the well's familiar comfort and its magical water before the ensuing centennial council. The entire priestess community would soon debate the continuance of Avalon's protective mists, as tradition had required for centuries, but this time it would be with her guidance as their High Priestess. She straightened her back and squared her shoulders. She had to think clearly and calmly to lead this crucial discussion. She had to lead with a wise heart for the sake of her priestesses. For Avalon.

Kneeling beside the well, she dipped the silver cup into the holy waters and drank. She sighed and relaxed her tense shoulders, letting it refresh her. Inhaling deeply, she closed her eyes, readying to meditate, when she heard the soft scrape of slippers walking across the grassy mound.

"I thought I might find you here," her one-time tutor said.

Vanora knelt on her heels and put her hand on Marissa's shoulder. "You are indeed prepared for this."

From the deep cave of her sorrowed heart, Marissa registered her surprise at Vanora's support. "I hope so, my Elder."

"You did well officiating the Funerary rites. The upcoming council concerning Avalon's veils is next. A heavy responsibility. It is much to take on for a newly appointed High Priestess. Know that Ciara and I, and all the Elders, will help you." Vanora offered a rare, encouraging smile.

"Do you believe I can do this? Do this well?"

"Your mother and I have readied you. It is in your blood."

"Yes. But do you believe in me?"

"Your actions will show your wisdom. Your mother always said you were the strongest of us all."

Marissa sighed. Vanora hadn't given a direct answer. But she hadn't said she doubted her ability either.

"You will learn and grow into your role. As do all High Priestesses," Vanora added.

"May it be so." Marissa looked into her Elder's eyes. "You know I want to be what our priestesses need."

"I know," Vanora replied. She patted Marissa's shoulder and rose to leave. "Trust in our Goddess. Trust in the wisdom of your heart," she said, before she walked away.

Marissa sank into the ensuing silence and the cover of night. The burbling well water and the nightingale's chorus receded to the background of her awareness. Thoughts ebbed and flowed. True, she'd known how to officiate the funerary rite for her mother *and* for Michael. The council discussion about Avalon's veils was another matter. She would be looked upon as a beacon of wisdom for the community. The thought brought another bout of unease that churned her stomach. There was more. She sensed something brewing. A change. Avalon was asking something of her because of her mother and her lover's death, and she didn't know what it was. She closed her eyes to pray and contemplate.

"Goddess, let me hear the wisdom of Your heart coming through mine," she pled.

She waited a long time in silence. Stilling her movement to better hear the voice of her heart's intuition. Her skin tingled and her womb-space warmed when guidance finally emerged in prose.

> *When truth and love are buried deep*
> *Under starlight's watchful eye they'll keep*
> *through many lifetimes' sleep.*
> *To be found again when the time is right*
> *for humankind to see with awakened sight*
> *and be brought out once more into the light.*

Marissa furrowed her brow. She tried to puzzle out what the words meant. Did this have to do with the vision the Goddess had once given her about the Creation Bowl? Did it involve Michael's secret wooden bowl and their shared destiny? What did it have to do with Avalon's council meeting and the upcoming decision about the mists?

She opened her eyes in sudden understanding. She'd heard the guidance correctly. *No,* she argued silently. *How can I advise this? Is it dangerous? Besides, lowering the veils will never pass the council vote.*

The prose repeated in her heart and mind, this time more loudly. *When truth and love are buried deep . . .*

Once she'd listened again, she put her head in her hands. "No!"

The Goddess's voice, strong and pure, like the song of a thousand stars, resonated around her in blue and silver luminosity. "Believe in the wisdom of your heart, nested inside My golden heart."

Marissa drew a slow breath, focusing her attention inside her again. She traveled the inner path to her heart once more. There, she saw the mantle of leadership on her shoulders, like a heavy shroud. But all High Priestesses bore this responsibility, she told herself. Vanora's counsel came back to her. *Trust.* She realized she had to trust herself, more so, trust her heart and her Goddess-guided intuition to be the wise leader Avalon needed.

She peered inside her heart once more and saw that she still bore the mantle of leadership, but it felt lighter. Golden. Connected to her heart with shining filaments.

She listened one more time to the prose that had come to her. *When truth and love are buried deep . . .*

When the last words reverberated in her heart and mind, she murmured, "Trust my visions. Trust my guidance."

The swirl of blue and silver diminished, the Goddess satisfied Marissa had heeded Her words. The nightingale's song floated back into Marissa's awareness and the wind whispered through the apple grove. While Her guidance had been at first furtive, its meaning was now clear. Marissa knew this to be the change she'd sensed brewing earlier. She had her decision. She trusted it. She knew what she would advise at tomorrow's council.

Chapter 67

The Isle of Avalon
1539 C.E.

The priestesses assembled beside the Red Well. The day was mild, the roar of the ocean waves crashing below Avalon's hill a reassuring cadence to Marissa ears. She swallowed down any remaining anxiety about her investiture and the following council meeting, and allowed the smoky frankincense and sandalwood incense to be fanned around her body with the long crane feather, aiding her into trance. Her expression softened and her heartbeat calmed.

At Vanora's direction, the group processed one by one up the knoll from the well. The air was filled with the refrain of chiming cymbals, melodiously plucked lutes, and airy flutes, trilling in symphony with the morning birdsong. Four priestesses trailed at the rear of the line, each beating a resonant drum, its rhythm inducing everyone's arms, hips, and pelvis to sway in dance.

Marissa's body undulated to the tempo as she passed through the sanctuary's massive gateway. She led the way into the courtyard, Vanora and Ciara directly behind, and waited for the rest of the priestesses to file in. They gathered in a circle in front of the enormous, sacred Apple Tree. Marissa inhaled deeply, taking succor from the tree's regenerative greenery and the honeyed scent of its ever-present golden apples.

She raised her chin to feel the uplifting warmth of the morning sun. Her skin felt soft, still rose perfumed from her predawn purification bath. The music, the incense, the procession, all helped her to feel fluid, attuned to nature, aligned with the Goddess. Her silk ceremonial mantles wafted gently against her body. The priestesses had adorned themselves in varying shades of blue, all the hues of the sea and sky. Hers was ocean turquoise, while others wore tints of dawn cerulean, daytime azure, twilight sapphire, and midnight indigo. The morning breeze lifted their mantles, the air caressing the delicate fabric into gentle folds.

Vanora called for a moment of reverent silence, then the chants and prayers began. As Marissa sang, her deep sense of devotion fueled her trance.

I am daughter of the Goddess
Great Mother of the Stars and the Sea
Priestess of Her Ways
I carry on Her flame
For all to share.

The Goddess's love infused and embodied Marissa in warm, radiant waves. Her feet felt like roots burrowing into the rich, moist earth. Her womb and the waters of her body resonated with the silver-lighted magic of the moon. She was fiery, her heart ablaze like the sun. Celestial, the stardust that made up her body sang the song of the stars in the night sky. She felt airy and spacious, and at the same time stable and anchored into the earth.

Vanora led her to the middle of the circle, as Ciara lit the central flame in a copper tripod filled with seawater. The fire flickered along the water's surface, a mystical fusion of water and fire. Facing Marissa, Vanora dipped her finger into a tiny stone pot of holy oil. Lifting her first two fingers, she anointed Marissa's forehead, lips, neck, chest, womb, pubis, and spine with the aromatic blend of sweet rose and musky spikenard.

"The Goddess of the Stars and the Sea blesses you and anoints you High Priestess of Avalon," she intoned with each rub of oil.

The scented markings surged with power. Ripples of energy radiated from each anointed spot and spread throughout her body. Her heart swelled open. The Goddess's love awaited her beyond all that was not aligned with it.

Vanora stepped behind her and pushed her hair aside, placing Avalon's pendant talisman around Marissa's neck—the ancient Vesica Pisces wrought in mysterious silver metal that never tarnished or weakened, which carried the power of her predecessors.

"We inaugurate you as High Priestess. Your investiture is sealed with this necklace, ancient talisman of our heritage, handed down from the first priestess, Geodran of Atlantis," Vanora formally declared.

The necklace glowed warm against Marissa's chest. Her fingers traced the two interlocking circles of the sacred necklace and stopped at the yoni-shaped symbol, outlined where they intersected.

Vanora spoke again. "The conjoined circles of this necklace are an icon of unity. Unity between earth and sky. Between the Goddess and her male consort. Between darkness and light. Life and death."

Marissa added further meaning silently to herself. *Between fear and tenacity*.

One at a time, each priestess stepped forward to kneel before her, to receive the blessings of the Goddess through her, as their newly appointed High Priestess. She lightly rested her palm atop each of their heads, allowing the Goddess to use her hands as Her own. Blessings and love from the Goddess passed through her as she let herself be the vessel for the raw power. In a remote corner of her mind, she thought, *Maybe I can really do this after all*. With each blessing, she felt power surge in her womb-space, then release. The power of the Goddess thrummed in her blood and bones in a way she'd never felt before—building, heating. A surge and release with each priestess's head she blessed.

When the ceremony concluded, Marissa felt strengthened by the benevolence of the benedictions that had passed through her. The music started up again, this time buoyant and lively rather than the sinuously slow tempo of the earlier procession. The priestesses danced into two lines, eventually fashioning into two interlocking circles that mirrored the holy talisman Marissa wore around her neck. She stood in the middle, yoni-shaped space that was created by the two connected circles. The power generated by the danced configuration charged through her body, forming a vortex of power she dedicated to the Goddess.

After the priestesses danced, the younger ones brought out the prepared trays of oatcakes and honey, along with cinnamon baked apples and golden mead, putting them out on the trestle tables situated along the courtyard walls. Slowly shedding her trance, Marissa took deep breaths, stretching her back, and wiggling her hands and toes. She stared at the magical flame in its tripod for a moment to stabilize herself before she joined the celebratory feast.

She was breaking her fast with a sweet oatcake when movement and form caught her attention, startling her. In her peripheral vision, just beyond the Apple Tree, she imagined she saw Michael, alive and well. But she immediately realized it was only a shadow cast by cloud and sun, a ghostly illusion born of her grief. Her willful heart pounded and bucked with unfettered memories. They flashed across her mind: him smiling at her with that intimate twinkle in his eyes, his tender lips on hers, him wielding a hulking sword, watching him fall and take his last breath. She relived the fresh memorial of Barinthus's barge cresting over the horizon, carrying her beloved to the golden Otherworld beyond the ninth wave. Her soul silently keened. Tears traced a now familiar path down her cheeks.

Ciara, sensing her twin's distress, was beside her in an instant, putting her arms around her shoulders. Marissa gave a weak smile. "Thank you. I will manage."

"Are you sure?"

She nodded, trying her best to look confident. She turned to the assemblage of priestesses, and, sensing the love and power generated by them, inhaled deeply, garnering her power to speak to them as their newly appointed High Priestess. The time for their centennial council had come. She had prepared herself as best she could to officiate this meeting, and trusted in the guidance she'd received the previous evening by the Red Well.

The crowd murmured, already informally discussing the question of keeping Avalon's protective veils. Vanora signaled for them to form a circle around Marissa once more, then positioned herself on one side of Marissa while Ciara stood on the other, the Apple Tree looming behind them.

Marissa reached for the Vesica Pisces pendant lying against her chest. Words echoed silently in her head. Was it the voices of her priestess ancestors? Her mother's voice? The Goddess? *Trust the talisman. It will bring you the power you need as Avalon's High Priestess.* She clasped and unclasped her hands under her robes, hoping her voice would be strong and sure when she spoke. Then she smoothed her mantle and cleared her throat.

"Two funerals in two days." Her voice betrayed her, faltered.

Her priestesses waited in silence, heads bowed. Breathing into her heart and womb-space to help compose her nerves, she strengthened her resolve, reaching up again to clutch the pendant. She lifted her eyes to gaze upon each of her fellow priestesses in turn. Some faces were lit with trust, others shaded with the slightest hint of uncertainty, waiting to appraise their new High Priestess and how she would manage her new role. Even if some priestesses still thought of her as the impetuous child she had once been, she knew what her advice would be this day, what changes she truly believed were necessary and right.

"Two funerals in two days," she repeated, her voice stronger this time. "Two beloved people. Our treasured High Priestess, my mother Alianore. And our friend, Michael, who spent a summer with us in his youth. Michael. My love." Her lips trembled but she continued. "I vow to do my best as your new High Priestess. To be the leader we need during these troubling times. The world of man has intersected with ours, bringing us this grief." She paused, to allow time for their lament.

Turning inward, she silently invoked the Goddess. Focusing into her sacred heart, she waited for the divine presence to speak through her.

"We are one with the bounteous earth that is alive beneath our feet. And we are one with the stars that dance above our head at night," she began.

The mystical flow connecting her body to everything below, above, and around her began to move through her. The flow danced up her spine, poured through her veins, streaming throughout her body in synchrony with the verdant sap flowing inside Avalon's magical Apple Tree.

"Before we take on the duty our ancestors requested of us, this centennial decision about Avalon's veils, we must connect. To each other, and to the Goddess. So, I ask you to first look deep inside. Be aware of your inner senses and your intuition." She waited a moment before continuing her instructions. "Go into your holy body. Feel it right down to your bones. Go into your heart. Put your hand on your chest and feel its beat. Full of life."

The priestesses followed her directions, placing their hands on their chests.

Marissa's whole body vibrated. "Connect your heart to your belly, to your womb-space." Her voice grew louder as she continued. "Fan the flames of that sacred space."

Inside her body, her own womb-space flared up in response. The central flame in the middle of their circle flashed and blazed higher in its copper cauldron of ocean water, the fiery devotion of those present fueling the magical flame floating atop. Marissa sensed when her sisters in the Goddess entered into deep body trance. They stilled their movements, breathing as one. Silence prevailed.

She prayed into this still void, at first silently, only to herself. "Tell me, Goddess. What do I say to them now?"

The priestess musicians added their gifts to the meditation. They took up a steady drumbeat in time with the earth's pulse. A flute interwove its high notes with the drum's beat. A triangle of tiny bells was tapped, adding a silvery tone like crystalline star song.

Drum. Flute. Bell. Water and Earth. Fire and Air. Conjoined.

Marissa's womb-space pulsated. Her heart expanded in her chest. She was ready. She brought the Goddess's Presence forth into the sacred circle, transmitting it through her body, communicating it through her words.

> *I am in and I am down.*
> *I am blood and I am bone.*
> *I am in you. In every part of your body,*
> *where love pulses the drumbeat of your heart.*
> *Where temple bells ring the song of your bones.*
> *I am black, moist earth. I am the cave in the mountain of your belly.*
> *Feel your belly blaze hot.*
> *I am water, I am the sea.*
> *I am She who resides in all. Come home to me. Come home to me.*

Marissa felt her body surrender to the thrum and sway of vibrant energy streams. Her arms raised and opened wide to invoke the Goddess's sustained presence. The air around her grew luminous with swirls of iridescent silver and blue.

The Goddess was not finished with her yet. She began reciting Avalon's living poem of the Goddess's body.

> *I sit so my vulva kisses the earth.*
> *I pull open my Yoni, tunnel entrance to my womb temple, Cauldron*
> *   of Birth.*
> *In my cauldron there is utmost stillness.*
> *I am birth. I am death. And rebirth again.*

I am Creatress. I am the Love inside all living things.
I am the black soil of the earth.
The greening of the plants and the wild things.
I am Mother. I am all matter. I am mar. The ocean and the sea.
And the stars shining in the innermost spaces.
Come home to me.
Through portal of pleasure or heart cracking open in pain,
find me and be comforted. Rest in my arms.
I am She who loves and cries and loves again.
I am She. Come home to Me.
Crown of stars on My head. Rolling seas at My feet.
I am She. Come home to me. Come home to me.

Marissa exhaled slowly, the Goddess's message now emptied from her body. Ciara slid an arm around her waist and bolstered her. The music softened and stopped.

She sensed the Goddess's palpable presence alive within each of the priestesses, radiating all around them in golden incandescence. She looked around the circle and saw some of the women crying, some with hands over their hearts or womb-space, eyes bright, mouths parted in veneration for the Goddess. Marissa was heartened. It was a very good sign, as they would all need to feel Her guidance for what they were about to discuss. She trained her eyes on the central flame. When her body settled, her breath quiet and her mind clear, she pulled away from Ciara's supportive arm and turned her focus to their centennial meeting's agenda.

"We are now ready to face this question, as our forebearers have done every hundred years. The question that addresses whether the mists veiling Avalon, dividing us from the world of man, should remain intact for the next hundred years," she said, opening the council debate.

The priestesses nodded their heads in acknowledgement of the solemn duty at hand.

"We are given this task to assess the relevance of our boundaries because centuries ago, the High Priestess Rhianna erected these veils to protect our vulnerabilities. To keep us safe. Her decision was sound." She halted briefly, preparing herself for the dissent sure to follow her next statement.

She made sure her voice was loud and sturdy. "High Priestess Rhianna's decision was indeed sound," she reiterated. "For that time." She allowed a pause to let her words sink in. "As your newest High priestess, I propose we take down these dividing curtains."

Vanora gasped. Ciara cried out. A heavy silence fell. Marissa instinctively put one hand on her womb-space, and the other on the talismanic pendant. "Let me explain my proposal."

Vanora interrupted. "Marissa. High Priestess," she bowed her head. "As an Elder, I feel I must advise against this. For the very reasons you just stated. Two funerals in two days. Times are no more safe for women priestesses than they were nearly a thousand years ago when Rhianna first conjured the magical boundary."

The crowd murmured their assent.

Ciara whispered in her ear. "Marissa, what are you doing? Does your grief cloud your judgment? We cannot trust men." She shook her head. "I mean, the world of men."

Marissa stroked her twin's flaxen hair, tucked a stray tendril behind her ear, then turned to face the circle of women once more.

"Yes. It can be dangerous. I will not deny that. Please realize I do not mean that we put ourselves in harm's way. But I have had a greater vision. Instead of hiding away, invisible to the world, I say that the very danger we speak of needs us. The world needs us. The world needs the love, the healing, and the heart of the Avalon priestess. We must plant the seed of that love now in the world in order for it to properly flourish in the future."

Again, a murmur went up, perhaps less vehement this time, giving Marissa a thread of hope. She raised her hand to ask for quiet.

"We will entertain all of your comments and concerns," she said.

Many of the women turned to Vanora to speak on their behalf again. "If we take down the magical veils, we would endanger our lives, our way of being," the Elder began. "How are we to do our healing work if we cannot do so in safety? How are we to protect ourselves from the hostile world of man?"

Many nodded their heads, a few adding, "Hear, hear."

Vanora glanced at Ciara, then looked deep into Marissa's eyes. The Elder's wizened eyes communicated what her words did not. They spoke the concerns she had always voiced to both Marissa and Alianore—her misgivings in regards to Marissa's impetuousness and her ability to lead. Her belief that Ciara was the more trustworthy and reliable one.

The unspoken words pierced Marissa's heart, battering at her resolve, exposing her underlying fear she wasn't fit to be High Priestess. Her hands trembled, her knees grew weak. Only for a moment. She took a deep breath and refused to buckle. She recalled her tribulation a few days earlier, in the Divination Cave, where she'd transformed her self-doubt and received guidance. The Goddess had told her, *Keep your heart open. Put your heart in my heart. That is all you need.* She recalled her intuition last evening at the Red Well, the divination spoken in prose, and the Goddess telling her to trust Her guidance.

She clung to that counsel and stayed in her heart. There she regained confidence and confirmed her wisdom. "I have purged my heart. I have opened to the Goddess and listened to my intuition to come to this decision. I know in my bones it is the right thing to do." She persevered, removing the hand resting on the talisman and placing it over her heart. "We will never expose our inner sanctum," she pronounced clearly and with confidence, assuring them. "Very few in the world of man would be able to see it or find it anyway . . ."

Trudence, another Elder, interrupted. "Perhaps so, but they can see and find our village and our homes. Like they once did in Rhianna's time, when marauders nearly killed all the priestesses."

"Trudence, you have lived behind the veils longest of all of us," Marissa said, in acknowledgment of Trudence's ninety years of age. "Times are changing, and we must change with them. My first reaction to my mother's, our High Priestess's, murder, and then losing Michael so soon after, was to hide away. And never come out again. But my heart and my soul tell me we have important work to do as priestesses now more than ever. And we must do this work amongst our fellow human beings. Not separating ourselves from them. We must begin to teach them our Path of the Heart in earnest."

She waited, trying to read the response to her argument before she clarified the details of her convictions. "The world needs that power. We can lead by example, by sharing our sacred ways. Without flaunting or condemning the differences between Catholic, Protestant, and our Goddess tradition."

Trudence spoke again. "The seasonal holy days are some of the few times our priestesses cross the safety veil created those centuries ago. We already covertly officiate and participate in ritual celebrations with the Glastonbury villagers. And there are also times we part the veils when those who still believe in the old religion venture forward to call across the borders, pleading for assistance in healing their ill or with conveying their dead to the Otherworld. Is that not enough?"

Some of the other priestesses nodded in agreement.

A young initiate, Etienette spoke up. "At the Summer Solstice ceremonies, I heard the villagers of Glastonbury talk. Many of them long to connect to something godly they can touch and feel. They say they love it when we come to them to help celebrate the old ceremonies."

Another priestess spoke up, adding, "They don't want a religion where Mass is spoken in Latin. They long for something like the ancestors used to feel in the old days, before Rhianna closed the veils. The days when we walked freely amongst them as priestesses of the Goddess."

Marissa grew excited. "Yes, we can show them how to commune with the Goddess in their world again. I have also heard their longing. In the voices of their religious reformation. If we stay hidden, we are no better than the Catholic clergy they condemn for excluding them from any truly holy participation."

She scanned the circle. "Yes, I propose it is time for change. Instead of hiding, we must walk amidst the world of men." She held up her hand to stem the murmur of protest. "Not openly flaunting our priestesshood. Not that. But making ourselves more available, even if that is done in a hidden, secretive manner. It is the best way to practice our devotion. A dedicated, practical approach is what is called for in these times. What good is our wisdom, our knowledge, if it cannot be more fully shared with the world?"

Ciara stepped forward, her voice steady and defiant. "Sister, I oppose this radical change. I've been in the world of men for longer than anyone here, having gone to Wales and lived amongst them, even if for a brief time. They are not ready for us. They are not ready for our ways. I have seen it firsthand. They will slaughter us . . . as they did Mother."

Ciara's words hit deep. Her heart sank. But she could not let her grief deter her from what she truly sensed to be right and guided.

Vanora asked, "Have you seen something in vision, Marissa? Something that gives you reason to want to make this change?"

Marissa looked down. She felt the beginnings of the familiar spasm in her gut that happened when Vanora questioned her ideas and revelations. Instead of giving in, she anchored herself in her heart's choice. If she didn't believe in her Goddess-sourced decisions, how could she expect others to follow?

Raising her eyes to meet Vanora's, she lifted her voice. "I have been guided, when I communed with the Goddess in the Divination Cave, and again, kneeling beside our sacred Red Well. I have seen us helping the world, right here in the village of Glastonbury. Healing. Teaching. Opening our doors to teach any young woman with the desire to learn our ways. This decision comes from my heart and my prayers. From feeling it down to my bones that this is the right thing to do."

Several more of the priestesses nodded their heads in alliance.

She continued, encouraged. "Let me reassure you. I propose we take down the veils, but place strong protection spells around our island. We will hang talismans for safety. Only those with pure hearts will be able to enter. But we will make ourselves more accessible. Even if we reach only a few. We have to start somewhere. We *must* be more accessible. Until a time when our teachings can be safely and openly embraced in the world."

She exhaled as more of the women gathered nodded. Comments were offered, moving the discussion along.

"I feel reassured now knowing you don't mean to throw our village to the wolves and cast protection aside."

"In Rhianna's time, they had not laid out spells and talismans. Perhaps if they had done so, many would have been saved."

"I still want the cover of safety the mists afford us."

Marissa felt the fiery sensations in her womb build again, her power kindled. Golden heat emanated from her in resplendent waves. Her eyes grew distant, her gaze turned inward. The Goddess spoke through her once more, in a voice that enveloped them all in its power and wisdom.

Carry the flame for the future.
Keep My path alive.
Teach it to others.
For one day the time will be ripe,
My love will reawaken humankind.
My teachings will rise again.
Taken from the grave of neglect and dishonor.

A grave where the Path of Love has germinated.
To awaken from the ashes of destruction and rise as a phoenix in a
*   new world.*
Taking flight to kindle the flame of peace and compassion.
At a time when the world can hear this new vow of love.

Marissa paused, her body telling her there was one last important piece of the message to relay.

If the truth of My love seems to die
And looks buried—know that to be a lie.
Beneath the black earth, it is merely asleep
Readying to be reborn when time demands.
But for now, plant its seeds so its message will keep.
When the path of love seems buried deep,
I charge Avalon with its wisdom to keep.
For one day there will be a quickening
and the path of love will be revived.

Silence again ensued as the priestesses listened to the Goddess's words coming through Marissa. She refocused, letting herself peer into the hearts of those gathered. "We have heard from all sides. Now it goes to the vote. Who agrees with this proposal?"

As was the practice before a council vote, she stepped up to each priestess and blessed her, saying to each one, "Allow your choice to emerge from the wellspring of the Goddess deep within your heart and womb."

Some consent was voiced immediately, some more slowly, others shook their head no. Vanora followed close behind, tallying the votes on a small slate tablet. Once she had counted the votes, she strode to the center of the group, turned in a slow circle, and checked once more for accuracy. She cleared her throat before she spoke. "It is a close vote. But the majority is clear."

Ciara's eyes were closed tight, hands clasped before her. The priestesses watched Vanora, waiting to hear the pronouncement. Marissa held her breath.

"The veils of Avalon are to come down."

Chapter 68

Glastonbury
October, Anno Domini 1539

Marissa breathed in the damp lake air and the fresh smell of the grassy reeds along Glastonbury's shoreline. Morning mist collected on her cloak, forming dewdrops. In the distance, church bells rang, and she could make out the faint intonation of the abbey's perpetual choir.

She scanned the road beside the lake, awaiting Matthew and Humphrey, the two village lads who'd accompanied her mother and sister to Wales. No sign of them yet, but she'd crossed the lake early, eager to begin her travels. She adjusted her robes above her horse's stirrups. She had opted to wear men's woolen hose under her skirts. They would absorb the moisture of the horse's sweat and help keep her dry and more comfortable for the long journey to Wales.

Her mare bobbed its head and neighed softly. She petted its long silky neck, murmuring, "Good girl."

Closing her eyes, she tilted her head back, letting the gentle sunrise warm her face. The soft hoof beats of horses and jingling reins alerted her to Matthew and Humphrey's arrival.

She opened her eyes. "Greetings."

"Good day to you, Mistress," Humphrey said. He jumped down from his horse to collect the extra travel satchels she had brought along, securing them to his mount.

Matthew leaned over to her. "We'll do a better job of accompanying you than we did your mother, I vow to you," he whispered, for her ears alone.

"What happened with my mother was the result of ignorance and blind prejudice. It wasn't your fault," she replied, laying a reassuring hand on his shoulder.

He sighed and cast his gaze downward. She could tell he carried the heavy stone of guilt, much as her sister did.

"Wait!" a woman's voice called out behind them.

Marissa searched the shoreline. She knew that voice as well as her own, yet still her breath caught when she spotted her sister. Ciara briskly stepped out of the boat she'd taken to traverse the lake.

Matthew's face lit up, but Ciara barely acknowledged him, giving a polite but curt nod of recognition. Marissa's heart sank once more at her sibling's turn of manner, her closed demeanor. Ciara had barely forgiven her for opening Avalon's doors to the world. And even more so, for encouraging the priestesses to bring their healing and devotional ways directly to the surrounding villagers. Their heated arguments after the community vote had rendered a wall between them. One that Marissa wished they could tear down.

Marissa smiled, genuinely glad to see her twin, and watched her pick her way through the reeds. When she reached Marissa's mount, Ciara lifted a small wrapped packet.

Marissa accepted the parcel. "What's this?"

"I prepared a small kit of herbs and ointments. Some tinctures. Ones you might need for travel. Lavender and arnica for sore muscles. Others for minor ailments . . ." Her voice trailed off.

"Thank you," Marissa said softly.

Ciara lifted her gaze. Marissa searched her twin's face, looking for signs of reconciliation, for softening of the recently set corners of her sister's mouth. She did catch a brief glimpse of the tenderness they once shared in her eyes. Also reflected there was the depth of her sister's festering heartache born of disappointment and loss.

"Be careful," her twin urgently insisted before her voice turned cool and her newly acquired brusqueness set in again. "Any healer worth their salt would prepare you such a healing kit for your long journey. Fare thee well."

Their fingers brushed as Marissa accepted the parcel. A spark flashed between them and her body stiffened and stilled, suddenly consumed by a premonition. In the vision, Ciara sat in a lone chair before a hearth fire, its flames accentuating a face furrowed with age and old sorrows, her once flaxen hair now white. A caustic brew of long-held discouragement suffused her sister's heart with a murky grey tinge. Standing beside her was her son Michael, matured into a man with a dignified air about him, garbed in the blue and white robes worn by the priests in service to the Goddess of the Stars and the Sea.

"The roads through the mountains of Wales are thawed. I must leave now, but will visit you again soon, dear Mother." He tenderly set his hand on her shoulder.

Ciara looked up with weary eyes, patting his hand, and offered a wan smile. "You are my one joy, my son."

The air crackled around Marissa, and she jerked as the brief vision ended.

"Ciara . . ." she gasped, clutching her own heart against the hardened ache she'd sensed in the foreboding.

"What is it?"

Marissa knew there was not much more she could say, nothing else she could do to ease her twin's grief and aloofness. But she had to try. "I beg you, tend your heart with gentle care. Keep it open, even though . . ."

Ignoring her outstretched hand, Ciara stepped back, her eyes steely. "Enough." She turned and headed back to her boat.

Tears stung Marissa's eyes. She yearned for the once sweet and light-hearted Ciara.

"Come back to me, my sister," she whispered.

Humphrey tightened his saddle and mounted his horse. "We're packed and can take our leave," he said, unaware, or perhaps politely ignoring the sisters' exchange.

Marissa twisted in her own saddle and added the healing kit to her side pack. She adjusted her robes once more and stared straight ahead. They would travel west and then north. To the hills and mountains of Wales. She would complete Michael's task for him as she had promised, fulfilling her part in their shared destiny. She would bring the Creation Bowl to the secret abbey hidden amongst the mountains of Wales, where seven monks awaited the esoteric treasure. She had foreseen the handover transpire in prophetic vision. The faces of the seven old men shining with awe, their gnarled hands reverently receiving the relic. She would turn that vision into reality. For Michael.

Reaching inside her robes, she patted the bowl inside its linen covering, safely stowed in a shoulder-strap bag, close to her body for safekeeping. She sensed its otherworldly Faery origins—the wild greening of nature, the warmth of the sun, the cool silver moon. It felt potent, tingling, and warm against her body. That original, magic power mingled with the bowl's mystical Christian undertones from its time in the world of man. A powerful combination. She understood the bowl's significance. It aligned with her priestess tradition of the regenerating cauldron of the Mother Goddess. For this reason alone, it was worth safeguarding.

As she'd been shown in vision, and Michael's Brotherhood had confirmed, humankind would one day acknowledge the bowl's healing power to open the heart. A power that could heal the darkness of the world, sometime in the future, when the time was right and the world was ready to receive it. It was her shared destiny to protect the bowl. Still, she did this for Michael. Her forever beloved.

Though tears wet her eyes, she smiled at her two guardsmen.

"I am ready to move on."

Chapter 69

Glastonbury Abbey Commemoration
and Fund-raiser
Present Day

The late morning was bright and clear, a warm sun making its way through a cloudless sky. The perfect weather for the abbey's commemorative ceremony, Sophie mused.

People streamed through the abbey's massive front gates, handing over their entrance tickets for the Revival Commemoration. Mrs. Henderson stood back and watched, a smile on her face, obviously pleased with the turnout. The monies would go to the abbey's treasury for much needed renovation funds. The day would celebrate the abbey's honored reputation, her life's work. Sophie gave Mrs. Henderson a cheerful smile. This day would prove fruitful for them all, even with her planned surprise.

Daniel stood to her side, his arm casually around her waist. The gesture felt good. Daniel felt good. She gave him a sideways glance of intimacy and trust. He knew what she was about to do and supported her decision.

"They admire your work," she said to him, noting the appreciative expressions and praising words of the guests who passed through the museum's gallery, filled with Daniel's photos and paintings of the abbey. Art critics and laypersons alike had come up to him, congratulating him.

"Your reputation is well earned and well affirmed by this project," Sophie said.

And my own journalistic reputation? Well, that remains to be seen, she thought. She no longer cringed or bowed under the weight of peer scrutiny.

With her article in hand, soon to be read aloud to the crowd, then soon to be published, she approached the raised speaker platform on the west grounds, between the abbey and the museum. She offered another cursory glance to Mrs. Henderson, nodded, and smiled. She was glad the curator had already seated herself, for Sophie wasn't so sure she'd not faint on hearing this final speech, after her orders to keep her report mainstream and nothing 'woo-woo.'

Sophie climbed the five side stairs to the podium, thoughts still running through her mind. In her defense, her report was not 'woo-woo.' She had corroborated much of the monk, Michael de Boulle's, story, as he'd conveyed it to her and Daniel. He'd pleaded to let the true story finally be told. She would do just that.

No longer would she listen to the constraining advice of well meaning but shortsighted editors and fellow reporters. She was not writing a story for the tabloids, as they might accuse. They couldn't say that once they heard her substantiation anyway. Even if they did accuse her of that, if they did ostracize and blacklist her, she would not be easily bruised. She had an amazing story to tell. The journalistic industry could no longer frighten or deny her.

Yes, she would be honored to stand by her promise to Michael de Boulle. Tell his story, the heretofore untold and hidden occurrences during the dissolution and takeover of Glastonbury Abbey.

The young monk stands at the back of the room. He knows Sophie does not see him. No one does. Daniel faces the stage, faces Sophie, his back to him. The young monk knows this is his last chance to rectify the mistakes of a ruinous fate. His tawny hair is tonsured, the color matching his rough-hewn robes. He cinches the cord tied about his waist before he folds his hands inside the arms of his cloak.

He watches the beautiful woman climb the steps to the speaker's podium in the Abbey Museum. His dear one. She arranges her papers and adjusts the microphone.

Sophie slipped the microphone in place, the stand adjusted to her tall height. She took a sip from the water glass next to the microphone, then flicked a glance at Daniel, who nodded his head in encouragement. Standing proud, she faced the audience of local patrons.

"Hello. My name is Sophie Morrison."

She dipped her head to the crowd's enthusiastic applause.

Then she began. "I'm a reporter, and I'm here to tell the true story of the abbey's dissolution. What happened that day was brutal. We know that. But there is much we had not known. Until now. I've uncovered new layers and am here to finally share this confirmed story. A story that wants to be told. A story that needs to be told."

Reading excerpts from her recently penned article, her voice rang clear and confident.

"In the year 1530 A.D., eight-hundred monasteries, nunneries, and abbeys flourished in England.

By 1541, there were none.

Over ten thousand monks and nuns dispersed or died during the widespread destruction of these monastic establishments, as ordered by King Henry VIII and carried out by deputies of his Vicar-General, Thomas Cromwell. The Glastonbury Abbey was one of the wealthiest that the king had his mercenaries confiscate, plunder, and burn. Monastic defamation and suppression was Cromwell's calculated maneuver to exorcise an overly influential Roman Catholic Church from the British realm, and strengthen the king's position as the new head of the Church of England. It was just as likely King Henry's agenda was to line his dwindling coffers.

British mystics and occultists say the history of southwest England's small village of Glastonbury merges pagan ancestral lines with esoteric Christianity. They claim Glastonbury is a magical, otherworldly land. They call it by the ancient name of Avalon, declaring it the New Jerusalem, the new holy land. Perhaps that was why the Celtic Druids, the Goddess worshipping priestesses of old, and the early Christians in Britain, revered it. As do modern-day pilgrims who travel there to drink the healing waters of its sacred wells, climb its labyrinth-demarcated hill called the 'Tor,' and contemplate the majestic vaulted ruins of the once great Glastonbury Abbey.

King Henry VIII's actions left an indelible mark on the spirit of England. This much is true. However, one young monk left an imprint that ran much deeper. He lived and worshipped at the mysterious Glastonbury Abbey before its pillage. He asked that his story be told."

She then divulged the inside story. The hidden story. For Michael. Her once beloved. When she concluded her presentation, she laid her article on the lectern. The audience was silent. Her heart pounded despite her newfound confidence. One audience member clapped. Daniel stood and clapped. Another audience member clapped. Then one more. And another, and another. Soon, the round of applause roared. Sophie felt tears in her eyes and blinked hard. She caught Daniel's gaze, feeling his support.

Mrs. Henderson eyed Sophie with a mixture of surprise and anger for the paranormal slant she had recounted. The curator's anger turned into a resigned sigh when she realized the audience was now giving Sophie a standing ovation. Mrs. Henderson replaced her at the microphone once the clapping tapered off. She slipped on her reading glasses and narrated William Blake's poem, *Jerusalem*, the famed ode to Glastonbury.

> . . . I will not cease from Mental Fight,
> Nor shall my Sword sleep in my hand:
> Till we have built Jerusalem,
> In England's green & pleasant Land

Some of the audience recited along with the well-known verses.

The monk turns to stand pensively before an easel displaying a painting depicting the abbey burning during King Henry's desecration. The picture's vivid orange and yellow flames seem to explode out the stained-glass windows of the ancient, magnificent abbey. He reaches out to touch the painting. But his hand passes through the canvas. He turns to watch the beautiful reporter exit the platform stage.

A smile plays at his lips. "My dear priestess," he whispers, before he slowly fades.

Sophie and Daniel stood in the final reception line, shaking the hands of the well-wishers who had attended the abbey's commemorative ceremonies and fund-raiser event. The affair had gone well, pulling in much needed monies for the abbey's costly maintenance, along with attracting many bright-eyed pilgrims, tourists, and local council members.

Daniel gave Sophie a sideways glance, arching one eyebrow. With a slight tilt of his head, he pointed in the direction of the private apple orchard on the other side of the grounds. Sophie nodded her agreement, she too wanting to take her leave. To be alone with Daniel and confirm their plans. The pair surreptitiously backed away from the reception line and strode to the orchard, hand in hand.

Once there, she closed her eyes and inhaled the scent of ripening apples. Daniel pulled her back against his chest and encircled her in his arms.

"I have the car packed," he said, nuzzling her neck.

"Mmhmm," she murmured, relishing the reassuring feel of his arms around her.

Her life was about to change once again. One of the many changes, small and large, since she'd come to Glastonbury. She exhaled softly, content for the first time she could remember. A sudden breeze ruffled her hair and caressed her cheek. She thought she heard the melodious ring of a thousand bells. It was a sign, she was learning, that proclaimed the Goddess of the Stars and the Sea's blessing. A Goddess she was growing to know, to remember, since Her revelatory visitation at Glastonbury's Chalice Well, just the other day. The memories of the Goddess had been surfacing slowly and gently. Feeling more like intuitive knowledge than memories, really. She was getting used to feeling Her presence. Much like she was getting used to this new path life laid before her.

She tilted her head to look at Daniel, her eyes searching his. Blue eyes that were his, and yet not his, gazed back at her.

A smile played at his lips. "It's fulfilled, my dear priestess," he whispered.

Sophie's heart shed a heavy burden she hardly knew she had carried.

Within a realm parallel to life, finally, at long last, the petals of peace blossomed in the young monk's heart. Their golden warmth spread through Michael, easing him forward, toward eternal rest in the luminous golden Otherworld. A long time coming.

"He was just here, wasn't he?"

"Michael? Yes," Daniel answered. "I hadn't seen him since we agreed to tell his story. Not until just now. I think he could finally move on." He turned her so she faced him. "Are you glad you did it? That you wrote the article you really wanted to write?"

She didn't hesitate. "Yes."

He swept an errant strand of hair behind her ear and clasped both of her hands in his.

The familiar surge of energy when he touched her swept up her arms, warm and gentle, as if she'd forever known the feel of his hands.

"Well, we have our story. We have the clues Michael gave us," she said. She squared her shoulders, feeling her new purpose course through her veins.

"Are you ready to find the Creation Bowl? Make sure it was kept safe?" he asked.

"I am. And maybe I can write a follow-up piece to let people know what the bowl means for the world. What it has to offer, and why we desperately need the compassion it can awaken," she said with enthusiasm.

"Great idea. Maybe even a book about it." Daniel held her close.

She laid her head against his chest and listened to his heartbeat, strong and vital.

"Are you ready to complete Michael and Marissa's great task? Shall we go to Wales and bring the bowl back to Glastonbury Abbey?"

Sophie smiled and nodded. "I'm ready to move on."

Barry busied himself digging and planting pansies in the far garden at the north side of the abbey, a fair distance from the commemorative festivities. The Abbey Lodging House rose tall and brooding behind him. At the other end of the grounds, he could see the day's ceremonies were coming to a close. The readings were concluded, the art gallery showing was over, and the crowd was dispersing. He'd have plenty of cleanup work to do after the ceremony, even with the volunteer helpers. For now, he allowed the contentment of gardening in the moist earth and the flowering greenery to fill his soul.

The shade of the cedar and hawthorn trees provided a comfortable respite from the afternoon heat, but Barry stopped to take a swig of water anyway. He wiped his lips with the back of his hand and laid his canteen beside his satchel. He paused, feeling her otherworldly presence before he saw her. A slow tingle traced its way down his neck and the scent of hawthorn blossoms filled the air.

He raised his head and turned slowly, knowing he could see her best with a soft gaze. First the billowing green mantle came into focus, trailing hawthorn flowers in its wake. Then her long silver hair and luminous green eyes. Eyes that were usually cool and calm now showed traces of concern, and fine lines of worry furrowed her pale skin.

Barry stood, brushing the dirt from his coverall knees. "Hello, Shayla."

Shayla shifted her gaze from his to watch Sophie and Daniel in the distance, where they stood under the dappled cover of the apple orchard. They looked so different in appearance than when she had first known them as Marissa and Michael, nearly five hundred years ago by human reckoning of time.

She took in a steadying breath. The new personalities of Sophie and Daniel would not know her, though she had not aged much. For her, it had only been a few years in the realm of Faery since leaving Avalon. A few years since she had tearfully turned away from Marissa and Ciara to fully embrace her Faery roots. But her love for them, for Avalon, had never diminished.

She sighed. "I know they now wear the faces of Sophie and Daniel. But I will forever know them as Michael and Marissa. As I knew and loved them in Avalon."

Memories vied for her attention. The couple's soul destiny had imprinted on hers back then. She had linked to them through love during their shared friendship in their lifetime together long ago. More so, she had linked to them because she had marred their fate with her interference. Interfered not only in their destiny, but their love. Incurring a soul debt that had haunted her ever since. A soul debt she'd desperately longed to repay and make amends for. Something she had hopefully now rectified.

"Were we successful?" she asked Barry. Her voice was the wind's whisper through the oak trees, her honey-scented words floating across a soft breeze against Barry's forehead.

Her hands were clasped tightly before her, her lips trembled. She asked again, her voice more eager this time. "Did my plan work? Do they find love again in each other? Is she content?"

Barry turned to watch Daniel and Sophie embrace under the apple trees.

He confirmed the accomplishment of Shayla's penitent quest. "Yes. Your plan was successful."

Shayla sighed in relief. She smiled, a true smile for the first time in centuries. "Ah. Good. Michael and Marissa have finally found each other's hearts again."

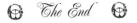 *The End*

Acknowledgements

How could I have authored this novel without the feedback from my extraordinary writing critique group? We called ourselves the Destiny Writers and met weekly for 14 years of creativity and encouragement. My deepest gratitude to Shoshana Alexander our group leader, as well as my dear and talented fellow authors, Tiziana DellaRovere, Alissa Lukara, Maggie McLaughlin, Lori Henriksen, and Nancy Bloom.

Thank you as well to my editor, the incredibly talented Kate MacGregor. Your insightful input made my diamond in the rough manuscript shine.

Big gratitude to Maggie McLaughlin for formatting my manuscript, uploading it to Kindle and print, and for your aid with the many details involved in getting my novel out into the world.

Thank you to the creative, gifted, and magical Renee Starr of The Beautiful Business Co, for her beautiful cover art. www.thebeautifulbusinessco.com

Thank you to Theresa Crater and Vic Smith for your generous beta read and editing suggestions.

I am grateful to the Goddess of the Stars and the Sea, who inspired me all along the way.

And thank you to my beloved Christopher. You are the love of my life.

About the Author

Jodine Turner is a multiple award winning, best-selling author of Visionary Fiction and magical fantasy. While living for a year in Glastonbury, England, the ancient Isle of Avalon, Jodine began writing the Goddess of the Stars and the Sea series about the magical Avalon priestesses throughout the ages to today.

Jodine is a founding member of the Visionary Fiction Alliance. She believes Visionary Fiction speaks the language of the soul and makes ancient esoteric wisdom relevant for our modern times, helping to transform consciousness.

Jodine met and married her truelove in Glastonbury. They presently live in northern California along with their four magical cats.

www.jodineturner.com

https://www.facebook.com/JodineTurner.Author/

Other Works by Jodine Turner

The Awakening: Rebirth of Atlantis

The Goddess of the Stars and the Sea is awakened from Her dreamtime with the knowing that a change for humankind approaches. The final days of Atlantis are marked by deceit, lust, and greed. The once vibrant culture, blessed with advanced knowledge bestowed upon it by a race of star beings, now suffers with a corrupt governing body and a degenerate priesthood.

The Goddess intervenes to assist humanity and calls upon the young priestess, Geodran, to be Her helper. Geodran struggles to fulfill a destiny larger than her own personal desires, a destiny bestowed upon her by her mother, the High Priestess Jaquine. In a moment of maternal desperation, Jaquine had promised her unborn child, Geodran, to the Goddess, in return for the babys safe birth, thus sealing her daughters fate.

Geodrans journey is a heroic quest to bring forth the next era of human civilization.

The Awakening is the first in the *Goddess of the Stars and the Sea* trilogy.

The Keys to Remember

In this award winning continuation of the Goddess of the Stars and the Sea trilogy, humankind is once again on the threshold of a spiritual evolution. In fourth century England, six year old Rhianna is kidnapped and raised in a Christian Abbey but has never forgotten grandmothers prophecy Your destiny lies with the Goddess of the Stars and the Sea. She alone must mid-wife the next stage of spiritual evolution, as dark times approach for humanity. Powerful forces within both the Abbey and the priestess community conspire to keep Rhianna from her rightful destiny and her true love. The price of her heroic quest is far higher than she expects.

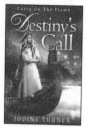

Carry on the Flame: Destiny's Call

Humanity is in the midst of the greatest crisis in their evolution. Sharay is the one chosen to show the way forward and help humankind move through the fear and dark times of today's world. Born into a lineage of priestesses in modern day Glastonbury, England, Sharay's way is blocked by her jealous Aunt Phoebe, who uses black magic against her to steal her fortune and magical power. When Phoebe commits Sharay to a psychiatric ward and accuses her of murder, Sharay struggles with the temptation to fight Phoebe's vengeance with her own. Through the ancient Celtic ceremony of Beltaine, Sharay experiences profound sacred union with the Welshman Guethyn, who shows her how to open her heart. But Sharay must learn to transform her hatred for her aunt in order to claim the mystery held deep within her cells that will allow her to fulfill her destiny and prove that the ultimate magic is the power of love.

Carry on the Flame: Ultimate Magic

Born into a lineage of priestesses in modern day Glastonbury, England, Sharay is chosen by the Goddess of the Stars and the Sea to help humankind move through the fear and chaos of today's world. To do so, she has to face her grief,loss, and her own dark side. Her way is blocked by her jealous Aunt Phoebe,who uses black magic against Sharay to steal her fortune and her magical powers. When Phoebe accuses her of insanity and murder, it's the elder, eccentric wizard Dillon who sets Sharay on the Celtic 'Imram,' a quest designed to awaken her magical abilities as a priestess. And it's Dillon's grandson Guethyn who shows Sharay how to open her heart in the Beltaine Ritual, the ancient Celtic ceremony of sacred union.

Hunted by the police, stalked by a demonic Tracker conjured by her aunt, and torn from everyone she loves, Sharay struggles with the temptation to fight Phoebe's dark powers with her own. She must transform her fear and hatred for her aunt in order to uncover the mystery held deep within her cells that will allow her to fulfill her destiny—a secret only she can discover. When separated from Guethyn's protection, Sharay continues on her Imram alone, in this spellbinding conclusion to *Carry on the Flame*.

To my readers.

Reviews are the best way to tell an author Thank you and show that you enjoyed their book. Would you leave a review on Amazon.com? It can be short—"I liked it" is fine. Thank you, you are so appreciated!